ELENA RANSOM

AND THE LOST SON

by

J.S. WOOD

Illustrations by BRoseDesignz

Small Frye
Publishing

Atlanta, GA

To Nicole, Jeannie & Angela

Prologue

1

———

2

———

3

———

4

———

5

———

◘ Prologue ◘

Stone. Sand. Sandstone. Silence. Emelie moved along through the descending passageway with her hololight extended in one hand, taking no notice of her footfalls against the brick steps because her ears were filled with the sound of her own breaths cycling through the full-faced helmet covering her head.

Emelie soon changed course into the ascending passageway. She made her way through a grand gallery with its painted mosaics and stone carved statues. Still, she noticed nothing, hurrying along with labored breaths.

The leather satchel around her shoulder bumped against her leg in an aggravating way, but the sleek tactical suit she wore was perfect for her swift, short steps. She adjusted her tactical vest as she neared the main antechamber. She slowed to a stop.

Emelie activated the external audio module on her helmet. She held her breath, listening intently for any signs of life in the king's chamber, but after a moment she realized she was undeniably alone. She hurried into a modest room that was supported by square, sandstone columns. Emelie set her hololight in the center of the room and watched the beams spread out in all directions until there wasn't a dark corner in the king's chamber.

She set her satchel on the floor. Emelie pulled back her sleeve to reveal a round-faced object that was attached to her wrist. She slid a finger toward the Broadcaster. A small object, the size of a drop of water, flew to the center of the room where an Optivision screen appeared in midair. Emelie stood very still as laser lights from the Touchdot began to scan the room. Less than a minute passed before Emelie located what she desired.

Emelie grabbed the satchel off the floor and walked towards the north-facing wall. She removed a pair of black gloves from her tactical vest and pulled them roughly over her fingers. Then, she methodically tightened the oxygen helmet mask to her face. Finally, she opened the satchel and withdrew an amethyst ostrich plume.

Emelie reached to the north wall and wrenched a brick free. Quickly, she extracted a separate ostrich plume from the crevice that was identical to the one she'd just pulled from her satchel. She held the new feather aloft, as if repulsed. She stuffed the new feather unceremoniously into her satchel. Then, she crammed the other plume into the crevice and reinserted the brick. However, it was already too late.

Emelie felt a sharp tremble beneath her boots. Ash collected on her facemask as the columns began to disintegrate around her. She stood perfectly still, facing up towards the ceiling. Waiting. Waiting. And then, daylight appeared above.

Two jets of energy burst from the bottom of her tactical vest. Emelie was propelled up through the king's chamber and through the opening that had been created from the quake. She flew up and up, through crumbling sandstone and mountains of powdery sand until finally she reached the light.

The sun rising over the great pyramids of Giza was temporally blinding, but Emelie continued on and took a moment to watch as the remarkable structure collapsed on itself. She then maneuvered her body back towards the city.

In the light of the day, Emelie could see a wide river snaking out, aligned by hundreds of buildings. Thousands of people were pushing along through the streets between the towers. She activated the external audio module from her helmet again.

Immediately, a wave of screaming panic arose like a cloud of smoke, permeating everything. She turned the sound off at once and focused all her attention on the apartment building ahead. With precision, she directed her body towards the roof and landed with ease as if she'd stepped off a sidewalk.

As she headed through the rooftop door, she deactivated the facemask, which folded away seamlessly and disappeared into her tactical vest. She descended three flights of stairs without breaking a sweat. Then, she opened the door to apartment number forty-seven.

"Norman. I'm back!" Emelie called from the entrance. "Such pandemonium in the streets. I've honestly never witnessed such bedlam, even though we studied the outcome so implicitly."

She eased through the apartment, gathering speed as she went, her eyes ever searching.

"They're all trying to escape the city, like that will somehow spare them. I wish they'd die already so I wouldn't have to listen to the moaning." She clicked her tongue impatiently. "Can you hear them out there?"

Emelie listened intently, but all remained silent.

"Norman? Are you there?" She kept walking, her eyes scanning. "I'm finished with my task. We need to call for extraction." Yet still, there was no response. "Norman, are you listening? Where are you?"

Emelie cleared the last hallway and made her way into a large living area at the back of the apartment where she found a man sitting rigidly in an armchair, his eyes were transfixed on a holographic screen that displayed images of the chaos outside.

"Norman! What are you doing?"

Emelie scanned the room and noticed that their two-year-old son was sitting in a corner, completely entranced with a PocketUnit.

"Did you hear me? We need to call for extraction."

Emelie pulled the leather satchel from her tactical vest and held it up for Norman to see. She set it down on a table and looked at her husband expectantly. However, the usual hardened, cold eyes that she expected to see from him were gone. He looked at her with a sad, pleading gaze.

Norman stood slowly from his chair, crossed the room, and grabbed his wife's hands earnestly.

"Emelie, I think we should reconsider."

"Reconsider what?" Emelie demanded, snatching her hands away from him.

"What we're doing for Imperator. I do not believe it is too late to seek an alternative. Perhaps we could go to Truman now, tell him what we've done, and see if we can receive sanctuary."

"You want us to go into *hiding*?" Emelie said, her voice rising to a shrill pitch. "After all the work we've done!

"Em, think about Gribbin," said Norman. He looked longingly at his son. "What kind of life can he have? Can we have?"

"What about the years we have spent cultivating trust with those we meant to betray? Do you remember how long it took me to breach Kenneth and Anne's files so we could ascertain the location of the artifacts? And, I wasn't even able to extract all the information from them yet.

"And let us not forget how I took great pains to hide the artifact that was entrusted to us so that no one, not even Imperator, would ever be able to find it. So, after all the undercover work and lies we have told to protect our family, you want us to turn our backs on Imperator? He is the future."

"Imperator has threatened to end our lives if we don't follow his plans flawlessly. How is it possible that we could keep this up forever? What if we make one little mistake and..."

"I don't make mistakes, *ever*!" Emelie said hysterically. "Except maybe when choosing you, a spineless coward, for a husband."

"We still have time to choose to do what is right, Em. Look at what Imperator is doing! He's murdered all those people out there and millions more will die," Norman said, his voice overcome with grief as he gestured to the Optivision screen. "I cannot do this any longer. I'm going to Truman with or without you. But either way, I'll be taking our son."

He grabbed the leather satchel off the table. Then, he started towards the little boy on the floor. At that moment, he heard the sound of a weapon engage. Norman turned slowly, staring blankly at his wife. He realized the assault pistol in her hand was pointed at his chest.

"You are *not* defecting," Emelie said calmly.

"What are you going to do?" Norman said calmly. "Kill me?"

The sound of the weapon discharging filled the apartment. Emelie walked across the room towards the body that was now crumpled on the floor beneath where her husband had stood. She looked at Norman resentfully.

"You know, he said that you were too weak," Emelie said to her already dead husband. "He warned me that one day I would have to *take care* of you. And so I have."

Emelie looked over towards the corner of the room where her son was still engrossed in his PocketUnit.

She activated an Optivision screen from a nearby window dimensional and a moment later the face of a Humanoid appeared.

"Agent Cristo calling for immediate extraction," Emelie said.

"Extraction for your location has been rescheduled," the Humanoid replied in a monotone voice.

"Rescheduled!" Emelie said sharply. "Impossible. The city is falling to its knees. Redirect me to Code 12202011 or Base 02142009.

"Those directories have been temporarily disengaged."

"Disengaged! Those *directories* are Imperator's personal contact lines."

"As I said, we are not able to provide any assistance to your location at the present moment," the Humanoid continued in a monotone voice.

"What are my temporary orders?" Emelie asked, sounding borderline hysterical.

"We can offer no assistance. Good day."

The Optivision vanished on the spot. Emelie attempted to reengage the screen, but was met with complete failure. She stood straight up and lifted her chin slightly. No one was coming for her. For the first time in years she didn't have any orders. She'd been left to fend for herself.

Fortunately, working for Imperator had enabled her to be immunized against the viruses that were being deployed around the world. But still, where would she go and what would she do? Imperator would be able to locate her no matter where she went.

Emelie's resolute footsteps carried her straight into the washroom. She wrenched a bodysuit free from the closet and covered herself, instantaneously transforming her womanly figure into that of a middle-aged man. She rifled through a drawer of high-necked, black-banded collars until she found a suitable piece and buttoned it roughly around her throat. A moment later, her face and head distorted until a black haired man was staring back at her in the mirror. She'd just reached for a suitcase when she stopped short.

"Being on the run with a future Grimsby trainee presents a tremendous complication," Emelie said aloud to herself. "I could escape better through the city if I leave the boy."

Emelie hurried back towards the living room and peered around the corner. Her son had moved from his corner and was now sitting beside Norman's dead body, yet the two-year-old was still consumed with the game on his PocketUnit.

"I should go alone," Emelie whispered to herself. "He'll never even notice I'm gone." She considered that option for a moment. "Though, the best route is to leave through the Renegade escape channel. However, if I go that way there's a possibility that Truman would catch me. Without Norman and the boy I will have no leverage."

Emelie tossed the suitcase over her shoulder and hurried across the room, lifting the little boy to his feet.

"Come along, Gribbin."

"Who are you?" the little boy asked, not recognizing Emelie's disguise.

"A friend of your mom," Emelie answered in the best male voice she could imitate.

"Where are we going?" the little boy asked.

"We're going to take a little trip out of the city," Emelie replied.

"What about Daddy?"

"He's taking a nap and will join us later," Emelie said impassively.

Emelie hurried Gribbin down the stairs of the apartment building and out into the chaotic streets. Fear coursed through every fiber of the city, but Emelie was purposeful as she moved through the sick, the crying, and the dying as though she had a map of planned movements memorized.

At length, Emelie cut through a side alleyway, pulling Gribbin through behind her. They came to the mouth of a drain tunnel that was covered with an iron gate.

"What are we doing now?" Gribbin asked as Emelie lifted her arm, revealing the Broadcaster on her wrist.

"We're going into hiding," she replied shortly.

A second later, the iron gate unlatched. She helped Gribbin up into the tunnel. As soon as they were both inside the tunnel, she turned to make sure that the door resealed itself. The, she hurried Gribbin along for many long, strained minutes of silence, except for the pitter-patter of her son's little feet.

After several hundred yards, the tunnel came to a fork and Emelie came to rest, feeling relief that they almost reached their final destination. She leaned against the wall, dropping her son's hand, and took a deep breath.

A light suddenly appeared. Emelie noticed that Gribbin had taken the PocketUnit out and was already playing a game.

"Boy," Emelie said in a firm tone. "I'll be right back. You stay right here."

When Gribbin didn't answer or even look up, Emelie smiled slightly and turned to leave. As she began to jog down the tunnel to the left, Emelie heard a deep, strong voice echo through the tunnel.

"I've been waiting for you."

Emelie flipped around quickly, staring blankly at a man in a waistcoat with a pencil thin beard. He was holding Gribbin in his arms.

"Truman!" Emelie said, feeling disbelief. "I wasn't expecting to see you, or any of the Renegades for that matter." Then, remembering that she was disguised, added, "How did you recognize me?"

"I recognized your son," Truman replied, hugging Gribbin closely on his hip.

"We were following the evacuation procedure," Emelie said seriously. "We are on our way to headquarters right now."

Truman stood very still, unblinking. Then, he set the boy down against the wall away from where they stood.

"Where is Norman?" Truman asked as he rounded on Emelie.

"We had a confrontation," Emelie said automatically. "He told me that he had been spying for Imperator and that he wanted me to come with him. When I said I wouldn't go he said he was going to take Gribbin with him. I couldn't let that happen, you know?"

"What did you do?" Truman asked in an accusatory way.

"It was an accident!" Emelie said earnestly, desperate to play her part well so that she could survive. "I had a weapon to defend myself. It went off as he struggled to get it away from me."

Truman took a step towards Emelie.

"You said that Norman was a spy. Do you know what, if anything, he told Imperator about our work?"

"I d-don't k-know..." Emelie stuttered. "I mean, how am I supposed to know what they discussed? It's not like I..." But her speech faltered under Truman's deep gaze and she had to look away.

"Who did you betray? Which family?" Truman said, his voice rising slightly.

Emelie hesitated a moment, but perhaps Norman had been correct that Truman could offer her asylum if he believed her. "He wanted the Cup, Truman. Only the Cup and nothing else."

"The Cup!" Truman hollered in anger. "But Jonathan and Abigail's plantation is half way around the world. How could I even get there in time?"

"Imperator said he'd kill my son! My only son," lied Emelie. "What was I supposed to do?"

"Your son? Your son!" Truman said furiously. "Imperator has already contaminated the Nile. That river unites over 160 million people. What do you imagine is going to happen to all of those sons?"

"I was so wrong," Emelie cried. "I called for my extraction, but no one would come for us. Imperator was never planning to keep me as a confidante. Please, have mercy."

"It is not *my* mercy you need," Truman replied. "I will speak with *Him* to see what He wants to do with you."

Truman turned and walked away, off into a shadow, but out of the same place came Tiny the Humanoid.

"Tiny," Truman said from somewhere Emelie could not see. "Stay with Emelie and do not let her or the trainee out of your sight."

Tiny the Humanoid lifted her arm, pointing a sleek black weapon at Emelie's head.

Emelie stood in silence, staring at Gribbin, as her thoughts spun wildly. She was certain that her inability to get in contact with Imperator meant that he no longer required her services and that he was content to let her die. She determined that she could never return to Imperator's service. However, Emelie did not want to go with Truman unless she was guaranteed immunity for her crimes. But, what if he wouldn't give her immunity? Then, she would need to go out on her own with Gribbin, as she had already planned to do.

The only way Emelie could think to escape now was if she killed Truman. However, she knew that he was a highly skilled asset and, even if she was able to catch him off guard, she was sure Tiny had orders to defend him. Furthermore, if she killed Truman and somehow restrained Tiny it would be impossible to reprogram the Humanoid, thus leaving a trail for someone in the Renegades to find her.

As Emelie was trying to decide how she could use Gribbin as a hostage, Truman returned from the shadows.

"Omegus has offered forgiveness," he said. "But you must hand over your artifact. Furthermore, your privileges are revoked. You are no longer a member of the Renegades."

"I can't give you my artifact. Norman destroyed it," Emelie lied.

She couldn't tell by Truman's face if he believed her. Truman grabbed Emelie by the throat, ripping the collar from her neck. In an instant her face appeared again as normal.

Then, Truman removed a long, thin tool from his waistcoat. He pointed it at her throat and pulled the trigger. Emelie cried out in pain.

"What was that?" she coughed in a hoarse voice.

"A device that will allow me to track your whereabouts," Truman replied.

"Isn't that what Trademarks are for?"

Truman gave Emelie a look of indifference and said, "I think we both know how those can be manipulated. You will be sent to live in Atlanson near my family where Gribbin will be safe. Imperator will soon find out that Norman is dead. We will need to come up with a solution to reestablish a spouse in your home. Clearly, you cannot be trusted with being married to an actual human being," he added scathingly, "but I'm sure that Kenneth and Anne can make a suitable Humanoid replacement for you."

Truman seized Emelie's elbow and quick-marched Emelie down the tunnel until they came into an underground chamber with several hovercrafts. He escorted Emelie and Gribbin to the largest of the vehicles and placed them inside with Tiny sliding into the operator's chair.

"Your new last name is Pigg," Truman told Emelie. "Your new family history, background info, replacement personal identities, and details about your new occupation will be waiting at your new apartment.

"The device I inserted into your neck gives me the ability to locate you, even into eternity. Imperator will never know it is there unless you tell him. Therefore, do hesitate before you think about betraying the Renegades again. The consequences for you would be dire."

Emelie swallowed hard, but she was secretly grateful that she'd gotten off so easily. She wasn't looking forward to life in Atlanson and she certainly wasn't looking forward to being a parent, but it was a sentence better than the plausible death that Imperator had planned for her.

"Tiny, take Emelie and Gribbin to Atlanson and leave them with Hannah for now," Truman said authoritatively. "Do not let her" — he looked pointedly at Emelie — "communicate with anyone. Once you have dropped them off, Tiny, you will need to leave straight away for Washington D.C. I will let Kenneth know you are coming."

"What are you going to do?" Emelie croaked.

Truman looked at her with a hard gaze. "That is none of your concern."

Fourteen Years Later

1

Not Interested

Elena Ransom gasped and then held her breath, biting her bottom lip as she deliberated her options. The hovercraft she was operating was going categorically faster than she wished to go, but she wasn't willing to give up her advantage so she pressed on, trying to avoid the towering mountainous ranges in her path.

"I know what you're doing." Kidd Wheeler's voice sounded through the receiver on Elena's control console. "But you're not going to beat me. We both already know that so don't get your hopes up."

Elena wanted to focus solely on the simulation, but she couldn't let him get away with thinking he was better than her.

"I've gotten much better," Elena responded tersely. "Don't be so sure that I'll lose."

Her nail bitten fingers moved quickly around the control column, yanking the hovercraft out of a nosedive as Kidd's hovercraft whizzed in circles around her.

"You look out of control," Elena commented as she maneuvered around a sharp turn.

"That's because you don't understand how to operate your aerocraft to its fullest capacity."

Elena forcefully shoved some red curls behind her ear and tried to focus on the next turn, which included a loop and another nose dive through a cavern, but Kidd's seemingly out-of-control craft was zipping around her at such speeds that she found it hard to concentrate.

"You're going down, Ransom!" Kidd's voice echoed in her ears.

"I'm not sure it's a good thing that you sound excited about my demise."

"Not about your demise, but I am trying to protect my ego. I can't let you win at racing or I'll feel incompetent."

"You should already feel that way, Wheeler!" Elena said, smirking as she struggled to maintain control of the ever increasing speed of the hovercraft.

At long last, she finally recognized an opportunity. Feeling elated, she sped towards a cluster of trees towards the left.

"Don't go through the forest," Kidd warned. "The tornado simulation whips through there at random. You could get caught in a storm and get blown off course."

"It's the best short cut to the finish line. You don't think I'm strong enough to fly out of it?" Elena questioned.

"No, you're not," Kidd replied honestly.

"Don't tell me what to do, Wheeler," Elena said defensively.

Elena heard Kidd make a frustrated sound. She watched his hovercraft suddenly change trajectory, cutting her own hovercraft off. She waited until the last possible moment. Then, she pulled out of the lane and back onto the course that Kidd had previously been taking.

"What are you doing now?" he shouted as his hovercraft disappeared into the trees.

"I'm winning," Elena stated confidently.

With the finish line in her sights, Elena looked to the left at the forest, almost willing the tornado with her mind. And then, as she neared the end of the course she saw angry clouds fill the sky and hover over the forest.

A moment later, Kidd's hovercraft spun up the side of the cyclone and then dove away from it towards the finish line. But, it was too late. Elena's hovercraft completed the last few feet, ending their race.

Elena couldn't contain her smile. She rubbed her hands over her face and then brushed her red curls behind her ears. She climbed out of the simulation hub, meeting Kidd on the main Simulab floor.

"I can't believe you won!" Kidd said angrily.

"I didn't win, I beat you," Elena said, laughing a little. But then she noticed the look of frustration on his face. "What?"

"I can't believe you tricked me!" Kidd said, still scowling. "Flying is my *thing*. No one should ever beat me at it."

Elena surveyed his black hair and dark eyes as he grabbed his rucksack up roughly from the floor. She noticed for the first time that he'd grown a bit taller in the past few weeks. But, then again, she was only just starting to observe things about him that weren't charged with negativity.

"Oh, come on," Elena said impatiently. "It's the first time I've won. Don't be grumpy because you lost to a girl."

"You're not a girl," Kidd said, his grimace slowly turning to a smirk. "You're an entirely new species of awesome."

"That's better," Elena said smugly.

"There you are!"

Elena spun around. Her friend, Abria Bowen, was striding toward them with her blonde hair flowing in waves around her face. Abria had also grown a bit taller since their third year at Grimsby School of the Republic had ended. Her face, though painted with a perfect varnish of makeup, looked a little more mature. Her arms were overloaded with shopping bags.

"I've been looking for you everywhere!"

"What's going on? Did the store run out of lip gloss?" Elena asked smartly.

Abria rolled her eyes and faked a laugh. Then, she wiggled a finger in Kidd's face and asked, "What's going on here?"

"What do you mean?" Kidd asked, looking dumbfounded.

"You're doing something weird with your face," Abria replied.

"Smiling?" Elena offered.

"Yeah, that's it," Abria said, nodding. "It's weird. So stop it."

This only made Elena and Kidd smile more.

"Don't you two ever get, like, bored of this?" She gestured at the Simulab. "This is the seventh time I've found you here and we've only been in Atlanson for three days. You should really get out and explore the city. It's so crazy beautiful here."

"You know what, Blondie, you're right."

Kidd grabbed Elena's hand and pulled her out onto Decatur Road where a row of Simulab gaming hubs were filled with people participating in virtual jogging, kickboxing, martial arts, and swimming.

"Do you realize how much shopping there is to do here?" Abria continued on as she followed them through the street. "Grandma Haddock and I have already been to a dozen stores trying to get ready for someone's birthday." She winked at Elena. "And she has expressly promised that she'll take me to all the other stores in the entire city."

"It's possible that I could care less about this conversation, but I don't see how," Kidd said playfully.

Abria cocked her head to the side.

"You know, it's just so weird...your new smile and this sort of joking manner. I guess it will take some time to...Oh WOW!" Abria's head had turned almost all the way around as she stared into one of the shop windows. "Would you look at that fabric? I simply *must* have a dress made while I'm here. Grandma Haddock said that Atlanson has the best seamstresses in the world."

"I feel like crying," Elena said suddenly.

"Why?" Abria asked, looking earnest.

"Because I'm literally bored to tears," Elena said dryly.

Abria giggled. Then, her voice tinkled like crystal as she said, "I was sent here to tell you that Austin wants us in Sector 7 for debrief about what Fergie and Pigg found out about the Cup of Jamshid."

"Anyone else starving?" Kidd asked, completely ignoring her.

"Oh, thank you for saying something!" Elena said. "I thought I was the only one that felt that way."

"You feel like getting a grilled pizza?"

"You know me so well," said Elena, smiling.

"Hello?" Abria said impatiently. "Didn't anyone hear what I said about Austin wanting to talk to us?"

"Anyone else getting a little bored talking about artifacts?" Kidd asked. "I'd rather have another skateboarding lesson before dinner."

Elena smiled and nodded. All the urgency she'd once felt to complete her parents' work had evaporated after she and Kidd almost drowned getting the Cup of Jamshid out of the Smuggler Station from the bottom of the lake on Kidd's family farm. In fact, she'd had several nightmares about the Smuggler Station. One dream included evil sea creatures that held her down as the Station was sinking and another dream where she'd drowned while holding the Cup because it had been too heavy to swim with.

Elena hadn't worked up enough courage to tell Austin that she wasn't going to help him search for artifacts any longer and that she was not planning to visit the Firebird Station at school again so that she wouldn't be tempted to resume the search.

"I'm just the messenger," Abria said as the friends cut through a back alley between the Rising Loafer Bakery and the Murphy's Paw Kennel. "If you don't want to work on artifacts anymore talk to Austin about it," she added as they approached a metal hatch door.

Kidd opened the door. Elena watched as Abria managed to squeeze herself and all her shopping bags through the door. Then, the three friends walked through the world of machinery, electric modems, and power grids that formed the deep underworld of Atlanson to the far corner of Sector 7 where a crude clubhouse stood between stack pipes and silver ducts.

The once smaller clubhouse had recently been transformed so that it could accommodate all Elena's friends plus the pupil stations that Fergie Foreman had set up so they could work on program writing for the artifacts.

As they stepped into the clubhouse, Elena said in surprise, "Pigg, you're here!"

Pigg ran his fingers through his ebony hair and looked a little nervous. "I'm not, strictly speaking, supposed to be out of the house."

He opened a Whimsical candy block and stuffed some of it into his mouth while he spoke. "My mom said that she'd skin me alive if she ever caught me spending time with any of you again, but she couldn't really do that, right? I mean, to skin a person *alive* would be extremely messy, not to mention incredibly loud with all the screaming and everything. Still, I used extreme caution to get here and I have an evacuation route for returning home safely."

"Hey there!" said Austin Haddock as he sat in the chair beside Fergie Forman's pupil station. "Let's sit."

Fergie sat straight-backed in a chair and didn't even look up in greeting, but worked feverishly through several Optivision screens with images of all the artifacts Elena and her friends had collected from all over the globe.

"Where's Bowen?" Elena asked.

"Oh, he said he had stuff to do," Abria said, waving her hand dismissively.

"Then, why do we have to be here?" Kidd asked.

"I wanted you to see what Fergie and Pigg have been working on," Austin said.

Kidd rolled his eyes at Elena.

However, even though she understood how he felt about not wanting to talk about artifacts, she couldn't resist helping Austin. They were friends and that alone meant she owed her attention, even though skateboarding with Kidd would have been more fun.

"Pigg and I have made significant progress on developing a program to read the artifact codes now that we have the Angel statue in our possession," Fergie said in a formal tone as she tucked her short, black hair behind her left ear.

"To think, this all started because of the Ransom Dossier," Pigg said reminiscently, as if lost in thought. "If Elena had just left it hidden or we had decided not to go after the Alpha Manuscript then we might have had a semi-normal time at school."

"Who wants *normal* when you can impulsively fly away from a horde of stampeding Humanoids?" Kidd asked and Elena had a clear visual of Washington D.C. and them running from the White House after they'd taken the Catalan Atlas.

"Oh, when those Humanoids started chasing us I thought we were dead," Pigg said nervously.

"Well, I never want to experience sinking to my death like what happened in New York," Abria said. "I mean, that was the worst feeling, like, ever!"

Elena shuddered as she remembered how Liberty Island sank under the New York City harbor, crushing their hovercraft with tons of sand. She absentmindedly grabbed the multidimensional, star shaped drop necklace that was hanging around her neck and pressed the sharp edges with her fingers.

Elena's dad had given her the Kairos necklace on her thirteenth birthday, but she had no idea the secrets the necklace would hold until she'd watched the Kairos work for the first time. She remembered how it had opened and the clock inside had spun wildly while she and Austin were standing inside a hidden chamber below the Statue of Liberty. The Kairos had succeeded in revealing the Amulet artifact they'd been searching for.

Elena noticed that Austin had started to rub the scar on the base of his chin, something he did when he was overly concerned or thinking too much.

"But we've had some major successes," Austin pointed out. "Like finding the Ampoule that revealed the blank pages of the Ransom Dossier, which helped us learn about the Tablets of Destiny."

"Yeah, but then we got tricked by Melly," Abria pointed out.

"Remember how Melly smacked the floor when she fainted?" Elena said, almost giggling as she recalled the moment they'd incapacitated their fellow Firebird so they could sneak through her closet to find clues.

"You mean, after you drugged her," Kidd corrected her.

"Whatever. She deserved it," Elena said.

"She was so heavy. I wasn't, like, expecting that," Abria said reminiscently.

"Okay, I know that Melly didn't help us and that we got sidetracked when we went to Tavington's farm, but then we found out about the Cup of Jamshid," Austin said.

"So, what do we know about the Cup," Elena asked, trying to push thoughts of Kidd drowning out of her head.

"We know from ancient Persian mythology that the Cup of Jamshid was filled with an elixir of immortality," Fergie said as she pulled up images of the Cup on the Optivision screen. "And that was used in scrying."

"What's *scrying*?" Abria asked.

"The practice of looking into an object for the purposes of divination or fortune-telling. In this case, the Persians believed that all seven heavens of the universe could be observed and this studying would reveal deep truths," Fergie said in a formal tone.

"We also know that the ancients believed that whoever possessed the Tablets of Destiny would rule the world," Austin said. "We still don't know where the Tablets are, but we've got to keep looking for them because we know Imperator wants them."

"So, what do we know about the Angel statue we found in Istanbul?" Kidd asked.

When Kidd said "Angel" a chill ran up and down Elena's spine.

"Ugh! I'm still having nightmares about how the cistern below the city collapsed on me," said Elena. "It was so hard to recover from being temporarily paralyzed."

"I know it was painful, but I built you that pool," said Kidd. "Didn't that help a little?"

"No, I meant it was hard to recover because Abria was constantly in my face telling me to stretch and exercise and whatever."

"Ha, ha..." Abria replied dryly and then she made a face at Elena. "At least you can walk."

"We do not possess any specific details about the Angel, as of yet," Fergie continued as if there'd been no interuption. "However, if we take all the other artifacts into consideration, the Cup that tells the future and the Tablets that are to be used to rule the world, it seems only logical that the Angel contains some type of properties for invoking absolute control over the earth. Or perhaps telling the future so that one has enough knowledge to rule the world."

"Anyone else worried that there's a person out there that wants to rule the whole world himself?" Pigg asked nervously.

"He already does rule the world," Elena said bitterly.

"That is not technically accurate," Fergie said formally. "If he knew for certain that he controlled the entire world he would not be fervently searching for mythological artifacts."

Kidd suddenly stood and stretched, groaning loudly.

"Anyone else done with this today? It's not like we can figure anything out from the underground of Atlanson."

"You're right," Austin agreed, though Elena noticed that he looked disappointed. "Besides, Grandma Haddock wants us home for dinner."

As everyone else exited the clubhouse, Elena stopped Pigg at the door and asked, "Think you could sneak over for my birthday party? Grandma says it's going to be spectacular, though she won't tell me what she's planning. But at least we'll all be together."

Pigg shifted his gaze away.

"I can't. Mom refuses to come. And I'm afraid if I lie and come to your house she'll catch me. Remember what I was just saying about her skinning me alive? Gives me the shakes thinking about it."

"But," Elena said, feeling astounded. "You've never missed one of my birthdays, I mean, not since I've known you."

"I'm really sorry," Pigg said, turning red in the face. "But you know how irrational my mom gets. I don't want to make her unnecessarily enraged. She lives in a constant state of being irate to begin with. I don't want to make things worse, you know?"

Elena did know. Emelie Pigg had never looked like she wanted to be at any of Elena's past birthdays. And there was the time she yelled at Elena's mom for suggesting that Pigg join them for physical training. And of course Elena would never forget how furious Emelie had been when she'd found them soaking wet from the rain simulation.

"What does your dad say?" Elena pressed. "Can't he bring you?"

Pigg shrugged and said in a non-committal tone, "Oh, you know Dad..."

Elena certainly did know Pigg's dad, too. Norman had always been very quiet, patient, and steady. Pigg's parents were such an unusual couple, in that they always acted as though they simply tolerated one another's company.

"Look, I've gotta go," Pigg said as they climbed back through the iron clad door into the alleyway.

Before Elena could even ask when she'd see him again, Pigg had sprinted to the end of the alley and disappeared into the crowded Decatur Road.

"You know what?" Elena said to Austin and the others. "I really think that Pigg's mom is getting crazier each year."

"Lena..." Austin sighed.

"No, seriously!" Elena insisted. "Remember when we got back from New York and Hannibal came to the Haddock apartment? She was livid."

"Well, she had every right to be angry," Austin pointed out. "We had done something illegal."

"I kno-wha," Elena said in an irritated tone. "But then she tried to get him switched outta the Firebird Unit like a half dozen times. I swear, she's crazy."

"Can we talk about something else?" Kidd said suddenly, sounding impatient. "What does it matter what Big E...I mean...what Pigg's mom is like?"

Elena felt her cheeks grow warm in embarrassment. "It's just, he's never missed one of my birthdays before."

Ever since Pigg had not been chosen to advance with Elena, Austin, and the rest of their friends to Special Ops at Grimsby she'd experienced varying waves of concern for how much the future with all her friends was about to change.

"Hey," Austin said, breaking into her thoughts. "How about we celebrate with Pigg at the Firebird Station when we get back to school?"

Elena shook her head stubbornly and stared up at the ceiling, which was a sophisticated hologram that today displayed a sea of storm clouds mixed with rainbows. "No, that's okay. It doesn't really matter. Whatever we do for my birthday is gonna be great."

Suddenly, a holographic figure approached Abria asking if she wanted to step inside her shop to buy a bottle of perfume. Behind the hologram, the walls flashed three dimensional advertisements of women modeling the trending fashions.

"No, thanks!" Abria said sweetly. "I've already spent too much today."

Somehow Abria managed to escape the allure of consumerism. She skipped to catch up with Elena and the others.

"I hope that Declan is back at the Haddock apartment," Abria said. "I really want to show him all the pretty things I bought today. I know he probably won't care, but as my twin he's required to give me some attention. Besides, the boy needs a little distraction lately."

"From what?" Elena asked as they stepped onto an elevator and started up the side of her resident tower.

"Err…oh, you know…just normal moody teenager stuff," Abria said, lifting her shoulders into an uncommitted shrug. Then, she buried her face into one of the shopping bags.

Elena looked out the glass window of the elevator to the spectacular polished rotunda roofs, avant-garde style office suites, and parks with playing fountains and thought about how Declan had been noticeably absent from a lot of their gatherings over the past three days. He'd made excuses about not feeling well, but Elena was starting to think that it was something more.

Kidd and Declan were staying in rooms at the Haddock apartment while she, Abria, and Fergie were staying at her parents' apartment. Somehow, even though she knew her parents weren't there, returning to Atlanson seemed easier with all her friends there.

Elena felt Kidd's hand slip into hers. She smiled at him as they all stepped off the elevator. Then, she noticed Grandma Haddock standing in the hallway looking pleased. It'd been a long time since Elena had seen her without a look of worry on her face. Her long black hair was glistening and she had a fresh application of makeup on her face.

"Oh, Sweetheart, there you are. I have something special to show you," Grandma Haddock said to Elena. And then, looking at Austin and Kidd, she added, "You boys go in and wash up for supper. I'll have the girls back in a few minutes."

Grandma Haddock scanned her Trademark into the Ransom's apartment door and it slid open silently.

"I am so excited about this gift," Abria said, giggling with delight. "I can't wait until you see! And, oh my, I can't tell you how jealous I am!"

"No need to be jealous, Dear," Grandma Haddock said. "I already said you are welcome to borrow anything that Elena does not choose."

Elena's brow furrowed in confusion as they filed into Truman and Hannah Ransom's bedroom. Then, her mouth dropped open as she saw the walls aligned with racks of fancy frocks, show stopping shoes, sparkling handbags, and demure hats.

"These are my mom's dresses and things," Elena said, looking puzzled.

"I know," Grandma Haddock replied. "I had them sent out to be cleaned and then set up in here for you to look through. You are her size now. I thought you might like choose a few things."

"Where would I wear these dresses?" Elena asked. "We have uniforms at school and then I normally wear combat boots and trousers, you know..."

"I meant that I would like you to wear one tomorrow night for your birthday party," Grandma Haddock said a glimmer in her eye.

"Oh, right, my party..." Elena said slowly as she walked towards the racks, now keenly aware that Grandma Haddock did not want her wearing her normal attire to the birthday dinner.

Her fingers slid slowly through the gowns of silk, and frocks of colors, and patterns of delight.

"My mom sure was fine."

"She was," Grandma Haddock replied genuinely. "The finest of all."

"She was superb!" Abria said exuberantly, caressing them to her cheek. "I mean, would you just look at these shoes? They're like a work of art."

"You should wear those," Elena said with a smile. "They would look totally, like, awesome on you."

"You mean it?" Abria asked in awe.

"Of course, choose anything you like," Elena said. Then she turned towards Fergie and added, "Are you too serious for fashion?"

"With a friend like Abria I cannot afford to be too serious about any subject," Fergie replied formally, but with a smirk.

▭ 2 ▭

A Birthday to Remember

"It's your birthday!"

Abria's tinkling voice filled Elena's ears. She opened one eye slowly as Abria plopped down on the edge of her bed.

"I talked it over with the guys last night and we're taking you out for a fabulous breakfast."

"Right now?" Elena asked groggily.

"Well, obviously we'll wait for you to get dressed, but yes, right now," Abria said. "And then we're going shopping! So exciting! And Wheeler said something about Simulabs, but Austin said something about skateboarding so we'll just let them settle that. But we havta be back early so we can get ready for the magnificent dinner that Grandma Haddock has planned for you!"

"Could you maybe give me five more minutes to wake up?" Elena grumbled. "It is *my* birthday after all."

"Yes, of course!" Abria said in a bubbly voice, but then she caught the look on Elena's face and whispered, "I'll just go now. Take your time."

Abria eased out of the room while Elena threw the covers over her face. She settled comfortably into her bed for a moment when she heard movement from across the room.

"Abria!" Elena called from under the blankets. "FIVE. MORE. MINUTES!"

"Still a grouch in the morning after all these years? You really need to work on that."

Elena threw the covers off and sat up quickly. "Austin, you know if I changed too much we wouldn't be able to be friends."

Austin smiled and sat on the edge of Elena's bed. "Abria tried to warn me not to come in here..."

"You should've already known that," Elena inserted.

"Wow! Someone needs to brush her teeth." Austin smiled and she punched him in the stomach. "But anyway, I needed to do this with you alone." He extended his hand with a wrapped gift. "In ancient culture, a sixteenth birthday held special significance..."

Elena quickly unwrapped the paper. She opened a box to reveal a seven-inch long writing instrument with a replica of the Kairos at one end.

"It's beautiful!" Elena breathed.

"It's called a King's Quill," Austin said.

"Where did you get it?"

"From Grandma," Austin replied. "Your parents left it with her before they died. Along with this..."

He handed her a piece of folded parchment.

"It's been a long time since I've seen a piece of paper," Elena said as she unfolded the creases.

"Happy Birthday, Sunshine," the note read in her dad's handwriting. "The King's Quill symbolizes authority and a responsibility for your own life. Your mom and I hope that you will find it helpful in the years to come. Love you always."

Elena absorbed the instrument with her eyes. If a King's Quill meant it was time to take responsibility for her own life then she wasn't sure she was ready to accept such a gift. The struggle to preserve her parent's legacy since their untimely death had been a challenge for Elena and it was a task she wasn't sure she could continue.

"I wish Dad and Mom were here," she said sadly.

"Me, too," Austin replied. "I'm glad you're here though. And that we can spend your birthday together."

"Me, too." Elena stared at the quill again. "Think I could hide this in my clothes to get it back to school?"

"I already had Pigg make you a special body bubble," Austin said. "Now, get dressed. And brush your teeth."

Moments later, Elena had finished getting ready. She and Austin left her apartment with all her friends, except Pigg. They made their way to Decatur Road where they played one of the new, multigamer Simulabs.

Then, they stopped at several vending carts to grab snacks. Atlanson was alive with young faces; teens home from school and young ones about to start Grimbsy.

Eventually, they went to Sector 7 for a skateboarding race. And, though Abria insisted that Fergie wasn't flexible enough for balance on a board she learned several moves that even made Elena jealous.

Finally, Elena sat at her favorite table for lunch at Ranchers Cantina and filled up on all her favorite foods while Declan and Abria shared stories about the different themed birthday parties their parents had thrown for them growing up. Elena and Kidd listened in silence, holding hands under the table. She couldn't remember feeling happier since her parents died.

"Time to get ready for dinner," Abria said airily after she swallowed her last bite of fried bread with honey drizzle.

"Abria! We've just finished lunch," Elena said sassily. "How could it possibly take us six hours to get ready for dinner?"

"Don't you worry about that," Abria replied. "I have the entire afternoon planned out."

Elena couldn't help but roll her eyes and groan. But before Elena had a chance to shout "good-bye" to Kidd, Austin, and Declan, Abria grabbed her left arm and Fergie grabbed her right. Then, the two girls hurried her out the door and down the lane.

First, Abria took Elena into a shop on Peachtree Street that she'd never even noticed before. A dozen women sat in a row of reclining chairs and each had an android serving them. Some robots were cleaning feet, some were cleaning hands, some were serving a bubbly liquid in tall flutes, and others were massaging oils into legs, arms, and faces.

"What are we doing here?" Elena said, feeling slightly overwhelmed.

"We're having our nails glossed and our feet prettified!" Abria replied jovially. "Now, I bet you're really glad you kept your toes after that frostbite scare during Level 2 studies."

Elena held up her nail bitten hand and said, "I don't have nails."

"Not to worry! Not to worry!" Abria replied, shoving Elena down into the first open chair. "They can take care of that."

Elena marveled at the speed in which an android appeared and stripped off her jump boots and socks. Her feet were placed in a small tub of warm water while another android grabbed one of her hands.

"Your nails are very short," the robot said.

"Obviously," Elena said dryly.

"This will hurt," the android replied as it proceeded to attach acrylic nails to Elena's finger tips.

"Use the dark blue polish with the sparkles on her hands and feet," Abria instructed from Elena's left. "It's gonna be so perfect with your dress."

Elena looked to her right and snorted a laugh at Fergie who looked as uncomfortable as she felt.

"So, by the look on your face I'm guessing that Abria didn't warn you about our little pre-dinner party outing," Elena said to Fergie.

"On the contrary," Fergie replied in a tone of formality. "I was informed, or rather I should say *warned*, but I was powerless to say 'no' given that it is your birthday."

"You're right, it's *my* birthday," Elena said loudly. "That means I can say 'no', Abria."

"You can't today because today isn't just about you. Grandma Haddock has gone to a lot of trouble to make sure your birthday feast is completely, like, a-maz-ing." Abria replied. "It's only right of us to return her kindness by making you look the part."

Hours later, Elena stood in the full length mirror in her parent's bathroom. She barely recognized herself. Abria had managed to pile some of her red curls onto the top of her head while the rest spilled beautifully down to her shoulders. The makeup that Abria had used covered up some of her freckles and her eyes were transformed in a striking fashion.

Elena remembered the last time she'd seen her mom in the midnight blue gown that fell in delicate, sparkling waves of material to the floor. Her parents had just finished getting ready for a special ceremony at her mom's hospital. Her dad had brought flowers and was dressed in a black suit.

Now, Hannah Ransom's dress fit Elena perfectly and even the high heeled shoes she'd chosen glittered just right in the light. She tugged at the Kairos hanging around her neck.

This was the first birthday she'd really celebrated since her parents' death. When she turned fourteen, they were in New York City getting the Amulet from the Island Station under the Statue of Liberty.

When she turned fifteen they were on their way to Istanbul and her Decoy Humanoid had taken her place at the party table in Atlanson.

"Okay, now that you're done, I've got to go finish getting ready," Abria said.

Elena looked at Abria in disbelief. Her friend already looked all kinds of gorgeous.

"How much longer can it possibly take you to get ready?"

"You shouldn't rush perfection," Abria scolded her. "Besides most people don't have the luxury of being as naturally beautiful as you."

"You have me blushing," Elena said dryly.

The doorbell suddenly rang through the apartment.

Abria squealed to the top of her lungs, "They weren't supposed to be here for ten more minutes! I still haven't finished making sure that every single strand of my hair will stay up in this meticulously beautiful twist."

Elena laughed as she looked at her friend. "Don't worry. I'll get the door."

She walked into the hall and saw Declan looking into the monitor in such a goofy way that she completely forgot they'd been estranged for a few days. She couldn't help but laugh as she scanned her Trademark to open the door.

"Wow!" Declan exclaimed at the sight of her, but then both he and Elena blushed. He scratched the back of his neck uncomfortably. "Um, I meant to say 'Hi' and it came out wrong. Let me try that again." He paused for a brief moment and repeated, "Wow!"

Elena smiled shyly. She noticed Declan was wearing a formal, high collared tunic with tailored slacks.

"And you look dashing." Elena paused and stuck the tip of one of her fake fingernails in her mouth. "Did I say *dashing?*"

"Yes, you did say that. How embarrassing!" Declan teased.

"Where's everyone else?"

"Wheeler said he had to run out to get something. Everyone else is waiting on you at Austin's and," Declan held his arm out, "I'm to escort you to your birthday dinner in the *proper fashion*, as Grandpa Haddock put it."

"Wait for us!" Abria said, her voice laced with joy as she and Fergie arrived at the front door.

Fergie's hair was slicked back away from her face and she wore a sleek form fitting black dress that was draped in jewels. But Abria was the most stunning of all with a periwinkle pink gown and a head full of blond curls spilling down her back.

"Aren't you going to say anything?" Abria prompted Declan.

"Perfection!" Declan said admiringly. "Now, my ladies, we have a party to get to."

He held both his arms out to the three girls. They all linked arms together and walked the few steps down the hall to the Haddock's front door, which was just opening.

"Lena, you're stunning," Austin said admiringly.

Elena didn't even try to hide her smile.

Then, her mouth fell open as she walked into the Haddock apartment. The place had been completely transformed. Crystal chandeliers hung from the ceiling and white draperies graced the tables and chairs. Pearly lanterns were strung about. An ostentatious table was set with candle light, white branches that sparkled, and vase after vase of white flowers.

"Oh, Elena!" Grandma Haddock gushed. "You are a vision! You are as classy as your mom. She'd be so proud of you."

"Grandma, what is all this?" Elena asked.

"This, my dear, is called a 'King's Feast,'" Grandma replied. "And we couldn't do any less for your sixteenth birthday. The dinner will include twelve courses of delicious food."

"The Haddock apartment has never looked more stunning!" Abria gushed to Grandma Haddock.

"Thank you for all your decorating help, Dear," she replied. Then, she turned to Elena and said, "As it turns out, Abria has an eye for décor and beauty."

"My lords and ladies," Grandpa Haddock said in a booming voice. He, too, was dressed in a tailored tunic with sleek slacks. "Let the feast begin."

"But, where's Wheeler?" Elena asked.

"I'm here!" Kidd declared as he came racing from the back hallway. "Sorry, I'm late."

Elena was too distracted to be curious about his whereabouts as she was ushered to a chair that was decorated for a queen. She marveled at the first Humanoid that arrived with a white plate dotted with a white spoon swimming with a piece of white fruit garnished with greenery and a zest of lemon.

"First, we have tea-smoked lychee," Grandma Haddock said. "And then next we'll have a bite-sized delicacy in fried cups."

"Why's it so small?" Declan asked, examining the soup spoon that was set before him.

"Everything will be taken in small bites tonight so one does not get too full during each course," Grandma Haddock explained. "That way one can enjoy the entire twelve courses."

"Well, this guy would like a plate full," Declan replied.

"Trust me," Grandpa Haddock said to Declan. "You don't want to tell Mrs. Haddock how to throw a dinner party."

Declan smirked and became silent.

"When Elena was born she was the most beautiful baby anyone had ever seen with her full head of curly, red hair," Grandma Haddock said reminiscently as the Humanoids brought more plates of food to the table.

"How do you know? You weren't there," Elena laughed, but then she noticed a strange look on Grandma's face. "Were you there?"

Grandma Haddock laughed uneasily and said, "Of course I wasn't actually present, but I've seen holofotos. Oh, but you were smart and brave, scrappy and inquisitive."

"That sounds like our Elena," Abria said joyfully.

"She was great at solving puzzles, even when she was a baby," Grandpa Haddock added. "And was always attentive when her dad would tell stories. Oh, Truman Ransom was a lover of history and a uniquely gifted man."

Elena felt strangely uncomfortable, almost like Grandpa and Grandma Haddock had known her family a lot longer than they'd led her to believe. But before she could ask a single question, a Humanoid arrived with something that Grandma Haddock called a consommé, which Elena felt was a fancy way of saying "soup."

The consommé was followed with seared fresh tuna and smoked salmon with cream cheese, sliced marinated onions, and capers. Then, they had a round of oysters.

"Are these things *supposed* to taste slimy going down?" Elena asked, as what felt like a slug slid down her throat.

"Yes, it's a delicacy," Abria said authoritatively. "We eat them all the time at home, except there the oysters taste fresher. I supposed it's because we, like, pluck them out of the sea and suck them straight down."

"Ewww!" Elena exclaimed, feeling sickened in her stomach.

The next Humanoid brought out a colorful assortment of marinated artichoke hearts, roasted red peppers, salty olives, rustic artisan breads, natural deli meats, and rich cheeses. Toasted focaccia bread with sardines and sweet onions lined another plate with sliced tomatoes and garlic-stuffed green olives. And yet another platter had shaved prosciutto with chunks of fresh cantaloupe, a bowl of mixed roasted nuts, and grilled vegetables with marinated mozzarella.

"Now you're speaking my language," Declan said, as he gazed at the new assortment of treats.

"What's this one called again?" Elena asked, looking at the different colored meats and cheeses.

"Capocollo and caciotta cheese with green olives," said Grandma Haddock, clearly pleased.

"I could eat it all day," Elena said, shoving another bite into her mouth.

"Don't get too full," warned Grandma Haddock. "We still have seven courses to go."

Throughout the meal, Grandpa and Grandma Haddock told anecdotes about Elena and her parents. Elena laughed so often that soon her cheeks began to hurt.

Then, Abria and Declan entertained them with stories from their first three years of school; about being stuck in the mud during their first Gauntlet, about all the horrible water training during Level 2, and about Elena pushing other students off the platform in Level 3 training.

Elena was now laughing so hard at the reenactments that tears leaked from her eyes. As her eyes began to blur, she noticed a person standing in the corner of the room. She immediately became somber and rubbed her eyes so that she could see more clearly.

Elena knew that she was still in the Haddock apartment, but she was also standing in an entirely different place that would have frightened her more had it not been for the fact that Hannah Ransom was standing there.

Elena was aware that somehow the Cognicross program in her head had started operating while she was sitting there, but she was feeling slightly panicked because before this moment it had only ever worked while she was asleep. She took a minute to remind herself of something that Austin had once told her about the Cognicross:

—

"You have a device in your brain that triggers dreams for you. Most likely the device is programmed with stories that were created specifically for you to know. The program is called Cognicross because it combines a cross between human cognition and a simulation."

Elena centered herself. If the Cognicross was working at this moment, she was confident that there was a reason. She took a deep breath and looked intently at her mother.

"Mom? What are you doing here?" Elena asked in a strained voice.

"Elena, so happy that you could join me," Hannah replied, opening her arms in a loving way at once.

Elena stumbled across the room and fell into her mom's safe embrace. She breathed in Hannah's lavender scented hair.

"I am very happy to see you, my sweet girl," Hannah said.

Elena suddenly looked around, feeling confused by the abrupt change of scenery.

"But, where are we?"

"At my work, of course," Hannah said as she turned and gestured toward a room filled with ghostly bodies.

Each of the bodies was suspended in midair and was being monitored by Optivision screens. Elena noticed Hannah was wearing the same high collared uniform that she wore when she worked at the hospital, but this place looked nothing like the hospital.

"This isn't where you work," Elena said sensibly. "And I would know because Austin and I spent hours and hours there when we were younger because he wanted to learn how to use that Suturand you gave him for his birthday that one time."

Elena started to laugh at the memory, but then hesitated because even her memory of Austin seemed out of place.

"Mom, this place is super creepy," said Elena. "Where are we? And who are all these strange looking people?"

"This is my work," Hannah said and then she turned and started in a brisk walk through the rows and rows of pale human bodies.

Elena hurried to catch up, but Hannah never looked back.

"Where are you going?"

"To my lab," Hannah said over her shoulder. "It's through here."

Elena stepped after her mom into a room filled with strange equipment and Optivison screens from floor to ceiling, except for one entire wall that was made from glass and looked out over the room filled with the ghostly bodies.

"What's all this for?" asked Elena.

"This is part of our work," said Hannah. "Part of your work for the Renegades."

Elena hung her head sorrowfully.

"Mom, I can't do that stuff anymore," she said softly. "I almost died a few days ago. It wasn't the first time either. I can't look for artifacts anymore. My friends could get really hurt."

Then, Elena felt a shiver of terror course through her body as Hannah screeched, "Come find me!"

"Lena? Lena, are you alright?"

Austin's sharp tone caused Elena to jump in her seat. She became conscious to the fact that she was sitting at the elaborately decorated table in the Haddock apartment. Her birthday dinner was still going on, yet her meeting with her mom was beginning to blur from her vision.

"Are you okay?" Kidd asked, squeezing her hand.

Elena blinked rapidly and cleared her throat.

"Oh, yeah. I'm so sorry for spacing out there. I was thinking about my mom," Elena said.

Grandma Haddock gave her a sympathetic look and said, "Of course you are. Well, now that the eleventh course is finished we will take a short break so I can check to make sure the coffee service is set up correctly while the Humanoids prepare the birthday cake. Feel free to stretch, but don't go too far!"

Kidd leaned towards her and whispered, "Are you sure you're okay?"

Elena nodded, determined to put the disruption with her mom out of her head.

"Okay, well, I'm going to the restroom."

"I'll wait here," Elena replied, forcing herself to wink in a playful way.

After Kidd left the table, Elena watched Declan leave the room in the opposite direction. So, while the others stood around the living room talking she followed the hall towards the back of the apartment, determined to get her mom out of her head. She found Declan in one of the secondary bedrooms.

"Hey," Elena said, coming into the room. "You decided not to stay in Austin's room?"

Declan barely looked up at her and vaguely replied, "Yeah, it was easier for us all to have our own rooms. Wheeler's room is next door if that's who you're looking for."

Elena moved into the room slowly. "I haven't seen you a lot at meals and things the past few days." She waited for a moment, but when he didn't respond she continued. "In fact, I think tonight is the first meal I've seen you at since we got back from school."

"You've been unusually busy with Simulabs lately," Declan replied. "So, I didn't guess you'd notice."

"Look, I know we all hated Wheeler, especially me, and it must be weird now that we're sorta...um...*together*. But I was hoping that it wouldn't change our friendship."

"Are you asking me to be *friends* with Wheeler?"

"Maybe not friends, but friendly."

He shook his head and sighed. "I think you're missing the point of my absence lately."

Elena's brow bent into confusion. "What's going on? Is something else wrong?"

Declan looked up, his gaze on her so steady that Elena felt her cheeks warm. "You're unforgettable in that dress."

Elena wasn't sure why, but she looked away, feeling embarrassed. "Grandma Haddock had some of my mom's old things cleaned for me."

"Abria told me," Declan said steadily. "That was nice of her."

"Yeah, Grandma has always been pretty great like that," Elena replied. "Abria picked out the dress and shoes. Then, she made me get my hair, makeup, nails, and toes done. You should have seen her at the salon. It was like it was her birthday, or something, she was so excited."

Elena realized that she was beginning to ramble nervously, but she couldn't stop herself from talking.

"I hate these fake nails, by the way. I know they're supposed to make me look pretty, but I've already poked myself in the eye with them about three thousand times and I could barely hold my fork at dinner because they feel so unnatural. Well, I mean, I guess they are *unnatural* because…you know…they're fake…"

Elena couldn't understand why she was still talking about her nails, but fortunately Declan interrupted her.

"Here," he said, walking towards her with a rectangular object in his outstretched hand. "A gift for your birthday."

Elena accepted a heavy, hardback book into her hands. She opened the cover and flipped through the first few pages, which were filled with beautifully illustrated children's stories.

"Where did you get this?" Elena breathed.

"When we were in Istanbul I found a whole library, but this one was sitting open on a table. After I brushed off the dust, I saw this…"

Elena saw a womanly figure that looked like a blend between a warrior equipped with weapons and a royal with a crown of jewels.

"She's very fierce looking. She made me think of you," said Declan. "But then you got hurt and we had such a crazy year I thought I'd hang onto it for a while."

"I'm glad you did. This is the perfect gift." Elena sighed. "Look, Bowen…"

"Hey Ransom!" Kidd's voice calling from down the hall interrupted her. "Time to cut some cake."

Declan looked at Elena expectantly. She wasn't sure what she was going to say next, so she blushed and looked away.

"I guess I should get back. Thanks again for the book."

When everyone was gathered back around the formal dining table, three Humanoids arrived carrying the most elaborate cake Elena had ever seen.

"Grandma, who's going to eat all this cake?" Elena asked as the cake was being served.

"Don't you worry, I'll make sure its eaten, even if I have to eat it all myself," she replied with a wink.

Elena smiled genuinely and hugged her tightly.

"Thank you so much! Oh, and Grandpa, too. This has been the best birthday since." — she stopped short of saying "since my parents died" — "I mean it's been the best birthday I've had in years."

"Is it alright if we take the birthday girl out for a while?" Austin asked his grandparents.

"Of course," Grandpa Haddock said.

"But we want all of you home by curfew," Grandma Haddock added. "And Elena, don't make plans for lunch tomorrow. Grandpa and I are taking you and Austin out for a picnic in the park."

Elena nodded as she and her friends left the apartment and climbed onto the elevator.

"I. Am. So. Full!" Abria said, holding her stomach.

"And I'm starving," said Declan. "I know that was a lot of food, but each course was only two or three bites at most. I say we go to that place where all the meat is carved off the rotisserie as it's ordered."

In next to no time, Elena and her friends were sitting down to yet another meal for the day.

"I can't believe we have to, like, be back at school in a few days," Abria said as she flipped through options on the menu screen.

"Yeah, it seems like we've been gone for a really long time," Declan said.

"How are we gong to get the Independence back to school?" Kidd asked Austin.

"We aren't," Austin replied. "If it's okay with you, I suggest we leave it in the access tunnel here in Atlanson. I don't see how we'll have time to get it back to school. Our Humanoids are already on board. They can stay here as well."

"It's fine with me," Kidd said.

Elena smiled. She felt relieved that the Independence would be staying in Atlanson because it would make it harder for Austin to ask them to go on another quest to find artifacts. She turned her head to look out the window and caught sight of a very familiar person standing across the street.

The petite, pretty girl had long blonde hair and bangs swept over her forehead. Her expressive eyes were fixed on Elena.

"Look!" Elena pointed. "There's Melly."

Austin and the others all scrambled around the window.

The last time Elena had seen Pamela "Melly" Linus was on a busy street in Harleston Village. And that was after Elena and her friends had gone looking for Melly's family in Crowfield Plantation only to discover that the Linus family had never existed in Crowfield. Melly's very existence was confusing.

"What's she, like, doing here?" Abria said.

Elena had already kicked off her shoes and pulled her dress up over her knees.

"I don't know, but I'm going to find out."

And then, she took off running out of the restaurant, straight for Melly.

¤ 3 ¤

The Future Awaits

As soon as Elena started running, Melly took off as well in the opposite direction. She could hear Austin calling her name, but she didn't stop. She was desperate to know what Melly wanted and wasn't going to let anyone or anything stand in her way.

Elena struggled in pursuit as she pushed through the crowd of people. But soon enough, Melly's blonde head was lost. Elena could do nothing to catch up. She doubled over grabbing her ribs, until eventually her friends found her on the street.

"I didn't realize that Melly could run so fast," Elena gasped. "I don't understand why she wants to get away from me."

"Why? It's not like you two are, like, friends or anything," Abria said. "And just look at the mess you've made of your hair!"

"But Melly *wants* me to *see* her!" Elena said, the edges of her words heavy with frustration. She looked at Austin. "Remember when she ran from me at Harleston Village a few months ago? I don't understand why she wants me to know that she's out there, but she won't talk to me."

"I'm wondering why you're so, like, crazy about it," said Abria.

"Yeah, Ransom, let it go," Kidd said.

"You're right," Elena said, shifting her eyes away and feeling disappointed. "I think I'm done for tonight. I'm going home to relax."

"Oh-wa, I was hoping to walk through the square again," Abria said.

Elena looked at Abria and pouted.

"How about I escort the birthday girl home so the rest of you can stay out a little longer," Austin said, taking Elena's arm.

Elena looked at Kidd, but he waved her on, so she turned to walk away with Austin.

"Do you want to tell me what's going on tonight?" Austin asked.

"What do you mean?" asked Elena.

"Well, at dinner you completely zoned out," Austin reminded her. "And now you have this thing about Melly. Is something wrong?"

Elena bit her bottom lip, struggling to decide how to say everything that was on her mind.

"Well, first it's weird that Pigg wasn't at my party. Then, at dinner I had this thing, sort of like a Cognicross of my mom, except that it seemed like it was happening in real time instead of something from the past. And then we came out and saw Melly, but every time I see her she runs from me. And I don't know why, but that all seems connected. It's super weird, right?"

"Life's certainly been weird lately."

"And it's weird that Bowen hasn't been around much at all since we've been home," she added. "Why has he been so distant?"

"It's not that Bowen hasn't been around," said Austin. "It's that you've been more preoccupied with a *certain person* we all love to hate. I think that person is also the reason that I can't get you to come to any meetings about artifacts."

Elena didn't want to tell Austin that the real reason she wasn't attending meetings was that she'd given up on the pursuit for artifacts, so she said, "I'll admit that I really hated Wheeler and he's the last person I thought I'd end up with, but he's different than I thought. Now that I know what he's been through I sorta understand him better." Elena sighed. "Today was supposed to be happy and carefree and it's ended up a mess, just like the rest of my life."

"Your whole life isn't a mess," Austin said. "Sure, we've got a few things to figure out and, yes, some crazy things have happened this year, but overall we've got a lot to look forward to."

"I wish I could be as optimistic as you," Elena grumbled.

"Well, there's still time to improve. You are only sixteen, after all."

A while later, Elena lay in bed thinking about Melly and worrying about what school was going to be like now that Pigg wasn't going to be around as much. Then, she thought about how quickly her feelings for Kidd had changed and wondered if perhaps she was losing her mind. She thought about the Cognicross of her mom and the supernatural conditions of the dream. Had an element of it been real? It had certainly felt real to her.

Soon, she was standing in her dad's office. She was overjoyed to see him sitting at his desk, but she didn't dare go to him because he was speaking to the Ransom Dossier.

"Imperator has learned of the Firebird Disc, though Roman has assured me that he does not know the function of the Disc," Truman Ransom said. "Roman continues to create innovative strategies for protecting the Disc. He is confident that Imperator will not find this artifact and that, even if he does locate it, he won't know how to use it."

Elena felt as though she'd heard him say this before. Perhaps in a past life. But when she thought more, she realized that the Firebird Disc was familiar to her. Then, she noticed that her dad was writing something using a very familiar instrument.

"Sunshine, you can come over here," Truman called.

"Dad, what's the King's Quill for?" Elena asked as she walked toward him.

Before he could answer, Melly arrived. Elena tried to approach her, but was surprised when Melly sat in Truman's lap. He spoke as if Melly were his daughter. When Elena tried to interfere, she found that she was unable to move nor speak. However, her mind was raging against her body, willing it to move.

"No! You can't have him," Elena screamed at Melly in her mind.

Soon, Elena gained slight consciousness and realized that her bed sheets were wrapped around her in a confining way. She felt slightly alarmed at the amount of sweat that had soaked her hair in the short minutes that she'd been sleeping.

Elena rolled over uncomfortably. Maybe her dad wanted her to know something more about the Ransom Dossier or the Renegades or the Firebird Disc. The internal battle that she continued to struggle with came to the surface yet again.

She was sure that her parents had created the Cognicross specifically for her mind, which meant that all the programs on it were a warning of some kind, or a clue, or a piece of information that they wanted her to have. But, she no longer had any desire to pursue an understanding of it.

Elena was bothered that she didn't seem to have any control over when she got the information and what it meant. How would she be able to tell the difference between her actual thoughts and what she was programmed to see? She was tired of thinking about the artifacts and she certainly didn't want her parent's work to dominate her choices any longer.

Early the next morning, Elena tried to push the memory of her dream out of her head as she and Kidd ate breakfast at a little restaurant on the square that overlooked the park. She was just telling herself again that it was time to move on from artifacts and continue living in the here and now, when Kidd pulled out a little box and slid it across the table to her.

"So, I realized that the breathing apparatus I gave you at the lake was not the best birthday gift," Kidd started.

"Because I told you..." Elena interrupted.

"Anyway, I made you a gift, but I didn't want to give it to you in front of everyone else."

Elena smiled and lifted the lid. She pulled out a length of leather that was woven with shaped pieces of metal.

"I made it with scraps from Sector 7," Kidd explained as he tied the leather to her wrist. "So you can always have a piece of home with you no matter where we go in the world."

"It's perfect," Elena said honestly. "Thank you! But seriously, I'm hoping that we don't have to go anywhere any time soon."

"Me, too," Kidd replied. "Except, there's a new hot air balloon Simulab where we can compete in a race around the world. Wannta try it?"

"I'd rather skateboard."

"Good choice!"

Elena and Kidd talked about frivolous things as they walked through the underground to Sector 7. They skateboarded for a while and finally sat at the top of the skate ramp, looking down over their little kingdom.

"So, I've been meaning to ask you about your aupaire," Elena said as she nibbled on one of her nails. "What was she like?"

"My aupaire?" Kidd asked, looking puzzled.

"Yeah," Elena replied. "Remember when we were in the icy forest simulation during Level 2? I was having that really bad dream and you woke me up. You said that when you had bad dreams as a child your aupaire would wake you that way."

"Actually, I barely remember her," Kidd said dismissively. "But I do remember how pretty you looked in that dress last night."

Elena smiled rigidly, wondering why he didn't want to talk about his past, though she didn't feel comfortable persuading him to share more.

"It felt weird to wear my mom's dress. I have such a vivid memory about the last time she wore it."

She wanted to tell Kidd more about the recollection, but instead she noticed that Kidd was leaning in towards her face. As a reflex, she clapped her hands firmly against her mouth and pulled away. Sector 7 was the one place in the world that she felt she could be herself. She wasn't sure if kissing Kidd there really fit into that.

"Um…" Elena said from behind her hands. "What are you doing?"

"I was going in for a kiss," Kidd said, pulling away awkwardly. "I was clearly rejected. I'll try not to be too embarrassed about it as long as you don't tell anyone."

"I don't mean to *reject* you. I'm not sure I'm ready to…" She couldn't think what else to say. "And anyway, we've only been *a thing* for a few days. It wasn't long ago that I wanted to punch you in the face every time I saw you, remember?"

Kidd smiled and absentmindedly scratched his nose where Elena had once broken it.

"It's not a big deal, Freckles. Let's call it a day. You have your picnic with the grandparents soon anyway."

Kidd stood up stiffly. Elena wanted to say more, to try to make him understand, but she wasn't sure how to talk to him. If he'd been Austin she could have said what was on her mind. But, Kidd wasn't Austin.

Kidd grabbed her hand and helped her to her feet. In complete silence, they made the way back to the park where Grandpa and Grandma Haddock and Austin were waiting for a picnic lunch.

"See you later, Freckles," Kidd said before turning to walk away.

Grandma Haddock had already spread the leftover delicacies from the previous night's dinner party all over a blanket. Elena could see the looks of excitement on Grandpa and Austin's faces so she let the incident with Kidd flee her mind and squatted onto the blanket beside Austin.

"It really was a wonderful birthday," Elena said to Grandma Haddock. "Thanks again so much."

"We're grieved that your parents couldn't be here to see the fine woman that you've grown into," Grandpa Haddock said kindly.

Elena blushed and her eyes began to tear, but she kept eye contact with him instead of looking away.

"Eat! Eat!" Grandma encouraged.

As Elena enjoyed many of the foods from the party the night before, the four talked and laughed for a long while, sharing memories of Elena's parents, and school breaks from when she and Austin were little, and outings they'd taken together.

Towards the end of the picnic, Grandpa Haddock said seriously, "We did have a reason for bringing you out here. We wanted to speak with you briefly about Special Ops."

"Special Ops is beyond physically demanding," Grandma Haddock said. "It's also emotionally challenging."

"We wanted to see if you had any questions about school. We want you to feel as prepared as you can be," Grandpa Haddock added.

"Did you go through it?" Elena asked.

"When we were going through the first generation of Grimsby training, Special Ops wasn't available then," Grandpa said.

"But we watched all of your parents go through the program," Grandma added, frowning slightly. "They had extensive post traumatic stress counseling afterwards."

"If I can survive three years of Marshall, I'm sure I can handle anything they've got for me this year." Elena began to laugh, but Grandpa and Grandma looked somber.

"Is there something you need to tell us?" Grandpa Haddock asked suddenly, almost like she wanted Elena to say something specific.

"Like what?" Elena shrugged feeling confused.

Grandma Haddock paused for a moment and then looked at Elena earnestly.

"For instance, we are slightly concerned with how you're dealing with the loss of your parents. You've never spoken of their death. Plus, the last time you were home you seemed a little distant."

Elena wanted to say that the last time her Humanoid Decoy had taken her place in Atlanson so she and her friends could cross the ocean into the country of Turkey, but she held her tongue.

"You two have gotten into quite a bit of trouble in the past few years," Grandpa Haddock added.

Elena gave Austin a thin smile.

"I know we've been...*challenging*," Elena began carefully. "But we're turning the pages to a new chapter."

"Yes, we're not going to cause anymore trouble," Austin said sincerely.

When the grandparents still didn't look convinced Elena looked them straight in the face and said, "You're right, okay? My parents' death has created all kinds of feelings, like loneliness and carelessness, to name some. But things are better now, I promise."

"And, you have this boyfriend now..." Grandpa Haddock started.

Elena's mouth fell open. She looked wide-eyed at Austin.

But before she could accuse him of having a big mouth, Grandma Haddock said, "We could tell by the way you're spending time with that boy."

Elena started to blush and cleared her throat loudly. "Well, it's something really new. I mean, I think we've sort of decided not to hate one another for a change. I'm not sure I would say *boyfriend*."

"Elena," Grandma Haddock interrupted. "We don't want to embarrass you and we certainly don't need an explanation about a boy that you may or may not like. We want to make sure that you and Austin are safe and that you'll feel comfortable coming to us if you have concerns about Special Ops."

"Of course we'll come to you," Austin said genuinely. "And we'll always need you."

Grandma Haddock cupped Austin's face with her hand. "We're so proud of the man you're becoming."

"Okay, okay," Grandpa Haddock said in a kind, but direct manner. "Enough of this. I think they get the point."

As Elena helped Grandma Haddock pack up the remaining food, Austin asked, "Can we go find our friends?"

"Of course," Grandpa Haddock replied and then added with a wink, "But tell Abria she really needs to stop buying up everything in all the stores."

Minutes later, Elena and Austin parted ways with the grandparents and began to walk back towards their resident tower.

"Why do you think they're so worried about Special Ops?" Elena asked. "We've been at Grimsby for three years. If we can get through Marshall we can get through anything."

Austin shrugged, but didn't say anything.

"What's with you?" Elena asked, suddenly aware that he was actually shrugging her off.

"It's nothing," Austin replied.

"Tell me," Elena implored, pulling his arm so he would stop to look at her.

"It's just that a few days ago we were all about searching for artifacts, finding more clues, and learning what it all meant. And now you're spending a lot of alone time with Wheeler. It's like you're not interested in finding what we need to know to defeat Imperator," Austin said.

"Well, we're kinda together now," said Elena. "Isn't that what you're supposed to do? Spend time together."

"I guess so," Austin said.

"Is something wrong with that?"

"Your relationship has changed our group dynamics a bit," Austin admitted.

"In a bad way?"

"Not necessarily," said Austin. "We used to do things all together. And now, someone has to come out searching for you two if we want to talk about the artifacts, or whatever. Not to mention that I can barely get Bowen in the same room with you two. I'm starting to think about how these dynamic are going to effect us in Special Ops."

"Sometimes it's nice to hang around with someone who doesn't talk about artifacts, or boys, or physics all the time."

"Just don't lose yourself," Austin warned. "Wheeler can't be your everything."

"I don't even understand what you're trying to say."

"I'm trying to say that one person shouldn't replace everyone or everything else in your life."

"He's not. We're getting to know one another without all the malicious intent that existed between us before," Elena said. "It's going to take a lot of work."

Austin flung an arm around her shoulder and said, "I really didn't think you'd be the first one of us in a relationship." As Elena rolled her eyes, he added, "I like being wrong sometimes. It's good for me."

■■■

"My mom was horrible!" Pigg screeched after he found Elena and the rest of their friends on the Grimsby Channel headed for school the following week. "Every morning we'd sit in silent meditation for an hour. What she expected me to reflect on that long I still have no idea.

"Then, she'd lecture me for another hour in the importance of safety at school. And how glad she was that I didn't get into Special Ops. And that I needed to choose better friends now that I'm not with the rest of you.

"And about not getting involved in things that draw extra attention to myself. And of course my dad was nearly silent as he normally is. I started sneaking off to Simulabs so I could get away from her. Plus, I needed to keep up with my strength and endurance. But, then she caught me and started having our Humanoid follow me..." Pigg paused midsentence and eyed the bulging rucksack on Abria's lap closely. "What'd you have in there?"

Abria smiled. "I went a little crazy shopping in Atlanson. There were just, like, far too many charming stores. I simply couldn't leave everything behind. I don't know when I'll get the chance to take all this back to the Galilee Province, but in the meantime I can enjoy my purchases at school. I just had the best time here! I'm seriously thinking I'll make Atlanson my home after our Level 6 commencement."

"Why would you be thinking about graduation?" Elena asked sharply as she felt the train pull away from the station. "It's three years away."

"I know, but after I watched the new Grimsby Initiation Memorandum about how it will be my decision to choose a career path based on our Level 4 training it got me thinking about my future." Abria looked at Austin and added, "I suppose you're going to be a, like, Healing Surgeon."

"I always thought that's what I wanted to do, but I'm also leaning towards a career in government," Austin said.

"What career do you want, Bowen?" Pigg asked as he stuffed a Whimsical candy wedge in his mouth.

"I was thinking maybe an architect," Declan replied.

"We don't have to decide today," Elena said impatiently. "Let's see if we can even survive orientation first."

As the others got up to make their way to the dining car, Elena noticed a frown appear on Kidd's face.

"What's wrong with you?" Elena asked.

Kidd looked hesitant for a minute, but replied, "Tavington contacted me."

"How?" Elena asked, feeling startled.

"It doesn't matter," Kidd said, shaking his head slowly. "He knows that we took my dad's neurolizor. I have a feeling that he'll come for it at some point."

"But, he can't get to us at school, right?" Elena asked.

Kidd shrugged. "I hope not."

"Okay, so let's not worry about him," Elena said, trying to sound cheerful and calm.

"Elena, would you please come with me to get some food?" Pigg had appeared from behind them. "This is my first time going to the dining car that's meant for upperclassmen. Austin said it would be fine if I go with them, but I want to make sure that I don't, you know, draw attention to myself, or eat so much that I make myself sick."

Elena laughed. She went off with Pigg to find something to eat, but soon enough they were pulling into the station at Grimsby School of the Republic.

Elena could feel a pulse of excited energy in the air as she stepped off the train with all the new students and Level 4 trainees.

"Well, I'm off this way," Pigg said, looking sadly toward the gate for the Level 4 trainees. "I've got to get registered with the other members of the Aves Company."

Elena nudged him in the arm and said, "You'll be great. Plus, you already know the Firebirds and most of the other trainees from Raptor, Harrier, and Falcon."

But Pigg didn't look a bit cheerful until Abria hurried over and tossed her arms around his neck.

"Hey, we'll see you for dinner, right?" she asked.

As Pigg walked off grinning sheepishly, Elena heard a strange commotion.

For a moment, she didn't realize what was happening or where the disturbance was coming from, but suddenly there were several older looking students moving between the crowd, pushing people forward and hollering.

"Level 4 Goonies this way!"

"Hustle! Hustle! HUSTLE!"

"Move it! Hustle! Stand in formation OVER THERE."

"YOUR FUTURE AWAITS!"

Elena locked eyes with Austin.

"*Goonies*? What do you think..."

But there was no time to talk because a squad of upper-classmen were physically shoving the Level 4 trainees toward their new resident tower.

▭ 4 ▭

Dino Roman

The Level 4 trainees were corralled into a courtyard at the base of their new resident tower. Elena was nervously quiet as she looked around trying to figure out what was going on.

Then, six students marched to the center of the courtyard. Each of them had their hair gathered into a spikey configuration the tops of their heads, but the sides were shaved so closely to their scalp that Elena had a hard time telling if they were dark or light haired. In fact, from her position she couldn't even tell if they had brown or blue eyes.

Then, the tallest boy called out, "Stand at attention!"

As Elena moved into formation with her friends, she noticed that the boy had hard, lifeless blue eyes.

"I am Dino Roman, Level 5 Special Ops trainer. You will refer to me as Roman or Sir. Is that clear?"

Each one of his words was punctuated with a harsh, strict tone. Elena was so surprised that this boy was addressing them as their leader that no sound came out of her mouth when it opened. She wasn't the only one.

After a poor response by everyone, Dino Roman screamed out, "Are you hard of hearing? Wake up, Goonies! You will refer to me as Roman or Sir. IS. THAT. CLEAR?"

His stern words sent a shock wave through Elena and she joined with the others as they said, "Sir, yes Sir!"

"As part of the Special Ops program, you will now be responsible for your own education. You will access your individual syllabus for the entire year by scanning your Trademark into any pupil station in the Media Lab. You are expected to perform above standard on every subject.

"In addition to your education, you will be expected to adhere to your Enrichment schedule. You will be required to be present at every training period on your schedule. Do you understand?"

Elena was not sure she understood everything that Dino Roman had said, but she joined with the others as they replied, "Sir, yes Sir."

"Your other Level 5 trainers are Sabrina Bauer and Brennan Colt."

Dino Roman indicated the boy and girl to his right, but Elena thought they looked exactly the same.

"And your Level 6 officers are Link Hawkins, Collum Duke, and Charleston Woods. Together, we are *Archon*. We make all the decisions here. We even decide when you're allowed to breathe. You will respect and not question our authority!"

On and on Dino Roman barked rules at them. He didn't draw breath for what seemed an eternity. Elena remembered feeling angry and intimidated when she'd first met their previous Drill Instructor, but the more Roman spoke the more confident she was that he was going to be worse than Marshall.

Elena began to chew her nails, feeling worried about the new demands in Special Ops and wondering if Pigg's orientation was going to be this harsh. She looked around and noticed several familiar faces, including Oscar Hunter. Every trainee looked just as nervous as she felt.

"We are not interested in your personal life or relationships," Roman continued. "There will be zero tolerance for public displays of affection of any kind. There will be no gossiping. There will be no fraternizing during training times. Take time to learn the names and faces of everyone here. We could be placed inside a Tribulation at any moment. Therefore, the more you learn about your fellow trainees the better off you'll be. You are dismissed to the Media Lab and Uniform Lockers."

Then, as suddenly as they'd arrived, the leaders of Archon left the quad in a straight line back toward the resident tower.

"Oh. My. Rude much?" Abria gasped as Elena and her friends came together. "And did you see their hair? Or lack thereof? If we become one of Archon do you think we'll have to wear our hair like that? Because I can't even imagine cutting mine. I mean, I'd look totally, like, terrible. Don't you think I'd look terrible?"

"Roman seems like a really wonderful human being," Elena said sarcastically, completely ignoring Abria. "We were standing there forever. How long did he yell at us?"

"Thirteen minutes and twelve seconds," Fergie said in a tone of formality.

"Well, one thing is perfectly clear to me," Elena said firmly. "I'm going to have to work hard enough to be one of Archon next year."

"Why's that?" Austin asked.

"I can't stand the thought of taking orders from Roman indefinitely."

"Did you hear that part of his little speech where he said we couldn't, like, gossip or have any physical displays of affection?" Abria said, sounding indignant. "So, he basically expects us not to be teenagers?"

"I expect you to be obedient!" Roman barked as he came up from behind them.

Abria turned slowly and flashed him a winning smile. "*Obedient* is such a serious word and..."

"Disobedience has serious consequences," Roman said steadily as he crossed his arms over his chest.

As Abria's face fell, Elena almost started to laugh until Roman turned towards her, eyeing her frizzy red curls and asked, "And what happened to you, *Ugly?*"

"Excuse me?" Elena said shrilly, instantly growing red in the face.

But before she could do anything else, Austin, Declan, and Kidd converged on Roman, essentially pushing Elena out of the way. She wanted to claw her way over the boys so she could punch Roman in the face, but they'd grown so much taller in the past few weeks that she was unable to do anything.

"We were honored to be accepted in the Special Ops program, Roman," Austin said formally. "And we will execute our orders. However, I hope I won't have to remind you again that we also deserve respect."

Roman's face hardened to the point that Elena was sure it might spilt into two pieces as he said, "I've watched you, Haddock, for quite a few years now. One could almost say you've been an *obsession* of mine."

"That's creepy," Elena remarked.

"Therefore, I hope that I won't have to *remind you again* that I won't be manipulated by you," Roman finished without acknowledging Elena's comment.

"My intent is not to manipulate," Austin said authoritatively. "I'm stating plain facts that if you abuse your trainees there will be unavoidable repercussions. A good leader knows that."

"Watch yourself, Haddock," Roman growled in warning. "I'm not accustomed to threats from *Goonies*."

"Again, not making threats. Just stating facts."

Roman gritted his teeth. "Go now and collect your gear from the Uniform Locker. That is an order!"

"Sir, yes Sir," Austin said as he, Declan, and Kidd backed away without taking their eyes off Roman.

But Elena was already stomping away in such a hurry that the others had to race to catch up with her.

"Geesh, that was totally, like, hostile!" said Abria. "And I can't believe he called you 'ugly' to your face. I'd die to have your hair."

Elena stopped suddenly and turned around, facing the three boys.

"What did you think you were doing?" Elena yelled. "I can handle myself! I don't need you three to stand in between me and some guy."

"You're mad at us?" Declan said in disbelief.

"And you," Elena said, pointing at Austin. "How are you so all-of-the-sudden comfortable talking to someone in authority that way?"

"He's not an Instructor, Lena," Austin said. "I've researched Archon and watched the orientation of our training at this facility. This isn't the same as before. In essence, we're not any different from the upper-classmen. Even though they're older, we share the same responsibilities and have the same work orders. This place is a self-governing system and, in this kind of a governing faction, leaders can be overthrown. Best to let Roman know now that he can't impose a totalitarian rule on us."

Elena's mouth fell open as she considered his words.

"I think having friends has made me soft," she eventually grumbled. "Even a year ago I would have pushed you three outta my way and impulsively punched Roman for calling me 'ugly.'"

"We know, Ransom," Kidd said. "Why do you think we stepped in? No point getting demerits the first hour of school. There's plenty of time to earn some tomorrow."

"What are *demerits*?" Elena asked.

"Oh girl," Abria said, flipping her hair over her shoulder and starting back up the sidewalk towards the resident tower. "One day I hope you'll watch the Grimsby Initiation Memorandum so the rest of us don't have to fill you in on, like, everything."

As the friends walked towards the Uniform Locker, Elena couldn't help but notice that the interior décor of their new resident tower could not have been more different than the one they'd used over the past three years. Instead of breathtaking frescos on the walls and ceiling, she saw bare walls and cold, hard floors.

However, as usual, Austin, Declan, and Abria attracted a lot of attention from several of the upperclassmen. Some of them actually seemed to know Austin personally.

For the others, Abria had no problem introducing herself and involving herself in a couple seconds of conversation here and there. Elena was happy to walk along quietly behind them with Kidd and Fergie at her side.

"I wonder how Pigg's doing?" she said absentmindedly as they stepped onto a Grimvator and started slantways for the Uniform Locker.

"I'm sure he's fine," Kidd said dismissively and then asked playfully, "So, do you think this Uniform Locker will work with two people inside?"

"Why?" Elena said slyly. "You want to go in with Austin?"

Kidd smiled. "That's not exactly what I had in mind."

Elena giggled as she scanned her Trademark into one of the doors on the long corridor in the Uniform Locker. The stall opened and she entered a small room with a mirror and dozens of thin panels instead of walls.

Once the door had locked behind her, Elena's face appeared holographically on an Optivision screen in midair. Then, laser lights scanned her entire body.

Once this was complete, a drawer popped open from the wall. Elena removed an armor wear combat shirt, buckle breeches, and combat boots. Everything was black, with hints of camouflage but nothing flashy and no Unit logos to distinguish the outfit.

Elena pulled all the pieces of her new uniform onto her body correctly. Then, the laser lights came on again and scanned her body once more.

A Telecaster appeared holographically and said, "Elena Ransom, please remove the uniform and place it neatly inside the drawer. You may get dressed in your regular clothing. Your wardrobe will arrive in your room momentarily."

Several long minutes later, Elena exited the stall and found that Abria and Fergie were already waiting for her.

"Ugh! The uniforms are, like, so dismal," Abria said. "Black and gray fatigues, yuck!"

Elena smirked. "I actually like the uniform. Black. Finally, something I look good in."

"Oh, puh-lease!" Abria scoffed. "No one wants a boring uniform."

"I'm not sure anyone cares as much as you," Elena pointed out.

"The suits are designed to provide us with camouflage in the field," Fergie said sensibly.

"But I just don't see why…" Abria started to say, but Austin interrupted her.

"We still have to get our schedules." He threw an arm around Abria's shoulder. "Surely your disappointment over the uniforms can be discussed while we walk, right?"

Minutes later, the friends arrived in the Media Lab. This part of the building looked similar enough to the lab from her first three years. Row after row of pupil stations lined the space to make walkways. But there were also clusters of cushiony chairs and long tables with a half wall of glass that rose out of the center of the table.

Feeling thankful that they no longer needed Smartslates, Elena scanned her Trademark into a window-dimensional. However, instead of a familiar looking schedule, she saw a detailed hourly schedule for each day accompanied by several long lists of duties.

"What is *Cocoon Learning*? And why do we have classes six days out of the week instead of five?" Elena asked, feeling scandalized.

"Look at this Enrichment schedule," Abria said. "What is *Sanitation?*"

"It means cleaning," Fergie replied.

"Just a minute!" Abria gasped. "Are they seriously going to expect me to clean something around here? That will, like, totally ruin my nails."

"Awesome! There's a class on engineering," Declan commented.

"Medial rotation, finally!" Austin said. "I've waited three years for this."

"Does any of this look right to you?" Elena asked Kidd.

"No. Every single hour of our day is scheduled with something, even in between meals, classes, and training," Kidd whispered. "We'll never be in class together. We'll barely see each other."

"They have an elective for the creation of simulations and code writing," Fergie said, distracting Elena from Kidd's comment. "Perhaps I can acquire the knowledge needed to complete the cipher for the program to read the artifacts."

Elena couldn't help but roll her eyes. "Fergie, did you see this schedule? We're not going to have time to do anything! Not even sleep."

"Remember when you felt stressed about the Level 1 schedule? But we got the hang of it and it all worked out," Austin said encouragingly. "We're gonna havta take this one day at a time. So, for now, let's get our room assignments and we'll meet up at dinner. And remember, let's talk to Pigg at dinner as much as possible."

Elena felt a bubble of dissention rising up in her throat, but she swallowed it down. She scanned her Trademark into the Grimvator after Abria and Fergie. As the enclosure moved backwards to their new dorm room, she remembered feeling awe-inspired when she first arrived to the Firebird suite for her Level 1 studies. The room had been beautiful and ornately decorated.

However, when the Grimvator doors slid open, Elena felt even more discouraged than when they'd first arrived. This space was the exact opposite of the Firebird suite in every comprehensible way. Long rows of bunk beds topped with gray blankets and pillows lined the chrome-paneled walls.

"Um...did we take a wrong, like, turn?" Abria asked. "Because I know they don't expect all of us to sleep in this tiny little room with all these dreary crowded beds. Right?"

Elena looked at her with actual sympathy.

"Yes, Abria, I think they actually want us to live here with all those other girls on these dreary beds."

"I counted eighteen beds," Fergie said.

"They're joking, right?" Abria said as she started running through the adjoining corridors.

Elena followed Abria around. She learned that the resident hall was like spokes on a wheel with the washroom in the center. The bunk hall on their left housed the thirty-six Level 5 girls and the thirty-six Level 6 girls occupied the hall on their right.

"Oh no!" Abria screamed suddenly.

She ran the length of their bunk hall and stopped. Abria scanned her Trademark into what Elena assumed was her closet. After peering inside, Abria gasped and fell to her knees.

"They. Took. Away. Everything!" she sobbed, sounding horrified. "I can't have anything pretty, pink, or sparkly? How am I supposed to get ready in the morning without hair products and makeup? Oh, and look at this pathetic little closet."

At that moment, the other girls from the Aves Company began to wander into the room a few at a time. Elena recognized Adrien Segars from Raptor, Moriah Kirkley from Falcon, and Stacia Bassi from Harrier right away. Elena wouldn't have considered them friends before. However, since they'd now be sharing a room with girls from the Animalia and Maritime Companies she felt it wasn't smart to hold grudges on past training experiences.

"Hey, ladies," Adrien Segars said to Elena and Fergie as she dropped her carrier bag on a bunk near where they were standing. "Congrats on making it to Special Ops, though I didn't have any doubts you'd get in."

"I'm relieved that we share part of the room with familiar faces," Stacia Bassi said. "Those girls from the other Companies look a little fierce to me."

"Okay...okay...just breath..." Abria said to herself, drawing Elena's attention away from their new roommates. "Everything is going to be okay. I can't do anything about my closet." She turned dramatically to Elena and Fergie with a manic look in her eyes. "I'm going to make friends. Be back in a bit."

And with that, their blonde friend disappeared down another corridor.

Elena found her bunk, which fortunately she shared with Fergie.

"Do you want the top or bottom?" Elena asked.

"Top is fine," Fergie said, as she scanned her Trademark, opening her closet door. "Our uniforms are already in place."

"Did you see that bathroom? I thought it was bad enough to share with the five other girls in the Firebird suite, but sharing with seventy-two other people is a little insane."

"Someone is approaching," Fergie said sharply.

Elena looked up with a solemn frown. She and Fergie wouldn't be able to avoid the pack of girls that were making their way down the bunk hall toward them.

Elena didn't recognize any of them personally, but she knew from experience that the Animalia girls were typically taller than other teens their age and the Maritime girls were all blonde haired with sickly pale skin.

For a reason that Elena could only assume was for the protection of familiarity, she also noticed that Adrien, Moriah, and Stacia grouped around her and Fergie in a defensive way.

For a few moments, no one spoke and everyone stared intensely.

Elena was about to break the awkward moment with a comment about how rude it was to glare at someone without introducing themselves first when Abria's tinkling voice filled the room.

"Aves girls, meet the ladies from Maritime and Animalia."

"I'm Rachel Reddington," said the tallest girl from Animalia. "And this is Apryl Sommers. We're top of the class."

"You mean, you *were* top of your class until we were sent here," said one of the shortest Maritime girls with piercingly blue eyes. "I'm Neylon Faulkner and this is Mandara Tilden.

"I don't need someone from Maritime to tell me how to speak," Rachel said in an aggressive tone."

"And we don't need anyone from Animalia to think that they're better than everyone else here," Neylon replied.

"You might want to save some of that attitude for the others," Elena said bluntly, interrupting the other girls.

"What's that supposed to mean?" Neylon Faulkner asked shortly.

"I'm not usually that great with numbers, but there are seventy-two Level 5 Special Ops and seventy-two Level 6 Special Ops. That means there are one hundred and forty-four trainees that are older than us and, I'm sure, willing to make our lives miserable. You heard what Dino Roman yelled at us, right? It's not going to be easy and we have to do everything ourselves. So, save your energy girls. You're gonna need it."

Neylon Faulkner made a noise of derision and rolled her eyes, but walked away with Mandara Tilden without saying anything else.

"See what I mean," Rachel Reddington said to Apryl Sommers as she pointed at Elena. "This girl knows what she's doing."

Then, Rachel looked at her intently. Elena wanted to smile, but nothing registered on her face because she was still feeling suspicious.

"I'm glad you made it into Special Ops, though I never doubted you would," Rachel told Elena. "It'll be nice to have someone innovative on our team for once."

"What do you mean?" Elena asked.

"I *mean*," Rachel replied, almost impatiently. "Sommers and I are pretty good with natural instincts, but during Level 3 you flew that plane out of rotation and landed it on one of those islands. And I watched what you did in the snow simulation during our Level 2 studies twelve times to try to figure out how you were able to get Pigg and the rest of your team outta there. Then, there was that one capture the flag simulation where you took initiative and knocked Hunter flat on his back. It's clear that you're one of the only girls here that can think on her feet."

"You make it sound like more than what it was," Elena said, honestly feeling modest.

"I watched all your play backs, many times. I'm not making it more than what it was, which was awesome," Rachel insisted.

Elena felt a lot of her suspicions subside and was slowly deciding that she and Rachel were going to be good friends.

"So, should we all go down for dinner, like, together?" Abria asked.

Rachel Reddington looked at Apryl Sommers and they both nodded. But their first meal back at school was not like the beautiful affair that Elena had remembered from her previous three years of school.

First, they waited in a long line to get to the entrance of the food service line. When Elena got to the front of the line she noticed that her fellow trainees were giving out a pre-proportioned meal served on shiny inox plates and water in a cup of similar looking manufacturing. As Elena carried her tray into the Mess Hall she saw that the room was plain and lined with long tables.

"I guess gone are the days of all the pretty things," Abria said glumly as they found the boys sitting at a table already discussing the events of the day.

"So, Haddock, are you flattered that Roman has been stalking you or are you as grossed out as we are," Declan asked as Elena took the vacant seat beside Austin.

Austin laughed.

"Roman isn't the only one that's been stalking you," Kidd said, lifting a fork to his mouth. "I overheard some of the other Level 6 guys say they've researched your methods over the years. You're becoming quite famous."

"Elena is, too, apparently," Abria interrupted with a sad look on her face. "Rachel Reddington went on and on about her when we met the other girls on our floor. Yet, no one seems to be concerned about the fact that literally every personal belonging has been taken away from us."

"Where's Pigg?" Elena said, craning her neck for a better view of the room. "Have you seen him come in yet?"

But no one had seen him.

As they ate they gossiped about their new roommates, talked about the Enrichment schedule and Dino Roman's speech, and made guesses about what tomorrow would bring.

When dinner was over, Elena followed along with the others to the dishpit where they left their plates, cups, and utensils before heading off for an early bedtime.

As the guys walked the girls back to their dormitory, Elena asked Austin in a whisper, "Should we be worried that Pigg never showed for dinner?"

"I'm sure he's fine," Austin replied. "Maybe they eat in a different room from us."

"Today, I discovered that Thomas Apted is the most gorgeous guy I've ever seen," Abria began to tell the others. "I know he's from Maritime, but I'm hoping that our Company distinctions don't matter any longer."

"I discovered that this place is even more insane than I was expecting," Declan said.

"I ascertained that the school schedule is going to push the trainees to the core of human depravity," Fergie added. "I have never been so grateful to be a machine."

"I think the more I get to know Dino Roman the more I'm going to hate him," said Kidd.

"I've discovered I have quite a reputation," Elena said smiling. "And it's not a good one."

"I've discovered that Special Ops is going to be a challenge on every single level," Austin said seriously. "How about we go to the Firebird Station to decompress a little before everything starts back up tomorrow?"

Elena caught Kidd's eye and they shared a look. They had talked a few times in private about not wanting to pursue looking for artifacts after they almost drowned removing the Cup of Jamshid from the Smuggler Station. Elena's fear of death sometimes choked her neck like it was trying to suffocate her.

Elena didn't know why she couldn't talk to Austin about her feelings. Maybe she felt ashamed that she was too afraid to help finish her parents' work for the Renegades. Or maybe she didn't want to feel like she was letting Austin down. But she didn't want to discuss what was bothering her and why.

"Oh, I'm feeling a little over all of it today," Elena said, using a voice that sounded more tired than she actually felt. "Plus, who knows what's going to happen the first week of school. I might skip the Firebird Station altogether."

Austin looked at Elena knowingly, but she blushed and looked away.

¤ 5 ¤

Special Ops Girls

"GET. OUT. OF. BED. GOONIES!"

Elena bolted straight up, slamming her palms against her ears to try and block out the obnoxious siren that was reverberating off the walls. She looked over and noticed that even Abria was still in bed.

"Sanitation crew on me," Roman hollered from somewhere far off in her consciousness.

Elena could only vaguely remember her schedule from the day before, but fortunately Roman called out her name from the list for the sanitation crew so at least she knew what she needed to be doing.

"The rest of you get to your Enrichment activities!" Roman screamed.

Elena was beginning to rise from her bunk when she heard Neylon Faulkner say, between yawns, "What are you gonna do? Stand there while we change into our uniforms?"

"No uniforms! If you wanted to be in full uniform you should have gotten up before I came in here!" Roman yelled.

"But it's not even 0500 hours," Neylon Faulkner said harshly. "How could we possibly…"

"Sanitation crew on me!" Roman hollered even louder to silence Neylon. "Everyone else to Enrichment activities."

When most of the girls had finally exited the hall, the blaring siren ended and Roman rounded on the sanitation crew.

"Get your supplies and start working on your wash room," Roman ordered.

"Excuse me?" Rachel Reddington said. "We have to do what?"

"Clean. The. Wash. Room." Roman repeated in an extremely rude tone. "It's not going to clean itself."

"But, why do we have to do it?" Rachel asked.

"What'd ya think?" Roman asked. "That little creatures dressed in sack cloth would pop in and out to make sure this place is running smoothly?"

"I thought we'd have a staff of Humanoids to do these things for us," Rachel replied with a somewhat embarrassed look on her face.

"Listen up, Goonies!" Roman screamed to the entire corridor in a way that made Elena want to cover her ears again. "We don't have help here. *You* don't have help here. *You* want to eat? You cook. *You* want a clean bed? You wash sheets. We go to class on our own. We perform in Basic. We obey orders. My orders. So, if you're unfamiliar with how to scrub a bathroom or make mystery meat with roast potatoes then you ask someone to train you because this program doesn't suffer ignorance!"

Elena wanted to protest, but considering that she didn't have enough energy to roll her eyes she followed along with the other girls in silence as Roman lead them into a closet that was filled with bottles of different jewel colored liquids.

Elena had never cleaned a thing in her life, but she'd watched her Humanoid, Tiny, clean the Ransom apartment plenty of times. Bleary-eyed, Elena grabbed one of the bottles of jewel colored liquid and found her way to the washroom.

She noticed right away that a few of the girls really didn't know what they were doing because Neylon Faulkner sprayed herself right in the face and Rachel Reddington literally dumped her entire bottle all over the shower stall floor.

Roman didn't give any guidance. He didn't teach them how to use any of the cleaner or indicate what potion was to be used where. Instead, he offered a constant, angry critique of their work. He also frequently urged them to work faster, commenting on the minutes that were left before their breakfast shift began.

"You'd think they would have let us brush our hair or teeth or put some appropriate attire on before we started cleaning the wash room," Neylon said haughtily. "Not that there is any possible way to look attractive in what they've given us to wear."

"Could you not talk about clothes?" Elena grumbled as she scrubbed a layer of scum from the marble floor. "I'm technically not even awake right now."

"We haven't even eaten breakfast," Rachel Reddington said as she polished the walls. "I'm starving."

"I miss the sound of running water and the sweet natured Telecaster that used to wake us up every morning," Elena said longingly.

"Rudimentary manual labor is an important training tool," Fergie said formally.

"Rudimentary manual labor is exhausting," Rachel countered.

"Hold your tongues, Goonies!" Roman shouted over the low buzz of grumblings that had filled the room. "And, hurry up, Faulkner! You don't want to go down to breakfast in your jammies like a Goonie, do you?"

Somehow, the girls managed to get all the bathroom stalls, floors, mirrors, windows, doors, and hallways on the entire floor cleaned. After Dino Roman was satisfied with their work, he left the room so that the girls could dress quickly into their uniforms.

At 0600 hours on the dot, Elena sat down with Fergie and Rachel Reddington to a miserable breakfast of cold porridge in the Mess Hall. She hadn't seen any of her other friends since wake up call. She was too tired to talk so they sat in silence.

When Elena was almost finished, Kidd and Abria arrived at the table also looking equally tired.

"You look as tired as I feel," Elena told Kidd.

"I was about to say that to you." Kidd tried to smile, but he looked too tired.

Kidd took the empty seat beside Elena. She immediately laid her head tiredly on his shoulder.

"Ransom!" Dino Roman's booming voice echoed from across the room. "Get your head off Wheeler's shoulder. No physical contact!"

Elena begrudgingly sat up, but she still slouched forward towards the table. "Half of the girls in our dorm hall snore. It's like they're in competition to see who can be the loudest. I could barely sleep last night."

"I didn't hear anything," said Rachel Reddington.

"That's because you snore," Elena said and Rachel blushed.

"Yuck! I feel, like, so totally disgusting!" Abria complained. "I have kitchen duty today. Would you look at the state of my cuticles?" She held up her hand so they could see it clearly. "I mean...just pathetic. And I got water all down in my boots from the dish pit. I never realized before how truly gross people are."

Elena cut her eyes at Abria. "And the other half of the girls talked and giggled late into the night. I think I'd get more sleep if I stayed in the hallway."

"Let's not forget the rude awakening this morning," Rachel added.

"Link Hawkins and Collum Duke pounded on the sides of the bunks to get us out of bed," Kidd said. "Thomas Apted punched Hawkins in the face for taking his blanket and got demerits already. It was the funniest thing!"

"Well, I'm glad someone had a good morning because it's been miserable for the rest of us," Elena murmured.

"Bowen!" called Charleston Woods from the other side of the room. "Break time is over! Get back in the kitchen."

Abria rolled her eyes and whispered, "Archons are super fun." But, then she jumped up with a smile on her face and shouted, "Coming!"

"I've got to go, too," Elena grumbled, somehow managing to stand. "I've got to find my cocoon...whatever that is...for my first lesson."

"I'll walk with you," Kidd said, rushing to gulp down the last bites of his porridge.

Kidd and Elena took their bowls and spoons to the dish pit window. Then, they grabbed the next available Grimvator to the cocoon learning hall.

"Sorry you're having such a bad first morning," Kidd said.

"Where are you off to now?"

"I have my first lessons, too, but my cocoon lab is on a different floor. I guess they keep the guys and girls separate so it's not so distracting," Kidd replied.

"Ugh! This day just keeps getting better and better. And it's not even 0700 yet."

Elena dragged her feet off the Grimvator, half waved to Kidd and walked onto a hallway that looked similar to the Uniform Locker. She noticed a digital representation of her face on one of the doors, so she scanned her Trademark to enter the small, white-walled room. When the door closed she looked around feeling confused.

Unlike the Uniform Locker, this room did not have paneled drawers. After looking up and down, she finally noticed the scanner niche in the floor. She rubbed the Trademark code on her forearm onto the niche. A pupil station suddenly appeared with several Optivision screens. Each of the screens projected a different Instructor's face.

"Instructor Booker!" Elena exclaimed as she looked through the faces. "And Niva, Copernicus, and Emerald. Well, at least I'll have classes with a few familiar faces."

Elena read the information briefly and said, "You mean, I get to choose what I work on first? Maybe class won't be so bad after all."

But, as it turned out, even Booker's hologram couldn't keep Elena from feeling bored and lonely. As the Instructor talked about the Age of Exploration and Ferdinand Magellan, the first person to circumnavigate the earth, Elena was finding it hard to focus. Barely awake, she stared at Booker's talking hologram.

Feelings of isolation set in quickly. When she finally looked at the time, she'd only been inside for thirteen minutes. Discouraged, Elena thought about all the fun she once had in Booker's lectures with her friends, her favorite memory being the time that Frankie Smiley had drifted to sleep in his pupil station and fallen out of his chair onto the floor during the middle of the lecture.

An hour later, Elena answered questions about the three most important tools during the Age of Exploration, how Portugal and Spain were the leading nations for exploration, the famous Amerigo Vespucci, and the Amerindian civilizations.

At lunch, Elena sat again with Fergie and Rachel because she didn't see any of her other friends.

"Classwork was an absolute snooze fest!" Elena said.

"I agree," Rachel said at once. "And it seemed to take FOR-E-VER."

Elena wanted to laugh, but she couldn't muster enough energy. She barely had time to finish her pathetic lunch because at 1230 hours she made her way with Fergie and Rachel to the training facility as was instructed on their daily schedule.

"You're here!" said Abria in relief as she met them at the door of the training room. "At least I can get outta the kitchen for a couple hours today."

Elena had entered a large room that was fully equipped with every type of exercise equipment imaginable. Coming from the smaller Unit classes they had the previous three years, training with over one hundred girls in Special Ops seemed overwhelming. Sabrina Bauer and Charleston Woods from Archon were standing on some kind of raised dais above the girls.

Elena noticed a huge wall of glass on the opposite side of the room and saw that all the Special Ops guys were on the other side of it. They had already begun their exercise routine with Dino Roman, Brennan Colt, Collum Duke, and Link Hawkins.

"Attention trainees!" Sabrina Bauer shouted, calling the girls to order. "Form your lines."

"The exercises we do today are compound in nature," said Charleston Woods. "We'll work on strengthening our core muscles."

"Why are all the boys training over there?" Rachel Reddington asked loud enough for the entire room to hear.

"Before you may address a member of Archon during training, you must say 'Permission to speak,'" Sabrina Bauer said sharply.

Rachel cocked her head slightly to the side and said, "Permission to speak?"

"Granted," Charleston replied.

"Why are all the boys training over there?" Rachel Reddington repeated, while a few of the girls around them giggled.

"We are not permitted to train with the guys," Charleston said coolly. "We will maintain separate exercise arenas during most of the year. However, at some point, our lessons will coincide so that we have the benefit of watching one another in hand-to-hand combat tactics."

"You should know," Sabrina said. "From here on out we are in constant, direct competition with the Special Ops guys for every task we're given."

"Permission to speak?" Elena asked.

"Granted."

"Why don't we work together since we're all in Special Ops?"

"Actually, the system is set up so that we are all in direct competition with everyone, male and female, at every moment," Sabrina said. "It's the school's way of being able to accurately access our performances."

"Back to our training," Charleston pressed on. "Most of what we'll be doing for the first part of this class will be cardio centric. Then, we'll move into strength-based exercises. You will learn to use your body weight to provide resistance during the exercises. There will be a lot of jumping involved, so you will feel a lot of pressure on your joints, which means it's important to fully utilize the stretching segment we'll do at the end."

"You will most definitely become more agile and tougher by the third week of this class," said Sabrina. "But it will take a lot to get there."

"Let's get started," Charleston said.

Charleston and Sabrina took turns guiding the girls through a series of stretching and yogini poses with sturdy, strong commands. Then, they moved into a series of switch kicks, power jacks, and push-up jacks. The polymeric cardio circuit followed, and finally a core balance set.

Elena had certainly been sweaty during training before. Marshall had pushed them all past the point of smelling pleasant more than a few times. But this workout was so extreme that every inch of Elena's body was soaked in sweat. Her cheeks burned as much as her triceps, thighs, and calves. The red curls that had fallen from her hair clasp where now stuck to the back of her neck.

At the end of the lesson, even Abria looked completely disheveled and she normally looked like a beauty no matter what kind of training Grimsby could throw at them.

"Good work, ladies!" said Charleston. "Now, training on the Gauntlet begins next week. The obstacles are open twenty-four hours a day for practice. I highly suggest that each of you practice, either alone or in teams every single day until you master each obstacle."

"I can barely move!" Elena grumbled to Fergie and Abria. "How can they expect us to practice the Gauntlet?"

"Yeah, my muscles are totally, like, screaming," Abria said. "And I have to go straight to the kitchens to cook dinner. This is totally, like, the worst day of my life."

While Abria headed off to the kitchens, Elena and Fergie went to the Media Lab to do more classwork until dinner, which started promptly at 1700 hours. Elena sat down with Austin, Kidd, and Fergie staring at what she described as slop on a plate.

"I wish I could be in bed asleep already," Elena grumbled.

"Abria said she'd be in the kitchen all through dinner so to go ahead and eat," Declan said as he joined them at the table.

"This class of Level 4 Goonies is completely hopeless!" Kidd said in a mock of Roman's voice. "I expect you to do better tomorrow."

"I started my morning off cleaning and then had lessons all day," Declan said moodily. "Then, we did all this crazy training with Roman who is actually worse than Marshall, in case you were wondering. I'm not even hungry."

"I'm so tired I feel like I'm going to pass out into my food," Elena said into her plate.

"Did you hear that we're supposed to review footage from past training simulations after dinner?" asked Austin. "Something about how we're supposed to be prepared for the Gauntlets and how we're expected to perform each obstacle perfectly. Class doesn't even end until 2300 hours and Roman said that's only if we can answer all his review questions."

Soon enough, Elena and her friends had arrived in a classroom that was set with stadium seating and dozens of Optivision screens. Roman stood at the front of the room.

"Watch with your mouths shut!" Roman said as a greeting. "You'll get the idea."

Before Elena could think what he meant, the lights in the room dimmed and the entire space lit up with playbacks of past training on the Gauntlet. Elena watched the screens with her mouth hanging open. The sheer amount of jumping, running, and weight ratio management of most of the obstacles seemed completely impossible.

She saw staircases of logs, pits of water and mud, strangely angled platforms, and spinning platforms. Trainees used jumping pads, landing pads, swinging ropes, and floating mats. But there were also vertical walls that rotated, beams of every shape and size to balance on, springboards and hoops, trampolines and cargo nets, and climbing walls.

Even though Elena continued to be in awe as she observed the new and ever increasing challenges, she also felt equally exhausted. Watching the trainees made her feel terrified that soon she'd be on that course. She didn't even have enough energy at the moment to bend down to tie her combat boot.

At long last, it was 2300 hours and the hours of watching the Gauntlet was over. Kidd grabbed Elena's hand. He led her out of the classroom and down the hall through the maze of other students headed tiredly to their dormitories.

"Let me walk you back to the dorm," Kidd said. "I feel like I haven't seen you all day."

"That's because we haven't seen each other all day," Elena pointed out. "Instead, we've been busy in crazy town. I really didn't think it was possible to cram that much info into one day," Elena said. "But somehow the Special Ops program excels at it."

"We should get used to it eventually, right?" Kidd asked hopefully.

"Doubtful. Very doubtful."

Elena and Kidd were practically silent as he finished walking her back to the girl's dormitory.

"Good night," Kidd said, dropping her hand gently. "I hope you can sleep through the chorus of snoring noses."

Elena tried to muster a smile, but it came out wrong and looked more like a sarcastic grimace.

"Or don't have a good night," Kidd said, laughing.

"Sorry, sometimes my face overreacts to how I'm feeling on the inside, which right now is totally exhausted."

"Get some sleep," Kidd said as he turned on his heels.

Moments later, Elena literally fell into her bed and was asleep without brushing her teeth or changing out of her uniform.

⌑ 6 ⌑

A Day with Pigg

"WAKE UP! WAKE UP! WAKE UP, GOONIES! Time to start another fun-filled day."

Elena felt as though she'd just dozed into a deep sleep when Dino Roman's voice was booming and loud sirens permeated her subconscious, which shocked her back into her miserable reality. She jolted upward as several of her roommates groaned "Ugh!" from their beds.

"Sanitation crew on me!" Roman roared.

Elena looked over as blonde wisps of hair appeared in her peripheral.

"Put this on while you walk to the kitchen," Abria said, holding out an extra shirt to Elena. "Trust me, you're going to want the extra layer to peel off after the lunch shift."

"My everything hurts," Elena groaned. "I think I have muscles in places that I shouldn't."

Then, Elena glowered at Abria, who was bright eyed and fully dressed in uniform with a fresh application of makeup on her face.

"I thought they confiscated all your makeup," Elena said groggily as she grabbed the shirt with a little too much force.

"I guess it's a good thing Pigg made me that body bubble before we came back to school," Abria replied with a wink.

At the mention of Pigg's name, Elena gave Abria a sleepy smile. Then, she shuffled around, slowly pulling on clothes for the workday.

She somehow managed to find her way to the galley where, to her pleasant surprise, Pigg was waiting.

"We have kitchen rotation together. Isn't it great?" Pigg said happily, handing her a steaming mug. "Strictly speaking, we aren't allowed to introduce coffee into the trainee diet this early in the year, but I snuck some for you."

"Thank you," Elena said gratefully.

"Come over this way," Pigg said, turning to lead her through a maze of prep tables and cooking ranges. "We'll work back here so we can be away from everyone else. And you'll want to put your hair up because it gets pretty messy around here."

Pigg stopped towards the back of the kitchen at a table that was organized with fresh ingredients.

As Elena pulled her red curls into a bun, he said, "I stopped by the greenhouse this morning and helped myself to the entire herb section because yesterday's breakfast was lacking in culinary finesse."

"That's a really nice way to say that it was awful," Elena said. Then, she took a sip from the mug that Pigg had given her, closing her eyes as the warm bitters and cream coated her throat. "Yum..."

"I thought you'd like that," Pigg said with a smile. "It's like your mom would make when we were little."

Elena smiled too, thankful for Pigg's company and the reminder that her mom had been gifted at helping people feel better.

"This place is awful," Pigg moaned as he began to chop something orange in color. "I didn't realize how good we had it the first three years at Grimsby. Our beds are covered with drab, the bathroom has to be shared with everyone on the floor, and our new schedules are overwhelming. The only thing that may be redeeming about this place is that I have a kitchen rotation every week."

"Personally, I'm just so excited about all our new friends," Elena said sarcastically as she looked over the table again feeling overwhelmed by all the different components that created their meals.

However, as the minutes stretched on it was very clear that Pigg knew exactly what he was doing. She stayed beside him, trying to learn whatever she could as he talked non-stop about the best way to incorporate ingredients into food.

"I should've appreciated our meals before now," Elena said warily.

She watched Pigg's skillful hands as he molded brown mush into a brick. Then, he spread some of the mixture on rounds of toasted bread and gave Elena a cup of mixed fruit.

"You don't have to worry about the food now that I'm here," Pigg said reassuringly. "Try this."

He lifted the toast round towards her mouth. Reluctantly, she took a small bite. The brown concoction tasted creamy with the perfect blend of sweet and salt.

"How did you do that?" Elena said, the edges of her words indicating astonishment.

"Again, it's all about the science of putting together flavors," Pigg said. "Plus, I added in some essential oils to help everyone feel a little more energized today."

"You should be in the kitchen every day," Elena said admiringly.

"Actually, I'm going to be," Pigg said brightly. "In my group, we're allowed to choose a specialty after the first three weeks of training. I'll be in the kitchens for the rest of the year after that. So, I'll get to see each of my friends five days out of the week."

"Don't you mean six days?"

"I'm sure I don't have six friends."

"What about Wheeler?" Elena asked.

Pigg's face turned slightly pink. "Oh, I guess I could count him on the list. If he would just stop calling me Big Ears..."

Elena pursed her lips together, deciding that she would speak with Kidd as soon as possible about his nickname for Pigg.

An hour later, Elena stood in a row with other students and a large pot of porridge was set on the serving counter in front of her. When the food line opened, she began to dish out the breakfast in bowls as students passed.

Elena could tell by the glum expressions on all the faces that no one had slept enough the previous night. She was just starting to wonder if she could make it all day without a nap when she heard a familiar voice.

"Hey Freckles."

Kidd had arrived looking tired, but happy to see her.

"Hey!" Elena said, relieved to have him as a distraction. "Where're you coming from?"

"Medical," Kidd said. "I'm on for twenty-four hours straight, but we get to break for meals. So, at least we can see each other today."

"Well, I don't think kitchen duty is going to be too bad, actually," Elena said. "Pigg's back there making everything taste amazing."

"Keep up the great work," Kidd said and he winked at her before sliding his plate down to the next serving counter.

When everyone in the building had finished eating, Elena, Pigg, and the rest of the kitchen crew barely had ten minutes to gulp down their own breakfast before they started cleaning the kitchen with jewel colored cleaners.

After this was finished, Elena followed Pigg into the dish pit where a mountain of plates, cups, and silverware was waiting. A slow, miserable hour eeked by as Elena and a couple other trainees rinsed dishes before loading them inside an industrial sized dishwasher.

Then, tired and wet, Elena rushed off to her cocoon lab for lessons. She was extremely grateful for the shirt that Abria had given her and changed into it on her way to class.

Fortunately, her class work with Instructor Niva was short that day. Unfortunately, her class work was short because she had to get back to the kitchen to start making lunch for everyone. Pigg was already there, excitedly pulling ingredients together for the menu.

"What is it?" Elena asked Pigg, feeling a little uneasy as she looked at white beans, pink meat, and various vegetables.

"This is bean salad with bacon and chives," Pigg said pointing. "This is salmon and couscous and this is going to be turkey quinoa stuffed peppers. Apparently, it's supposed to give us a lot of protein before our physical training session."

"Oh, how did yours go yesterday," Elena asked. "Ours was absolutely horrible. Woods and Bauer led the exercises. I don't think I've ever been this sore from training."

She noticed Pigg's shoulders sag slightly as he said dismissively, "Mine was fine."

Elena looked him over carefully. She felt that she understood why he was being vague. She'd been like that with Austin before their first year at Grimsby. She assumed that school would be horrible and that she'd never be able to make friends because of her character flaws. But it was hard admitting it out loud to Austin.

"You can tell me honestly."

"Oh, I know," said Pigg earnestly. "It's just...you know...going to take some getting use to."

"You'll make friends soon," Elena insisted.

"Sure, of course," Pigg said, looking away again as he sliced a red pepper into thin slivers.

The kitchen crew took shifts to eat lunch, so Elena was able to sit down with Fergie and Abria, though she showed up at the table soaked from head to foot.

"What, like, happened to you?" Abria asked

"I had an unfortunate incident in the dish pit," Elena said gloomily. "But I've got to hurry to eat and then get back in the kitchens to finish cleaning before our training starts."

"Okay, so the pain in my legs has finally started to swell to a point where I may just cry today," Abria complained. "I hope Bauer and Woods don't work us too hard later."

Nevertheless, the training was extremely hard again. The rigorous pacing of switch kicks, power jacks, globe jumps, and suicide jumps had Elena wishing that she could train with Marshall again.

As soon as physical training was finished, Elena hurried back to the kitchens to start on dinner with Pigg while everyone else headed off to their Enrichment activities or class work.

Hours later, everyone had finished eating yet again and Elena began cleanup with the crew, yet again. When everything was finally clean and put back in place, she looked over the kitchen feeling that she'd be happy if she never stepped foot inside it again.

"I'd say that today was worse than yesterday, but you were here to make it better," Elena yawned at Pigg.

"It was good to see you, too," Pigg said. "Well, we're done cleaning in here. And I know you have to get to your next thing."

"What's on your schedule now?"

"Oh, I get the task of finishing all the class work I didn't finish earlier today. Should be tons of fun..." Pigg said sarcastically.

"Ohhh, you're learning to use sarcasm," Elena quipped. "How fun for me! See you next week."

Then, she hurried over to the stadium theater room and met her friends for another round of watching playbacks of past Gauntlets. However, this time, Roman stood at the front of the class the entire time, lecturing about the different stages of the courses. He spoke so quickly and with so much intensity that soon Elena was finding it hard to concentrate.

Soon, Oscar Hunter's hand was in the air.

Roman looked disturbed by the interruption, but allowed Oscar to speak anyway.

"You're talking too fast," Oscar told him. "How can we even follow..."

"The Tribulation could begin at any moment," Roman warned. "Last year it started after only three days of classes."

Roman said the word *Tribulation* with such a strange intensity that Elena felt a twinge run up her back.

"Yeah, it wasn't easy to go through the Age of Exploration with Henry the Navigator after only three days worth of studying," Brennan Colt added.

"What's the *Tribulation*?" Oscar Hunter asked aloud.

Dino Roman looked at him sharply.

"It cannot be explained to you Goonies in words, except to say that it's designed to stretch us, hurt us, and then break us. Take my advice. Keep your mouths shut and your ears open to everything we tell you. And, Hunter, if you can't keep up with the lecture perhaps you'd do better with a demotion back to your old Unit."

Oscar Hunter fell silent at once and was first to leave the room as soon as Roman's lecture was over.

"Why do you think Roman and the others sound totally, like, scared when they talked about the Tribulation?" Abria asked Austin as they all left the theater and made their way back to the dorms.

"It must be something pretty awful," Austin said. "Fergie, any chance of us hacking into the mainframe to find out more info about it?"

"Possibly, but not this evening," Fergie replied.

"Yes, some of us need to take a shower to wash off the stench of the dish pit mixed with sweat from the exercise torture we experienced earlier today," said Elena.

But Elena's hopes for a long, hot shower where disappointed when the shower timed out after seven minutes. She stood in the stall, shaking from head to toe. As her tired muscles spasmed out of control, she wondered how she was going to get through the next day.

▯ 7 ▯

Not Okay

The next morning, Roman started screaming for them to get up at 0400 hours. Most of the girls headed off to their Enrichment activities, but since Elena's class wasn't until the afternoon she was forced to try and catch up on work in a cocoon lab.

At 0600, Elena dragged herself down to the Mess Hall. Gulping down the meager breakfast she'd been given was a struggle.

She arrived at yet another cocoon lab at 0630 for a new round of class work.

"You know, Instructor Booker," Elena told the hologram standing in front of her. "I mistakenly thought that having sanitation and kitchen rotation first thing in the morning was the worst part of the Enrichment schedule. But now that I'm inside this room with you, with no the hope of a break until lunchtime, I've realized that this is worse."

"After you have selected the next module from your screen, you will see that a conquistador named Cortes landed on the shore of Mexico in 1519 AD," the hologram replied.

Elena sighed. She tried to feel interested as she watched a live representation of Cortes army moving inland toward the Aztec Indian's capital city and his dealings with the Aztec king Montezuma, but she was feeling enormously tired from getting so little sleep the past few days.

Next, Elena selected Niva's lecture about the territorial aggression between the Dutch, Russians, French, and British in the 1500s. But the Instructor spoke in several different languages the entire time, so Elena found it mentally challenging to keep up.

When Elena finally checked the time, she noticed that it was quite a while before lunch. So, she chose to watch Instructor Copernicus's lecture about the different celestial maps and instruments that the early explorers used as they began to conquer the unknown parts of the world.

Through a haze of tiredness, she managed to get back to the Mess Hall for a measly sandwich, which she ate at a table all alone.

Then, at 1400 hours Elena walked to her Enrichment activity, which only said "Engineering" on the schedule. She had no idea what to expect, but was pleasantly surprised to see Declan slumped down in a chair with his head slightly back. His blonde hair was disheveled, his eyes were closed, and his mouth was wide open.

Smiling a little more than she had in days, Elena plopped down loudly in the seat beside him. He startled awake with a snort.

"Hey, Ransom," Declan said sleepily. "So, today you decided to go with a dark shade of exhaustion on your face. How original…"

"Thanks for the compliment," Elena said, the edges of her words dull.

"You're welcome," Declan replied. "I'm all about engineering, but how can they expect us to care about learning anything when we're this tired?"

"It really feels like they're trying to kill us this time." Elena complained.

"Mouths shut and ears open," Link Hawkins said, calling the class to attention.

Elena was quite surprised to see that Link would be teaching the class, but then again everything that happened at the school had been confusing so far.

"This year we'll focus on engineering the empires of Rome, Egypt, Aztec, Britain, North and South America, and Russia. This class will include lecture and then practical application."

As Link Hawkins started his teaching, Elena leaned toward Declan and whispered, "I want to sleep."

"Me, too. But consider, class will be at least an hour. So this is the first time all day that we're actually sitting down without the urgency of needing to get right back up again and on to the next thing."

"Good point," Elena replied. "I think I'll practice sleeping with my eyes open."

Therefore, she fixed her eyes on Hawkins with inactive thoughts and, for the first time since school started, felt a temporary moment of calmness.

After class, Elena sprinted to her physical training with Charleston and Sabrina, where they worked again on the same cardio set that targeted the core muscle groups. Plus they practiced balance, which sounded easy at first, but was extremely difficult.

At 1700 hours, Elena sat down at a table in the Mess Hall with Abria. She looked down at the brown loaf on her plate. She had no idea what it was, but she didn't even care because she was so exhausted.

"This is the worst schedule ever!" Elena said bitterly. "Today, I had to stand in that dimwit cocoon for five hours!"

"Just wait until you have kitchen duty," Abria yawned loudly.

"I already had kitchen duty," Elena grumbled. "I got totally soaked in the dish pit. I swear there was an inch of water in my boots."

"Oh, that's right." Abria yawned again. "You have that with Pigg, right? I'm losing track of my days and everyone's schedule. But I can tell when Pigg's in the kitchen because the quality of the food greatly improves."

At 2030 hours, after more lecturing from Roman about the Gauntlet and finishing up classwork, Elena walked into the shower. Her legs and arms were constantly trembling now. She stood perfectly still for seven minutes until the shower timed out. Then, somehow she managed to find a towel and her pajamas. She was asleep the moment her head hit the pillow.

The next day was more of the same. Roman started screaming for them to get up at 0400 hours.

Elena forced herself to gulp down breakfast.

She arrived at her cocoon at 0630 for class work.

After lunch, she sat through Sabrina Bauer's lecture about program writing and then had practical instruction group work with Abria. She used parts of physics and mathematics that she never understood before, but it didn't even matter. Elena could not focus either way.

At 1600 hours, Charleston Woods led the Special Ops girls through a polymeric cardio circuit, during which all the muscles in Elena's body were burning with pain.

When they were finished, Elena lay on the floor of the exercise room wishing that she were asleep in bed. She wasn't the only one on her back. In fact, most of the other Level 4 trainees were taking up the space around her, including Abria and Fergie.

"I. Just. Can't." Abria said quietly. "Everything hurts."

"My mom taught me some special stretches for helping with muscle issues," Elena said slowly. "But I'm in so much pain I don't think it matters."

"We should try it," Fergie said in a tone of formality. "I will help you get up. Then, you can show us."

With Fergie's help, Elena stood and began to teach her and Abria what she could remember about her mom's unique stretching. Twenty minutes later, Elena was starting to feel a little better, but it still wasn't enough to improve her mood.

At dinner, Kidd pulled up the chair beside her and asked, "You okay?"

"No, I'm not okay," Elena said, frowning as she hunched over because she was in too much pain to sit upright. "This is not okay. I haven't slept in days. And everything is hurry, hurry, hurry." She looked at Kidd, who was bright eyed like he'd had an influx of energy and cocked her head. "Why do you look okay?"

"Oh, I already had my Enrichment with Medical," Kidd said. "Some of the older students are eager to prescribe supplements to ease the strain of the rigorous routine. Plus, I got a really good nap in one of the spare medi-cots."

"Ugh!" Elena sighed. "I don't even have Medical for two more days."

"You can go there today," Kidd suggested. "You can be seen at any time and like I said, they're eager to give those little pills out."

"Nah, that's okay," Elena said dismissively. "I'll wait. Austin and I have that Medical together. It's weird that we don't see each other during the day, or any of our other friends, right?"

"Well, we have Enrichment together tomorrow," Kidd said. "I think it's called *Construction*."

"And there are no moments to relax during the day," Elena continued as if he hadn't spoken. "I'm constantly hurrying to the next thing. Plus, how can they expect us to do so much physical training along with a full day of work study and lessons?" Elena grumbled.

"I dunno," Kidd replied. "I actually fell asleep standing up in the shower last night. If Declan hadn't found me I would've drowned."

"Drowned? Standing in the shower?" Elena repeated slowly in a disbelieving tone.

Then, Kidd winked at her.

"Stop it. I'm serious," Elena said, though she smiled. "This is not getting any better or easier. We have to do something."

But since neither one of them had any ideas about who to even complain to they fell into silence.

After dinner they attended yet another Gauntlet review with Roman. Elena didn't even realize that she'd fallen asleep in her chair until Kidd nudged her awake when the class was over.

"Why didn't you wake me earlier?" she asked.

"You looked peaceful," Kidd replied. "I couldn't disturb you. Especially after you started snoring."

"I can't believe Roman let me sleep?"

"One of the benefits of sitting on the back row is that we're nearly out of Roman's sight line," Kidd said. "Another benefit is that Roman likes to hear himself talk so much. I'm not sure he'd be distracted if a herd of elephants tromped through the room."

The following day moved by in a blur. The only part that was significantly different was Elena's Enrichment activity about Construction with Kidd. Collum Duke taught them, explaining that they would use program-writing techniques to build models of the empires of Rome, Egypt, Aztec, Britain, North and South America, and Russia.

"We're responsible to build models of these places and it counts for 100% of our grade in the class?" Kidd asked in disbelief.

"That's what I just said," Collum replied. "Pay attention, Wheeler!"

Elena tried to smile encouragingly at Kidd, but she was pretty sure it came out as a grimace. She completed the remainder of her schedule in a haze of hand tremors and headaches.

And by breakfast the next morning, Elena could barely lift the fork to her mouth because even the smallest muscles in her wrist and fingers hurt. She doubted very sincerely that she would be able to muster enough energy to do the twenty-four hour required medical rotation for Enrichment.

But when she saw Austin waiting for her outside the Medical Station she brightened a little, feeling hopeful that the day would be better than some of the others she'd had in the past week.

"Hey there, Sunshine," Austin said happily.

"Why do you look so awake?" Elena asked in disbelief. "Aren't you exhausted? I think I've only had a total of three hours sleep this whole week."

"I don't know," Austin replied. "Something about Medical gives me an excited energy. Plus, it feels like we're a little closer to your mom in here."

"I wonder why I don't feel closer to my mom when we're in physical training. Oh yeah, that's right, it's because class is led by dimwits."

Austin laughed and tossed an arm around her shoulder. Together they walked into the Medical Station and Elena gawked in astonishment as soon as they came through the door.

The Medical Station her first three years at school had been pretty basic, with several rows of beds that were staffed with only a couple Humanoids. But this room was only the lobby of a much larger floor. Older students walked up and down several hallways and everyone seemed to be busy and in a hurry.

Elena and Austin gathered with the other Level 4 students as Sabrina Bauer greeted them and said, "Patient care is one of the most important parts of the Medical field. As you spend time with each patient you must take time to involve various disciplines to be able to discuss the patients' condition, determine a diagnosis, and prepare a treatment plan that pertains specifically to the patient's deoxyribonucleic acid profile. The same amount of medication can perform differently in two separate people."

Next, Sabrina directed Elena, Austin, and the other students down the main corridor to show them the facility.

"We see a lot of inflamed joints and muscles because of the rigorous activities we do," said Sabrina. "The skeletal structure often becomes damaged. Even simple things, like having a rib out of place in your chest, can cause a patient to feel as if he's having a heart attack. So, when you're talking with students about their injuries make sure you're thorough and enter lots of notes into their records."

Sabrina showed them an Optivision screen at the end of each bed. "This is the only way we'll be able to keep track of their progress and medications. You can spread out now to take a look around. Then, you need to begin the practice module number one."

Elena and Austin moved around to the opposite side of the room away from the other trainees.

"So, it looks like I was stupidly ignorant about what school would be like this year," Elena said as she accessed the Optivision beside the bed. "Grandpa and Grandma tried to warn us, but I didn't understand. How can anyone keep up with this schedule and remain sane? I mean, seriously, when are we supposed to sleep?"

"You'll have to figure out a time in your schedule to take a quick nap during the day. Fortunately, today we'll share our Medical rotation with eleven other Level 4 students so we can take turns sleeping," Austin said.

"And when do we eat?" Elena continued.

"Sometimes you'll have to eat on the run," Austin said, grabbing an apple from his pocket and holding it out to her. "And then you'll have one scheduled time a day to eat in the Mess Hall."

Elena took the apple with force.

"I'm experiencing culture shock right now so a little extra compassion from you is absolutely necessary."

"I'm not sure how much compassion we can fit in today." Austin replied. "I hate to say this, but I've rewatched some of those Gauntlet playbacks that Roman teaches us each night and it's clear that we're going to need to take our friends right away. We've got to start practicing before it begins to count on our grades."

"Austin! I am so tired that I can barely think straight. How can you even talk about practicing on the Gauntlet?" Elena asked, the edges of her words punctuated with exasperation. "What I need is something to help me relax. Wheeler was talking the other day about getting a prescribed supplement from Medical to help him. Do you know what it is?"

Austin directed Elena down a side corridor and into a dark room that was mostly empty expect for several bunk beds.

"Lena, you don't need supplements. You need to sleep," Austin instructed. "I'll wake you when it's time for you to take a turn rounding the hall to check on patients."

"How did you know where this room was?"

Austin looked a little guilty. "I have a confession to make. I've been up here a few times this week already. I wanted to see what kind of equipment was here and wanted to get a feel for the place. Then, I realized this is the only place in the building where Roman won't come so I've been taking naps up here."

"You could have shared that bit of info a little earlier," Elena grumbled as she flopped down onto one of the bottom bunks.

Within minutes she was asleep, but she was also standing on top of a sand colored stone wall. She looked all around. A rotund temple with a gold-topped roof stood to one side of her. All around she could see decaying trees, a city in ruins, and personal possessions that littered the streets. For some reason, it reminded her of the vacancy she felt in New York City and Washington D.C.

Suddenly, Elena became aware that a gunship had landed at the base of the wall. When the door opened, she watched the imposing figure of Imperator step down to the ground. He was shrouded in a black cloak and wore a silver-studded mask that made him appear fierce and indestructible.

Then, several dozen robotic figures emerged from the hovercraft, brandishing weapons on their metallic arms. The Droidiers moved toward the base of the wall in perfect unison, a flawless army that was devoid of any kind of emotion.

Elena was glad she was standing on top of the wall, far from Imperator. But then, suddenly he appeared at her side.

"I have come for the Firebird Disc," Imperator declared in a superior tone.

Elena felt that she knew where the Disc was, but also that she didn't. She was able to recall that her dad had spoken of it in the Ransom Dossier. She also knew that she'd read about it, but at the same time she didn't know where it was.

"I don't have it!" Her voice sounded scared, but she wasn't sure she actually felt true fear.

"But you know where it is!" Imperator insisted.

"I don't know what you're talking about!"

Imperator came towards her in a forceful way. She wanted to escape, but there was nowhere to run. He grabbed her by the throat and held her over the wall.

"And I know your dad has the Tablets of Destiny in his possession," Imperator continued. "You will help me!"

As she dangled in his grasp, Elena noticed that Austin, Pigg, and Fergie suddenly appeared, standing along an adjacent wall to her left. Then, Declan, Abria, and Kidd appeared on the wall to her right. As she was beginning to call for Austin, she noticed that none of her friends had eyes; rather, their eyes were white and sightless.

"I need you to get the Disc for me," Imperator breathed in her face.

"I can't! I don't know where it is!" Elena insisted.

Elena felt the squeezing of her neck and the tearing of her flesh.

"Bad dream?"

Elena's eyes flew open. Austin was standing over her. His eyes looked brown and normal as they always did, but they were filled with concern.

"I guess," Elena replied groggily.

"You were screaming so loud I could hear you down the hall," Austin informed her. "I would say it was bad."

"What time is it?"

"0300 hours," he replied. "Again, sorry to wake you, but my shift has technically ended, which means you're on call until your shift ends at 0600 hours."

He yawned loudly. "I need to get some sleep before breakfast."

Elena left Austin and walked down the hall aimlessly. Her dream was still fresh in her memory and it had terrified her to see Imperator and her friends without the eyes that she knew so well. But, as she was descending into the anxiety of her feelings, she took a breath.

"No," Elena ordered herself firmly. "No more questions about Cognicross. No more worrying about any of those things. I'm done with all that."

▭ 8 ▭

The Obstacles

At long last, Elena's first week of Enrichment schedule, cocoon classwork, and physical training was over. However, Austin wasted no time asking Elena and their friends to spend their first restful day off with training.

"Want to go practice on the Gauntlet?" he asked during breakfast on the seventh day of the week.

"We've been going non-stop all week!" Elena said in disbelief. "And now you want us to go practice more?"

"You could use the, like, exercise," Abria said with a smirk.

"Hardy, har, har..." Elena faked a laugh. "You're so funny."

"I know we could all use some rest and certainly more sleep, but Roman keeps threatening that the Gauntlet is going to be a real challenge this year. And we only have two weeks left before we'll be there instead of sitting in Roman's lecture about it every night. I'd like to know what we'll be up against so we can have an advantage over the other Level 4's."

"Of course you would..." Kidd said.

Elena looked at Kidd and then at her others friends. She was tempted to rest, but Austin did make a good point. Therefore, after they finished eating, she begrudgingly headed out to the Gauntlet with her friends.

The obstacle course spread out in front of Elena as a daunting task, and all of it dripping with water as it had during her Level 2 training. Flashes of Gauntlet exercises that Roman had been showing them all week replayed in her mind.

"I guess we should start from the beginning and work our way around together," Austin suggested.

Elena looked at the first obstacle, which was a staircase of logs that led over a pool of water to a platform on the other side of a pit. It didn't look hard. In fact, it looked so easy that she was sure it must be some kind of trick. She was not interested in going first, so she kept her mouth shut.

"I'll go first," Declan volunteered.

Elena watched him jump from the landing pad to the first stair. His weight caused the stair to rotate on a lateral axis. Declan completely lost his balance and fell face first into the water below. As he came out of the water sputtering, Elena and the others laughed nervously.

"Laugh at me now, but wait till you try it," Declan said darkly as he came out of the pool.

"It can't be that hard," Kidd said confidently. But after his attempt at the stair, he also plummetted straight into the water.

When it was Elena's turn, she didn't even jump far enough to reach the stair and fell like a stone into the water. Frustrated, she tried again and again, but she never came any closer to landing properly.

"This is impossible!" Elena said, the edges of her words filled with aggravation. "How are we ever going to get past the first obstacle?"

"With practice," Austin said. "That's why we're out here. There has to be some kind of secret to solving this course. We have to figure out what it is."

"Perhaps we should spread out to try several obstacles at once," Fergie suggested in a formal tone. "Then, we can report back the details of each obstacle once we have mastered it."

"Great idea!" Austin said.

So, Austin and Fergie headed off together in one direction. Declan and Abria went off to another obstacle while Kidd and Elena stayed at the stairs.

"I hate these stairs!" Elena said, feeling discouraged.

"Me, too," Kidd replied. "We have to figure out how to land."

"Maybe we could try jumping from a different position," Elena suggested.

But no matter what they did, Elena and Kidd kept falling. And, even if they managed to balance on the first step, they were never able to jump successfully to the second step without falling in the water below.

A while later, Elena noticed more Level 4 trainees arrive. Rachel Reddington, looking confident, started on a rope that zipped down a track.

"Look at that," Elena guestured to Rachel. "She has no idea what's about to happen."

Elena and Kidd watched Rachel descend the track, let go, and attempt to catapult her body onto a mat floating in the water. However, once she landed, her weight caused the mat to shift and she was dumped uncermoniously into the water below.

"Watch Apted for a sec," Kidd whispered to Elena.

Not too far away, Elena saw Thomas Apted on a trampoline. He bounced high and then leapt forward to grasp the underside of a declining climbing net. But the net must have been slippery because his hands slid right off.

"I'm pretty sure he's fallen off that three times already," Kidd said. "And Bassi keeps trying to jump onto that spinning vertical wall, but everytime she ends up in the mud. I'm glad it's not just us."

More trainees arrived the longer that Elena and her friends practiced, but it didn't seem that any of them knew any more about how to successfully complete any of the obstacles.

Elena thought nothing could have been worse than the tippy dippy stair case, but when she had to jump four angled platforms that were alternately placed across the length of a pit of water, she just about lost her mind in anger.

"I can't anymore!" Elena stated at Kidd after three hours and only completing three obstacles.

"Let's get some food," Kidd suggested.

"What about the others?"

"They can find us when they're ready," Kidd said as he grabbed her hand and tugged her away from the Gauntlet back towards their resident tower.

But moments later, Austin and the others caught up with them.

As Elena and her friends gathered for lunch, she realized that this was the first meal they'd had together in a week.

"That Gauntlet was seriously, like, hard," Abria complained over her plate. She took a big bite of pork. "Yum! Pigg must have found his way into the kitchen today."

"Yes, no one else would think to use apple butter, cranberry, and pickled watermelon rind with the pork," Fergie said formally.

Elena and the others looked at her with dumbfounded expressions.

Fergie shrugged. "Gribbin has been challenging my palate for years. I am almost at the point where he trusts me to cook with him."

Elena rolled her eyes. "This week has been awful. And those Archon leaders are really annoying."

"Colt, Bauer, and Woods seem alright," said Austin.

"Yeah, but Roman, Duke, and Hawkins are horrible," Declan commented. "So, Haddock, when are we going to stage a rebellion?"

"What?" Austin said.

"Oh, come on! Don't tell me you haven't thought about overthrowing Archon to establish new management."

"I know you want to go in fighting, but if you're patient we can take them over in a better way," Austin said sensibly.

"How's that?" Elena asked.

"We'll study their systems. Then, over time, we'll place doubt in the minds of the other trainees about Archon's ability to lead properly. Eventually, the trainees will rebel without us having to start a revolution of our own."

"How are we going to do all that?" Kidd asked.

"We haven't been here long enough for me to have figured that out yet," admitted Austin. "But soon we'll know what to do."

"Well, since we've spent the entire morning training in misery can we please take the afternoon off?" said Elena.

Later that evening, Elena climbed into bed with a sense of calm and warmth. She felt confident that everything would be fine in the morning. However, she had only precious few hours of sleep before...

"GET. OUT. OF. BED. GOONIES!"

Elena bolted straight up in bed. She slammed her palms against her ears to block out the obnoxious siren that was reverberating off the walls.

"What time is it?"

"GET. OUT. OF. BED. GOONIES!" Roman hollered again. "Sanitation crew on me. Everyone else get to your Enrichment activities."

Elena looked at Roman standing across the room. She wanted to clobber him.

"Ugh! More cleaning. It never ends!" Rachel Reddington complained.

"Whining about it won't make it better," Roman shouted at her.

"Why do you have to be so awful?" Elena asked Roman as she pulled some jewel colored cleaners out of the closet.

"It's a special talent I have," Roman said as if he were proud. "Now, get that mouth shut and get to work!"

"We're supposed to be getting more mature with age," said Elena to Fergie under her breath. "And yet *some of us*..."

Fergie smiled and helped Elena scrub down the bathroom shower stalls.

"Hey, do you know what's up with all the cocoon learning?" Elena asked Fergie. "It's like solitary confinement. Is Grimsby trying to bore us to death?"

"They are systematically testing for our weaknesses," Fergie said formally. "Those with auditory learning style will naturally excel. Those with kinetic will find the tasks more strenuous."

"Shouldn't they know our strengths and weaknesses by now?"

"There is always an opportunity to test individual vulnerabilities to see if a person has evolved or not," Fergie said.

"So, basically it's never gonna get easier."

"If this entire experience were easy there would be no point to learning to begin with."

"I don't agree with that. Some things could be a little easier for the sake of my brain cells, which hurt, in case you were wondering," Elena said. "Plus, everything around here happens so fast. After I was done eating lunch the other day I puked it up on the way to field training because I was running to get there."

"You are not the only trainee that is struggling to meet demands," Fergie said in a low voice. "When I was in Medical for my shift last week, I logged symptoms of headaches, memory loss, and hand tremors all due to sleep deprivation. Moriah Kirkley lost seven pounds last week alone, Stacia Bassi presented with symptoms of psychosis, and Apryl Sommers mentioned having hallucinations."

Elena thought about her own headaches and hand tremors over the past week and began to chew on a fingernail. "So, all those side effects are from not sleeping?"

"It appears to be," Fergie replied.

Elena decided to keep her ailments to herself because she didn't want to look weak. She continued the cocoon classwork in isolation that day, feeling barely awake as she stood encased by a dozen Optivision screens.

Booker lectured on Portuguese navigators, the Spice Islands, and the building of forts in the New World. Niva taught her the developing languages and the new ways of keeping records as sailors crossed the world.

But Copernicus's lecture was easily the worst as he said, "From 1524 to 1529, the Portuguese and Spanish rulers appointed three astronomers, three cartographers, three pilots, and three mathematicians to find the exact location of the antemeridian, which would divide the world into two equal hemispheres."

Given her lack of sleep, Elena could have cared less about the class. However, it seemed that Fergie enjoyed the lectures because she mentioned how interesting their classes had been when they met for physical training.

"Well, I thought it was an absolute snooze fest," Elena grumbled to her and Abria. "But I do finally understand why we were forced to learn so much about longitude and latitude and cartography. Today, I answered questions the entire time about famous navigators and celestial patterns."

The rest of the day went by in a blur of work and pain. After training with the other Special Ops girls, Elena developed a stomach cramp, which she assumed was from over exerting herself. Then, she had extreme difficulty concentrating and keeping the facts straight while Roman lectured yet again about the Gauntlet.

As evening approached, she felt a swell of fear. Not being sure how many hours she'd sleep before she'd be up again made Elena's heart pound and her head sweat. So, instead of sleeping as she should have been, she stayed up far too late listening to the other girls snore.

The following morning, Roman was screaming again for the girls to wake up. Elena stumbled tiredly off to the kitchens where Pigg was waiting for her second kitchen rotation. He looked so rested and happy that she was actually jealous.

"Good morning!" he said brightly as he handed her a steaming mug.

"You're looking well," Elena said grumpily.

"It seems that I've been a huge asset to the kitchen," Pigg beamed. "Roman told me a couple days ago that he wants me in the kitchen every single day. He said that he's letting me choose my Enrichment activity one week earlier than everyone else, but not to say anything about it. So, I'm only telling you. It's such a relief that I don't have to do any of the other Enrichment exercises any longer. I was especially lousy at Construction."

"I wish I could choose only one Enrichment activity," Elena grumbled. "But we have to do them all."

"Well, pull up those curls and let's get to work," Pigg said as he led Elena through the maze of prep tables and cooking ranges.

He stopped at a table in the back of the prep area. "Roman said I could continue going to the hydroponic farm and that I could take any fruits or vegetables I want as long as I keep the food tasting as good as it has been."

"That's really quite a compliment, especially coming from Roman."

Elena pulled herself into a sitting position on the counter and watched Pigg quietly for a few minutes as he grated some lemon into a bowl of ground meet. He looked so happy.

"How are you sleeping?" Elena finally inquired.

"Pretty well," Pigg replied. "I go to bed super early so that I can get up early and run over to the hydroponic farm. Now that I get to stay in the kitchens every day I have to plan my schedule so that I can get to the cocoon for classwork. But the classwork is easy so it doesn't take long."

"You aren't bored out of your mind in there?" Elena asked. "Because I find that I'm half asleep most of the time."

"I like being on my own," Pigg said simply. "It's quiet and no one can bully me in there."

"Well, what about friends?" Elena asked. "How do you make time for friends?"

"Strictly speaking, I don't have any friends yet," Pigg admitted. "But I'm very hopeful that my culinary skills will be endearing, at least to...Abr...the girls."

Elena smiled a little. "You hoping to get some dates?"

"No!" Pigg blushed. "And I'm not trying to replace you or anything, but I do miss having a sister-type person around all the time."

Elena also blushed. She punched him lightly in the arm. "Well, now that you'll be in the kitchens everyday at least I'll get to see you when I'm going through the food line."

Pigg hummed softly as he added breadcrumbs and a compilation of spices to the meat mixture.

As Elena watched him, she thought absentmindedly about the time that they'd tumbled down the hill during the icy wilderness simulation. Even in the woods, Pigg had always known how to cook, which made up for some of his other shortcomings, like not being able to handle things medically in the field. As she thought about how awkward it had been for Pigg to set her bad arm, she began to rub her shoulder.

"What's the matter?" Pigg asked.

"Oh, I'm tense from training," Elena replied. "And I can't tell if my headache is from not sleeping or from my shoulders."

Without speaking, Pigg pulled a couple bottles down from the side pantry. He mixed some coconut oil in a bowl with some herbs and then added some drops of oil to some water.

"Drink this," he instructed as he handed her the water. "And then rub some of this stuff on your shoulder."

"What is it?" Elena asked.

"The drink is a concoction of Roman chamomile that will help with the headaches and muscle tension," Pigg explained.

As she drank, she experienced a pleasant burning sensation in her throat.

"And the shoulder rub is a mixture of peppermint oil that will help with inflammation. I've been studying it a bit with Austin. I saw him in the hydroponic farm the other morning while I was picking my ingredients for the day. He said he's been working on something in Medical to help with some of the side effects of insomnia and sleep deprivation. I told him I was happy to test any product as long as it didn't interfere with my cooking."

Elena scooped some peppermint oil mixture on her fingers and slipped her hand inside her sleeve. She was amazed at the instant relief she felt as she rubbed her right shoulder, and hurried to rub some oil on the left as well.

"For lunch today we're having seared salmon with couscous salad to give us a lot of protein before physical training," Pigg said.

"How's that going this week?" Elena asked.

"Much better," Pigg replied. "I seem to be getting the hang of it. At least, Roman doesn't yell at me as much. I feel stronger, but I think that's mostly because I get to be in the kitchens all the time with the unlimited supply of food."

Elena couldn't help but laugh. "You better be grateful for human engineering or else you'd weigh a ton by now."

The following day, Elena really wished that she could stay in the kitchens with Pigg because she was finding it hard to concentrate during Program Writing with Abria.

She also had trouble staying focused during Enrichment with Kidd the day after. He tried to help her as much as he could while they wrote code for the construction of the Ottoman Empire, but Elena never fully understood what he was talking about. And Declan was effective in coaching her through engineering the following day, but overall Elena was getting moodier by the hour.

Every day that week, she struggled in physical training with Sabrina Bauer and Charleston Woods. Sometimes she could feel that her body was flat out rejecting the sessions, but then she'd look through the wall that separated the boy's training and felt thankful that she didn't have Dino Roman for a leader. Brennan Colt, Collum Duke, and Link Hawkins weren't much better either. All four of them seemed to push the guys extremely hard.

As always, Elena ended each day with dinner, Roman's lecture about past Gauntlets, and Kidd walking her back to the dorm. Sometimes they were both too tired and moody to talk, but he always wished her a goodnight. But then, another morning would come with loud sirens and Dino Roman's booming voice shocking her to the reality of another day.

The lack of rest appeared to have a positive effect on Abria, who seemed to have amplified energy, alertness, and an enhanced mood. Elena felt ashamed that she was increasingly tired and grumpy until she learned that she wasn't the only one having such a hard time.

"And while I was in Medical, Mandara Tilden was seen for high blood pressure, Thomas Apted had been admitted with seizures, and Jaden Kinard was prescribed a set of medication for, like, mania or something," Abria told Elena and Kidd during lunch one day. "Apted is so cute, even when he's spasming out of control."

Elena rolled her eyes. "The dimwit schedule that's making me crazy and you're talking about boys! I just can't deal with you."

"Want to go for a walk through the woods?" Kidd interrupted. "It might take your mind off things. Or at least, you'd have a wide open place to scream about it."

Elena wanted to walk, but she was too tired.

"Actually, I feel really terrible," Elena confessed. "I'm going to try to take a nap. See you at dinner."

As Elena rounded the hall towards the girl's dormitory, she noticed that Austin and Fergie were talking alone at the other end of the cooridor. When they looked up at her, she simply waved and hurried along, not wanting to stop for anyone.

Once she reached her bunk, she fell into an uncomfortable sleep, where she dreamed about her mom being surrounded by ghostly figures in some type of medical lab, which reminded her too much of the Cognicross she had at her birthday.

Her mom pleaded with her again and again, "Come find me!"

"You don't understand what it's like," Elena told her mom each time, as she sobbed. "I don't want to die."

◻ 9 ◻

Done

Every night over the next few weeks, Elena hoped that the following day would somehow be easier than the previous day, but then the morning would come with Roman's booming instructions. Sometimes, he would even wake the girls randomly in the night. Every night was different. The tiredness she felt was almost debillitating.

Elena's cocoon classwork, Enrichment schedule, and physical training began to run together in a haze of constant motion. More and more she lost complete concentration throughout the daily tests, including during Roman's boring lectures about the Gauntlet at the end of each day. Even if he called on her to answer a question, she cared less if she responded correctly.

One night, as Elena lay in bed wishing that she could fall to sleep quickly, Abria said, "Why does everything around here happen so fast? And on such a specific schedule?"

"Oh, I don't know, maybe to make us insane!" Elena grumbled.

"But yet not everyone has the same day off during the week," Abria continued as though she hadn't heard Elena speak. "We have to do all cooking, cleaning, and medical treatments in the school. So, that technically means that the school is never at, like, rest. It's running full steam ahead without rest." She looked at Elena and cocked her head to the side. "And let's face it, you're getting crazy enough to need a break from this place."

"Oh, what does it matter?" Elena said moodily. "We've been working endlessly for so many weeks that I've completely lost track of what quarter of school we're in. I barely sleep and it's hard to eat. It's hard to even think. What's it matter if we have a break?"

But before she allowed Abria to answer, she rolled over under the blankets on her bed and covered her hands over her ears.

The following day, Elena walked into Medical for her weekly rotation hoping to find a bed for a nap.

However, Sabrina Bauer had called the trainees together and said, "Today we're going to start medical training on simulated human bodies. You've already had basic field medical training with Hopper during your first few years. So, your instruction in here over the next few weeks should be pretty simple for you. Be advised that you're still required to treat any injured students that come through the door."

As Elena followed Sabrina through the halls with Austin and the other trainees, she felt thankful that Austin had hidden her away for a nap the weeks before because she hadn't had to deal with any injuries.

Sabrina led them to a room that was filled with rows of tables. A simulated human body lay on each of the tables with an Optivision open at its feet. None of the simulated bodies wore clothing nor had distinguishable anatomy, but Elena still felt slightly embarrassed.

"This is weird," Elena whispered to Austin. "Plus, it's a little disgusting that I can see every single organ on the inside of the body."

"Everyone gather around this first table," Sabrina instructed. "As you can see, this patient has internal bleeding coming from the spleen." She pointed at the Optivision to the section of the body that was in distress. "Using this cadaver as an example, what will need to be done?"

Austin raised his hand.

"We would give a directive to the Optivision for the robotically-assisted minimally-invasive surgery to begin, at which point the manipulators would make a small incision and repair the damaged organ."

"Very good, Haddock. You stay here with me for practice," Sabrina replied. "Ransom, I want you back up front to wait for incoming."

As Sabrina gave everyone else orders, Elena begrudgingly walked back to the front desk where Thomas Apted was already waiting with a bloody nose.

"What happened to you?" inquired Elena.

"I was punched in the face one too many times," Thomas complained.

"Why were you punched in the face?"

"Oh, Roman thought it would be a good idea for us to start training for the H2HC portion of the syllabus before you girls do. He said it would give us an advantage over you in training, but I think he's crazy."

"H2HC?" Elena questioned.

"Hand-to-hand combat," Thomas said with a surprised look on his face. "Didn't you already know that?"

Before Elena could ask any further questions, the door slid open and Jaden Kinard hobbled over the threshold holding his side.

"I'm pretty sure my ribs are broken."

Elena's eyes widened in horror, but there was no time to talk because the door opened again with yet another injury. In fact, it was constantly busy for the following hour as more and more boys filed in, each reaping the pain of Roman's first H2HC class.

After a few hours, Elena realized that she hadn't seen Austin around. She went on a search for him and found him, at last, in a dark room towards the very back of the Medical Station. He had goggles over his eyes, gloves on his hands, and was hunched under the light from an Optivision screen. She noticed he had several medical dishes that were sparsely filled with powdered materials and he was carefully using tweezers to combine the fragments in each dish.

"What are you doing in here?" Elena asked.

"Working on remedies for the trainees that are struggling with sleep issues," Austin said. "After you mentioned about supplements a few weeks ago I started doing some research. The ones provided by the school are supposed to help with insomnia and sleep deprivation, but I think the pills are really inducing anxiety and aggression."

"Why do you think that?"

"I've noticed some trainees with the adverse side effects of reduced emotional intelligence and constructive thinking skills, plus weakened immune systems. But others are almost too hyper and happy, which is also unnatural."

"Like Abria?" Elena smirked. "If the pills make some people worse then why does the school give them to everyone?"

"I'm not sure," Austin admitted. "But I scanned a book about medicinal herbs from your dad's library into my Broadcaster before we came back here."

"Why did you do that?"

"I was concerned after Grandpa and Grandma Haddock made such a big deal about Special Ops being so difficult," Austin said. "I actually scanned quite a few of his books just in case. But anyway, I've been working with Instructor Emerald to take herbs from the hydroponic farm. Fergie and I have been brewing remedies at the Firebird Station. I think we've almost perfected a new supplement that will help trainees get to sleep quicker and stay in deep sleep longer."

Elena felt her face go warm. While she'd been simply reacting to her new circumstances, Austin had not only anticipated a possible situation in Special Ops but made steps to bring healing to the suffering students.

"You're awesome, you know?" said Elena. "But why didn't you tell me? I could have helped."

"No offense, but you're no chemist," Austin said with a half smile. "Plus, I could tell you were exhausted. Fergie doesn't suffer from that human condition."

Elena smiled.

"And, you have said several times how you don't want to go to the Firebird Station, which I assumed meant that you don't want to get lured into searching for artifacts."

Elena blushed and looked down at her jump boots, feeling exposed and wondering how Austin always seemed to know exactly how she was feeling and why.

"I am trying to respect your boundaries on that even though I would like it for you to be there with me. So, instead I want you to take this tonight." Austin handed Elena a little green pill. "After our last class with Roman."

"You want me to *test* your new *invention*?" Elena asked, feeling dumbfounded as she accepted the pill into her palm.

"Yes. And then let me know how it works for you," Austin said. "You're the perfect trial case because you're constantly complaining about feeling tired."

Elena rolled her eyes at him. "Even if it works a little I'll consider it a huge improvement."

But, as it turned out, the concoction helped Elena fall into a deep, restful sleep. In the morning, even as Roman was screaming for everyone to get out of bed, she woke feeling physically better than she had since she arrived at Grimsby.

"You're a genius!" Elena gushed at Austin as he met her for breakfast. "I slept so well that I don't feel tired."

"That's good news!" Austin said.

"We designed the pill to rebuild, restore, and rejuvenate brain chemistry," Fergie said in a formal tone.

"Well, whatever you did, it worked!" Elena said.

"But we're not sure how long the effects will last, so you'll need to make mental notes all day about how you're feeling."

Elena promised that she'd give him a thorough report as they made the long trek with their friends out to the Gauntlet for practice. However, she was immediately distracted when she saw that the members of Archon were already out training. The Gauntlet had been transformed into a new series of physically demanding obstacles. The upperclassmen were in varying stages of the course and it seemed they were each trying to out perform the other.

"Another day of practice on the Gaunlet dripping with water," Abria said glumily. "Who designs these things?"

"I designed this one," Roman barked, coming up from behind them. He folded his arms at Abria. "Some say it's the most difficult Gauntlet ever constructed at the school."

Elena rolled her eyes and headed down the slopes with Kidd, Austin, Declan, Fergie, and Abria.

Elena couldn't help but watch in awe as Brennan Colt jumped from a springboard and grabbed onto a large hoop on a long declining track. Somehow, Brennan was able to use his momentum to jump from the hoop at the end of the track onto a platform that was several feet away.

Not far from him, Charleston Woods leapt forward off a trampoline and grasped the underside of a declining cargo net. Miracously, she was able to alternatively climb over and under the net without falling in the pit of water below.

And while all this was going on, Elena also watched a Level 5 girl slide down a giant chute and then grab onto a horizontal rope that was suspended some distance away. Using her body, she was able to grab a swinging rope. Then, she began to jump from one line to the next in a long procession of ropes that were suspended over water.

"Did you see what she did?" Elena said in amazement.

"Yes, but stop pointing," Austin said with a smile.

"Geesh! Let's start practicing," Elena replied.

Elena, Kidd, Austin, and their other friends started on a long stretch of track that was nearly impassable because of all the cascading waterfalls and walls. But they soon realized that they had to lift the wall up from the ground and pass under it to the other side to get to the next wall.

As they started, the obstalce seemed rather easy because all six of them were lifting the wall in unison. But after the twelfth wall, Elena was physically worn out.

Knees wobbling, she managed to walk across a series of unstable columns over the water. However, as they came to a progression of hanging chains, Elena decided she couldn't go any farther.

"We're supposed to swing across the water on those chains?" Elena said wearily. "But I just can't go on any longer."

"Me neither!" Abria said almost before Elena finished her sentence.

"Well, I'm okay to go on," Austin said.

Kidd and Declan nodded.

Elena, Abria, and Fergie watched the boys continue on through the course for a while longer. By the time the boys were finished, Elena was feeling particularly discouraged. She made a hand motion at Austin, Kidd, and Declan to join her, Abria, and Fergie on one side of the course.

"What's going on?" Declan asked. Then, he put on a playful voice and said, "Are we making plans to bust outta school or have you figured out a way to give Roman food poisoning?"

"Gauntlets were never this bad before!" Elena stated with a crazy look in her eye. "And this isn't even the worst part about being at school. The Archon leaders make all our decisions and we have to follow mindlessly along."

"Well, not mindlessly," Abria pointed out. "If you were mindless you wouldn't care so much that they control every single little detail of our, like, day."

"And have I even mentioned how many demerits I have?" Elena said, ignoring Abria completely. "Roman gave me demerits yesterday for rolling my eyes. Like I can even help that reflex!"

"Yeah..." Declan said slowly. "You're acting a little insane."

"This isn't an act!" Elena insisted. "I'm actually insane. Look at my eye twitching. I didn't even know that it was physically possible to feel sick and tired every moment of the day, even when I'm asleep."

"I guess the pill wore off already," Austin said, then he turned to Fergie and added, "We need to make one for the day-time, too."

"Do you think they ever kick anyone out of the Special Ops program?" Kidd asked.

"If we fail to meet the requirements, we will be demoted to our original Companies," Fergie said.

"I want to go see Hopper and find out what's going on here," Elena stated. "I want to know why there aren't any adults around. And I want to know who elects the members of Archon. Also, why all the classwork is done in isolation during, but then all the training is together? He's the only person that may give me a straight answer."

"What about Hannibal?" Austin suggested. "I've seen him around our campus a bit. He appears to be monitoring our progress to some extent."

"We can't trust him, Austin," Elena said. "He works too closely with the Headmaster. Plus, his tolerance for helping us is probably low given all the stuff we've already put him through."

"I am sorry to point out the obvious flaw in your idea, but at this stage in our training we are not permitted to enter the other resident towers," Fergie said. "Which means we will not be able to consult Hopper on any topic."

"What do you mean we're not *permitted*?" Kidd asked.

"One of the conditions of confidentiality is that they keep us separated from the younger students," Fergie replied.

"So, we can't, like, what?" Abria said. "Cheat?"

"That is one of the reasons," Fergie confirmed. "The school does not want us to divulge details of our training to anyone."

"Well, I need answers!" Elena said. "And I'm going to Hopper to get them."

"We could always scale the resident tower to his room," Austin said.

"That's a great idea!" Elena replied. "I'm ashamed I didn't think of that myself."

"When are we doing this?" Kidd asked.

"*We* are not doing anything. *I* am going tonight," she said with determination.

"Tonight?" Abria said in a startled voice. "Don't you want to think about it a little longer first? You could get into so much trouble. Plus, you'll lose sleep. And we all know how much you need to catch up on that!"

Elena made a face at her, but said, "I don't care about getting demerits from Dino Roman." She noticed the covert glances between her friends, but didn't care to talk further, so she said, "I'm going to my room now. The sooner I can get a quick nap before dinner the better."

After lights out that evening, Fergie manipulated the surveillance from the school's mainframe so that Elena could escape without being noticed.

"Good luck," Abria whispered from her bunk as Elena pulled on her jump boots.

"I'll definitely need it," Elena replied.

Then, she hurried down the hall and out onto the first balcony she could find. She climbed over the side of the wall and carefully stepped down the outside of the building, using the crevices of the structure as a stepladder.

Once on the ground, Elena moved through the shadows of the resident tower and the tall hedges towards her old dwelling. As she was coming around the last hedge, she ran smack into someone else and fell hard to the ground.

"Sorry about that!" Kidd apologized as he bent over to help Elena stand again.

"What are you doing here?" Elena exclaimed.

"I thought you might need some help."

"I told you that I was doing this myself."

"I know, but I thought you might want my company."

"Go back!" Elena ordered.

"No, I'll come with you," Kidd offered. "I'd like to hear from Hopper myself, anyway."

"Me, too," called a voice from behind them.

Elena's mouth fell open as she turned to look at Austin. "What are you doing?"

"Going to see Hopper, just like you," Austin replied.

"We're more likely to get caught now that more of us are going," Elena pointed out.

"It's not like you can stop us," Austin said.

"Good point," Elena conceded. "Let's go."

The three of them started, going as quietly and as quickly as they could. As they came to the base of where they needed to begin the assent, Elena heard the sound of footsteps racing toward them. She crouched low to the ground with Austin and Kidd on either side of her. Then, Elena noticed a wisp of blonde hair.

"Bowen! What are you doing here?" Elena demanded in a shocked whisper.

"Oh, good, you're here," Declan said as he came through the shadows. "I thought I'd missed you."

"It looks like we're going to be quite the entourage for Hopper tonight," Kidd said.

"No, we can't all go," Elena said firmly. "We're not even supposed to be out here."

"I agree," Austin said. "There are too many of us now. But how do we decide who goes."

"I'm going! This was *my* idea," Elena said to Austin.

"Hey look," said Declan. "Hopper told Haddock about the Firebird Station in the first place. And he told Ransom the truth about Imperator and everything. So, you both should go."

Declan looked at Kidd and then they both looked at Austin.

"Fine," Kidd agreed. "But we'll stay here until you get back. I want to know what Hopper tells you and I'm not waiting until morning to hear it."

Elena and Austin started up the side of their old resident tower using the stepladder crevices that were part of the facade. Once they reached an empty portico, they quietly made their way into the building. Then, the friends raced quietly through the hallways until they finally reached Hopper's door.

Elena held her breath as Austin knocked once.

A moment later, the door slid open silently, and there stood their old resident advisor. Hartwell Hopper's curly rainbow colored hair was just as wild as ever. His scraggly, long goatee did nothing to hide the silver ring through his nose. He looked at them with a mixture of surprise and disapproval.

▭ 10 ▭

A New Outlook

"How did you get in here? Hopper sighed. "Your Trademarks don't work on the entrances anymore."

For a moment, it seemed he was trying to sound impatient at their clear disregard for school rules, but his eyes were kind so Elena felt sure they wouldn't be in trouble.

"You taught us how to climb up and down the building our first year here," Austin reminded him.

"Oh yeah," Hopper said, smiling. "I probably shouldn't'a done that." He punched Austin in the arm and slapped Elena on the back. "It's good to see you though. Come on in."

Elena had never been inside Hopper's apartment before. She was somewhat surprised to find it in perfect order. Hopper was always so relaxed that she almost expected to find his living space a mess. She felt somewhat uncomfortable as she sat down on the neat and structured couch.

"How have things been?" Hopper asked, but then he noticed the look on Elena's face and added, "Clearly, it hasn't been going well."

"Hopper, you've got to try to help us understand what's going on over there," Austin said. "Why is the schedule so intense? Why are we being educated in isolation?"

"And why isn't there adult supervision?" Elena interrupted. "Seriously, isn't Headmaster Bentley worried that we'll kill and eat one another?"

Hopper rolled his eyes and said, "Dudes, you're never alone. We have surveillance on you twenty-four hours a day, seven days a week. The Headmaster is actually watching you closer now than he ever did before."

"Why?" Austin asked.

"Each of you is being vetted for your unique abilities, so that he can determine your future," Hopper said, but after noticing their confused looks he added, "Career placement."

"Headmaster Bentley *chooses* our career for us?" Austin asked.

"Not exactly. The evaluation he makes over the next three years will go on a permanent record for each of you," Hopper explained. "From these records, business owners or government officials will seek their workforce."

"Who cares about our career at this point?" Elena asked in a frustrated tone. "Can we get back to the actual problem? We're being traumatized on a daily basis! How are we ever supposed to make it through training?"

"You need to learn how to compartmentalize," Hopper advised.

"I don't know what that means, but it doesn't sound pleasant," Elena grumbled.

Hopper smiled. "Look, you need to learn how to not let your external situation affect your attitude. Compartmentalization will allow you to focus on your situation while suppressing any overarching, negative feelings about your daily schedule."

"Clearly, you haven't met Dino Roman," Elena said. "He's horrible! Every time I see him or he's in my presence I want to punch him in the face."

"Dudes, I know Roman really well. He was a Firebird the year before you. I know he's intense. And what do angry, intense people hate more than anything?"

Elena shrugged. "Feeling constipated?"

"Joy and laughter."

"Joy? There's *nothing* enjoyable about being around him," Elena insisted.

"Then, find some. We used to prank one another to relieve stress during Special Ops," Hopper said.

"Prank? What's that?" asked Austin.

"Oh you know, hang other people's clothes from the ceiling, or rub toothbrushes in salt, or steal all the towels from the shower room," Hopper said with a goofy grin on his face. "Stuff like that."

Elena and Austin looked at one another in disbelief.

"Do whatever you havta do to create laughter and lightheartedness," Hopper added. "I'm telling ya, if you shift your focus from defensive grumbling to proactive coping it's going to make your time a lot easier."

"So, you want us to manufacture fun?" Austin asked.

Hopper nodded and said, "Now you're getting it!"

Minutes later, Elena and Austin climbed out of window and back down the side of the building.

"I thought Hopper was going to help us," Elena said to Kidd and Declan. "But he didn't say anything useful."

"Actually, the thing about compartmentalizing was very good," Austin said. "I think your dad has a book like that in his library. If only I would have thought to scan it..."

"So, what are you saying? That somehow magically we'll be happier with Roman?" asked Elena.

"No, not that," Austin said with a huge smile on his face. "But we don't have to always be on the receiving end of the trauma. We can create some havoc ourselves. And I think you'll find that creating chaos will bring you a little joy."

A slow smile began to spread across Elena's face. "It always does."

However, as it turned out, Elena didn't have time to create chaos over the next few days. She continued to be in a constant state between being asleep and awake most nights and wished that Austin would hurry to create more supplements. Elena's dreams were frequent and mostly recurring, either about the Kairos turning into a giant clock that chases her until she's crushed by its weight or her mom begging Elena to come find her.

Elena's nerves were on edge all throughout the day, every day. Three times during cocoon classwork that week she had to close the sessions out early because her heart began to race, or she had numbness in her hands, and she had trouble breathing.

She was constantly snapping at her fellow trainees when they made any mistakes during Enrichment activities. And to make matters worse, the physical training part of her day continued to get more intense as Charleston Woods announced that they'd soon start hand-to-hand combat training.

"Listen up, ladies!" Charleston called as Elena gathered with the girls for their next training class. "Bauer is sick, so Link Hawkins is joining us to help facilitate as we begin to teach H2HC."

Elena was not happy that Link had joined them, but she was thankful that Dino Roman hadn't been given the task.

"First, we'll warm up. Then, I'll teach you several basic H2HC techniques." Link barked.

"You mean, I'll teach them," Charleston said steadily to Link.

"Whatever...we can do it together," Link said. "There are certainly enough girls in the class. I'll take all the pretty ones."

Elena appreciated it very much that Charleston rolled her eyes as she squared up against Link to show the rest of the girls a proper example.

"H2HC is about balance, focus, and anticipating your opponents next move. Rotate your hips and upper body as you pivot your right foot." Charleston moved slowly in demonstration. "Exhale sharply as you extend your right fist straight out from your chin. Then, rotate the fist to land with your palm down."

Charleston and Link practiced the technique at a steady pace. Elena thought it looked like a cross between boxing, kickboxing, wrestling, and judo.

"Now, for a hook," Link said. "You'll need to pivot your feet clockwise as you drop your right heel and lift your left heel. Your body should rotate as a solid block when you pivot. Then, your left arm tightens as you swing your left fist towards the target. Remember to exhale and breathe!"

Elena watched Charleston and Link take turns lightly punching and kicking one another under the ribs and in the abdomen. They also moved steadily around the fighting mat in a give-and-take fashion that Elena recognized from the years of classes her mom had given her back in Atlanson.

"Okay, enough of that," Charleston said. "Pair off with someone and practice these couple moves we've shown you."

"Don't you think Hawkins is just the cutest?" Abria asked, grabbing Elena by the arm.

Elena had overheard many of the girls in the dorm say that they thought Link was cute and she'd heard them gossiping in to the night about tactics for trying to get him to notice them, but Elena thought he was too arrogant to be considered as anything more than a nuisance.

"Not really." Elena winced in disgust. "Do you see how the ceiling lights reflect off his high forehead? It's not really that attractive."

"But, he has those great cheek bones," Abria said in his defense. "And, I know his hair is spiked up, but it looks thick and wavy."

"Abria, please, you're going to make me sick," said Elena. "If you like him so much, how about you go join his training group."

Abria smiled and skipped off in his direction. Elena was happy to remain behind with Fergie. They moved off together to one side of the room and began working together.

Periodically, Charleston would call out helpful tips, like, "Maintain your stance, Kirkley. It will help with power and mobility; Reddington, make sure to exhale sharply on every punch; Keep your body still as you extend that one fist, Faulkner; The right cross will be your strongest punch."

Elena was glad she and Fergie were left relatively alone because she got the benefit of teaching her friend all the moves she'd learned from her mom.

After a long while of practice, Elena noticed that Link Hawkins had started assessing the other pairs of boxers that hadn't trained in his group.

"A left hook is a dangerous punch." Elena overheard Link say to Rachel Reddington. "But you need to time your impact better."

He didn't stop there.

"Sommers, you need to relax more and aim better. Faulkner, your balance is way off. Someone could knock you over with a feather. Tilden, don't just stand there after you punch! You need to focus on recovering your punching arm and planning your next move."

Elena turned back toward Fergie in their fighting stance and said, "Now I understand why they separate the boys and girls during training. It's so the girls won't kill the boys for being loud-mouthed dimwits."

Suddenly, Elena felt pressure on her hip. As she was involuntarily twisted around, she smacked Link's hand away.

"Don't touch me there!" she hollered in his face.

He smiled in a taunting way. "You're not standing properly."

"And from that you concluded that it would be okay for you to *touch me*?" Elena said angrily. "Keep your hands to yourself!"

Link walked away looking satisfied with himself, but Elena was the opposite of pleased.

"I can't believe he'd think that unsolicited touching would be fine with me," Elena told Kidd as they walked toward their Enrichment class after training. "I mean, honestly, look at my face. Does this look like a face that encourages the violation of personal space?"

"But you actually weren't standing correctly," Kidd pointed out. "All the boys got out of training early, so we watched the end of the girl's session."

Elena's face burned red in anger. "As someone who has broken your nose, I think I stand fine."

"Why did you have to bring that up?" Kidd said, suddenly moody.

"Why do you have to attack the way I do things?"

"I wasn't attacking you."

"That's what it feels like when you say I stand wrong."

Kidd looked as if he wanted to say something else, but then he closed his mouth and looked off down the hall away from her. Elena had no desire to stand there in silence, so she walked away, deciding that she was going to skip the Enrichment with Kidd. Instead, she went in search for some peace.

"Hey! What are you doing here?" Austin asked. He was standing in the dish pit at the back of the kitchens, dripping with water. "You skipping class this afternoon?"

"Not everything," Elena replied. "Only my Enrichment with Wheeler."

"Uh oh..." Austin said. "I know that face. Why're you angry?"

Elena blushed and then sighed. "During H2HC, Hawkins told me I was standing wrong. But when I tried to tell Wheeler about it he said the same thing."

"Why'd you care what Hawkins says?" Austin said.

"Because it's like saying that mom taught me wrong," Elena said, revealing vulnerability in her voice.

Austin smiled in an understanding way. "Did you tell Wheeler that?"

"Nope, I just yelled at him." Elena said.

"That's really mature," Austin laughed. "I'm sure you weren't standing wrong. Your mom would have known to teach you a perfect stance based on your weight and frame and dominant hand. It wouldn't be the correct stance for everyone and it wouldn't be textbook, but your mom taught us both well and in the way we needed."

Elena instantly felt cheered by his words.

"Remember how Hopper said that you need to learn to compartmentalize your feeings? I'm not sure yelling at Hawkins or Wheeler accomplishes that," said Austin.

"I'm trying, I'm trying," Elena complained.

Elena's ability, or rather inability, to compartmentalize her feelings was soon tested to its fullest because that evening Roman started their formal training on the Gauntlet's entirely new course.

The other Archons were there as well, but it was clear by Roman's directions that he was the one running the practices.

"You will perform every single obstacle according to my standards or you will stay until it's perfected!" Roman hollered at the Level 4 trainees.

They'd only watched Archon go through the Gauntlet once before. As Elena looked over the course laid before them, she didn't feel that their training had been enough for Roman to expect perfection.

Elena, Kidd, Austin, and their other friends were first directed to four platforms that were positioned alternately, left and right, across the length of the pit.

"Those platforms look to be at a 45° degree angle," Declan said. "Pointed straight down into the water."

"It looks impossible!" Abria said. "I mean, how are we even supposed to, like, stay on there?"

"We'll have to jump back and forth between them as quickly as we can," Austin said. "I'll go first."

Austin started off well. He jumped quickly, back and forth between the platforms, making it all the way across the obstacle without falling in the water once.

"It's like that other obstable we did on the first practice course," Austin hollered to them.

Elena had every intention to launch her body back and forth across each platform as Austin had, but when it was her turn she landed clumsily on the first platform and fell carelessly into the water below.

Elena could hear her friends laughing as she came out of the water.

"You shouldn't laugh until you try it," Elena warned.

In next to no time, Fergie, Abria, and Kidd had all joined her in the water. Declan, on the otherhand, breezed through the obstacle like Austin had. They kept on trying with Austin and Declan directing them until they were all finally able to make it across the platforms without falling into the water.

"What's this all about?" Elena asked as she looked at the next obstacle with a rope and some kind of floating dock in a pool of water.

"I think we're supposed to ride the rope down the zip line and finish on that floating dock. At least, I think I remember that from some of the playbacks that Romans showed us."

"This doesn't look too awful," Elena said. "I'll go first."

Elena grabbed a rope tightly. But, right before she jumped from the platform, she could hear Roman from a nearby obstacle.

"You are slow and weak!" Roman shouted into Oscar Hunter's face.

Then, the edges of Roman's body blurred into a silouette. As she leaned into the zip line, she was also standing in an entirely different place. A place that she'd seen many times before.

A medical looking lab was filled with ghostly bodies spread out in every direction. Each of the bodies was suspended in midair and was being monitored by an Optivision. Hannah Ransom was there, wearing the same high collared uniform that she always wore in this Cognicross.

"Elena, so happy that you could join me," Hannah said, as always, opening her arms in a loving way. "I am very happy to see you, my sweet girl."

"I don't want to do this with you again, Mom," Elena sighed. "As always, this place is super creepy and you never tell me who these people are anyway. Why do you keep bringing me here?"

"Come find me," said Hannah.

"What do you mean, *find you*? You're dead, Mom. And, like I've told you before, we're not really having this conversation."

"Come find me!" Hannah said more insistently.

"Lena! Lena! Are you okay?"

Elena could hear Austin calling for her, but it seemed to be coming from a long way off.

"Ransom! Can you open your eyes? Are you hurt?"

Elena could hear Kidd trying to get her attention. What did he mean, could she open her eyes? Weren't they already open?

She blinked and blinked until her mom's lab disappeared. Elena slowly realized that she was lying on her back, looking up into concerned but friendly faces.

"Get off your back, Ransom!"

She knew that Dino Roman had hollered at her even before she saw his face.

"Take it easy!" Declan growled at him. "Ransom fell off the obstacle and knocked her head in."

"I don't care what happened to her! Get her up off my course if she can't continue, but she's not going to lie there taking up space."

"Do you think you can sit up?" Austin asked as he waved his Suturand over her face.

"Yes, I feel completely fine," Elena said truthfully.

Kidd and Austin put their hands under her arms and lifted. As she sat forward, Elena noticed Roman glowering at her from the next obstacle over.

"That's it..." Elena said quietly to Abria and Fergie. "I'm tired of Roman! And I'm tired of this place."

"Oh, yeah," said Abria. "And what are you gonna, like, do about it?"

"I'm going to start having fun," Elena said. "Even if it kills me."

"What did you have in mind?" Fergie asked.

"First, we'll need to enlist help from some girls on our hall," Elena said.

☐ 11 ☐

Pranking

"I need your help," Elena told Rachel Reddington, Moriah Kirkley, and Apryl Sommers as they were getting ready for bed that night. "I have this thing I want to do."

"What thing?" Rachel asked.

"I want to play a prank on Roman," Elena said.

"What's a *prank*?" Apryl asked with a confused look.

"It's sort of like…" Elena started, but then she threw her arms up in the air in frustration. "Okay, I don't know exactly what it is, but Hopper said we should try it. It's something that's supposed to create laughter, or fun, or something. I don't know. Fergie and Abria have already agreed to help, but I need lots of rucksacks and people to help carry them."

"Rucksacks? For what?" asked Moriah.

"First, we're going to sneak over to the Mess Hall and get all the tin cups we can carry out of the dish pit," Elena said. "And then we're going to line the cups in the hallway right outside the boy's dormitory after lights out. There's no way they'll get through the hall in the morning without making a mess."

Rachel, Moriah, and Apryl shared looks of concern.

"We can't be out of our room after hours," Rachel said.

"That's where Fergie comes in," Elena said. "She'll take care of the survelliance so we won't be seen. So, will you help me?"

"Are you sure we won't get caught?" asked Apryl.

"Absolutely certain," Fergie declared in a confident tone. She removed the Broadcaster from her pocket and attached it to her wrist. Then, a little dot the size of a drop of water shot from the device into midair.

As Fergie began to access Optivision screens from the Touchdot, Rachel asked, "What is that?"

"It's called a Touchdot," Elena said. "From it Fergie can gain access to Grimsby's mainframe and tell the surveillance what we want it to do."

"Where'd you get it?" asked Rachel.

"From my parents." Fergie lied so automatically that Elena felt impressed.

"Wow! You've been busy!" Moriah said.

"What'd you mean?" Elena asked.

"If you learned how to acquire access to the school's surveillance already you're ahead of the rest of us," Moriah replied.

Elena didn't want to tell them how long she'd been able to hack into the school's system so she focused on Fergie's work.

"I have gained access to the mainframe," Fergie said while looking at the different codes that lit up the Optivision screens. "We can proceed to the kitchen."

Fergie followed the Touchdot as it led the way out of the girl's dormitory. As it flew down the hall, its laser lights scanned every area while the girls followed closely behind.

"If we get caught, I hope they put us in solitary confinement for a month so we don't have to do all the dimwit Enrichment and cocoon classwork," Moriah whispered.

Elena couldn't help but smile.

The girls took the first Grimvator they came to straight to the Mess Hall. The kitchen felt very different without the lights on and hundreds of teenagers filling the space with noise. They went straight into the dish pit and began to fill their rucksacks with tin cups.

"This has to be the most reckless thing I've done in my life," Apryl said. "Seriously, what if we get caught?"

"We won't get caught," Elena said again. "Trust me. I know from experience."

"I don't even want to know what that means, Ransom," Rachel replied as she gave a wink.

In next to no time, Elena and the other girls stood at the edge of the boy's dormitory hallway. As quietly as they could, the girls began to lay out the hundreds of tin cups they'd collected, covering every inch of the corridor.

"It will be impossible for them to leave in the morning without chaos," Elena whispered proudly.

"I hope that Roman trips and falls flat on his face when he comes out in the morning," Abria said.

"Too bad we won't be able to see his face," Rachel said.

"But we will," Fergie whispered. "I will simply access the surveillance footage tomorrow after the event. We will be able to replay it again and again for the entire school to see."

When the girls had finished their work, they barely got three hours of sleep before Roman was in their room hollering for them to get out of bed. He looked angrier than usual so Elena was confident that the prank had worked. Especially since, instead of starting their Enrichment activities, Roman called all the Special Ops trainees to the hall outside the boy's dorm for a meeting.

Elena noticed that a large section of the floor was scattered with tin cups, as if someone has tripped and slid.

"I don't know what happened here," Roman said in a deep voice as he gestured toward the mess. "But some of you Goonies think that it's acceptable to break rules and manipulate the data on the survelliance. I'm going to ask the culprits to come forward now."

Elena looked around the room with a dumbfounded expression on her face, just the same as everyone else.

Roman pressed his thumb and forefinger on the bridge of his nose, sighed, and closed his eyes firmly as if he were experiencing a headache.

Then, he exhaled dramatcially and said, "Let me make this clear for you. If the Goonies responsible don't come forward then everyone will be punished."

Elena felt that she and the other girls from the pranking crew should have won an award for maintaining straight, almost confused looks on their faces.

"What are you going to do?" Charleston scoffed. "You can't give everyone demerits."

"Yes, I can," Roman replied.

"No, you can't," Charleston said boldly. "We don't know who did this. It could have been your own Ops team. I'm not going to allow you to punish my girls when no evidence has been presented. I demand a majority vote."

At her words, Roman glared at Charleston in such a way that Elena feared for the girl's physical well being.

"All those in favor of punishment raise a hand," said Charleston.

Of the members of Archon, only Roman responded.

"All those in favor of dimissal raise a hand," Charleston continued.

The rest of the Archon members raised their hands in unison.

"I won't forget this, Woods," Roman said bluntly.

"I certainly hope not," Charleston replied in a confident tone. "It's a good day for the rest of us when you look foolish."

Roman turned away from her and yelled, "Listen up, Goonies! I forbid rule breaking of any kind. Clean this mess up now! All of you!"

Then, he turned and stalked out of the room.

"Was that you?" Austin whispered, as he and Elena's other friends gathered together.

"To be fair, I did have help." Elena smiled.

"That was awesome!" Declan said. "I wish I could have seen him when he first found the cups."

"Oh, you will later," Elena promised. "Fergie has that all figured out."

"So, what's next on the list?" asked Kidd.

"You'll have to be surprised," Elena said with a wink.

"You know, pranking can ellict retalitory type feelings in others," Austin replied with a smile.

"I'm counting on it," Elena replied.

As they all left the hall for their Enrichment activites, Declan's wish to see Roman finding the cups came true a little sooner than expected. Suddenly, from every window dimensional in the hall the survelliance footage of Dino Roman coming out of the dorm an hour earlier began to play.

Elena watched Roman round the corner. He slipped on one of the first tin cups. As he started to fall, he slid forward, knocking into a dozen more. The tins scattered, clattering loudly as more and more knocked over.

Elena couldn't help but laugh at the look on Roman's face as he realized the entire hall was covered with cups. She wasn't the only person to enjoy the scene. The entire corridor burst into a fit of unrelenting laughter that lasted throughout morning Enrichment and continued on as she overheard whispers of other trainees seeing the footage from the kitchens and Medical.

But easily, the best part of the day was that the boys did not wait to respond to the girl's prank. That evening, after Roman's lecture, the girls walked back to their dormitory and into a scene that caused Elena's jaw to fall open. A huge pile of clothing had been left in the center of one of the hallways.

"I checked and I'm pretty sure that all of the clothes were taken from every single closet in the entire dorm," Charleston said as she pointed at the pile with a very mischievous look on her face. "Look, I don't know which of you girls started this little game, but obviously the boys are eager to join. So, I'm all in now."

"Me, too," said Sabrina Bauer. "I mean, seriously, who doesn't like a little flirtatious pranking?"

Elena wasn't interested in the flirtatious part, but she was all about thinking up another prank for the Special Ops boys. As all the girls on the floor began to sort the clothing, several of them started tossing around ideas, such as filling all the boys tactical packs with dirty socks instead of supplies, or somehow suspending clothing from the ceiling, or stealing all the bath towels off the entire floor.

Therefore, even with the sleep deprivation that was almost debilitating, Elena arrived in the kitchens the next morning ready to cause some trouble. Pigg, however, was not supportive of the idea.

"You want to do what?" he asked with a confused look on his face.

"I want to prank the boys. You know, I could yuck up their food or maybe I could hide all the silverware so they have to eat with their hands."

"That doesn't sound like a good idea," Pigg replied.

"I heard some of the other Special Ops girls say that they're going to remove all the toilet paper from the boy's bathroom during breakfast." Elena laughed. "I can't wait to see Roman's face once this day is over."

Looking horrified, Pigg said, "Well, don't get me into trouble. I find enough trouble on my own."

Elena was busy rolling her eyes as Pigg tried to hand her an entire pan of tofu patties, but they fumbled it horribly between them. The pan crashed to the floor, spilling the patties in a partially neat row. Pigg's eyes widened in disbelief as Elena hurried to scoop the damaged food back into the pan.

"That wasn't the kind of prank I was expecting, but it will do." Elena smiled.

"We can't serve that!" Pigg whispered. "It's contaminated!"

"Sure we can. We can serve it to the boys," Elena said. "Besides, it was only on the floor for five seconds."

She dropped the pan on the counter and began to portion bags of rice pilaf for lunch. "One would think that prepping pre-portioned meals wouldn't be so difficult."

"Or so messy," Pigg said with a disgruntled flinch as he watched her. "Do you have to do that? I mean you're flinging food all over the place."

"You're right. I'll let you do this. Besides, I need you to help me with something else," Elena said.

"With what?"

"I need you to teach me how to hack into the school's mainframe," Elena said. "If I'm going to start pranking, I need to make sure that I can't get caught."

"Why can't Fergie do it for you?"

"Oh, she can, but I'm not with her right now. And she can't help me all throughout the day anyway. I need to be able to learn for myself so I can prank whenever I want. Look, I brought my Broadcaster so you can show me."

Elena held up her wrist so he could see it.

"Okay, but what are you going to say if anyone asks how you learned it?"

"That I didn't learn this from anyone with the name Gribbin Pigg," Elena teased.

While Pigg chopped onions, garlic, carrots, and celery he instructed Elena on how to hack into the school mainframe from her Touchdot. She had several Optivision screens going at one time. Even though she told him often to slow down so she could take notes, at the end of her first lesson she felt really confident about what she'd been able to learn.

After breakfast, Elena hurried to finish her cocoon learning sessions so she could get back to the kitchens to ask for more instruction from Pigg.

"We need to stop now," Pigg finally said. "The lunch line is about to open."

"Okay," she said begrudgingly as she put her Broadcaster away. "But I expect more training later."

As the lunch line opened, Elena saw a group of Level 6 guys headed toward the food line. She immediately grabbed the canister of salt.

"Um...what are you doing?" Pigg said in a slightly panicked voice as he grabbed her hand.

"I'm adding more salt to this pan," Elena replied. "To the point that no amount of water will take the taste out of their mouths for the rest of the day."

"Don't do that!" Pigg cried. "You'll ruin the food."

"I want to ruin it," Elena explained. "It's my prank for today."

"Elena, I'll let you do a lot of things, but I won't let you compromise my reputation as a chef."

"Pigg, just because you have an obsession with food that's psychotic doesn't mean that I have to participate."

"E-le-na puh-lease!" Pigg begged.

Elena shook her head and rolled her eyes.

"Fine! But you owe me. I need you to teach me how to manipulate all the window-dimensionals and Optivision screens in the building at the same time so that I can replay the pranks. Fergie did that yesterday and it was perfect revenge on Roman."

"Now that I can do!" Pigg said, sounding relieved.

"So, how have things been with classes and all?" Elena asked, abruptly changing the subject as more students entered the food line.

"Things have been fine, I guess," Pigg replied vaguely.

"Yeah. Are you making friends?"

"Not really." Pigg wouldn't even look her in the face when he added, "But I'm also not getting my head stuffed down the toilet anymore so I must be doing something right."

"Who put your head in the toilet?" Elena demanded.

"The classwork is way too easy," Pigg said, ignoring her completely. "I spend most of my time in lectures so I don't have to talk to anyone. But I really think…"

Pigg stopped short at the sound of a strange commotion coming from the dining hall.

Elena and Pigg raced out to the main eating area. A dozen students were flinging food at one another from across the room. Elena saw at least three different boys dumping their drinks down the backs of girls' shirts and Stacia Bassi had smashed her meatloaf into Jaden Kinard's face.

"What's all this?" Pigg asked.

"Looks like successful chaos to me," Elena shrugged.

As Elena started to laugh she noticed that Pigg looked horrified.

"That's funny, right?" Elena said, nudging him in the shoulder.

"All that amazing food…"

Elena grabbed a fist full of whipped potatoes from the nearest plate and smashed it straight in Pigg's face. She was hoping for a smile, but Pigg gave her a sad sort of look and walked back to the kitchens shaking his head.

However, soon enough, Roman burst into the Mess Hall screaming at everyone to stop. And, even though he got a face full of mashed potatoes, that didn't stop him from hollering out demerits to everyone in his path.

That evening during Roman's lecture, he tried to punish several other people for the food fight and for the clothes debacle in the girl's dorm, but the trainees were already worked so hard that it didn't matter if they received more demerits. And then the replays of the pranks started and Roman lost complete control of the room.

The following day, during program writing Enrichment with Abria, Stacia Bassi, and Moriah Kirkley, Elena was trying really hard to concentrate, but the thought of Roman's angry face kept replaying in her mind. Instead of studying, she wanted to think up more pranks.

"Guess what?" Abria whispered, leaning toward her.

"What?" Elena said absentmindedly as she stared at the Optivision screen with the layers of codes to decipher.

"Never mind. I'll tell you later," Abria said after she was unable to gain Elena's attention.

"Okay," Elena replied, not even bothering to look up.

"You don't want to know now?" Abria asked impatiently.

"Not really," Elena said. "I have a lot to do. I'm already so distracted with thoughts of how to torture Roman that I've ruined this code about seven times already."

"Elena, playing pranks isn't the only way to have fun around here," Abria said. "You can also have fun gossiping."

"That's what our friendship is for," Elena said dryly. "For you to keep me entertained."

"It's true that your life would be boring without me," Abria confirmed. "But when I come to you with salacious gossip I expect you to be a little interested, for my sake."

Elena turned toward her with a look of expectation.

Abria looked excited and said, "So, Oscar Hunter locked Apryl Sommers in the closet with all the sanitation cleaning products. Then, when he went to open the door later, she squirted him in the face with one of the blue concoctions and he had to get up to Medical because his face started swelling.

And Fergie changed Thomas Apted's info in the system so he couldn't login to his classwork."

"And Stacia and I have decided to hide all of Link Hawkins clothes and give him a map to find where we hid everything," Moriah said as Stacia nodded.

"I'd say that things have definitely gotten out of, like, control. And it's all thanks to you," Abria said.

The smile on Elena's face could not be contained, but she said, "You do realize that everything you just told me in *gossip* was about pranking, right?"

"Oh well..." Abria said, looking as though she were trying to think of something else to add. "Collum Duke almost cut off his left pinky finger during construction the other day. There was so much blood and I was, like, ewe gross! But all the guys thought it was fantastic. Guys are dimwits, but then Anita Huey is falling all over herself trying to get Apted's attention. I mean, show a little respect for yourself; you're, like, two years older than him. Let him come to you."

"Are you jealous?" asked Stacia.

"Of course I'm not jealous of her," Abria said, flipping her hair haughtily.

"I heard she's jealous of you though," said Moriah.

"Of course she is. I'm gorgeous."

As the three girls burst into giggles, Elena dropped her chin in her hand and said, "I really didn't understand any of that conversation. Where's Fergie when I need her to translate?"

"Then, how about we talk about your relationship for a while," Stacia suggested.

"Oh, I've tried, but it's completely hopeless," Abria said, rolling her eyes. "She's all like, *Ugh! Don't ask me questions like that,* and then completely shuts down."

"Well, the last time you asked if Wheeler had kissed me yet," Elena said. "Why would I want to talk about that with you?"

"It's what girls do," Abria said. "We talk about stuff. And it doesn't havta be embarrassing. Like, take me for instance. Frankie Smiley kissed me before we left school last term and there was absolutely no chemistry there. Plus, he didn't get into Special Ops so a relationship would be almost pointless. Plus, now I have my eyes on...Elena, where are you going?"

Abria paused midsentence because Elena had closed out her Optivision session and jumped up from the table.

"This conversation is insane," Elena grumbled.

"Elena, to reiterate what Abria said earlier, part of school has to be devoted to gossip," Moriah said. "How else will we know what's going on around here?"

"I honestly don't care," Elena said as she walked away.

In truth, Elena still had no desire to talk about her relationship with Kidd with anyone. Plus, in general, she was distracted by the mood on campus. She could feel something bubbling under the surface after only a couple days of pranking, something that felt like a mixture of happiness and frustration.

Roman had become almost insufferable during his afternoon lectures. He seemed to have exhausted footage on past Gauntlets because he'd started showing the trainees playbacks of different Tribulations. He gave them such odd, confusing tips on how to successfully complete the simulated exercises that the trainees were constantly giving one another puzzled glances.

"That's a little vague," Oscar Hunter blurted out one day. "We could do a whole lot of dimwit things without even knowing it."

Roman cut his eyes at Oscar at once and replied, "For you, Hunter, dimwit is even opening your mouth."

Elena pursed her lips together angrily.

Then, as Roman started to lecture again, she leaned toward Oscar and said, "I heard that you stole all Roman's clothes while he was in the shower. I'm impressed."

"Well, that's good because I live to impress you," Oscar replied sarcastically, but then he winked at her. "He's only mad because he's been Ransomed."

Elena gave Oscar a look of confusion.

"Oh, you didn't hear? Since everyone figured out that you're the one that invented the pranking around here, we started calling it being *Ransomed*."

Elena smiled and shook her head slowly. "I'm really flattered. So, what are we going to do next? I'm thinking..."

"Are you Goonies going to persist in talking throughout my entire lecture?" Roman barked at Elena and Oscar. "Because I can have you each bound and gagged."

Elena closed her mouth again, wishing that there were something more they could do to annoy Roman.

⌂ 12 ⌂

Weapons Training

The following week, Elena was looking forward to her next kitchen rotation with Pigg. She thought she'd figured out a way to convince him to help her food prank people, but when she arrived in the galley she couldn't find him anywhere.

"Hey, where's Pigg?" Elena asked Anita Huey, who was in charge of the kitchen that morning.

"Pigg was permanently reassigned to Technology. He won't be back in kitchen rotation," Anita replied.

Elena turned away wondering if his reassignment had to do with him helping her hack into the school's mainframe to help with pranking.

As soon as breakfast began, she slipped out of the kitchens and found Abria and Austin sitting at a table.

"Pigg's not in the kitchen anymore," Elena said with a slightly worried edge to her words. "I bet Roman had him moved, but I hope it's not my fault because of all those pranks."

"It can't be. Everyone's pranking," Abria said dismissively.

"Austin, should we worry about Pigg?" Elena asked. "He was teaching me how to hack into the school's surveillance. Do you think Roman found out and did something nasty to him?"

"Do you always have to take the pessimistic view of everything?" Abria asked. By now you should know the answer is *yes*."

"Pigg will be fine," Austin interrupted.

"I know, but Grimsby managed to take away the one thing he absolutely loved. Food."

"Ransom!" Anita Huey called from across the room. "Kitchen! Now!"

Elena jumped up at once to hurry back to her workstation, hoping that at some point she'd run into Pigg later that day.

However, as the weeks elapsed and the Grimsby campus began to transition from cold winter weather to pleasant spring afternoos, Elena was beginning to think that she'd never see Pigg again. She hadn't found him in the halls, on the campus, or even in Emerald's hydroponic farm. Her schedule was so structured that it was hard for her to find time to look for him anywhere else.

Roman continued to wake the girls all hours of the night, but Elena felt stronger and more rested than ever. Her body had grown accustomed to being interrupted, but also the supplement that Austin and Fergie had perfected was now being used by nearly everyone. And even though month four was beginning with no break in sight, Elena felt better every day.

She was feeling so terrific, in fact, that she barely thought about anything else but pranking. That is, until one afternoon while she was doing left over classwork with Abria and Fergie, and Rachel Reddington entered the Media Room in a flurry of exhilaration.

"Hey!" said Rachel. "Did you hear? We're going to start weapons training this evening!"

Elena felt a prickle of excitement on the back of her neck. "Anything to get us out of Roman's boring lectures or off the ridiculously hard Gauntlet training is good news to me."

"Are we training with the guys?" asked Abria.

"Who cares? We get to use weapons!" Rachel said excitedly. "We're to report to the weapons room at 1900 hours."

However, when Elena arrived with Abria and Fergie for weapons training she noticed right away that the term "room" had been used incorrectly. The trainees were standing in an oversized arena that was divided into different zones for weapons training. Each area contained a wall of handheld devices that varied in size, shape, and color.

In the far corner of the arena, Elena noticed that Headmaster Worthen Bentley was sitting with Hannibal and Hopper in some sort of spectator's area high above everything else. Even from a distance, the Headmaster's high, tight collar and harsh facial features intimidated her.

Elena joined Austin, Kidd, and her others friends and gestured towards the men.

"Why are they here?"

But before anyone could reply, Roman barked, "As you now know, our weeks of physical training have culminated. We will now enter a term of weapons training."

In Roman's right hand he held up a silvery-barreled weapon that covered his wrist and extended out a foot beyond his hand. In his left, Roman held up a round flat object that was the size of a coin, which Elena recognized as a neurolizor because Booker had taught that to her the previous year. She had also witnessed Kidd using one that had belonged to his parents in the Smuggler Station before it flooded.

"All the weapons work using neurotechnology. The artillery, type of ammunition, and even the direction of your aim can be control by wearing the neurolizor. It should be worn on the back of the neck at all times to give you better control."

He placed the small round disc on the back of his neck. Then, Roman lifted the weapon and said, "This particular piece produces a customizable energy pulse to render an enemy unable to continue in pursuit. Observe."

As Roman stepped into the active field, the room filled with dozens of warrior figures that appeared to be constructed with some type of electronic signature. The figures were also holding varies types of weapons.

"Look up there," Fergie said, pointing. "Those projections are simply relayed from the Optivision screens above the arena."

Elena didn't even have time to ask what Fergie meant because the figures approached Roman in an attack formation. He lifted his weapon toward the advancing figures.

Before Elena could blink, some form of laser light began to emit from Roman's weapon. As each of the lasers connected with the digital soldiers, the figures exploded into a million electronic bits. When Roman was finished destroying all the projections, he turned with a look of accomplishment on his face.

"So, if you shoot a human with that, does the person exploded into tiny pieces?" Oscar Hunter asked.

A murmur of uncomfortable chuckling broke out, but Roman did not look pleased at the question.

"I've never tried it before, Hunter." Roman glared at him. "Would you like to find out today? I'd be happy for you to act as my target."

The entire class of trainees fell silent at once.

"Now, the other members of Archon will demonstrate some of the other weapons that are available for training," Roman declared.

Sabrina Bauer stepped up first. Elena could easily see the neurolizor on the back of her neck because her head was so bald. She was holding a sleek black cannon with sharp, knife like sides.

As Sabrina's training began, Elena leaned toward her friends and whispered, "They're teaching us to train with weapons?"

"Yeah, why would they do that, Austin?" Abria asked. "We're only sixteen years old."

"I don't know," Austin replied. "But I heard Hopper say that the school only started advanced weapons training last year. Before that, everyone used the point and shoot laser pistols during the simulations. You know, the ones with the sensored vests."

Elena's brow creased into a frown. "Why does this sound like something that has to do with Imperator?"

"Well, Hopper did tell us in our first year that this place was training us to fight against him," Austin reminded her. "Maybe the type of weapons we trained on before weren't enough."

Elena's stomach gave a jolt of fear. If thousands of people had been trained for many years with the wrong weapons, how would they ever be able to defeat Imperator when the time came?

As Brennan Colt charged toward the virtual soldiers with a long, barreled weapon, Elena tried to whisper something else to Austin, but she suddenly heard her name shouted over the sound of the vaporized simulations.

"Ransom! You talked through that entire demonstration. Since you seem to know it all, how about you come up here and show us how it's done?" Roman barked.

Elena rolled her eyes at Austin before she started toward Brennan and took the weapon from his outstretched hand. She should have felt nervous, but there was something about the way that Roman and Brennan gazed at her with their arrogant expressions that caused defiance to rise up instead of fear.

Elena slid the stocker part of the weapon over her wrist as her finger closed around the trigger. The barrel felt awkward, heavy, and unnatural. She turned back toward Austin for a moment and gave him a look that she hoped he'd understand as "help."

When she turned back, she expected to see Roman's scowling face and a room full of simulated attackers, but instead there was a man with a pencil thin beard wearing a waistcoat.

"Dad!" Elena exclaimed.

"Hello, Sunshine," Truman Ransom replied.

Elena looked down at the weapon in her hand, then back up at her dad.

"I've been here before, haven't I?"

"In a way…" replied Truman. "Your mind has been preconditioned to withstand and understand the most complex parts of your training at Grimsby."

"You couldn't have given me better programming for those first few sleepless months I had because of Roman?"

Truman chuckled. "Unfortunately, most of your training has to be done the hard way. However, you should find that as you are pursued and attacked your Cognicross will respond effectively."

At these words, Elena could now see that she was still inside the same training room at Grimsby and that all the digital figures with weapons were moving toward her. But Truman still stood at her side and her weapons suddenly felt as though it were a part of her arm.

As her attacker approached, she engaged them in a way that almost felt as an effortless dance. With her dad standing at her side, Elena moved her body to escape the onslaught of the attack and used her weapon to eliminate the projections that were presented before her.

When the simulation ended Elena wanted to thank her dad, but he'd already disappeared. Feeling proud and elated, she turned for Roman's approval, but he was staring at her with a look of pure loathing.

Then, Roman turned toward the other trainees and shouted, "ALRIGHT GOONIES! For the last hour of class we're going to show you how to hold the weapons and use them at the shooting range. Arm yourselves!"

As Elena walked over to the weapons area to join her friends, Abria hurried over and gushed, "That was, like, the most totally awesome thing I've ever seen!"

"Did you see Roman's face?" Declan laughed. "He was in total shock."

"I'm in total shock," Elena admitted. "When I first got up there I didn't know what was going to happen, but I was sure I wasn't going to be any good at it."

Austin laughed and tossed an arm around her shoulder. "Well, I didn't have any doubts that you'd figure it out."

Elena, her friends, and many of the other trainees moved along the wall of weapons slowly. Several Optivisions displayed how each of the weapons worked. She saw some that were clearly designed for Maritime style fighting under the water and different types of hand-held devices for Animalia. But the weapons for Aves were extremely impressive because they could be used on land, in water, and also when traveling at high speeds through the air.

"Bring your weapons toward the shooting range and make well-ordered lines," Roman suddenly hollered. "Girls to the left! Boys to the right!"

Elena felt anticipation threatening to suffocate her as she, Abria, and Fergie moved off into a line together. The simulated weapons range was currently a blank stretch of wall and floor, but far above everything sat the Headmaster, Hannibal, and Hopper in a viewing box.

"How do I look?" Abria asked as she struck a pose with her weapon.

"Perhaps you should care less about how you look and more about how you aim," Elena replied dryly.

"Oh, come on!" Abria said. "How're we ever supposed to have fun in weapons training if you won't humor me a little and tell me that I look amazingly powerful and awe-inspiring holding this thing?"

Elena looked down her nose at her friend, but Abria only giggled.

"I believe Elena's point is well taken," Fergie said in a formal tone. "You should focus your attention on the fact that Reddington lost her footing on her first shot at the target and has now fallen into a heap on the floor."

Elena looked to the place where Fergie was pointing and she wanted to laugh, but Roman was already descending on the situation with condemnation.

"You are absolutely hopeless!" he shouted at Rachel. "How do you expect to defeat your enemy if you lose control of your weapon?"

"Why don't you step over here and find out," Rachel replied, her face burning red with embarrassment and anger.

Roman walked straight over to her and grabbed her off the floor with his hand firmly under her armpit.

"One hundred demerits for the attitude, Reddington," Roman said in a measured voice. "Now get back in line!"

As Roman tossed Rachel away from him, Elena felt the urge to lunge forward and attack him. Instead, she felt a hand grip her left shoulder and another close on her forearm.

"Leave it," Abria warned in a whisper.

"Agreed," Fergie said. "Roman's time will come."

Elena sighed. She resolved herself to standing in the line quietly with the other girls as they waited for their turn to shoot at the targets. However, many of the trainees were having trouble holding their weapons, much less aiming them. And Roman seemed determined to criticize everyone on how they were holding their weapons instead of actually teaching them how to use them, which gave Elena even more anxiety.

"That's not how to hold it properly, Kirkley!" Roman barked. "You're never going to hit anything that way, Wheeler!"

In addition, the ever changing simulation on the range with a never ending list of foes began to play tricks on Elena's psyche. One minute, Moriah Kirkley was fighting a series of fur covered attackers on a snowy mountain range and a minute later Adrien Segars was trying to shoot at a twenty-foot giant wearing full body armor.

"That looks frightening," Kidd called to Elena from the row beside her.

Elena gave him a smirk. "I bet I could get every one of those without even blinking."

"Sure," Kidd said in disbelief. "Is that before or after your magic weapon is able to get through that body armor? Face it, these simulations are designed so that we'll fail."

"Hunter hit himself in the forehead swinging his own weapon up," Elena pointed out. "So, I don't think it's only the simulation that's the obstacle. Plus, Bowen didn't hit a single target. That's all on him. I'm good at this."

"Don't be overconfident before you go up there," Kidd said, frowning slightly.

Elena was suddenly overwhelmed with the feeling that Kidd might be trying to hold her back from something. She wasn't trying to be boastful about the shooting range. She simply knew she could perform well because her dad had given her the tools.

But Kidd's frown and the way his eyes shifted uncomfortably caused her cheeks to turn pink with confusion. Could it be that he didn't want her to do better at the simulation than him? Or was he trying to protect her pride from being hurt if she were to fail at it? She wasn't sure of his motives, but she was certain that whatever he was trying to say or do he was doing for himself.

"How were you so good at this the first time around?" Fergie asked Elena as she stepped away from the range.

Elena watched Fergie's simulation, a naval vessel filled with armed sailors disappear, as she said, "Truthfully, I could feel that my dad was with me. I think he programmed my mind so that I'd be fully equipped when I face Imperator, knowing that could be at anytime."

"And knowing that it'll probably be sooner than later," Elena thought to herself as she headed toward the range, forcing her eyes to stay fixed on her target instead of Kidd standing behind her.

She had no way of knowing what she'd face in a moment, but she did know that Headmaster Bentley, Hannibal, and Hopper would be watching her; making notes for a future that she wasn't sure she wanted.

Then, Elena's mouth fell open as the range in front of her transformed into a rocky slope that was dotted with very familiar figures. She wasn't the only person in the room to gasp as digital projections of her own classmates started toward her, firing their weapons. But easily the worst part of the simulation was that Austin was in front, leading the charge against her.

Elena looked up into the viewing box and straight into Hannibal's eyes. It was impossible for her to read the look on his face, but she hoped very much he'd be able to see the contempt that had engulfed her.

"Ransom! What are you waiting for?" Roman hollered for the entire room to hear.

Elena couldn't think of how to reply to his question. The only thing she was certain of was that she didn't have to play whatever sadistic game the school had invented for her. She relaxed the weapon on her arm, turned on her heels, and marched with her head held high back toward the wall of weapons.

As she set her weapon down, she heard Roman call after her, "So, you're accepting a fail for the day?"

"Yep," Elena replied without even bothering to look back as she strutted for the door. "And I give you permission to give me as many demerits as you'd like."

"I'm pretty impressed with your first time out on the floor," Kidd said as he followed Elena out of the training room.

"Thanks!" Elena said as she slipped her hand into his. "So, what are the chances that we could use any of these weapons on Roman?"

"Don't even think it," Austin replied as he joined them. "Besides, don't you already have over one hundred demerits?"

"It's one hundred twelve, actually," Elena said proudly. "I wonder if anyone has ever been kicked out of Special Ops for excessive demerits."

"Yes," said Fergie as she and Abria also joined Elena and the two boys. "But trust me when I say that you don't want to be one of them."

"I currently hold the record for having the most demerits for physical displays of affection in the entire history of the school."

Elena's mouth fell open. "How could you even possibly know that?"

"And what did you get them for?" Kidd asked, smiling slyly.

"Wouldn't you like to know?" Abria replied playfully.

"So, anyone want to go for a walk?" Kidd asked, winking at Elena.

Elena really needed to go to the Media Lab to study, but she felt so tired from weapons training that she was sure she wouldn't be able to concentrate on schoolwork.

"I'm in," Elena said as Kidd grabbed her hand and swept her out to the hallway.

"So, we could walk or jog," said Kidd. "Or we could go sit by the lake and do nothing."

"There's Pigg!" Elena exclaimed as she pointed down the hall. "I haven't seen him in weeks! I'm going to talk to him. Want to come?"

Kidd shook his head and tried to smile, but Elena could tell he was disappointed. Still, she took off running toward the back of Pigg's head.

"Pigg! Wait for me!" Elena called as she made her way through a crowd of students changing classes. When she finally reached him, she said, "Hey! I've been looking all over for you for weeks."

When Pigg turned toward her, Elena gasped. He had an angry bruise under his eye and a fat lip. When she looked closer she noticed that his normally nervous brown eyes were set in absolute fear.

"What happened to you?" Elena cried in astonishment.

"Oh, Roman oversaw our last training and pushed me a little too hard."

"He hit you?"

"No, it was more like he slammed me down on the mat one too many times. I think it's because he found out I was helping you learn how to hack the system to do pranks. He really didn't appreciate the time we put his head on the dancing girl all over the window dimensionals. Plus, then he got mad because I accidentally deployed my life vest and it expanded to the point that they had to cut me out of it before I choked to death. Everyone was laughing, except he really didn't think it was funny."

Elena's face burned red with anger. "He shouldn't do this to you no matter what kind of pranks we do!"

Pigg shook his head, turned away from her suddenly and said, "Look, I've gotta go."

"No, wait! I haven't seen you in forever," Elena said, grabbing his shoulder. "What's been going on? Huey said you don't have kitchen duty anymore."

Pigg shrugged in an uncommitted way. "They changed my schedule all around."

"Well, how have your classes been?"

"Fine, I guess. Just the same as everyone else."

"Okay, fine!" Elena said, suddenly angry at his indifference towards her. "Don't talk to me. I came to tell you I miss seeing you."

She turned to walk away in anger, but Pigg called out from behind her, "Elena, I'm sorry. I'm having a hard time lately."

Elena turned back around and looked at him sympathetically.

"I know it's been hard. It's been hard on all of us. But you're only alone if you want to be."

Pigg looked like he wanted to confess something, but then he turned and ran away from her. In fact, he ran off so quickly that Elena didn't even have time enough to consider if she wanted to follow him to talk some more.

Disappointed by how Pigg had disappeared, Elena wandered aimlessly for a while trying to figure out what she should do. Eventually, she made her way to the Media Lab thinking that she could catch up on some of her procrastinated work, but instead she found Kidd sitting alone at a pupil station.

"Hey, whacha' doing," she said grumpily and she sat down beside him in a huff. "You decided to work, huh?"

"Yeah, I had some stuff to catch up on," Kidd replied without looking at her.

She tried to stay quiet, but a sigh escaped her mouth.

"What's up with you?" Kidd asked, barely looking up from the holographic lecture of Instructor Booker.

"I tried to talk to Pigg, but he literally ran away from me," Elena said. "I don't understand what's going on with him. I mean, we've been friends since we were five. These three older boys were bullying him at the park one day. When I saw what they were doing I felt bad for him, so I went over and started punching the other boys. They got all scared and ran off. It was so great. A couple weeks later, school started and Pigg found his way onto my Optivision screens. We've been friends ever since."

Elena looked to Kidd for a response, but he was still staring at his classwork.

"I haven't seen him for weeks and he just ran away from me. I don't know how to get him to talk to me," Elena said in a leading way.

"Why does he *need* to talk to you?"

"I just...he doesn't *need* to..." Elena said, as she began to stumble on her words. "I don't understand why he's acting like we're not friends anymore."

"Maybe he's jealous that he didn't make it into Special Ops," Kidd suggested.

"I don't think he's jealous," Elena said thoughtfully. "I think he's sad, maybe even borderline depressed. I mean, he lost all his friends all of the sudden and..."

"Yeah, we all lose things and then we learn to move on," Kidd said shortly. "Let it go."

"But I haven't seen him in forever and then he just ran away from me. What do you think I should do?"

"I don't know," Kidd said dismissively as he made notes on a separate Optivision screen.

Elena watched him carefully for a minute and then said, "I mean, I could go hunt Pigg down, tie him up, and make him talk to me until I feel better."

Kidd didn't even flinch.

"Or I guess I could ignore my feelings and wait until he comes to me."

"I don't get why you care so much about it," Kidd said, not looking over.

"Because he's like a brother to me," Elena said, her voice rising a little. "And it hurts my feelings that he suddenly won't talk to me."

"Look! What are we trying to accomplish here, Ransom?" Kidd asked.

"I'm not trying to accomplish anything," Elena said defensively. "I'm telling you what happened so I can try to figure out how I feel about Pigg."

"But we've been going around and around for twenty minutes."

"I didn't realized there was a time limit for how long I'm allowed to talk," Elena said nastily.

"Maybe there should be," Kidd said, looking impatient. "Listen, I've got a lot of work to do. I don't have time to worry about Big Ears right now. Can we talk about this later? Or can't you go and find Austin, or something?"

Elena couldn't think of how to respond so she stood up to leave.

"Hey, sorry," Kidd said, finally looking up from his work. "Do you want to stay and study together?"

"No, thanks," Elena said shortly. "I have somewhere else to be. I'll see you at dinner."

Elena left the Media Lab and walked straight to Medical. Her conversation with Kidd made one thing clear. If anyone could help her with Pigg, it wasn't going to be him.

After walking through the entire Medical floor, Elena finally found Austin working in a back room. He was wearing goggles over his eyes and gloves on his hands and he was bent over a liquid that was bubbling in a glass jar.

"Hey, Sunshine," Austin greeted her, though he didn't look up until she didn't respond. "How'd you find me?"

"You're always in here every chance you get," Elena grumbled.

Austin pulled the gloves from his hands and the goggles off his face and asked, "What's the matter?"

Feeling relieved that Austin wanted to talk, Elena said, "I saw Pigg earlier and he would barely talk to me. He would barely even look me in the face. Plus, he has a black eye and a fat lip that Roman gave to him. I'm really worried about him. Have you seen him at all?"

"Yep. I go and talk to him every day," said Austin as if it weren't a big deal.

"And he actually talks back to you, using words and everything?" Elena said incredulously. "What am I doing wrong?"

"Pigg's feeling out of place right now. It's nothing you did," Austin said. "So don't give up on him. He needs us now more than ever."

"But why will he talk to you and not me?"

"I think he feels embarrassed, like he let you down or something by failing to get into Special Ops."

"What? That's crazy!"

"He's under a lot of pressure now that they keep him secluded in the program writing room most of the day. Maybe next time you see him you could simply say that you're proud of him and you miss him."

Elena sighed, feeling bad for being mad at Pigg when she saw him. "How come you always know what to do?"

"I'm smarter than everyone else," Austin smirked.

"Oh yeah...if you're so smart, maybe you can tell me what to do about Wheeler. He's so..."

Elena paused. In truth, she had no desire to talk about her relationship. even with Austin, when Kidd was confusing enough for her on her own. She sighed.

"Never mind."

"Tell me," Austin encouraged.

"No, it's nothing. I'm tired again and I'm upset about Pigg. Anyways, so what did you think about weapons training?" Elena asked, eager to change the subject.

■ ■ ■

In the sixth month, on the first day, Elena finally felt like she was able to manage her schedule. The Level 4 trainees still performed exhaustive training sessions on the Gauntlet and in weapons training and the pace was still hurried throughout each day, but overall school was more tolerable for her.

The weeks continued to hurry by in a torrent of cleaning, kitchen duty, physical training, and code writing that made her brain hurt. And though Roman continued to be difficult to deal with during the extensive weapons training classes, Elena hadn't seen another simulation that required her to shoot her follow classmates, so she was excelling through every challenge.

Elena still hadn't seen much of Pigg and when she did he always made up an excuse so he could get away quickly. Even though she felt confused by Pigg's behavior she made a point not to speak with anyone about it, especially Kidd because their time together continued to be somewhat strained for reasons that Elena was too nervous to ask him about.

"I don't understand why we keep talking about Pigg." Kidd would say anytime she brought him up. Or he'd say, "What are we trying to accomplish here, Freckles?" when she'd try to complain about Roman or the hours of solitary classwork that continued to be absolutely boring.

Elena was honestly beginning to feel that she annoyed Kidd every single time she opened her mouth. Therefore, she was beginning to learn to keep her thoughts to herself when she was around him. The less talking they did, the more pleased he seemed to be in general.

Eventually, Elena caught up to the mid-1500's in her classwork, but she was still far behind Fergie in the curriculum and she continued to feel amazed by her friend's ability to process information so quickly.

"Yesterday, I was studying about Italian physicist and mathematician Evangelista Torricelli study 1608 to 1647 about…" Fergie started, but Elena interjected, "Well, I feel like a dimwit. I haven't even finished the 1500s yet. This whole learning at my own pace thing clearly isn't good for me."

"You can't look at it, like, that way," Abria said as she took a chair at the pupil station that Elena and Fergie were working from in the Media Lab. "Fergie is always ahead of everyone in her work."

"No, I don't think you understand how miserably bored I am," Elena said. "I mean, without Fergie there's no one to encourage me to pay attention."

Fergie gave her a thin smile and said, "I have discovered what we need to know about the Angel statue that we recovered from our trip to Istanbul."

"Oh…" Elena said slowly. She hadn't really thought any about the artifacts since they'd started school and she had no interest in knowing what Fergie had learned.

"The statue is called Gabriel's Horn," Fergie began in a whisper. "The name refers to the religious tradition identifying the Archangel Gabriel as the angel who blows the horn to announce Judgment Day."

"Judgment Day?" Elena said quizzically. "Sounds like that's going to be a fun time for everyone."

"The horn is a geometric figure with infinite surface area and finite volume," Fergie said.

"What does that, like, mean?" Abria asked.

"The simplest way to explain is to say that the Horn is a paradox," Fergie replied. "We have no way to know if or how this artifact will be used, but we do know it has the code we need."

"Fergie, I don't get how you and Pigg can do all this code writing so easily," Elena said.

"Obviously, it is not complicated for me because of my hard wiring," Fergie replied. "Pigg, on the other hand, possesses a rare gift. He was single-handedly instrumental in developing the portion of the artifact code that prevents it from self-destructing in case we add an incorrect sequence of numbers, an accomplishment that I myself could not have completed. My parents gave me limitations so I would be more human-like. Pigg has a natural ingenuity that cannot be limited."

Elena smiled in a sad way.

"Has anyone, like, seen Pigg lately?" Abria asked.

"I haven't, now that he's been taken outta the kitchens," Elena said bitterly. "It makes me wonder what they're doing to him." She sighed and put her chin in her hand. Then, she looked at Fergie quizzically and asked, "Why're you working through history so quickly?"

"I am trying to gain as much knowledge as I can to help Austin with the artifacts," Fergie said simply. "Additionally, I overheard Woods say that this is the longest they've gone without having a Tribulation. Since we do not possess enough information about the Tribulation or how long it lasts, I would like to get as much classwork in as possible before that time arrives."

"I wonder what it means that we haven't had a Tribulation yet," Elena said as she yawned.

"You are tired," Fergie observed.

"While you and Austin have been working to save the world I've been spending a lot of energy compartmentalizing my feelings like Hopper said so that I can enjoy my time rebelling against Roman's attitude problems. It's exhausting to be so happy all the time."

Fergie smirked a little.

"Seriously though, even with all the crazy stuff Roman does to us, I feel the happiest I've felt in a really long time," Elena admitted.

"Does Wheeler have anything to do with your feelings of euphoria?"

Elena wanted to say "yes," but the truth was that she didn't want to tell anyone that Kidd had become quieter over the past few weeks. She never knew what kind of mood he was going to be in when she saw him. Sometimes they could laugh about pranks, but other times an argument would start between them even when they talked about the simplest things.

Also, Kidd often encouraged her to skip classwork so they could go hiking in the woods, but when she declined he'd get upset. Elena was starting to get tired of his attitude.

Elena's secret struggle with Kidd was never more evident than later that day as she gathered with Abria and Fergie in the physical training room. She was attempting to learn how to handle the weapons with the longer barrels with smoother movements when she noticed Kidd standing in her peripherals. Elena wanted to ignore him, but soon he was standing almost in front of her.

"So, you gonna tell me what's going on with you?" Kidd asked. "You've been really quiet this week and today I can barely get you to look at me."

"Nothing's wrong. I'm fine." Elena lied.

"Seriously, are you mad at me or something?" Kidd asked.

"Yes, I'm mad at you," Elena replied in a calm, steady voice.

"For what?"

"For basically dismissing me every time I try to talk to you about Pigg, or anything else for that matter," Elena said.

"I told you I've been busy lately and have a lot of classwork to catch up on," Kidd said.

"That doesn't make any sense," Elena said. "That's just one of your excuses and you always have one."

"I don't want to always talk about Big Ears, okay?"

"Why? What's the big deal if we talk about how I feel?" Elena asked.

"Do you want to see Pigg more than you want to spend time with me?" Kidd asked. "Because it seems like that's mostly what we talk about lately."

Elena stared at him in silence. The truth was that she did want to talk to Pigg more than spend time with Kidd. She felt an almost desperate need to help Pigg, but she didn't want Kidd to know that.

Fortunately, Elena didn't have to answer Kidd's strange, leading question because loud sirens sounded off throughout the entire training arena.

"What's that for?" Elena shouted over the noise, but Kidd didn't need to answer because at that moment Charleston Woods arrived on the floor.

"Goonies! Grab your weapon of choice," Charleston hollered. "Time for our first Tribulation of the year."

Elena steadied a weapon in her hand as Kidd grabbed a short-barreled weapon from the wall. Then, she hurried into formation along with the other seventy-one Special Ops Aves to a hall of Grimvators.

The Grimvators descended and descended, farther than Elena had ever been before. When the doors opened, she stepped into a white-walled room with no beginning and no end. In spite of that, hundreds of Optivision screens were hovering in mid-air above the white-washed floor.

"Where are we?" Elena asked.

"We're several levels below the building," Charleston Woods replied. "This is the main area for holograph learning. Or, what we call, Tribulation."

"Over here, Goonies!" Roman barked. "In a few moments, we'll begin our first Tribulation as a team. Our minds will enter the same program together. Over time it will be hard to tell that we're in the simulation, but make no mistake! While we are inside, we are in a race against the Animalia and Maritime Special Ops trainees to find clues that eventually determine our tasks and final outcome of the simulation."

It was only after Roman mentioned that they were in competition with Animalia and Maritime that Elena realized for the first time that the two other groups of trainees appeared to be standing in separate sections of the room. The Aves would be up against one hundred and forty-four trainees that were solely focused on trying to destroy them.

Elena could see Sabrina Bauer and Link Hawkins talking to the Animalia group while Brennan Colt and Collum Duke talked to the Maritime crew.

Headmaster Worthen Bentley, Hannibal, and Hopper stood over them in a viewing chamber similar to the one in the weapons training room. Knowing that the Headmaster would be overseeing her first ever Tribulation made Elena slightly nervous.

"If your brain becomes disconnected from the simulation due to illness, starvation, death, or a varied number of other circumstances, you will gain consciousness in this room," Roman continued. "Then, you may watch the rest of the Tribulation from the viewing room or any of the window-dimensionals in the building.

"Be responsible. Be vigilant. Be warriors!" Roman barked. "Now, go scan your Trademarks into one of those Optivision screens so we can get started."

Elena didn't feel like Roman had given them enough information, but she followed along with the others and scanned her Trademark into the first available Optivision screen. Instantly, Elena felt her mind being transformed, or rather, *transported* through time and space.

She soon became aware that she was standing on an aerocraft with everyone else in the Aves Company. She was hooked to the ceiling in such a way that she was completely unable to move, but she could tell that she was wearing a jumpsuit, tactical vest, a pair of jumpboots that she could wiggle her toes in. She was fully equipped with gear for a long trek and the weapon she'd chosen was somehow strapped to her side.

"Sea creatures can't fly!" Roman shouted over the rumble of the aerocraft. "Land walkers can't fly! But winged creatures can fly, swim, and conquer land on foot. And that's exactly what we're going to do. Make your way to the beach!"

Elena's breath caught in her chest as the floor to the aerocraft opened beneath her feet. Quite unexpectedly, she dropped from the harness into a sky of blue.

▭ 13 ▭

Tribulation I

Elena felt in awe of the sheer scope of the simulation that spread out before her feet. An entire world of trees and sea expanded beneath the Aves Special Ops trainees far beyond what she could see. The scale of the Tribulation was beyond anything she'd experienced or expected.

As Elena deployed her parachute, she saw a beach and a steep cliff face. She tried to steer the parachute because she wanted to land on top of the cliff. However, no matter what she did, she landed on the beach with the other trainees at the base of the cliff.

"This is the worst place we could've, like, landed," Abria said as she began to pull her parachute back into her tactical pack.

"They put us here on purpose," Elena said bitterly.

Elena noticed that Roman had already stowed his parachute and moved off to one side of the beach with Charleston Woods. They seemed to have opened some type of Optivision screen that didn't look the same as any screen she'd seen before. They were talking quietly, but Elena managed to overhear the words *token*, *climbing equipment*, and *time*.

Elena waited impatiently with the other trainees until Roman and Charleston headed back in their direction.

"Listen up, Goonies!" Charleston declared. "During a Tribulation, we are always in direct competition with the two other Special Ops teams. We're all looking for a token of some kind. The tokens look different every time, but they always bear the Grimsby logo. Each time we find a token before the other Special Ops teams we get an advantage over them."

"Are you saying that these tokens are located anywhere within the simulation?" Austin asked.

"Yes! So, keep your eyes open and your mouths shut because, so far, we have no map," Roman growled at them. "And, I will repeat again! I'm not losing to sea creatures or land crawlers for any of you. Come on, Goonies! We've got to conquer our first obstacle to get to the first token before the others."

"But, shouldn't we look around the beach first?" Charleston asked.

Elena turned on her heels and scanned the area. She couldn't see anything, but maybe Charleston had a point. Since they didn't have a map, perhaps it was best to comb the beach before they scaled the cliff.

"For what? There's nothing here," Roman replied.

Elena stared up at the side of the cliff face. She'd done plenty of climbing at school and in simulations before, but this cliff wall appeared to be a challenging maze of rocks and trees with no clear way up.

"Who are the best climbers?" Roman asked.

Kidd gave Elena a look of contempt as he stepped toward Roman with a boy trainee from Level 5 and a girl from Level 6.

"Does it make you nervous that we're starting blind?" Elena asked Austin.

"Blind with very little info," Austin said. "Yeah, I'm nervous."

"It could be worse," Declan said with a quirky smirk. "The whole wall could be dripping with water."

"You three get up that wall first," Roman ordered the first climbers while handing them a bag that Elena recognized from one of their previous Gauntlets as the climbing gear. "Secure the nuts, hexes, and climbing ropes. The rest of you fall into lines from tallest to shortest."

Elena started to chew a nail as she watched Kidd ascend the wall with the others. She'd completely demolished three nails by the time the first three climbers were at the top of the cliff. Once ropes had been let down, Roman began to usher the first trainees forward.

When it was Elena's turn, she laced the climbing rope comfortably through her fingers, pulled with her arms, and pushed with her legs. However, even with the support of the rope, the climbing was challenging. Elena was soon out of breath and wishing that she didn't have such a heavy pack on her back.

She'd just reached what she guessed was the halfway mark when she heard an enormous shriek echo all around. Elena's head jerked to the left. She saw a body falling fast from a higher elevation.

"Help her!" Elena heard several voices holler from various ropes, but the girl was falling at such a speed that it was impossible to do anything.

When her body smacked the ground below, the image of her immediately disappeared. Elena heard Abria gasp loudly.

"Don't worry," Charleston called to them. "She has simply awoken in the simulation room where we started. She's perfectly fine and unhurt."

Then, Elena heard Roman bark callously, "Clearly, she wasn't a skilled climber."

As Elena began to roll her eyes at Roman's comment, she noticed a small rock wriggling in the wall in front of her. She looked around to see if there was trembling coming from somewhere deep in the earth. Considering that she'd experienced earthquakes in a previous simulation, she knew the school was willing and able to use the environment against them.

When she didn't see anything else unusual, she turned back to the rock face. The pebble was now shaking violently enough to be nearly falling out of the wall. Suddenly, it seemed that the small rock jumped out of the cliff by its own free will.

Elena's brow furrowed as she turned to watch the stone fall. She noticed that it fell with purpose and in such a way that it was leading her eyes out to the water. The small stone hit the water with such a heavy force that it caused a gigantic wave to lap against the shore below.

Elena was about to dismiss the entire situation as a hallucination when she spotted something down in the water where the stone had fallen. The item was large, rectangular, and glowing with the Grimsby logo.

"The token!" Elena hollered up at Austin. "I can see the token in the water below us."

Elena could hear movement all around her through the trees that grew from the cliff face as everyone turned toward the water. Then, she heard a message being relayed up the cliff to the place where she knew Roman was waiting.

Moments later, Elena saw Roman descend rapidly on a newly dropped climbing rope.

As he rappelled, he ordered, "Goonies! Get up that rock!"

Elena immediately continued her assent with the others. At long last, she was standing atop the cliff looking out over the vast ocean below. She turned, expecting to see a forest of trees, but instead the landscape had transformed into a town of sorts. Rows of small buildings and houses seemed to have been forgotten by time because the paint was peeling from the exteriors and weeds were growing in long twisted tangles around everything. The vacancy of the place all seemed a little too familiar to Elena.

"Austin, does this town seem familiar to you?" Elena asked as she turned to catch his eye, but then she noticed that Austin was standing off a little from the others.

Roman had pulled himself to the top of the cliff. As Elena began to wonder how he could have scaled the wall so quickly, she realized that Austin had positioned himself closely to where Roman and Charleston were talking.

Austin stripped off his pack and put it on the ground. He appeared to be organizing it, but she knew him well enough to know that he was eavesdropping on their conversation. Elena moved toward Austin at once and flung her pack down beside him.

Covertly, Elena watched Roman handling the object he'd pulled from the water. The token was shaped like the Grimsby logo. The token hovered in front of Roman while an Optivision screen appeared from the center of the logo. Then, Roman and Charleston looked as though they were reading.

"We didn't win the first token!" Elena overheard Roman tell Charleston.

"What's our consequence?" Charleston asked as she moved her fingers around the screen.

"They've taken our water away for the day," Roman said roughly.

"But look at the map," Charleston whispered, pointing at a terrain that seemed very familiar to Elena. "We landed here. Animalia is hiking along this route and Maritime's vessels landed on the shoreline there."

"Our next target is probably in the next town over," Roman said.

"But, how can we be sure?" Charleston asked. "They've never given us a token this early in the game and usually each one is spaced far apart."

"It doesn't matter. We've got to get to the next token before the others! I don't want to lose our rations, too," said Roman. "Divide the Goonies between the buildings. We need to get supplies first since we can't get water."

Austin looked at Elena and her brow furrowed in confusion. She hoped that sometime very soon she'd understand exactly what they were doing inside this simulation.

As Roman closed the Optivision screen, Elena and Austin were quick to rejoin Kidd, Declan, Abria, and Fergie.

"What were they talking about?" Declan asked at once.

But Roman had already turned toward the trainees and hollered, "We didn't get to the first token in time. We've had water taken away as our disadvantage. Be on the lookout for the next token. We need to find it before Maritime or Animalia locate theirs or we'll get another consequence. Haddock, Ransom, and Wheeler! I want you in that first house. The rest of you spread out through the houses to look for supplies and anything you can use as a weapon!"

As Elena turned into the first house that Roman instructed her to, she noticed that Declan, Abria, and Fergie were headed into the next house over.

Elena had another strange feeling of familiarity as she searched through the vacant living room and bedrooms.

"I found some food!" she heard Kidd call from the kitchen, but Elena couldn't tear her eyes away from several photographs that were hanging in frames on the wall. They looked like people she'd seen before, but she couldn't remember where.

When the Aves trainees came back together, Roman didn't even bother to look at what they'd collected.

"Let's get that next token!" he ordered.

"Do you know where it is?" Oscar Hunter called to him.

"No," Roman replied flatly. "But that doesn't mean we're going to stop here. We've got to find it first."

Roman hiked along on a long asphalt road with Charleston by his side. The trainees followed behind them for long hours in the uncomfortably hot sun. Roman never paused to rest.

The wide-open spaces were dotted with clusters of abandoned towns that were overgrown with weeds and buildings that were crumbling. Neighborhoods were filled with abandoned vehicles. City streets were littered with broken store windows. Office buildings were dilapidated with peeling paint.

Even with all the decay, Elena observed that the land was fertile with wild animals. The entire simulation again seemed a little too familiar to her.

"This pack is too heavy and I can't get the shoulder straps to work right," Abria complained.

"I'll hold your pack," Declan offered.

"I don't want you to hold my pack," Abria said. "I want this dimwit simulation to be over so that I can get to a place that's more comfortable."

"I'm sure it can't be too much further," Austin said in a bolstering way. "I mean, we've already been walking forever so it really can't get that much worse."

"Yeah, sure…" Declan replied sarcastically.

"Is anyone else concerned that we have not been proceeding at a pace that would allow us to attempt to locate another token?" Fergie asked in a tone of formality. "At the rate we are traveling, we could have easily overlooked several."

"That's a good point," Austin said. "But I doubt Roman would listen if we mentioned it."

"Does this simulation remind you of anything?" Elena asked. "I feel like I've seen this all before."

"Yeah, it looks like the *outside*," Kidd replied in a whisper. "You know, when we were on our way to New York."

Elena couldn't believe that she hadn't realized it before, but Kidd was absolutely right. The town at the top of the cliff had looked similar to a town they'd driven through in the Independence on their way to New York City three years ago. The scenery, roads, and even the teams of wild animals were all the same as it had been on their first trip outside the dome.

"But, how would the programmers know to make it look like this?" Elena asked. "No one has been there before."

Kidd only shrugged his shoulders.

"Who cares about the programmers," Abria grumbled. "I need water. And a foot massage."

Elena rolled her eyes as Kidd turned to her and asked, "Want me to carry your pack a while?"

"Nah, I'm alright," said Elena. "I mean, I am exhausted and a little head crazy from Abria needing a food massage, but I'll be alright."

After a very long day of hiking, Elena heard Charleston call out, "Roman! It's getting dark. Shouldn't we stop to make camp?"

"There's no stopping until we reach the next token," Roman replied. "If we don't get the token we could receive another consequence from the other Ops teams. We push on until we drop."

"I wonder what the consequences will be for sending us in here with a psychopath," Fergie whispered to Elena, and she actually smiled despite feeling tired and bitter.

"Well, I'm dropping," Charleston said. "Some of us need to eat so we aren't completely useless."

"And others of us really need to, like, use the natural facilities," Abria said.

"If you need to eat or drink do it while we're hiking," Roman said shortly. "And if you need to *potty*, Bowen, figure out a way to do that without slowing me down."

As Roman charged ahead, Elena looked at Austin and her other friends and said, "First, he sent us up the cliff without even looking around. We missed the first token and lost all our water for the day. And we've been hiking forever. He's such a bad leader."

"What does he honestly expect is going to happen if we're all sleep deprived and, like, starving?" Abria asked.

"Mutiny," Declan said.

"I say we start one right now," Kidd added.

"Not yet," Austin said calmly. "We've never been in a Tribulation before. It's not wise to change the dynamics of the game too much before we know what game we're playing. We've got enough in us to keep going. Plus, aren't you a little curious what finding the next token means?"

"Not curious enough to die for it," said Elena.

"You heard what Roman said," said Declan. "If we starve to death we wake up back at school and then we can eat whenever we want."

"If we go back we won't have to take orders from a psychopath," Elena added.

As the others chuckled, Fergie said practically, "It would take an extraordinarily long time to starve to death."

"Not if we're dehydrated from hiking first," Austin said darkly.

A long weary night of hiking followed. Fortunately, each of their tactical packs was equipped with a headlamp so that they didn't have to hike in complete darkness. Unfortunately, Roman never once slowed down so the rest of the Special Ops team followed along at a miserable pace. Elena felt quite sure that jumping Roman from behind and forcing him to forfeit was going to happen at some point.

As dawn broke, the Aves team was exhausted and dehydrated, but Roman kept them marching.

"We have hiked approximately forty-seven miles," Fergie said formally. "With very little rest, I might add."

"How do you know that?" Elena asked as she adjusted the straps of her tactical pack on her back.

"We have been hiking at an average rate of three miles per hour multiplied by fifteen hours plus factoring in the time it took to climb the rock wall and the changes in elevation plus the slower pace due to exhaustion and lack of proper nutritional refreshment."

"My pack feels so heavy that I keep tripping over my boots," Delcan said.

"My curls are stuck to the sweat on the back of my neck," Elena offered.

"Gross!" said Abria.

"I'm pretty sure that the skin has rubbed off the big toe in my left boot," Kidd added.

"Can we talk again about starting a mutiny..." Elena started, but Austin shouted, "Listen!"

Elena closed her mouth and then heard the most beautiful sound in the world. Water! And, she wasn't the only one.

A group of Aves trainees had broken away from the marching line and were making their way through an overgrowth of trees off one side of the road.

Elena could hardly believe her eyes when she came through the foliage to see a glorious lake of blue, complete with a cascading waterfall. Before she blinked, several of the boys stripped off their boots and socks and had rushed into the water.

"Hurry to fill your canteens and cool off before Roman gets here," Austin urged.

Elena and the others obeyed at once.

As Elena waded into the water, she heard Oscar Hunter shout, "I see a token over here in the water!"

Elena looked to the spot where he was pointing and she saw a large, rectangular item under the water, glowing with the Grimsby logo.

But then, Roman's booming voice broke through the trees.

"What's going on here? Who gave you permission to get into that water? Get out of that water immediately!"

"But Roman!" Oscar shouted. "I've found another token in the water."

"Bring it up!" Roman ordered.

After Oscar retrieved and handed over the glowing token, Roman said, "This is the first time the orders have been repeatedly hidden from view. Why do I get the feeling these cryptic clues are here because of all the new Level 4 Goonies?"

He looked in Elena's direction where she was standing with Kidd, Austin, Declan, Abria, and Fergie. Elena and her friends all pointed at one another at the same time. Roman simply glared at them.

"Call me *Crazy*..." Elena whispered at her friends as Roman turned away from them.

"Okay, *Crazy!*" Abria said playfully.

"But I don't think he likes us very much," Elena said.

"What makes you think that?" Kidd asked. "Is it the constant screaming?"

"The threatening to kill us?" Declan added

"Or the blatant disregard for the feelings of others?" Fergie said.

Roman opened an Optivision in midair and a series of codes appeared that Elena could not read.

"What's happening?" Oscar asked Roman.

"We did it! We got the second token before the other teams," Roman exclaimed. "This is why we march all night and why we obey orders."

"Because we won the challenge we get to choose a limitation for one of the other teams," Charleston explained. "This Optivision screen gives us a list of options."

"I'm giving Maritime gout," Roman replied. "They are severely lacking in medical skill. This should wipe out about half of the seventy-two trainees."

Elena looked at Austin. He looked as concerned as she felt. Giving Maritime a disease that would reduce their numbers so drastically could lead the other teams to seek revenge. They moved a little closer to the Optivision screen to get a better view.

"So far, we've found two orders with maps," Charleston said to Roman. "But given the length of time between tokens it could be tomorrow before we find the next one."

"That's why we need to get going," Roman replied. As he turned toward all the trainees, he barked, "Get your gear! We're moving on."

Hours later, the Aves Company was passing through yet another overgrown town when Abria suddenly complained, "We've never hiked this long without a break."

"I'm hungry. I'm tired. I'm thirsty," Elena grumbled as she adjusting the straps on her rucksack. "And it's way too hot out."

"Haddock, what are we going to do?" Declan asked. "We need to think of something. We can't keep going on like this."

"I think we should move through the groups and tell everyone to stop at the same time," Elena interrupted. "Roman may or may not stop if we do, but at least we could take a break."

But, before Austin could even reply, Roman barked unexpectedly, "Goonies! Time to make camp for the night. Set up at the edge of town, away from me."

"Thank you!" Abria exhaled as she tossed her bag off her shoulders.

"It's too hot for a fire, but I don't see any other way to get our sweaty socks dry," Austin said as he began to remove his boots.

"Wow! That's quite a smell," Elena said, plugging her nose.

"Oh please, I'd like to see what your feet smell like," Austin teased.

As small fires were lit along the path, Elena gathered with Austin and her others friends feeling tired.

"Anyone else bitter about the lack of progress we've made during the Tribulation so far?" Kidd asked as he settled beside Elena.

"I wish they'd let someone help them decode the map," Austin said longingly as Elena looked over at the Optivision that Roman and Charleston were huddled around.

"Roman's pushing us too hard," Kidd grumbled.

"We need to try to get you into a position of authority," Elena whispered to Austin.

"Austin is perfectly capable of asserting himself into a position of authority without our assistance," Fergie pointed out.

"Yeah, I know," said Elena. "But it wouldn't hurt to let Roman know that we want Austin to give advice."

To the right, there was a sudden commotion. Even though it was dark, Elena could tell that Oscar Hunter was limping toward their fire.

"What happened to you?" Austin asked Oscar.

"Oh, I was coming down that hill back there and I twisted my knee."

Oscar slowly sat down beside Austin, in a way that looked like he was in pain and asked, "What are you talking about?"

"I saw the options when Roman was giving Maritime gout. He could have easily given them more food or water. Clearly, he has the power to play decently, but he's choosing not to," Austin said.

"Maritime took water from us after they got their first token!" Elena pointed out.

"Yes, but that could be in retaliation for another simulation where Roman caused unnecessary duress," Austin said. "Remember, this is only our first Tribulation, but the older trainees have done this together several times before."

"Look at that!" Declan said.

He'd clearly not been paying attention to their conversation because he was pointing at an Optivision screen that had lit up a large portion of the ground. Roman and Charleston were reviewing some kind of detailed plans.

"Do you see that?" Declan asked Austin.

Elena looked at the Optivision screen. A separate set of instructions seemed to acclimatize on the screen, a set of instructions that would have been impossible for Roman and Charleston to see from where they were standing.

"They're reading the map wrong," Austin stated in a tone of realization.

Declan jumped to his feet and made his way towards Roman and Charleston at once with Elena and the others following closely behind.

"Roman! We just noticed the map!" Declan said urgently. "There's a separate set of instructions."

As Roman turned, Elena noticed that he looked at Declan in a way that indicated he did not appreciate the interruption.

"Step back, Goonie!" Roman barked, pushing Declan away roughly.

"But you're reading the map wrong," Declan insisted.

"We've done this a few more times than you," Charleston said sensibly.

"Bowen is right," Austin insisted. "There's a secondary set of instructions under that map with completely different coordinates telling us to…"

"How could you possibly know that?" Roman asked.

"From where we were sitting we had the best position for reading it," Austin explained. "There's a separate…"

"Haddock!" Roman shouted. "I'm going to stop listening to you now so that I can read the map and then give everyone the plan. Take your Goonies back over there and be quiet."

"But if you would listen…" Elena began to say, but Roman began to glare at her.

Austin grabbed her arm and pulled her gently. She and the others followed him back to their fire.

"Austin, what are you doing? Elena asked. "Tell Roman that he's wrong so he can fix it."

"Lena, he's being arrogant. No amount of talking can change his mind now. We can still be good examples to the others even if we're not leaders." Then, Austin turned to everyone else. "If we wait, Roman will learn where his fault lies. Only then will he be able to see the truth."

"You want us to wait?" Oscar said in disbelief.

"But we could all, like, fail the simulation because of him," Abria said sensibly.

"If we do fail, it's not on us," said Austin. "It's a lesson Roman will have to learn the hard way. I know that Roman and Woods have been given instructions. They're leading us somewhere and for a specific purpose. We can only keep going and trust that at some point we'll understand why we're out here. I know it's hard, but let's rest. Who knows what tomorrow will be like."

"I hope you noticed what Roman did there," Fergie whispered to Elena as they laid back on their tactical packs.

"Oh, you mean he acted like a total fool?" she replied.

"Yes, that, but did you also notice that Roman declared Austin the leader over the Goonies when he gave Austin the order to have us removed from the map?"

A slow smile spread across Elena's face. She hadn't realized it before and Dino Roman didn't realize it either, but he'd given Austin authority over all the Level 4 trainees by his simple words *take your Goonies back.*

"I told you that Austin did not require our assistance in gaining leadership status," Fergie said.

The next few days stretched on in an agonizingly slow way. When the Tribulation began, Elena didn't feel that it was much different than the adventures she'd had in simulations during her Level 2 studies where she was left in the bitter cold wilderness or the Level 3 simulation where she'd traveled to different floating islands.

However, the extent of the Tribulation was beginning to have an extreme negative affect on all the trainees. Elena couldn't remember ever hiking so many miles. And, with no clear indication for how long the simulation would last, she grew weary along with everyone else.

Even though the Aves Special Ops trainees hiked through heavily wooded areas, fields, and small towns, there was never enough food for all seventy-one of the them.

Within a couple more days, some of the trainees had gaunt, drawn faces with dark circles under eyes. Many of them had been sun burned and everyone had cracked lips. And, Elena noticed that Oscar Hunter's limp seemed to be getting worse.

"Can you help Hunter's leg?" Elena asked Austin one afternoon.

"I wish I could," Austin said. "I've looked at it several times, but I'm not sure how he damaged the muscle. Even my Suturand doesn't show me all the problems and we have nothing out here to help repair serious health issues."

"After all the simulations we've been in and all the Gauntlets we've run," Abria said, coming up beside them. "And after all the training we've had I feel confident in saying and I know you'll be totally, like, surprised, that I despise hiking."

Elena smiled, though it didn't last long.

Roman began to send Kidd out into the wilderness with small groups of hunters to scout ahead for food, but Elena's belly was still never full and her tongue was almost always dry.

Plus, anytime that any one of the trainees asked Roman for the plan he'd lose his mind to anger and start hollering at people. Therefore, Elena noticed more and more trainees being disrespectful to Roman.

"Why do you insist on being stupid?" Roman shouted one morning after Oscar had asked where their next meal was coming from.

"Actually, being stupid is my natural tendency," Oscar replied coldly. "It can't be helped so get over it."

Despite the general negative attitude, the Special Ops team had gotten proficient at erecting and breaking camp. Roman had given everyone a specific job, whether that was setting up lean-tos, lighting fires, hunting, cooking, or washing dirty clothing.

And though many of the girls grumbled often, Elena was thankful that they weren't stuck in a frozen wilderness like she'd been during her Level 2 studies.

Once in a while, when Elena was washing socks or preparing a meal, she remembered the years she'd spent in physical training. During those quiet moments, she'd notice an odd break in the atmosphere, almost like an interruption with the code of the simulation. This always made her think of how Pigg had always been one of the best at code writing.

"I wish Pigg were here," Elena said one evening as she sat around with her friends, feeling thirsty and lethargic from lack of food. "We wouldn't be starving to death if he were here. Somehow, he'd have managed to find us some food in this place.

"Let's hope that Wheeler and the others will come back with, like, a pile of dead animals or we're gonna be dead too," Abria said.

And then, as if Kidd had somehow heard Abria's wish, he and the other boys that had been hunting were walking back toward camp with several small animal carcasses and a line strung with freshly caught fish. The Aves trainees had quite a banquet of fire roasted meat and fish, but Elena's elation over the feast was short-lived.

That night, a rain simulation started. It lasted for days on end. And, even though Kidd and some of the other boys were proficient at hunting, the rain made finding food nearly impossible.

Elena learned quickly that hiking in the rain was miserable. The only time that Roman allowed them to stop was if they happened upon a decaying town. Then, they would break into small groups and light fires in dilapidated buildings so they could hang their socks and outer clothing up to dry.

"How long do you suppose we've been at this?" Elena asked one evening as they grouped together in a corner of a large abandoned warehouse.

"Precisely three weeks today," Fergie replied as she helped Abria lay out blankets on the dusty floor so they could sleep later that evening.

"I'm tired of all the days of making and breaking camp without any purpose or directions," Elena complained.

"Yeah. Haddock, shouldn't we at least try to talk to Roman again?" Declan asked as he stirred a measly dinner in the cook pot over a small fire.

"Haven't you noticed how crazy he gets when people try to talk to him about anything?" Kidd asked. "I think we should lay low until we find the next token and see what the directions are."

"But that's the point!" Declan said. "He won't ever show us the orders. We don't even know why we're here. We've only found two tokens and he won't even tell us how many more we need to find."

"I know it's been a long while since we've found a token. Maybe it's time we…" Austin began, but whatever he was going to say next was drowned out by Oscar Hunter's loud, angry voice.

"What's the goal here, Roman?" Oscar shouted, his voice echoing around the barren room. "Because it feels like we're wandering."

Roman had been pacing alone in a far corner. He stopped moving, turned very slowly, and walked confidently over to Oscar.

"You don't need to have goals," Roman barked at him.

"But all we do is hike all day, make camp, sleep, and then do the same thing the next day," Oscar argued. "What's the point?"

Elena couldn't help feeling the same way as she and her friends watched the argument from their side of the room.

"The point is for you to learn to obey orders." Roman said steadily.

Oscar looked like he wanted to continue to debate their current circumstances, but Roman had already begun to walk away. She watched Oscar adjust his balance uneasily on his hurt leg and then walk in the opposite direction of Roman shaking his head as he went.

Elena rolled her eyes and sighed in frustration, but like the rest of them, there was nothing she could do.

The following morning, the sun wasn't up yet, but Elena awoke feeling a slight chill. The floor of the warehouse was bitterly cold. From where she sat, she noticed that it wasn't raining outside the door so she decided to get away from everyone else to find some peace.

Elena walked away from camp the Special Ops trainees had made on the road and made her way through the trees as if the forest were calling her. She made her way over and under tree roots until she came to a spot where she could look out over a ravine.

She could just see the sky through the trees. And then, the sun! The colors of the sunrise were broken by the tree line, but it was still a sunrise. She stayed for an hour watching the colors change until finally she noticed Kidd standing not too far from her.

"Good morning," he said quietly. "What are you doing out here?"

"Thinking about my dad," Elena said honestly. "Sometimes he'd wake me up early before the sunrise simulation and take me to the roof of our building. We'd watch the colors change together." She smiled sadly. "It was spectacular."

Kidd sat beside her. Then, he extended his hand and gave her a small bouquet of wild flowers.

"Where did you get these?" Elena asked in astonishment.

"Here and there," Kidd replied.

She noticed that he'd started to lean toward her slowly, but at that same moment she saw a flash of light.

"Did you see that?" Elena said excitedly. "Over there, in the trees?"

"I was a little distracted," Kidd said in a disappointed tone.

"Sorry," Elena said vaguely. "But I just saw it over there!"

Kidd looked in the direction of her pointed finger. "Okay...what are we looking for?"

"I swear it was a clue of some kind. It was one of Pigg's signatures in program writing." Elena looked harder, but then sighed in disappointment. "It's already gone. I've got to get back to camp right away to tell Austin that I think Pigg's trying to contact me!"

Elena stood at once and nudged Kidd to join her. As they were coming back to camp they heard an inexplicable commotion and took off in a sprint.

They arrived to an unexpected scene. Everyone in camp was standing in a circle outside the warehouse. Dino Roman and Oscar Hunter were standing in the center of the others. They appeared to be in some kind of conflict. Elena could tell that Oscar was still in pain by the way he held his arm by his side. She could also tell that Roman was demanding that Oscar pick up a stack of logs.

▢ 14 ▢

Pigg's Signature

"Are you giving up?" Roman roared into Oscar's face.

Elena and the others looked on from where they were standing. Everyone knew that Oscar had been limping for several days and that his injury was beyond repair. She was perplexed about why Roman seemed so irrationally angry.

"Not giving up, Sir," Oscar replied. "I injured my knee a few days ago and it still hurts."

"Are you making excuses?"

"No, Sir!" Oscar insisted. "I physically don't have the stamina to…"

"I can move the stack," Austin offered, moving toward them, but Roman didn't even acknowledge Austin's presence.

Roman brought the heel of his boot down on Oscar's good knee. Oscar crumpled to the ground in a heap, holding his leg and howling in pain.

Elena immediately crossed the entire camp in a fast sprint and grabbed Roman's forearm forcefully.

"You can't treat him that way!" she shouted.

Roman rounded so quickly that Elena felt sure he was going to punch her in the face. But, instead, Roman shook his head in a disappointed way.

"Ransom, Ransom...the only trainee to ever physically challenge Marshall. Do you think that makes you better than me?"

Elena wanted to be a good example for Austin's sake, but she could feel her face burning with anger.

"Not *only* for that reason, Sir," Elena said boldly.

"You wear your insubordination like a badge of honor and it disgusts me," Roman spat. "After Hannibal assigned you to Special Ops, I watched every single account of your hours in Basic Training. Even your very first day. I confess that I didn't see much talent."

"Perhaps you were watching with an untrained eye," Elena replied. "It's time you stopped doing whatever you want to in this Tribulation. We're in here together. We're a team."

"Not everyone has to complete the Tribulation," Roman informed her. "Only one person from each Special Ops team." He held up a single finger in her face. "Just one."

A keen sense of understanding Roman's behavior through the entire simulation thus far came over Elena at once.

"Oh, and let me guess...you're *the one* who always gets through unscathed. Well, you can't scare me into submission."

Dino Roman lowered his mouth down to her ear and, with barely an audible voice, whispered, "But I can try."

Then, he walked away from her and shouted, "Listen up, Goonies. Every time we enter a Tribulation it's completely different. This is my seventh round.

"The first time we lost half the team on the first day. One time we were stuck in the exam for three months. By the time I accepted my position in Archon we had the simulations down to a science. So, listen to what I'm saying." He turned back to Elena. "And stop acting weak!"

Then, Roman looked at Oscar with a face of pure contempt and said, "Get your gear together and let's go."

Begrudgingly, Elena stomped back into the warehouse. She began to toss random items into her tactical pack as Kidd and their other friends collected all the rest of the gear. Then, all the Special Ops trainees followed Roman out of their campsite.

After several hours of marching, the Aves team reached the crest of the hill and Elena's mouth fell open. A city of tall buildings that seemed to scrape the sky was standing in the distance.

"Remind you of anything?" Kidd whispered in her ear suddenly.

"New York," Elena replied, feeling uneasy about how familiar the simulation had truly become to real life outside the dome. "Why would this be in a simulation?"

But when Kidd couldn't answer, she immediately walked over to Charleston and asked, "Woods, have you seen any Tribulations like this before?"

"Never a cityscape on this magnitude," Charleston admitted. "But, the programmers are always trying to challenge us. Sometimes they come up with absolutely absurd simulations and other times we get something that seems normal, but really isn't once we get up close to it," Sabrina finished. "We should get going, though. Roman doesn't seem to want to stop here."

And she was right. Roman had already begun to descend the hill toward the city. Elena and the others sprinted to catch up. Soon, she was walking between the skyscrapers feeling in complete awe of their surroundings. The city was laid out identically to New York City, complete with weeds growing from cracks in the pavement and possessions left haphazardly along the roads.

"It's so, like, weird being here again, isn't it?" Abria asked Elena and the others in a whisper.

"Yeah, I feel like we were just here," said Kidd.

"Do you think we'll see Fallon and his people lurking about somewhere?" Declan asked with a smirk.

"I don't know how to explain this," Elena said suddenly. "But I think Pigg is writing this simulation while we're in here."

Elena noticed Declan and Abria exchange a look of skepticism, but Kidd, Austin, and Fergie looked as though they wanted to hear more.

"There's this thing Pigg does in his program writing, it's like his signature. I keep seeing it all over the place," Elena said.

"Why didn't you mention this earlier?" asked Austin.

"Because it all seemed random. But now we're in this city that looks like New York and you already know why that's familiar. When we were inside that very first house Roman told us to check, I swear I saw some of the same photographs that I saw when we were in your apartment in New York. Plus, there was that stone that broke free from the cliff so we could find the first token. And there were the fish at the waterfall lake where we found our second token. I think Pigg's trying to communicate with me."

"So what if he's writing the program while we're in here?" Declan said. "What does that matter?"

"It matters because it means he might be able to help us find a way," Austin said.

"Listen up, Goonies!" Roman shouted suddenly. "I want you each to search a building for food, water, and weapons. We'll meet back up at the end of this block. Get started!"

Elena and her friends followed their orders well enough. They went into the first building on the row and looked through every cupboard and closet for supplies.

When they came up empty handed, Declan said, "How much you wanna bet we get demerits for not finding supplies?"

"It's been days since we've found a token," Elena said. "I really doubt any of this matters at all."

As Elena and her friends all grouped around, Roman looked over the meager supplies that the whole team had gathered and grumbled, "This Tribulation is taking too long. So, I'm changing the rules. Instead of looking for the next token we're going after the other Special Ops teams."

"Why would we do that?" Charleston asked.

"To take them out of the game one by one," Roman said. "The less players the better. Then, maybe we can get to the end of this Tribulation." He opened an Optivision screen from one of the tokens they'd collected. "Thermal scans indicate that Animalia and Maritime are in different sections of this city. Woods, maybe we should form raiding parties to try and separate their teams. Pick off the weak ones."

Before Elena had a chance to consider what Roman meant, she noticed something wiggling on the ground. As she moved in for a closer look, she realized that it was a small stone in the ground that was trying to break free from the earth. The portion of the rock wiggled and wiggled until finally it popped from the ground and flew into the air. She watched it go, shielding her eyes from the sun as it went.

The rock flew far down the block to toward a grouping of buildings and that's then she noticed a light, like a beacon, at the top of one of the skyscrapers.

"Look!" Elena shouted. "There's a token at the top of that building."

As everyone turned, Elena saw the thermal scans on the Optivision screen begin to move in a steady formation.

"They're going after it!" Roman blurted. "Quick, trainees! We need to get to it first!"

The Aves Special Ops team tore off down the street in a desperate run. After they'd covered several blocks, Elena could see the Maritime Special Ops team approach the base of the building.

She never stopped running, but Elena had a sinking feeling in her stomach that the Maritime team was going to get to the token first.

Her feelings were confirmed as she and the other Aves trainees reached the top of the building tower. Elena saw the Maritime crew huddled around the glowing token. The look on Roman's face was unfathomable.

"You Goonies wait over there!" Roman commanded, though he didn't even look at them as he strutted over to the Maritime team.

Elena tossed off her tactical pack and sat with the others, glad for a chance to catch her breath. She watched Roman and Charleston talking with Brennan Colt and Collum Duke. She couldn't hear the exchange, but she could tell it was intense.

Then suddenly, Elena was on her feet again as Roman grabbed Collum by the neck. Brennan reacted, but Roman punched him in the face with his free hand. Then, Roman quick marched Collum to the edge of the building and pushed him off.

Elena's mouth fell open as the Maritime trainees drew their weapons. Roman turned and pulled his weapon up so quickly that Elena didn't even see where it'd come from. Then, she noticed that several of the older Aves trainees had also drawn their weapons and were advancing on the situation.

Elena wasn't sure what to do until she saw Austin walking boldly through the center of the tension. She had almost forgotten that she had a weapon because they'd never used it, but she pulled the weapon from the side of her tactical pack and followed behind Austin.

"Everyone take a minute," Austin said aloud, though Elena was still trying to figure out what had just happened. "I know that no one wants to get hurt, so let's slow down. You can keep your weapons up Maritime, but give me a minute to talk with Roman."

Austin moved toward Roman in a steady, non-threatening way. Roman's eyes had a strange look of nervous tension that Elena had never seen before.

"Dino!" Austin said sharply, as if trying to draw Roman out of a trance. "You threw Duke off the building."

He took a step closer to Roman, who still had his weapon drawn. Elena wished Austin would back away, but since he didn't, she began to take a few quiet steps closer.

"The Maritime trainees witnessed you disqualify one of their leaders from finishing this assignment," Austin said firmly as he moved into an arm's length of Roman.

This made Elena extremely uncomfortable.

"Do you want to end the Tribulation right now? We can all go back together if you don't put your weapon down. I know you could do it, but is that what you really want?" Austin asked.

Roman grabbed Austin roughly by the throat, but Austin didn't struggle.

Elena tried to leap forward toward Roman, but she felt a firm hand close around her arm. She looked straight into Declan's piercing blue eyes, which were almost pleading with her to remain silent.

Unable to move, Elena turned back towards Austin and hollered at Roman, "Let him go!"

Roman looked at Elena sharply. Then, he seemed to come back to his senses a bit. At least, his eyes looked a little less psychotic.

From the clutches of Roman's grip, Austin managed to choke out, "You'll have a mutiny on your hands in a minute if you don't attempt to negotiate with Maritime."

Elena could tell that Roman was considering Austin's words carefully. Austin had always had a way with words that was both wise and affirming. He was giving Roman power while protecting the Aves trainees from the others.

"What exactly are you suggesting," Roman asked.

"I'm suggesting that we tell them our mission without the expectation that they disclose their own."

"That's against the rules," Roman said. "The intel is classified."

"Who wrote this simulation?" Austin asked.

Roman released Austin's neck and asked, "What?"

"Because I bet whoever wrote it intended us to destroy one other. Ever been in a simulation where everyone failed?"

Roman's look was blank.

"What you're suggesting is unprecedented," Roman said. He still looked distracted, but he added, "But it just may work. Wait here and I'll attempt negotiations."

Roman lowered his weapon to the ground and then advanced in the Maritime direction with his hands raised. Brennan Colt looked furious, but at least he let Roman approach.

"What are you doing, Austin?" Elena asked as he came back toward them. "Roman pushed Duke off the building!"

"Yeah and what do you think that means for us?" Austin asked.

Elena considered him silently and then said slowly, "He could do that to any one of us."

Austin nodded. "I'm gonna take a page outta your playbook. You've broken several conventions during our past simulations, but none of that resulted in failure. Roman is making choices that continue to have a negative effect on us. We'll never get through this Tribulation without help now. Maritime has all the food, we have all the medicine, and Animalia has all the survival gear. We need to work with them."

Elena looked at Roman and Brennan as they talked, both with their arms folded protectively across their chests.

"But how do you know he's even going to tell them our mission?" Elena asked.

"I saw it in his eyes," Austin said. "He knows it's the only option we have left. Unless he wants to fight with the two other teams for the rest of the simulation."

"I thought he was gonna punch you when you called him by his first name." Declan smirked.

A smile slipped across Austin's face. "Me too. But it was the only thing I could think to do to get his attention."

"I think it worked," said Kidd.

"I don't know," Austin said, massaging his neck. "He still grabbed me pretty hard."

"Look," Abria said quietly. "Roman's coming back over."

"Goonies!" he said sharply. "We'll camp in the next building over tonight."

Without words, the Aves trainees gathered their gear and set off for the place where they'd stay for the night.

However, even several hours after the nighttime simulation began, Elena was finding it hard to sleep. So much had happened in the past few hours and she wasn't sure how she felt about it. Fortunately, Elena noticed that Fergie was sitting upright in one of the blown out building windows.

"What are you doing out here?" Elena whispered as she took a seat near her friend.

"Contemplating the next best course of action," Fergie replied.

"Me, too," Elena admitted. "I can't sleep. Too much going on in my head."

"I am curious about what is bothering you the most. Is it the fact that Roman pushed Duke off the building, or the fact that we're wandering in circles because Roman will not disclose the plans, or the fact that we haven't had anything substantial to eat in three suns?"

"All of it," Elena said. "I'm realizing more each day how awful Roman is at leading. Yet, we still have to keep following him. I'm scared for us."

Fergie remained silent.

"If it comes down to it, would you push me off a building so Austin can stay in the game?" Elena asked.

Fergie seemed in thought for a moment and then said, "Perhaps we could jump together and pull Roman with us."

Elena grinned. "How can we get him near a window?"

After an hour of making random plans with Fergie about Roman's demise, Elena finally decided that she should try to get some rest. She was almost back to her sleeping bag when a voice called to her from the shadows.

"I didn't appreciate your insubordination today."

Elena stopped as Roman walked into the light of the moon that shown through a blown apart wall.

"That's a shame," she replied sarcastically.

"You saw what I did to Duke, right? That could easily be you."

"You wouldn't dare do anything to me in front of everyone," Elena said hotly. "Austin has more influence over the whole group than you'll ever hope to have. How do you think he'd react if you tossed me off a building?"

"Ransom, you have such a limited imagination," Roman whispered. His voice was thick with malice and so much more terrifying than his booming bark that all the hairs stood up on the back of Elena's neck.

"I don't need to toss you off anything. But one morning you could wake up bound and gagged in a random part of the city or out in the forest beyond the city. I would put you so far into the simulation that no one could hear you scream."

A tingle of panic rushed up her spine, but she raised her chin defiantly.

"Try it. Austin will always find me, no matter where I am."

She turned on her heels and stomped off into the darkness, vowing to tell Austin everything.

"Why are you so grumpy?" Austin asked the next morning as he handed her a tin cup steaming with hot tea.

"Because of our crazy leader," Elena replied, feeling glad that she had a friend that could tell her mood by the look on her face. "He cornered me last night and threatened to hide me somewhere in the simulation."

"Don't worry about him," Austin said confidently. "I think I've finally figured out how to..."

But what Austin had figured out was lost on a loud commotion. Elena turned to see Oscar Hunter slump to the floor. She and Austin were on their feet and to his side a moment later. Oscar's eyes were rolling and his body was shaking violently.

"What's happening?" Rachel Reddington asked. "I mean, we were talking one minute and now..."

"He's having a seizure," Austin said as he opened his shirt and removed the body bubble from his chest, which Elena knew was filled with medical supplies.

Austin held his Suturand over Oscar's face and read from the Optivision screen that had materialized in midair.

"What are you doing, Haddock?" Roman demanded. "Did you steal that Suturand from school?"

"Sometimes seizures can be brought on by sleep deprivation and stress," Austin explained, not even bothering to look at Roman. "If I can get him under control maybe..."

"Don't touch him!" Roman commanded. "Let him go. One less weakling in the game."

Austin paused for a moment and gave Roman a look that Elena had never seen him give anyone before: a mixture of pity and absolute disappointment. Then, Austin went quickly back to his work.

"I'm saving him," Austin firmly stated.

Elena noticed Roman's face turn red with anger. As he reached out to grab Austin, Elena brought her leg down on Roman's arm. The sound of the bone breaking in his forearm did nothing to stop Roman from switching his focus onto her. He grabbed her around the neck with his good hand and quick marched her over to the side of the building where they'd been standing the night before. Roman lifted her off the ground and held her through the missing portion of the wall.

Gasping for air, Elena noticed Kidd, Declan, Fergie, and Abria all make a movement towards them.

But Roman extended his broken arm and said, "Stop now! If you come any closer I'll send her back to where we came."

While Roman was distracted, Elena used her free hands to punch the sides of his ears. He cried out in pain and released her. As she fell, she tried to reach for the side of the building, but it was no use. Elena was falling from the skyscraper.

¤ 15 ¤

Kantele

Elena gasped as if she were coming out of a deep pool of water. As her brain began to focus, she still couldn't believe all that had happened in the past few minutes. She slowly became aware of her surroundings and realized that she was inside the white-walled gargantuan training room where they'd initially started the Tribulation. Many trainees still stood motionless in their spaces amongst the hundreds of Optivision screens that were hovering in mid-air.

When she was sure that her legs were working properly, Elena hurried to the exit where Sabrina Bauer was waiting for her.

"That was a rough way to exit the Tribulation. I guess you'll want to see what happened after you left. Follow me."

Elena definitely wanted to know what was happening in her absence. When she reached the room that Sabrina led her to she saw that it was filled with other students that had already failed out of the Tribulation. They gawked at her with horrified looks as she entered the room, but she ignored them.

Several large Optivisions played around the walls; some with coverage of the Maritime group, some with the Animalia crew, and another fixed with the Aves. Instead of taking a seat, Elena walked straight over to the screens with the Aves trainees. She could see that a fight was continuing to rage between Roman and several of the other members of the group, including Austin who was now being physically restrained from helping Oscar with Dino Roman's good arm.

"What's happening?" Elena asked.

"You mean since you broke Roman's arm?" Sabrina asked with a smirk.

"Well, after you fell, Bowen and Wheeler lost their minds and attacked Roman. While they were fighting, Haddock was still trying to help Hunter. But then, Abria stepped in to help Hunter so that Haddock could try to calm things down with the guys. This has been the most interesting Tribulation scene that I've ever watched."

"Your excitement over this nauseates me," Elena growled.

"It's not just me," Sabrina replied. "Everyone is in awe over the flat out crazy reaction to Roman trying to attack Haddock."

Elena put her own hands around her neck, remembering how it felt as Roman's hands squeezed.

"What's going on now?" Elena asked with a feeling of anxiety growing in her chest.

"Oh, so Roman said that if Hunter wasn't allowed to fail the simulation naturally that he'd start throwing everyone else off the building. Then, he put Haddock in a headlock and now we're waiting to see if he'll really toss Haddock off."

Elena held her breath, watching in desperation. She could tell that Abria was trying her best to help Oscar, but whatever she was doing wasn't enough because he still shook uncontrollably. Kidd and Declan were standing on either side of Roman, but since he had Austin in a headlock neither of the boys moved toward him.

As Abria started to cry, Elena could tell that Oscar wouldn't be able to hold on much longer.

"Please, let me help him," Austin pleaded with Roman.

"No!" Roman replied.

A minute later, Abria grabbed the sides of her face in distress as Oscar Hunter's body disappeared from the simulation.

After Oscar was gone, Roman released Austin from his grip.

"Do you want me to fix your arm?" Austin asked Roman as he massaged the side of his neck.

Roman grabbed his broken forearm with his good hand and yanked once. A bone-crushing crack reverberated through the room. Then, he laced his belt around his neck and slid his bad arm through the loop.

"I think that Haddock, Bowen, and Wheeler have earned a little time on a raiding party," Roman said nastily. "Animalia is near our location. I want you to find three trainees and send them back to school. That is an order! Do you understand?"

Austin took a deep breath and the three boys replied, "Sir, yes Sir."

Elena could barely contain herself as she watched Austin, Kidd, and Declan walk away from Roman and the Aves camp.

As the boys made their way down the staircases of the building, Declan asked, "What are we doing, Haddock?"

"We're going to get captured," Austin replied.

Elena wasn't the only one in the viewing room to gasp at his declaration.

"Why?" Kidd inquired.

"So we can tell Brennan Colt the mission we were assigned."

"Which is what?" Declan asked.

"All three of the Special Ops teams are looking for something called a Kantele."

"How do you know that?" Kidd and Declan asked together.

"I got Woods to tell me after she acknowledged that Roman is losing his mind," Austin replied. "She was a little reluctant until I told her my full plan. And now, instead of finding three Animalia trainees to *send back to school*, we're going straight to Colt to offer our help in ending this simulation."

Elena turned and looked around the room at the other students that had already failed out of the Tribulation. They had a mixture of admiration and respect on their faces.

Sighing with relief, Elena chose an empty chair and continued to watch with the others as the three boys made there way through the city ruins towards the Maritime base camp.

Elena noticed right away that the Maritime team had guard lookouts several hundred feet surrounding their camp. She wished there was a way that she could warn Austin about their defenses. She didn't enjoy feeling useless.

After watching Austin, Kidd, and Declan hike through the city for a while, Elena saw them approach the first of the Maritime guards. The three boys dropped their weapons to the ground and raised their hands over their heads. They were each patted down for weapons. Austin, Kidd, and Declan were then led over rubble, through buildings, and across a yard to a fire pit where some kind of animal was roasting over a fire. Brennan Colt was sitting near the fire and looked up at the boys with malice in his eyes.

"It shows poor judgment to be captured, especially considering Roman ended Duke. We owe Aves payback," he said to Elena's friends.

"Can't you put me back in?" Elena asked Sabrina urgently as she turned away from the scene on the screen.

"Nope. That's against the rules," she replied. "Once you're out, you're out."

Elena turned back to the screen, chewing a nail to the point that she tasted blood in her mouth.

Austin was thumbing the scar on his chin, which she knew meant he was trying to mentally work an angle.

"Are you planning to speak at some point?" Colt asked. "Because you're wasting my time."

"You're looking for something specific, aren't you? As part of your mission?" Austin stated boldly.

Brennan's face was unreadable to Elena.

"The Aves is looking for something, too," Austin continued. "We're looking for something called a Kantele."

"That's what we're looking for," Brennan confirmed. "But we don't even know what it looks like."

"Have you ever been in a Tribulation like this before?" Austin asked. "One where you were tasked with finding an object to end the simulation?"

"Never," Brennan admitted. "What are you getting at?"

"Roman won't allow any of us to help discover the location of the Kantele," Austin said, as Elena chose a new nail to bite. "So, we wanted to offer to help you find it. To help the Maritime win."

"Why would you do that?" Brennan asked.

"First, because Aves owes you since Roman ended Duke," Austin said. "But also, because we're ready to get back to school."

It was clear that Brennan was also eager to get back because he said, "What do we need to do?"

Over the next few days, Elena watched the Tribulation as often as she could. She was supposed to continue with her classwork now that she was out of the simulation, but she couldn't focus long enough to learn anything. It was all she could do to race from her Enrichment activities, which were required, and meals before getting back to the unfolding story on the Optivision screens in the Tribulation viewing room.

On one screen she watched Roman corner Abria and bark, "Why aren't Bowen, Haddock, and Wheeler back yet?"

"How should I know?" Abria asked.

"Aren't you friends with them?" Roman demanded.

"Yes, but what's that got to do with, like, anything?" Abria replied. "You're the one who sent them away. I haven't seen them since they left either. Maybe they were captured."

At this suggestion, Roman's face twitched.

"I volunteer to go after them," Fergie said in a formal tone. "I can track them to see where they are and report back to you."

"I'll go with her," Abria added.

Roman looked around at his group. Of the seventy-two Special Ops trainees from Aves, there were only forty-seven left. Elena could tell that he was considering his options, but she didn't care what he did.

From another screen she painfully watched Austin, Kidd, and Declan go around and around in circles looking for the Kantele with the other Maritime crew. She could see the object clearly on the screen, but the boys were so far from it. As she started to go crazy from not being able to help them, she finally realized that she knew one person at school that could help.

Elena burst through the viewing room door and sprinted down the hall. She had to find Pigg right away. She stopped every person she came across to see if anyone knew where the program writing room was, but all she received were a bunch of shrugs and strange looks.

Then, she tried searching through a schematic of the school on one of the window-dimensionals in the hallway, but she didn't see any rooms where Grimsby might be keeping a team of programmers.

Finally, she took to searching the halls again. She'd just decided to try the Mess Hall when she came around a corner and saw him at the opposite end of a hallway.

"Pigg!" Elena exclaimed as she sprinted toward him. "I'm so glad to see you. I need your help."

"Come here," Pigg replied in an urgent whisper as he pulled her into a vacant learning cocoon.

He looked extremely tired, but Elena was too distracted to ask him how he was doing.

"I was helping you during the Tribulation," Pigg revealed.

"Yeah, I know," Elena said, still a little breathless from hunting him down. "What's the matter?"

"They have me in this room with a few other boys and girls. We spend all day watching the Tribulation and changing the features of the simulation."

"You're changing the game while we're playing it?" Elena said, the edges of her words thick with disbelief. "That hardly seems fair!"

"We're forced to!" Pigg insisted. "Headmaster Bentley and Hannibal have been to our room every single day. Sometimes they stay for a few minutes and other times a few hours. They're giving us directions and telling us different story lines to try. It's been really awful."

"But, what's the point of the simulation in the first place?" Elena asked in frustration.

"I don't know," Pigg replied, sounding honest. "There's no mathematical reasoning to the testing. No rhythm or pattern that I can detect. But I did overhear three of the Level 6 programmers talking and it sounds like...well..."

"What?" Elena urged.

"It sounds like the whole point is to isolate the abilities of one person."

Elena shook her head in disbelief, thinking about how Hopper had told her something very similar her first year at school. He'd told her that Imperator was looking for one person that would fulfill some kind of prophecy.

"But there's more," Pigg said urgently. "Before you were put into the Tribulation, I started to do a little searching around on the server..."

"You mean you were illegally hacking the system?" Elena asked.

"I wouldn't *technically* say it was illegal. I mean, if they didn't want the files looked at they should have installed better security."

Elena couldn't help but smile.

"Anyway, I found this one server with information about all the artifacts we've been looking for."

"Well, that we already knew. Remember our first year? Austin and I overheard them talking about the Alpha Manuscript. Headmaster Bentley was looking for artifacts way back then," Elena shrugged.

"But, Bentley has all the files and details and things about searching for the Firebird Disc," said Pigg. "I've found all the work he's been doing on the mainframe."

Elena's mouth fell open in disbelief. "Are you sure? Can you get the info off the server?"

"I'm working on that, but it's very complex. And I don't want anyone to know that I've been sneaking around in there." Pigg wiped his forehead as if he were sweating. "And the other thing is that I found this new artifact called the Kantele. So, I decided to make it part of the Tribulation. Elena, they're searching for the Kantele because of me."

"What's the Kantele for?" Elena asked.

"I don't know," Pigg confessed. "The server doesn't explain much about it, but I knew I needed to capture the information somehow so I could remember to tell Austin. When I brought up the idea about placing an object in the Tribulation that the trainees would have to search for, the older programmers agreed right away," said Pigg. "They said they'd never done anything like it in the past. That it would be a unique and welcome change."

Elena considered his words carefully, but she was really most concerned with getting her friends out of the Tribulation as soon as possible.

"Can you do anything to make Roman go away?" Elena asked.

"I can't," Pigg said shaking his head.

"Can you lead Austin to the Kantele faster?" Elena asked.

A smile spread across Pigg's face. "That I can do. But I'll have to be very careful because I don't want it to seem like I'm helping Austin. I could get into serious trouble. Strictly speaking, we're not supposed to help the trainees. But the few things I showed you went unnoticed by everyone else so it might work."

"You're amazing, Pigg! Now, go get started right away!" Elena urged.

Once Elena left Pigg, she raced back to one of the viewing rooms. Many of the other Level 4 trainees were present, but Elena circled in front of them all and selected a chair close to the screens. She could tell right away that Pigg was writing some new code for the simulation because Austin suddenly switched directions in his quest.

"Where are you going now?" Brennan Colt asked Austin.

"I think I know where to find the Kantele," he said.

"How? There were no further instructions on that last token we found," Brennan said.

"I have a feeling," Austin said as the Maritime team got closer and closer to the spot on the screen where Elena knew the Kantele was waiting.

Then, quite suddenly, the Kantele appeared on the screen. Elena hadn't known what to expect before, but she was surprised to see that the object was made from wood and had the strings of an instrument. In truth, it looked like something she might find one of Fallon's people playing in the tunnels of New York City. Besides that, the object looked very familiar, almost like she'd seen it before.

On another screen, Elena saw Austin, Declan, Kidd, and Brennan arrive at the mouth of an alleyway. The Kantele was simply lying along the side of a dumpster like it was a piece of trash.

"There it is," Austin said, pointing at the Kantele.

Elena stared at the screen, barely daring to breath. She wanted more than anything to be standing there with Austin. Her heart was beating so fast that it felt it would explode from her chest.

"If we take the Kantele the Tribulation will end," Brennan said. "But I have a feeling your troubles with Roman are about to get worse."

"Worse?" Austin repeated with a quizzical look. "Have you seen what he's been like the entire time we've been at school? I doubt he could get worse."

"He can always get worse," Brennan replied with such a serious look on his face that Elena felt afraid for Austin.

"Don't do it!" Elena yelled at the screen. She felt the entire room of students turn to look at her, but she didn't care. "Don't do it, Austin! Go get Roman and show him how to take the Kantele for himself."

But obviously, no one in the Tribulation could hear her.

As Brennan took the Kantele into his hand, Elena was no longer watching the screens. Instead, she was running down the hall towards the room where she knew her friends would be exiting the simulation.

◻ 16 ◻

The Cheater

"I thought that would never end!" Elena exclaimed as she threw herself into Kidd's arms.

Austin, Abria, Declan, and Fergie were also just coming out of the room where the Tribulation took place.

"That was the absolute worst!" Abria exclaimed.

"Yeah, no one wants to do that again," Declan said.

"What were you thinking?" Elena asked Austin. "Why would you go against Roman like that? You know he's going to be vindictive when he finds out that you helped Maritime."

"I know," Austin said. "But you saw what he was like in there. We all needed the Tribulation to be over."

Elena nodded. "I know, but seriously we're going to havta be on guard all the time now."

"What are you doing?"

Elena turned and came face to face with a disappointed look on Sabrina Bauer's face.

"All of you should be in Medical right now," she said as she looked at Austin, Kidd, and the others.

"We're on our way right now," Austin told Sabrina.

"I should probably get going," Elena told Kidd as Austin and the others followed Sabrina. "I'm so behind on work."

"I was in the Tribulation at least seven days after you got out," Kidd said. "What were you doing the whole time?"

"I ran from meals and Enrichment to any window dimensional in the school to watch what was happening in the Tribulation," Elena replied. "There's no way I could do classwork. I mean, I did try once, but I was too distracted thinking about what was going on that I closed the session early and didn't go back again."

As Kidd laughed, Elena realized that she'd really missed him while they were apart.

She enforced her grip on his hand and said, "You know what, I think I will join you in Medical to make sure you're really okay."

As Austin, Kidd, and Elena's other friends were hooked up in Medical for their wellness assessment, they talked about some of the more intense parts of the Tribulation. Kidd laughed as he recounted her breaking Roman's forearm. Abria groaned and complained about all the hiking they'd done. Fergie recounted statistics from the route they'd traveled and Declan waved his arms around as he told a story that essentially mocked Roman's performance as a leader.

Then, Elena started talking about all the benefits of being at school while Roman was in the Tribulation.

"And, did you know that when Roman is in the Tribulation there's no one to wake us up in the morning?" Elena said. "I still woke up about the same time because of my conditioning, but still, it was like being on vacation."

The following day, after the last trainees from the Aves Company had been released from Medical, Kidd wasted no time asking Elena if she wanted to go out for a walk in the woods.

"Don't you need to catch up on your schoolwork?" Elena asked him.

"Nah, I'm taking off from all that today," Kidd said. "I worked a little ahead before the Tribulation started and have plenty of time to finish everything on my syllabus before the end of the year."

Elena and Kidd walked hand in hand through the quiet Grimsby campus and out into the woods. It was immediately clear that both of them were still thinking about the Tribulation.

"Did that Kantele look familiar to you?" Kidd asked.

"Yes."

"Like a large version of my mom's necklace," he said thoughtfully.

Elena nodded and looked away for a moment. It had been a long time since Kidd and she had talked about artifacts. She didn't want to ruin their afternoon, but she felt that she needed to tell him the truth about what Pigg had found while they were inside the Tribulation.

"I'm not sure if I should tell you this, but the thing is that Pigg found out that the Headmaster is searching for artifacts, just like we are. One of the new artifacts that we didn't know anything about is this Kantele. Pigg made this artifact part of the Tribulation to try and see if he could find out more about it from the Headmaster's records. It's so confusing and strange that it looks like your mom's necklace."

Kidd looked away from Elena and far off as if he were deep in thought.

"Do you think we should tell Austin?" Elena asked after a long silence.

Kidd shook his head. "It doesn't matter if you tell him or not. You and I aren't looking for artifacts any longer, right?"

Elena smiled sadly and nodded. Then, as she suggested that they get back to start classwork, Kidd began to lean toward her with a familiar look of expectation she'd seen a couple times before. Elena turned her face and his lips connected with her cheek.

"Ah, rejected again," Kidd said, looking frustrated.

Elena felt confusion bubbling up inside her. "Why do you seem upset when I won't kiss you?"

"Isn't it obvious?" Kidd grumbled.

"Obviously not to me, which is why I asked," Elena said. When Kidd wouldn't respond or even make eye contact with her she said, "Listen, okay, it's not about you."

"It feels like it is."

"That's because you're self absorbed," Elena said a little too unkindly.

"Let's just drop it okay?"

"Are you serious?" Elena said. "We can't even talk about it?"

"I don't know!" he said, sounding thoroughly frustrated. "What do you want me to say, Ransom?"

Elena wanted to tell him what she was thinking, but the look on his face made her withdraw to silence. When she still couldn't speak, Kidd walked away leaving her feeling dumbfounded.

Elena walked alone for a long while through the forest until she found her way to the Firebird Station. She wasn't sure why her feet had taken her there. She paused in front of a myriad of trees that were covered with creeping plants, grabbed a handful of foliage, and yanked it back to reveal a steel plated door with the Firebird emblem etched directly in the center. Elena felt a prickling on the back of her neck.

Elena had stopped wanting to search for artifacts after she and Kidd almost drowned at the Smuggler Station. She'd stayed away from the Firebird Station in an effort to distance herself from her parents' work for the Renegades. But, this place was also where she'd grown into a deeper relationship with Abria, Declan, and Fergie. It was a place where she felt accepted and well cared for. The Firebird Station was one place in the world where she felt that she could be her real self.

Elena pulled down a steel lever on the front of the door and there came a loud scraping sound of metal on metal. She heaved the door open and stepped inside. She walked slowly down the main hallway and then was surprised to see that Austin and Fergie were already there. They were off to one side of the bunker with their heads bent closely together. When they noticed Elena, she saw Austin's cheeks flush.

"I thought you'd be in Medical working on compounds," Elena said. "What's going on?"

"Nothing," Austin said, standing quickly. "Why?"

"You just got out of the Tribulation and the first thing you two do is come here. What are you two talking about?" Elena asked.

"We were talking about Pigg, actually." Austin's gaze held steadily on hers until she sighed and took a seat near them.

"I'm worried about him," she started. "While you were in the Tribulation I found him to see if he could help you get out of the simulation quicker. He looked stressed and tired and like he'd lost a little weight. It turns out he really was helping us the whole time. But that's because the programmers sit in a room all day watching the Tribulation and changing the details of the code while we're in there.

"Then, he told me the weirdest stuff about how he hacked into the school's mainframe and that he found all this research about the artifacts. And, he said that he wrote the part about the Kantele into the Tribulation because it was one of the artifacts that was listed in the research he found."

Elena noticed Austin and Fergie exchange a glance.

"What is it?"

"I guess we need to add the Kantele to our list of artifacts now, that's all," Austin said. "And speaking of the Kantele, where's Wheeler? I thought you were with him."

Elena shrugged. "I don't know."

"You two argue about something?" Austin asked, eyeing her.

"We didn't argue," Elena said. "We just don't agree on something, that's all."

"What?"

Elena looked from Austin to Fergie and rolled her eyes. "He wants to kiss me and I'm not ready, okay?"

"That is nothing to be embarrassed about," Fergie said formally. "It is a natural part of adolescence for a boy to want to kiss his girlfriend."

"Yeah, thanks, Mom," Elena said sarcastically. "Is it natural for the girlfriend to not be ready to kiss him back?"

"Why won't you kiss him?" Austin asked.

"At first it was because I wasn't ready. I mean, we'd just stopped hating one another so it felt weird to even be in a relationship with him. Then, things started to feel more comfortable, but school started, and Roman's making me crazy, and I've had sleep deprivation forever, and everything feels not quite right, you know? If I don't know how I feel, how can I go around kissing him?"

"That's a fair question," Austin said. "Did you tell him that?"

"I don't even think he'd understand," Elena sighed. "I wish we could take a break from this place. We've been here too long without a vacation."

But Elena's hopes that the Special Ops trainees would earn some kind of time off since the Tribulation had lasted nearly four weeks were soon destroyed as they started yet another week of classwork, Enrichment, and physical training.

To add to her frustration, more Tribulations began to take place, disturbing her regular schedule almost every other day.

The weeks stretched on with very long days of either working in Enrichment activities and cocoon isolation or being randomly thrown into a Tribulation that ranged from lasting several hours to several days. The trainees barely had time to recover in between all the schedule adjustments.

Furthermore, now that the Tribulations were taking place almost daily, each of the simulations was carried out by a different group of trainees. Sometimes Elena entered the Tribulation with only two or three other students from different Special Ops teams and other times she went in with the whole Aves team.

But easily the hardest part of the constantly changing schedule was the distance she was beginning to feel from Kidd and her other friends. She rarely saw any of them unless they had Enrichment together. And, even when they were together, the words she exchanged with Kidd were spoken in tones of frustration. Kidd had become so careless when speaking to Elena that she was beginning to despise communication with anyone.

However, Elena hadn't considered the fact that she might have been losing her mind until the next Tribulation she'd entered with the entire Aves Special Ops team. They'd only just arrived on a shipping vessel of some sort when Roman ordered them to surrender all their canteens.

"Why do you want our water?" Oscar asked.

"Put all your canteens together in the middle of deck," Roman ordered.

"Don't do this," Charleston said. "Everyone can be responsible to ration their water before we find our orders."

"Or I can manage it until we find our orders," Roman replied sternly.

"We're on the open ocean and the sun is out. How are we supposed to survive without hydration?" Oscar demanded.

"Exactly!" Elena blurted. "You're the worst leader ever!"

The effect of her words was instant.

"Ten demerits!" Roman shouted.

"You make sure everyone in our Unit suffers so you can get ahead!" Elena screamed over his attempt to call out demerits. "You're the most selfish, brainless, spineless dimwit I've ever known."

Roman tried to add demerits while she was talking, but every time he opened his mouth she screamed louder.

Finally, Elena felt a familiar, friendly grip on her shoulder. She took a long drawn breath as if she was struggling for air in her lungs.

"You know what," Elena said boldly to Roman. "Take ten more demerits because I know you can."

As Elena turned to face Austin, Roman called sharply, "Haddock!"

She turned back in time to see Roman point his weapon straight at Austin's chest. As Austin turned toward Elena and held his hand up at her as if to tell her to remain calm, Roman pulled the trigger. Austin's simulation disappeared on the spot.

Rage exploded out of Elena. She grabbed one of the catapult spears that was hanging along the side of the boat.

"Hey Roman! You've been Ransomed!" Elena shouted.

As Roman turned, she launched the spear with full force straight at him. The weapon lodged in his stomach and his projection disappeared.

After Roman was gone, everyone that had been standing around them gawked at her.

"Now, under my authority as a self-appointed member of Archon..." Elena started. "Keep your canteens."

"You can't do that," Rachel Reddington said. "You can't appoint yourself to Archon" — but then she looked slightly unsure and turned to Charleston — "Can she?"

"No, she can't," Charleston replied, looking at Elena with a mildly amused expression.

"Now that Roman and Haddock are out, there's an opening for a new Aves leader," Elena said.

But before Charleston could speak again, everyone turned to see that Roman was headed toward Elena in long, resolved strides.

"How did he get back inside the Tribulation?" Elena heard Oscar say right before Roman discharged his weapon again.

A moment later, Elena woke back up in the simulation room. Austin was standing there, looking disappointed.

"Why did you do that?" he asked.

"You know why," Elena said, shaking her head. "Roman's awful. He deserved it."

"Lena, I know we've all been under a lot of pressure lately, but you really need to learn how to control your temper."

"This is a really bad time to lecture me on my temper," Elena said shortly.

Suddenly, all around them, the other members of the Aves team began to wake from the Tribulation.

"What happened?" Austin asked.

"Roman probably sent them all back so he could win," Elena grumbled.

But, as she was speaking, Roman was also waking. A moment later, Austin's question was answered when Hannibal marched into the room.

"Attention Aves Special Ops! For the time being, I am suspending the Tribulation simulations for Aves trainees." Hannibal's face did not hide the fact that he was deeply displeased. "During this suspension, I expect you to catch up on your classwork, improve during physical training, and become more proficient at your Enrichment activities. I am disappointed with the inability of this team to work together as one unit. Now, all of you, get back to your normal schedules."

With that, Hannibal turned and walked out of the room. Elena looked over at Roman and smirked at his sour expression.

"How did Roman get back into that simulation?" Austin asked again as Elena and their other friends grouped together.

"He must be able to manipulate the system," Fergie stated in a formal tone.

"You should really be more careful how you treat Roman," Kidd told Elena as he made a covert glance over at Roman. "You're going to get yourself into even more trouble than you already have."

"I can take care of myself," Elena said dismissively.

"I'm so glad we can take a break from doing Tribulations," Abria said. "Things have been out of control for far too long."

"I really don't want to get back to class, though," Declan grumbled.

"No one does," Elena said as she and her friends exited the simulation room and began to walk the halls.

"How about we go work for an hour and then meet up outside and take the afternoon off?" Austin suggested.

The others nodded in agreement and then each one set off in a different direction.

Elena entered the first cocoon lab she could find. She really had no interest in listening to any of the lessons, so instead she replayed all the events of the last simulation in her mind.

However, as Instructor Booker taught about Mozart and the American Revolution, Pigg's face suddenly appeared on a completely different Optivision screen.

"Pigg!" Elena exclaimed. "You scared me out of my boots."

"Elena! I'm so glad I finally found you. I saw what happened in the Tribulation and I was worried about you," said Pigg, looking slightly relieved, though he also looked like he hadn't slept in years.

In the few short weeks since she'd caught him in the hallway, Pigg's eyes had sunken in with dark circles and his cheeks were extremely hollow.

"You look so....*different*," Elena gasped, struggling to find the correct word because she was so startled at the drastic change in his appearance.

"What do you mean?" he asked, cocking his head to one side.

"Your face is just..." Elena stopped mid-sentence to change the subject. "What are you doing?"

"I work all the time," Pigg said in a desperate voice. "I hardly ever sleep or eat. It's completely miserable."

"Sounds like you need to be rescued. How can I find you?"

"You can't," said Pigg. "All of our Trademarks are preregistered to the door. No one is allowed in and we're barely allowed out."

Elena was feeling horrified by his appearance, but she put on a fake smile and said, "Well, I miss you. I miss seeing your face in the kitchen. And the quality of food has more than suffered."

"You don't have to tell me," Pigg said glumly. "All our food is delivered to the programming room. We never go outside the room unless we're going to our sleeping quarters, which are located on the other side of the wall from where we work."

"That sounds horrible," Elena said. "Seriously, there must be some way that I can help you."

"If I can keep visiting you here while you're doing your classwork I think that will be enough for me," Pigg said. "The Goonies in here have absolutely no personality."

Elena tried to smile again.

"Ugh...I have to go," Pigg said suddenly. "But I'll find you again tomorrow."

Elena was so disturbed by their conversation that she ended her session early and went to find Austin.

"Have you seen Pigg lately? He looks terrible," said Elena after she'd found Austin working in the Medical lab. "I think he's being mistreated. I wish I knew how to help him."

Austin looked sad and actually turned away from her.

"What is it?" Elena asked, grabbing his arm.

"He didn't want me to tell you," Austin said slowly. "He asked me specifically not to, but I think you should know. Pigg is addicted to opioids."

"I can't believe that!" Elena stated, as a tingle of concern crept up her spine. "How could Hannibal allow that?"

"At the beginning of training, he was getting hurt so much during training that he started stealing from Medical every day. Eventually, I realized that he was taking the meds. I should have recognized the signs from the beginning. I know that he can manipulate the surveillance." Austin shook his head in a disappointed way. "Even though his physical training has stopped, he keeps breaking in to steal things. He says being numb to his environment is the only way he can manage."

"What's being done to help him?" Elena asked.

"I don't know if anyone else knows besides me. The school maintains that Pigg is taking an approved dosage of meds," Austin said. "I've tried to talk him into a more natural route for his pain management, but he says he's fine."

"We've got to get him off those drugs!" Elena insisted. "It'll kill him."

"It's not that simple," Austin said. "I think he's really depressed. We've got to help him, but now that he's so isolated from everyone it's really going to be a challenge."

"Well, he said that he'll find me again tomorrow during my classwork so maybe I'll talk to him," Elena said. "I'll tell him about all the stuff you and Fergie are making and how much better it is for him. In fact, if I get back there now he may find me again today so we don't waste another moment."

As Elena walked to the door, Austin said, "Lena, be gentle with...how you speak to him."

Minutes later, as Elena was hurrying through the halls, she heard her name and turned to see Kidd sprinting towards her.

"What's wrong?" he asked after noticing the look on her face.

"It's just Pigg," Elena said. "He's really struggling and I don't know what to do."

"I don't want to talk about him right now," Kidd said, grinning widely. "I had a great idea for our day off tomorrow. Let's wake up early and get breakfast in Harleston Village. After that, we'll go to the races and I won't even fly. We'll hang out and I'll tell you all about the different hovercraft models in the stadium."

Elena smiled. She liked to see him looking so happy and she didn't want to dismiss his idea, but she knew it was impossible for her to go.

"I know this is our first day off in forever, but I got really behind on Physics after the last Tribulation. You know how hard it is for me. I've already made a study date with Fergie all day."

"Come into town with me," Kidd pleaded.

Elena looked at him sadly.

"I really want to. You know I do, but I have to finish before exams. You should go and have a relaxing day. Then, we'll have dinner in the Mess Hall and you can tell me all about the races."

Kidd grabbed her hand looking disappointed, but he walked her to a cocoon lab without grumbling.

In the morning, Elena and Fergie sat at a pupil station in the Media Lab and pulled up all the lectures on Physics. The hours of studying were set before her, but she kept thinking about how much fun it would be to go to the races with Kidd. School had been so overwhelming that Harleston Village would have provided some much needed relaxation.

"You should go," Fergie said after Elena had answered her twentieth question in a nonchalant way. "You know this better than you think. You should go meet with Wheeler and have a good day off. You have earned some time away. We can always work on this after dinner."

In next to no time, Elena began to see sand colored homes with red brick roofs appear out the window of the Grimsby Channel that was on it's way to the Harleston Village station. She stepped onto the white sand streets and made her way through whimsically shaped green bushes, palm trees, lava rocks, cactus, and strange mountainous rock formations growing out of the ground.

The air was filled with cumin and coriander, but she didn't let any of the women in brightly colored skirts distract her with food from the umbrella topped booths.

Elena made her way steadily through the streets to Horlbeck Alley where she saw the racing stadium. The arena was already alive with an autoflyer race and thousands of screaming fans. She looked to the Optivision screens to see if Kidd was racing, but when she couldn't find his name on the boards she began to scan the crowds.

The seats were so dense with people that it was nearly impossible to see everyone and since she didn't know where Kidd liked to watch the races she gave the mission up as hopeless.

But then suddenly, she remembered that Kidd had mentioned a restaurant in town that served his favorite tacquitos. She left the stadium at once to see if she could find him there.

The day couldn't have been more glorious. The richness of the blue mosaic tiles that were inlaid into the city walls shimmered in the sunlight. The loud, unruly collection of voices that rang out through the streets as people were busy in the markets was almost comical.

Finally, she found the restaurant and was about to cross the street when she saw Kidd coming through the entrance. He had such a happy, relaxed look on his face.

Elena raised her hand to wave and call out to him, but a moment later Sabrina Bauer stumbled through a shop door into Kidd's arms.

Elena felt confused by their laughter and cheerful faces. Then, Kidd leaned over and kissed Sabrina on the mouth. The kiss lasted a moment, or perhaps an eternity. Then, the couple ran down the street, holding hands and smiling.

❑ 17 ❑

Paradigm Shift

For a few moments, Elena wasn't sure what to do. She sensed that there were noisy people all around her going about their business, but she heard a strange buzz ringing in her ears that cancelled out all other noise. She fiercely rubbed the tears that were gathering in her eyes away.

Slowly, she made a long, lonely walk back to the Grimsby Channel. She hoped that Fergie would still be working in the Media Lab so she'd have someone to sit with. However, when she arrived she noticed that Fergie was no longer studying. Elena sat at the pupil station in the farthest corner of the room and pulled up several Optivision screens.

Hours later, Elena noticed Kidd enter the Media Lab looking happy, but she quickly returned her eyes to her work. He plopped down at Elena's table and grasped her hand.

"Hey! You almost done? I'm starving. We should get dinner."

Kidd's carefree attitude caught Elena completely off guard. Was he really planning to lie to her about what he'd been doing with Sabrina Bauer?

She couldn't even look at him as she said, "I was in Harleston Village today. I thought I'd surprise you."

Out of the corner of her eye, she saw the smile fade completely from Kidd's face.

"I saw you kissing Bauer in front of that restaurant you like earlier today."

Elena felt Kidd increase his grip on her hand, but she yanked it away. Silence stretched between them until it became unacceptable to her.

"And you have nothing to say? Your tongue still caught up in her mouth?"

Kidd sighed. "I met Bauer at the tracks last year. I was sort of with her for a bit. Never at school, of course, but whenever I was in the village." Then, his tone changed to a defining insistence. "But she means *nothing* to me."

Elena felt her entire body tense at his words.

"She means *nothing*? I saw you holding her hand. You were hugging and kissing her." She hung her head. "The thing is, you looked really happy."

"Things with her are easy...I mean that it's less complicated...no, no!" Kidd stuttered as Elena looked at him intensely.

"You mean, it's easy because she'll kiss you," Elena said shortly.

"No, it's not like that," Kidd replied defensively.

"If she's so easy to be with, why aren't you with her?" Elena looked expectantly at him, but he just rubbed his hands over his face in an irritated sort of way.

"You know, I would wait for an answer, but that would indicate that I care more than I do."

Elena jumped up quickly from the table and made her way across the room. Secretly, she hoped that he would chase her down, yell at her, and plead his case. However, as she was painfully learning, Kidd wasn't available to give more in their relationship.

That night, Elena found herself wandering in an indistinct place. Shadows surrounded her and fog was beginning to gather, but still she could see Imperator moving through the gloom.

Instantly, Elena was curious about what he was doing. Imperator didn't seem to notice she was there so she quickly decided to follow him.

As Imperator made his way through the darkness, Elena came closer and closer to him. Until, suddenly, he stopped.

His back was to her, but Elena could tell that he was looking at something. She wanted very much to be able to manipulate her dream so she could see what he was looking at.

Therefore, Elena came around to his side silently, yet he still didn't seem to realize her presence. She looked down and saw two stone tablets that were etched with fine writing hovering in midair.

"Are those the Tablets of Destiny?" Elena asked, hoping and fearing that Imperator would answer her.

"Of course they are," Imperator replied.

"Can you tell me where they are?"

As Imperator turned to face Elena, fear bubbled up at the sight of his silver studded mask. Then, beyond his shoulder she noticed a sudden movement. Her mom and Austin had arrived. They were both wearing high collared hospital uniforms and looked seemingly normal except that their eyeballs were as white as snow.

Then, Elena gasped as she saw Kidd and Sabrina appear. They walked straight over to the table, sat on the Tablets, and started kissing.

Elena awoke feeling sweaty and prickly. But she didn't have time to recover from her awful dream or from the real memories of Kidd kissing Sabrina in Harleston Village because her Enrichment activities, classwork, and rigorous training started again.

During weapons training, Elena made covert glances at Sabrina. She'd come to accept Sabrina as a kind and genuine leader with a strong mind. But she'd never really considered how strikingly beautiful Sabrina looked, even with the sides of her head shaved and her hair all combed into spikes down the middle of her scalp. In addition, Sabrina somehow had the ability to influence others, even with silence.

Elena hated that she couldn't hate Sabrina. And she hated that she could see why Kidd liked Sabrina, that is, if he liked her. The two were never together at school, but Elena was too much of a coward to ask Sabrina about her relationship with Kidd.

"What's going on with you today?" Abria asked, coming up beside Elena. "You're very quiet."

"I'm always quiet," Elena grumbled.

"Yes, but normally you don't have a look of, like, contempt on your face unless Roman is around," Abria pointed out. "Why are you glaring at Bauer?"

Elena blinked and looked at Abria feeling slightly embarrassed.

"I'm not. No, reason. I mean, I'm fine."

Abria raised her eyebrows but didn't ask Elena any further questions.

Later that evening, while the Aves trainees were at the Gauntlet, Elena continued to feel distracted. She watched Sabrina's every move on the different obstacles, feeling determined to outperform her in some way. However, as always, the obstacles had grown increasingly difficult. New and more challenging ones had been added since she'd last been there.

As Elena struggled to do her best, she came down off one of the platforms and completely lost her balance. She was starting to fall when she felt a strong grip on her arm that steadied her. Elena looked, thinking that Austin was standing there, but instead she locked eyes with Kidd.

As a reflex, Elena shoved Kidd so hard in the chest that he stumbled back and almost fell over.

"Don't EVER touch me again!" Elena hollered.

Kidd looked sad and disappointed, but Elena didn't care. She did, however, notice that her reaction had gained quite an audience of onlookers.

Elena stuck her chin in the air, turned on her heels, and sprinted back towards the school.

"Lena!" she heard Austin call but didn't stop or even look back.

When Elena finally made it back to her bunk, she scanned her Trademark against the closet door. She grabbed a rucksack and tossed clothes into the bag while her mind raced around in disconnected circles.

Elena felt like her life was spinning out of control and there was only one place she knew where she could steady her thoughts. She needed to go home. She needed to immerse herself in her dad's library. She needed to remember who she was and where she came from.

"OH! MY! CHEATER!"

Abria had arrived at the end of the dormitory. She hurried down the hall to edge of Elena's bunk with Fergie beside her.

"Wheeler told us what happened. We want you to know that we're on your side." Abria's words were laced with empathy.

"Wheeler's behavior has created a paradigm shift of considerable magnitude," Fergie said in a formal tone.

"*A what?*" Abria squealed.

"A paradigm shift is a change that happens when one replaces a former mode of thinking with an entirely new mode of thinking. In this case, we were once inclined to think that Wheeler would be faithful in his relationship with Elena, but now that we have evidence to the contrary our paradigm has shifted to a new mode of thinking...that Wheeler is a lying scoundrel."

"Really, Fergie, is that necessary to point out right now?" Abria asked, but then, she looked at Elena and added, "What are you doing?"

"I'm going home," Elena replied in callous way.

"You can't just leave," Abria said. "You'd have to get permission."

"Technically, she is not required to get permission to leave school any longer," Fergie said. "Though our classwork is mandatory, we do have the liberty to complete it at our own pace. It is not advisable to excuse oneself from school unless we are given a formal leave of absence, but it is not prohibited."

"That was totally not, like, helpful," Abria stated bluntly.

"I don't care what I can and can't do anymore," Elena said, the edges of her words void of emotion. "There's a train leaving for Atlanson in twelve minutes and I'm going to be on it."

Even though Elena realized that her friends were staring, she couldn't stand to look them in the face. She swung the rucksack over her shoulder and walked towards the door. She reached the train minutes later, but before she could board Elena could feel that Austin was behind her.

"Lena, where are you going?"

"I'm going home," Elena replied, though she couldn't bear to look at him. "And I'm going there alone."

"Why? Because of Wheeler?"

"No!" Elena lied. "Because I need some time with my parents."

Elena could feel Austin's desire to argue with her, but instead he said, "I'd like to come with you."

"I'll be fine by myself," Elena lied again. "If I get lonely, Grandpa and Grandma are right across the hall."

She didn't look at Austin before she boarded the Grimsby Channel, but when she finally took a seat she noticed he was right out the window.

A little over an hour later, Elena stepped into her dad's office. She walked straight toward the elaborate shelving that stretched the entire back wall. The shelves were embroidered with rounded emblems. Elena slid the third emblem from the left open and inserted her finger into a hole. A moment later, a portion of the bookcase disappeared from the wall.

Elena walked into her dad's library, which was filled from floor to ceiling with books on shelves, stacked in piles on the floor, and lying lazily over cushioned chairs. She remembered the last time her dad had been with her there, but it brought her little comfort now.

Elena flung her rucksack down on the carpet and laid her head down. She stared up at the ceiling with its slopes and arches, constellations and symbols. Elena now knew that the ceiling was designed to work with the Catalan Atlas, but she had no desire to think about the journey she'd been on since her parents' death. Yet, in the stillness, her mind began to wander between all the secrets that had been part of her life for so long.

Most of the mysteries had originated from the Ransom Dossier. She wished her dad had never left it for her. She wished that she'd never been involved with finding artifacts. She even wished that she'd never started school at Grimsby School of the Republic.

Elena was suddenly desperate to get away from all the secrets in the library.

Leaving everything, Elena wandered out of her apartment to the leisure garden at the end of the hall. The garden was lined with manicured hedges and flower bushes. A trickling fountain sat in the center of the garden, surrounded by lounging chairs. She went straight to the ledge and stared over the edge into the city below. She'd never actually sat out there before. Usually, she only passed through it when she'd sneak out of her house at night to meet Austin.

As she watched the people walking home from work, Elena thought about her own life in Atlanson. She'd been raised with a strong, independent mind, yet she was still a slave to all Imperator had designed. And because she now knew that she had always lived under his command, she struggled the idea of destiny, even as she heard Anne Foreman's words in her head:

"Did you know that the ancient Greeks had two words for *time*? The first was Chronos, which referred to sequential time. But the other word, Kairos, referred to the supreme moment in time. And *that* is destiny...the perfect moment in time."

Elena pulled her Kairos necklace into her fingers. She wished that she could have more faith in the perfect moments in time, but instead she could only see Kidd and Sabrina laughing and kissing. Elena could only see the thousands of people on the streets walking around with their seemingly perfect lives, not aware of the fact that they were all enslaved. The people were so content. Why couldn't she be like them?

Elena watched the simulated sun setting in the sky. She saw the city lights brighten the streets and then the door to the terrace opened.

"Hey, I hoped you'd be here," Austin said. "I checked every where else and was starting to get worried."

"Why did you come?" Elena said, trying to make her voice cold. "I said I wanted to be alone."

"I could tell you were lying," Austin said. "I wanted to give you as much time alone as possible, but I think we both knew that eventually I'd be here to interrupt whatever twisty little thoughts you're having about life."

Elena continued to watch the city below.

"Lena, I know you're sad about Wheeler..." Austin started, but she interrupted him.

"No, it's not that," Elena insisted. "Before I left school, Fergie said something about a paradigm shift. It's like a change from one way of thinking to an entirely new way. I felt like that when I learned Pigg was doing drugs. And I felt like that after Hopper told us about the Renegades and their work. I'm constantly in a state of changing my thinking.

"And well, I've been sitting here for hours, watching people go about their lives. They have no idea that there's more than this."

Austin had now arrived at her side, but she still couldn't look at his face.

"Austin, all those people are happy. They're happy in their ignorance. They don't know anything is wrong. Maybe this life is good enough for them. Maybe people should be allowed to live in the bliss of their ignorance. No need for a paradigm shift here."

"Lena, those people aren't really happy. They don't have enough information about the world to be anything. Imperator forces human sterilization, he prohibits any form of human expression, he engineers us all to look the same, he forces women to terminate pregnancies, he controls and manipulates everyone into submission.

"If we let these people continue to live in ignorance then no one will experience the joy of having freedom. We would condemn them to a death that is not their own, but one that Imperator decides for them. Your parents would still be alive if it weren't for Imperator..."

Uncontrollable outrage burst from Elena's mouth. "No! They'd still be alive if they didn't get involved with the Renegades or if Imperator hadn't believed in some dimwit prophecy about some dimwit 'chosen' leader. I mean, what's the point, Austin! What's the point of all this? What's the point of living in this world?"

"For today, our purpose is to rescue them, Lena. To rescue all of them. And to be rescued ourselves," Austin said steadily. "To be free to have a *real life*. We shouldn't settle for an insufficient interpretation of life because we think that's all we get. We should strive for what is true! And we should share that truth with all the others.

"Do you remember how Fallon's people were? They created their own music, unique art, and food. Everything was authentic. They lived in peace of their own making. And, they lived in color. Every color skin, hair color, eye color, and every disabled or abled body was there. That's the way we're meant to live. We're meant to experience a full, authentic life, and thrive in it.

"Don't you think that the people of Atlanson, the Galilee Province, Crowfield Plantation, and all the students at Grimsby deserve that? Don't you think we deserve the right to decide whether or not we want to live the rest of our lives being told what to believe, where we have to work, how many children we have, and when we die?"

"Sometimes I miss how things were before," Elena said, weariness creeping around the edges of her words. "I used to think I was in control of my life. I mean, for the most part, we went where we wanted and did what we wanted." She sighed heavily. "After I almost drowned in the Smuggler Station, I was happy to forget about the artifacts. I mean, nothing good has really come from all this anyway."

"But consider," Austin said. "My father went missing, Imperator murdered your parents and Kate Bagley's family is gone. Declan and Abria's parents are in that hospital. Melly Linus's family never existed. Fergie's parents are dead. Wheeler's whole family was burned alive. And those are the people that we know about. How many more families have suffered because Imperator has us all in his grasp?"

"That's exactly what I'm trying to say. All these bad things have happened. And don't even get me started about how many lies and secrets that have been told," Elena said. "Finding artifacts doesn't matter. Imperator has control of everything. And all the people living in his world seem content. We should let that be."

Austin looked at her in a strange way and asked, "What aren't you telling me?"

Elena didn't want to be honest about the dreams she'd had lately, but she was also trying to make sense of them. Maybe Austin could help her.

"I keep having these dreams and they're disturbing. But in my last dream it felt like I was able to *choose* what I wanted to do instead of reacting to whatever was going on around me."

"We've talked about this before," Austin said. "Since you have that Cognicross in your head you'll have types of stories that have been preprogrammed for you."

"But, there's something different about these," Elena said slowly. "In one of my dreams, I was standing on top of a sand colored stone wall. A gunship landed and Imperator was there. You, Pigg, Fergie, and the rest of our friends were there, too, but all your eyes were white and sightless. Imperator kept asking me to tell him where the Disc was hidden. I think he expects me to have it and that he's going to come looking for it. He's going to come after me. It's only a matter of time." Elena trembled with terror. "He's going to capture me and split my head open to get whatever information he needs from me. I know he will."

The look of horror that briefly passed Austin's eyes wasn't lost on Elena, but he rallied quickly and enveloped her in a tight hug.

"No matter what happens, I won't let him take you. I promise."

"You can't stop him," Elena said, pulling away from the embrace she wanted so desperately to cling. "He's killed everyone. He does whatever he pleases. No one can stop him. And that's why I think I should go away. I could go into hiding somewhere out there, maybe even back with Fallon and his people in New York. If I'm gone maybe Imperator won't kill anyone else."

"Lena, we can't change the past, but we can change the future of where that past was going to take us."

Elena looked sharply at Austin. "Did you hear Anne Foreman tell me that once?"

"No, but she told it to me when we stayed with them that time," Austin replied.

Elena suddenly felt something in her brain sliding into focus. "Our choices can change the future of our broken past. I don't know how to choose the right thing."

"Help me with the artifacts," Austin pleaded. "As Anne would say, *through freedom we can find truth, peace, and a hopeful future.* Freedom is the key."

Elena nodded, not feeling sure if she wanted to help with the artifacts or not. She wanted to help her friend and to believe as he did, but she still wasn't convinced that the Renegades knew what they were doing or that the artifacts would somehow give them the answers they needed.

◇ 18 ◇

Right Decisions

The next morning, Elena and Austin caught an early train back to school. As they arrived in the Mess Hall they noticed Declan sitting alone. He had a smile on his face and a spoon in his hand.

"You look happy," Elena said gloomily as she and Austin took seats at his table.

"It's a beautiful day," replied Declan.

Elena looked out the window and frowned. "The rain simulation is on."

"Is it? I hadn't noticed," Declan said, grinning. "Want to go for a walk after I finish this amazing porridge?"

"Wheeler cheated on me and I feel like my heart has shattered into a million pieces. So, no, I don't want to go for a walk."

Declan's grin faded. "Wheeler's a dimwit. You're never going to be able to change that, no matter how much your heart aches. So, take a walk with me."

"You know what? I'm not even hungry," Elena said abruptly. "I'll see you later."

Elena didn't wait for them to reply before she left the table and headed into the hallway. She wasn't entirely sure what she was going to do first, but since she was still holding her rucksack she decided to swing by her dorm to put everything back in her closet.

As she was rounding the last hall before her dorm, she heard, "Ransom! Wait for me!"

Elena turned and felt her face grow embarrassingly warm as she came face to face with Sabrina Bauer.

"Maybe this is none of my business, but Wheeler and I are not a couple," Sabrina started. "We were never a couple. We met at the tracks last year and spent time together whenever we were in Harleston Village."

Elena suddenly realized that her mouth was hanging open, so she closed it at once.

"I didn't know you two were together. When I asked him about you the other day, he said things were complicated and he didn't want to talk about it."

Elena nodded and then lied, "It's fine really. We weren't really serious or anything. If you want to be with him..."

"Oh, I don't," Sabrina said quickly. "I really have no desire to waste my time being in a serious relationship. Wheeler's a fun escape from being around here. No offense."

As Sabrina walked away, Elena considered her words very carefully. Somehow, it did make sense to her that being in a steady relationship might be a waste of time.

"I mean, seriously, isn't there more to life than boys?" Elena said quietly to herself.

She slowly walked back to her dorm room, deciding that she was going to take control over her life. Elena knew that Austin was good enough to be one of the Special Ops leaders and she wanted to be right there, leading with him.

"I need to focus my full attention on classwork and schedule if I'm ever going to take Roman's place in Archon," Elena whispered. "And if I'm going to achieve that goal, I need to devote extra time to physical and weapons training. I'll start tomorrow."

On the first day of the first week of the eighth month, Elena started her day with a new sense of self. She watched and rewatched Instructor Booker's lectures on the Age of Reason, the American Revolution, and the War of Spanish Succession without complaining once.

During Niva's class, she interpreted French correspondence that gave details about the French and Indian War and in Copernicus's lecture she created ancestry charts from a list of French rulers with intentional focus.

During weapons training she chose a new weapon that she hadn't handled before and during the Gauntlet she decided that she'd attack every single obstacle with a cheerful attitude.

"You seem different today," Austin said as they rounded the third obstacle with ease.

"That's because I am different," Elena said and she smiled. "I've decided that I want to take Roman's spot in Archon. I'll have to work really hard to get there, but it's worth a try."

"I didn't know that was an interest of yours," Austin remarked.

"It's a new thing," Elena replied. "I've decided that I want to rule with you once you get elected as one of our leaders."

And so, Elena continued her days with a positive attitude, even though she could feel unspoken tension building between she and Roman every time they saw each other in the halls, at meals, or during physical training.

Elena didn't allow herself to feel discouraged during cocoon learning and often selected to learn more subjects from the syllabus. She continued pranking people as often as she could, but in general she was working so hard on school that she'd almost caught up with Fergie's place in the syllabus.

"You've been Ransomed, dimwits!" she shouted regularly at the boys as she ruined food, stole towels from the showers, and hacked into their study sessions to slow down their studying.

In addition, Elena was now always the first to volunteer to learn new skills during physical training. And she wasn't even disappointed when Instructor

Booker announced during her next cocoon lesson with him that she'd be starting group work that would last until the end of the year.

"You will be assigned to a group that will work together until this class ends. Your group will be assigned a country and time period to research," said Booker's hologram. "You'll combine your collective knowledge to create an appropriate simulation that accurately represents the historical data. In addition to this, you'll create an entirely new set of scenarios that will change the outcome of history.

"Essentially, you will be rewriting history using the benefits of modern technology. For example, in 1533 Spain invaded the Incan empire. Quizquiz was the commander of the Incan army, but his own troops killed him after they lost the city of Cuzco."

Elena's cocoon lit up with several Optivisions to display what her Instructor was describing.

"However, if we apply a new algorithm, allowing the Incan army to defend Cuzco, the outcome is very different." Elena watched the Optivision change as he spoke. "Your group will present the project that you write together at the end of this semester. Miss Ransom, your team is as follows..."

The screens in Elena's cocoon morphed yet again until she saw the faces of Fergie, Rachel Reddington, Thomas Apted, Donald Lawson, and Mandara Tilden.

"So, who did you get in your study group?" Abria asked as she caught up with Elena after cocoon learning.

"Reddington, Apted, Lawson, and Tilden," Elena replied. "I'm not sure I like any of them except Reddington and at least I get Fergie." Then she turned toward Abria and asked, "Who's in your group?"

"Apryl Sommers and Jaden Kinard from Maritime, Timothy Curwen and Neylon Faulkner from Animalia, and Wheeler.

"Good luck with Wheeler in your group," she said sarcastically.

"I'm sure it'll be just fine," Abria said lightly.

Later that same week Elena, Fergie, and the rest of their group started on the project that Instructor Booker had assigned them. She immediately started to see the extreme personalities of some of the trainees the first time.

During Tribulations and training, Thomas Apted and Mandara Tilden had been somewhat timid or hesitant about action, but as soon as they started group work it was clear that they wanted to lead every discussion.

"I certainly know more than you about Prussia in the 1600's," Mandara said haughtily.

"No you don't," Thomas replied. "I was the only one to pass that part of the exam with perfect marks."

"Well, I still think that if we weave a detailed story about the Electors of Prussia and the Junkers who worked with Electors and served as officers in the Prussian Army and do a section on how the Hapsburg rulers in Austria rivaled the Prussian rule to compete for control of German states, that should be plenty," Mandara argued.

And on and on they went for twenty minutes with very little interjection from the rest of their group.

Until finally, Fergie said, "Tilden and Apted! Though you have both made excellent cases for how the presentation should be handled you have left out the key component, of which, several of us, including myself, will be necessary for the completion."

"What's that?" Thomas asked impatiently.

"We will need programmers, a task I excel at and a task that neither of you do."

Elena couldn't help but smile slightly at Fergie's boldness. She was, of course, correct. Therefore, Fergie was able to speed the process along quite a bit after her declaration. Still, Elena felt weary of words once the meeting was over.

In addition to her group work, Pigg met with her every time Elena entered her cocoon learning room. She was worried about his deteriorating appearance, but Pigg never wanted to talk to her about what he was experiencing. He always kept on task with their training and he'd already taught her a lot about hacking into the school mainframe and security systems.

Sometimes, Elena had to beg Pigg to slow down his tutoring because he'd talk about techniques she didn't understand.

"Sorry! Sorry!" Pigg apologized. "It's so important that you learn all this because I have no idea what's going to happen next."

"What do you mean *what's going to happen next?*"

"I don't know, exactly," Pigg admitted. "I hear mutters of things that sound suspiciously like Hannibal is going to start Tribulations again."

Elena felt really nervous after Pigg said this but Austin, Declan, and Abria didn't seem the least bit concerned when she relayed the message to them later at the lunch table.

"I guess I figured we'd start Tribulations again at some point," Declan shrugged. "I mean, apparently it's a central part of the program."

Elena started to bite her nails nervously as Austin said, "I wouldn't worry too much about it. Hannibal has stopped it for now, but if we have to go back in at least we'll know what we're up against."

"Yeah, Ransom, instead of worrying about the Tribulation maybe you should focus your attention on being a better pranker," Declan suggested with a wink.

"You can't accuse me of not being a good pranker," Elena said indignantly. "Last week I snuck into the boys shower room and stole all the clothes and towels. I also shut down the electricity on the entire education floor while Roman was taking his exams. And who do you think hacked the system and plastered that picture of Roman in a dress on every Optivision screen and window dimensional in the building?"

"That was you?" Declan said, looking impressed. "I thought Fergie did that."

"Of course you did because I'm stealth like that," Elena said.

"How did you learn to do all that?" Austin asked.

"Pigg taught me the hacking part," Elena laughed. "But the ideas were all mine."

As everyone started to laugh, Elena had a flashback of her recent visit with Pigg. She remembered the strained look on his face and his words of warning that he wouldn't really tell her about and her face immediately fell.

Everyone else noticed the extreme change in her demeanor and also quieted quickly.

"How is Pigg doing?" Declan asked in a serious tone.

Elena blinked and shook her head. "I think he's fine. I mean, I'm sure he must be fine."

Elena tried to look convincing, but she was sure that her eyes were giving her away, so she quickly leapt up from the lunch table.

"I'm going for a quick run before my afternoon classes start," Elena announced and she bolted out of the room before anyone could stop her.

Elena jogged out into the woods. She needed to run to clear her head and there wasn't anywhere else on campus that she knew would be free of other trainees.

By the time Elena wound around through the trees to the entrance of the Firebird Station it was time for dinner, but she still wanted to be alone so she decided to go in and sit for a while.

She expected the Station to be empty, but when she entered she heard voices coming from the Research & Development room. Quietly, she edged her way down the hall until she realized that the voices belonged to Austin and Fergie.

Feeling curious about why they were at the Station alone again, she moved toward the door to get into a perfect eavesdropping position.

"And you're sure it will work?" Elena heard Austin ask.

"I am certain," Fergie replied. "I do have a few more diagnostics to perform, but the program will work flawlessly."

"Fantastic! Just make sure you keep it a secret, okay? I don't want anyone to realize what we're doing."

"I would advise you again to tell Elena," Fergie said. "She could be helpful and..."

"No," Austin said firmly. "I've already told you about the dreams she's been having. This is the only way to protect her from Imperator. Now that she's essentially discovered the location of the Firebird Disc, she and everyone else are in danger."

"Very well," Fergie replied. "I will begin another diagnostic now. Would you like to stay and watch?"

"I have to get back to school," Austin said. "I don't want Elena to catch us alone together again. She's already so suspicious. And after what Wheeler did to her, I know she'll have a hard time understanding why I've kept a secret from her this long."

"Then, you are planning to tell her?"

"Of course I'll tell her," Austin said. "I tell her everything. I need to find the right time."

Elena eased back down the hall toward the front of the Station. So, Austin was keeping secrets from her. And, not only that, but he'd lied about it. Elena wasn't sure how to feel.

Should she confront him? Should she make him confess? But then again, Austin said he was planning to tell her whatever he'd been doing with Fergie. Should she wait and trust that, whatever the secret, Austin had a good reason to keep it from her?

When Elena got to the front door of the Station, she opened it wide. Then, she called out, "Hey! Is anyone here?"

Austin appeared in the hall. "Hey there! What's going on?"

"Oh, nothing," Elena lied. "I was out for a walk and decided that I wanted to read my dad's dossier for a while. I'm hoping maybe I'll find something about my Cognicross."

"Want me to read with you for a while?"

Elena bit her lip. Even though he'd lied to her, she still wanted to be close to Austin. She didn't want there to be any distance between them. She wanted to trust him and visa-versa. But she also couldn't deny that she was insulted and angry that Austin was keeping things from her.

"Actually, I was hoping to be alone," Elena lied again. "I need some quiet."

"Okay, well I'm going back up to school," Austin said. As he came closer to the front door he paused to look her in the face. He squeezed her shoulder and said, "Happy reading. I hope you find what you're looking for."

After Austin left, Elena walked to the Research & Development room, but she didn't see Fergie anywhere. Feeling discouraged, she grabbed the Ransom Dossier and fell into the nearest chair.

Elena wished she could understand why Austin would keep secrets from her. And why had he told Fergie that she'd essentially discovered the location of the Firebird Disc? She had no idea where it possibly could be in the world.

"Another paradigm shift," Elena grumbled.

She felt beyond confused, but the main source of her discomfort lingered in her mind. Did she trust Austin enough to wait for him to tell her everything he'd been keeping from her? And did she trust that he had a good reason for doing so?

"Oh, hey!" Abria said as she came into the Research & Development room. Elena hadn't really been reading the dossier, so Abria startled her. "I didn't know anyone else was here."

"I didn't either," Elena said. "What are you doing here?"

"Oh, I was just out in the hangar helping Fergie with something," Abria said. "Actually, you should come out and see for yourself."

Abria led Elena through the tunnel that looked like it had been carved out of solid rock. When they reached the end, they stepped onto a platform and overlooked an enormous cave, which seemed strangely enormous without the Independence in its normal spot on the landing pad below.

At the base of the main staircase, Fergie stood alongside the frame of a two-seater hovercraft that was in varying stages of being built.

"What's all this?" Elena asked.

"Wheeler's building a hovercraft," Abria said jovially.

"Why?"

"He said it's so he has something smaller to fly so he can leave whenever he wants. I asked if he'd teach me to fly this one because the Independence scares me too much and he said he would. Isn't that exciting? I mean, I know we've done plenty of flying in simulations, but it would be so fun to actually operate a real one, right?"

Elena nodded. She walked slowly over to the hovercraft trying to decide if she wanted to turn around and go back the way she came. As she inspected the construction, she couldn't help but slide into the driver's seat.

"Wheeler said the funniest thing today about Hunter while we were in group work," Abria said reminiscently. "And then Hunter's face turned the brightest like, shade of red that it looked like it was going to explode, and..." She stopped mid-sentence and looked at Elena curiously. "What's that face you're making?"

Elena could feel tension creasing her eyebrows together. "Why're you talking about Wheeler in front of me?"

"Oh, come on, you can't hate him for, like, ever."

"I can try," Elena replied moodily. "But that's not really the point. I think I asked you twice already not to talk about him when I'm around."

"Elena, it's been quite a few weeks now since you broke up. I think it's time you forgive and move on," Abria said.

"Forgiveness has never been a quality that I've found useful," Elena said. "It makes people weak."

"Elena!" Abria shrieked. "What would Austin think if he heard you say that?"

"Austin knows me better than I know myself," Elena said plainly. "He's never shocked at the things I say."

"That doesn't mean he would like you saying it," Abria pointed out. "Let's go, Fergie. Wheeler said we will find the other parts for the guidance system over there. And he said he needs you to finish programming the main console so that he can install everything."

As Abria and Fergie moved to the opposite side of the cavern, Elena remembered the hours she'd spent in Simulabs with Kidd in Atlanson and the dates they'd taken to their favorite restaurants and the times they'd trekked out to Tavington's farm together. Eventually, her thoughts drifted to the Smuggler Station. They'd almost drowned together. She once believed that made she and Kidd closer.

"It had to have been my fault," Elena whispered. "I know I'm not exactly easy to get along with."

As discouragement threatened to come over her, Elena heard her dad's voice in her head:

"She didn't betray you because of something you did." Truman Ransom once told her after a friend had lied about her in a way that hurt her reputation. *"She made a choice that hurt you because something inside her was hurting. Human reasoning can be confusing sometimes, but remember that everyone makes a choice when they react to a situation. Sometimes we choose what is right, and sometimes we choose wrong."*

Elena wished, for her dad's sake, that she could learn to make right decisions, but she was afraid that it might never happen.

▭ 19 ▭

Betrayal

As the eighth month slipped away and the weather simulation changed from unbearably hot and humid to cooler mornings and evenings, Elena's routine was now so effortless that she was making positive strides in excelling to the top of most of their classes, Enrichment, and physical training. She'd finally caught up on all her classwork, though Fergie was, as always, weeks ahead of all the other trainees in their studies.

The leaders of Archon continued to push the trainees during all hours of the day and night and Elena's rapport with Roman had not improved, but she was deteremined to make the best out of her time at school.

As the weeks progressed through the ninth month of school, Pigg continued to teach Elena the finer points of the school mainframe. They never talked about anything personal and she never commented on the state of his appearance, which she felt was downright disturbing, to say the least. And, since she was too much of a coward to confront him on the opioids he was taking, she kept him up-to-date with the gossip around the school that Abria had relayed to her.

Then one morning, Pigg said, "So, I've been researching the Kantele. The artifact is from Finnish folklore in the 1500's. Apparently when it's played the music from it induces a deep sleep. I don't know what that has to do with the artifacts we've been collecting or why the Headmaster has done so much research on it, but it's what I learned, anyway. How about you? Have you learned anything else from the dossiers?"

"Well, I did find this one algorithm in the Alpha Manuscript…" Elena said slowly as she began to fight a battle in her head about whether or not to tell Pigg that she knew that the real Kantele was actually in the Smuggler Station at the bottom of the lake on Kidd's family farm. "Maybe you can work on it for me?"

"Why don't you ask Fergie to help?" Pigg wondered.

Elena bit her bottom lip. She was still feeling resentful about the alone time that Austin and Fergie had spent keeping secrets from her. But, she didn't want to tell Pigg all that.

"She and Austin have been spending a lot of time working on things without me. So, I thought I'd work on this without them to see if I can get something to show them. What do you say?"

"Of course I'll help you. If you bring the algorithm to our next study session, I'll take it from you. Okay, now back to our lesson…" Pigg pointed to something on the screen with his finger, "If you put this code in right here, you can manipulate the space in the school. You can even create things that aren't there. Like, let's say that you want to look like you're asleep in bed, but you're really off doing something else, you just put the code in here and a digital projection of you would appear in your bed."

"How is that possible?" Elena asked, feeling astonished.

"Because this entire place is a simulated atmosphere. I mean, the school likes to portray that we only experience simulations within the boundaries that they set, like in a classroom or when they sent us out into the frozen wilderness. In truth, the entire dome is a simulation, which means that the boundaries of the space can be manipulated and controlled if you have the correct information."

"You're so brilliant! You know that, right?" Elena said admiringly.

Even though he was a hologram, Elena could see that Pigg's ears turned a bright shade of pink.

Elena left Pigg that day feeling slightly encouraged. At least she still had one friend that she could count on. Still, she crawled to bed that night feeling anxious about Pigg's health.

As she lay in the dark, she chewed her nails and thought about what she needed to say to encourage her friend to change his mind about taking the medication that the school dispensed. As she was rehearsing her speech to him for the third time, loud sirens shocked the girl's hall awake.

"The school is under attack!" Charleston Woods exclaimed as she ran into their dorm.

"What do you mean *attack?*" Rachel Reddington asked.

"I don't know much about it," Charleston replied, looking intense. "I know that this specific sequence of warning sirens means that the school is under attack by a foreign invader! We need to get out of the building."

Elena was up on her feet in a moment and pulled on her jump boots.

"How do we get out of the building if we're being attacked?" Elena shouted over the siren.

"We have an evacuation procedure," Charleston admitted. "Let's get going, ladies."

The sound of all the girls pulling boots on and charging down the hall toward the exit filled the entire floor. But as Elena neared the door leading out to the main hall, she noticed that it had been barricaded from floor to ceiling with beds, chairs, tables, and other random pieces of furniture.

"We're trapped!" Sabrina Bauer declared. "What's going on?"

But before anyone had a chance to answer, the sprinkler system above their heads burst. A steady current of rain soaked their heads, clothes, and the floor.

"The guys!" Charleston exclaimed. "Only Archons have access to override the fire response system and the alarm bells."

"You think this is a prank?" Elena asked.

"That's the only logical answer," Sabrina said. "I mean, our exit has been blocked and now it's raining."

"Worst. Prank. Ever!" Charleston said, but she was already starting to laugh.

"I think I could crawl up there and squeeze through to the other side," Sabrina suggested. "Then, at least I could go shut off the water."

As Sabrina began to climb the tower of furniture, Elena turned toward Abria and Fergie. They both had smiles on their faces.

"This is such an awesome prank. I really wished I'd thought of it," Elena laughed.

"We'll figure out a way to get them back," Abria giggled as water dripped off her nose.

Elena turned back and noticed that Sabrina had made it to the top of a stack of mattresses. Then, she began to shimmy through the narrow gaps between a chair and some table legs.

"Oh, no!" Sabrina cried suddenly. "I'm stuck! Somebody help! Pull me back in."

At once, Charleston began to climb the structure. She tried to pull Sabrina back through the hole, but in all the maneuvering Sabrina actually fell out through the opening on the other side of the mountain of furniture.

All the girls on the hall burst into a fit of giggles as they heard Sabrina cry out in pain.

"That was an epic failure," Elena called to Abria and Fergie over the continued sound of the sirens.

"Oh, I'm laughing so hard I peed my pants!" Rachel Reddington cried.

Elena couldn't help laugh even harder as Rachel waddled out of the room. Then, she and the other girls began to dismantle the structure so that they'd be able to get out of the room at some point.

Eventually, Elena assumed that Charleston was able to get to the control room because the siren and sprinkler turned off. The girls had gone from laughter to extreme exhaustion in a very short time, but since everything in their rooms was now soaking wet they opted to change clothes and nap in couches and chairs all over the building.

When breakfast was finally served, Elena sat down with Abria and Fergie feeling tired but happy. They ate in silence until Abria finally stood from the table.

"Well, I'm off to group work," Abria said, smiling sleepily.

"Ugh! I can't believe you have to spend time with Wheeler after a night like that," Elena said.

"I really don't mind," Abria said. "He's really not that bad. And he's really good at the construction part of things. Sommers is good at code writing and Kinard is good at planning, so I think we're going to have a good project."

The wet and wild prank was the talk of the school that day. Elena couldn't get away from it because no matter where she went every single boy shouted, "You've been Ransomed, dimwit!"

In fact, there was even a playback on the Optivision when she arrived to her cocoon for classwork. She laughed as she rewatched Sabrina fall from the furniture structure, and fresh tears spilled down her cheeks as Rachel waddled from the room with wet pants.

By the time Elena had Medical with Austin later that week, she was beyond pleased with everything going on at school.

"Look at you," Austin remarked as he met her in the cadaver diagnostics lab. "You look so happy."

"Things have been great lately," Elena said honestly.

Even though Austin was still keeping secrets from her, she couldn't stop being herself with him.

"School has been working out so well lately. But I do miss home a bit. I think I'll go Telepost Grandma Haddock. Do you want to come with me?"

"That is tempting, but I spoke with her yesterday and I really don't want another lecture about why I look so tired," Austin said, though his smile was wide. "You can go now if you want. I'll cover for you."

"Okay, see you later," Elena replied, excited for the opportunity to skip part of Enrichment.

Elena hadn't been to the Telepost office once since she arrived at her new resident tower at the beginning of Level 4 studies, but she assumed it was in the same part of the building as the previous resident tower because when she selected Telepost from the menu, the Grimvator began to descend.

When she stepped out into the catacombs, the hall was just as deserted as it was in her previous resident tower. She walked along the halls slowly, thinking distractedly about Austin and Fergie, Pigg, and Kidd.

Finally, Elena came around the corner onto the Telepost hall and stopped short at a scene she couldn't quite place at first.

She recognized a wisp of blonde hair tangled through familiar looking fingers. Then, she noticed arms wrapped in a tight embrace. Slowly, Kidd's profile slid into focus and Elena realized that his mouth was connected to Abria's face.

Elena's sharp intake of breath was loud enough to disturb them both. Kidd and Abria turned towards her. Then, their mouths opened in surprise.

Elena ran as fast as she could back down the hall, but she was still in range to hear Kidd call out, "Freckles, wait!"

She didn't wait. Elena kept running, not feeling sure about what she wanted to do first. She'd just seen Abria and Kidd kissing. How could Abria kiss Kidd? Were they together? Nothing made sense.

Soon, Elena was out in the woods heading in the direction of the Firebird Station, though she wasn't sure if she actually wanted to go there just in case Austin and Fergie were there holding a secret meeting. She couldn't take any more secrets today.

Visions of Abria and Kidd kissing would not leave Elena's mind. She felt abandoned by her friend. She felt embarrassed about all the unkind words she'd spoken to Abria about Kidd. She also couldn't help but feel inferior to Abria's beauty. She was jealous that Kidd wanted to be with her blonde friend.

Suddenly, Elena knew what she wanted to do. She stopped before she got to the Station and retraced her steps back to school. She searched and searched until she located Neylon Faulkner.

"Hey, Faulkner, would you trade bunks with me?"

"To sleep near Abria? Absolutely! That will save me from having to cram together in her bed when we have our little late night chats about Apted," Neylon giggled. "But why do you want to move?"

Elena only shrugged her shoulders.

Later that evening, Elena was already situated in her new bunk when Abria arrived at her side.

"What are you doing?" Abria asked, though Elena couldn't look at her. "Are you sleeping down here now?"

When Elena didn't reply, Abria said, "I've been looking for you everywhere. Ever since...well...you saw us together."

"You know, if you wanted to be with Wheeler you should have just told me," Elena said flatly.

"I know, I know. But I was so, like, worried that you wouldn't understand. Or that you'd hate me, or something. And I didn't want to hurt you."

"Oh, so you thought lying would be better. And catching you would be the best way for me to find out," Elena said sarcastically. "Well, you're right about me not understanding. I don't get why you want him. You know he cheated on me, right? I mean, you remember we had that conversation, right?"

"He's changed," Abria said firmly. "People change."

Elena turned toward Abria, looked her directly in the face and said, "People don't change. People might make a different choice next time, but they don't change. Just like, I wanted to march across the street and punch Wheeler in the face when I saw him cheating on me, but I didn't because I'm trying to be less impulsive. That doesn't mean I've changed."

Abria hung her head and said quietly, "We like each other. You don't have to be so judgmental about it."

"Clearly you don't know me that well," Elena replied.

Abria looked teary-eyed.

"How long has this been going on behind my back?"

"Just a few, like, weeks," Abria said quietly.

"Weeks?"

"Maybe three," Abria admitted.

"That's really insensitive timing!" Elena spat. "We just broke up."

"I know, I know," Abria said, sounding ashamed. "But we had all that group work together and the late nights..."

"Just stop!" Elena said, holding out her hand for silence. "I really don't care."

She turned her back and pulled the covers tightly up to her chin. Elena waited for Abria to say more, but a moment later she heard her friend walk away. She sighed quietly, feeling genuinely sad. But then, she heard a commotion behind her. Turning, she found that Fergie was placing clothes in the wardrobe beside her new bed.

"What are you doing?" Elena asked.

"Tilden agreed to trade beds with me," Fergie replied. "Obviously, I needed to bring my clothing as well."

Elena's brow furrowed with confusion. "What about Abria?"

"I explained my reasoning for my new sleeping arrangements. She understands."

"Are you going to explain it to me?" Elena asked.

"Very simply, I do not want you to feel alone. Abria can keep good company with anyone."

"Thanks for reminding me of my obvious limitations in the area of socializing," Elena said with a sarcastic smirk.

"It is what I was made for," Fergie replied with a wink and a smile.

Elena rolled back over, grateful that Fergie wanted to be near her. Far too soon, she felt her eyes were heavy. In her tiredness, she saw Austin standing in front of the other trainees. His head was shaved. Behind him stood the other members of Archon, all except Dino Roman.

At first, Elena felt proud that her friend was in the leadership role that he certainly deserved. But the more Austin spoke about fairness during physical training, student's rights, and the freedom of speech she soon began to feel irrationally angry.

"In addition to these reforms," Austin said boldly. "We are now permitting all couples to display their relationships openly."

Elena noticed Kidd and Abria standing to her right. As if on command, they began kissing. She looked away from them and back to Austin.

"And you're going to have to get over it, Lena!" Austin said.

Elena couldn't help herself. She took off running toward Austin and caught him around the waist. She flipped him to the ground and tried to punch him, but he resisted. Elena wanted to claw and bite him, but he was quick to maneuver away from her advances.

At long last, she was able to out think his moves. She tricked him into being on the defensive on the left so that she could attack on the right. The trick worked. She began to pound him again and again in his face, chest, and stomach.

At first, it felt really good to hit him. In fact, she couldn't stop herself from hitting him. Finally, she paused long enough for him to look up at her with a bloody face and pitiful brown eyes.

"I forgive you!" Austin said.

Elena felt deepening pressure on her shoulder. When she looked, she saw Imperator standing there. He was shrouded in a black cloak and wore a silver-studded mask that made him appear fierce and indestructible. He was holding her shoulder, but he was staring at Austin.

"You have done very well," Imperator said. "Now, ask him about the Tablets of Destiny."

Elena looked back to Austin and shouted, "Where are the Tablets?"

"You know that I don't know where the Tablets are," Austin said calmly. "We were never able to find that artifact."

Imperator sounded impatient as he clicked his tongue. "Never mind! Ask him about the Firebird Disc. He knows exactly where it is."

Something in Elena's brain unraveled at the mention of the Disc. She remembered that Austin had recently told Fergie something about the artifact, but he didn't say he knew where it was located. Austin said that *she* had discovered the location.

"But, he doesn't know where it is," Elena said as she looked into Imperator's masked face.

"Of course he does," Imperator said. "He knows everything. You have him right where you want him. Finish your work! Make him tell you where it is."

A terrible battle, unlike any Elena had experienced, raged in her brain. She knew that Austin didn't know where the Firebird Disc was and she felt certain that her dad had hidden it somewhere. She knew Imperator wanted it, which made her even more certain that he should never have it.

Elena felt herself tumble suddenly through time and space. Her eyes opened in the safety of the girl's dorm room. She saw Fergie lying on the bottom bunk in the next bed over.

Elena rolled over, feeling sick. She wished that her dreams would stop, or at least be a little less menacing. She dressed quickly in the dark and left the room before Roman arrived to wake the other trainees. However, as she walked towards the Grimvators she found that Austin was waiting for her. His face was normal and whole as always. Still, she felt distracted by the thought of her horrible nightmare.

"So, you and Abria caused an obscene amount of gossip for teenage boys that I'd say was bordering on obnoxious last night," Austin said.

"How did you know that I'd be out here this early?"

"I thought you'd either be up pranking or too anxious to sleep. I'm sorry that I was right about you not being able to sleep."

"Did you know they were *together*?" Elena asked.

"No, it was a surprise to me," Austin replied. "Fergie didn't even know."

"Well, if Fergie didn't know then Abria knows she's doing something wrong."

"I know you must feel rejected," Austin said.

"I don't," Elena lied.

She tried to look in his face, but then remembered how she'd felt empowered as she pummeled him in her dream. She felt sick all over again.

"How about you tell me how you feel instead of pushing me away?" Austin said.

"It's fine," Elena said. "If they want to be together it's fine. But that doesn't mean I have to be around them while they're together."

"I know you won't feel better today, but one day it won't hurt so much. And your friendship with Abria will be restored, probably when you least expect it."

"I could never be friends with her again," Elena stated. "You already know that, which is why you're here. Don't force this, Austin. You can't force me to be friends with either of them."

"I'm not trying to force you. I'm stating a fact."

"You're not really the best person to lecture me about the value of friendship," Elena said bitterly.

"What do you mean?" Austin asked.

Elena wanted to tell him that she knew he was keeping secrets from her, but instead she bit her tongue and walked away.

☐ 20 ☐

Agent X

Several tense days passed, during which Elena refused to speak to Abria or Kidd. Abria tried several times to offer a tearful apology, but Elena couldn't stand to listen to her.

Fortunately, Elena's new bunk arrangements kept her away from having to listen to Abria talk about Kidd with Rachel Reddington, Neylon Faulkner, and the other girls at night before lights out. Also, for most of the week her schedule had never really intersected with Kidd or Abria's schedule. So, she could easily avoid seeing each of them and avoid seeing them together.

During program writing Enrichment with Abria, Elena now sat at the opposite end of the room. And in her construction Enrichment with Kidd, she traded seats with another Level 4 trainee so she didn't have to sit at the same table with him any longer. Elena felt his eyes on her a lot, but she forced herself not to look at him.

Nevertheless, there were times when Elena found it difficult to avoid seeing Abria and Kidd together. She hadn't caught them kissing again, but they were always hand in hand in the halls between classes and on the way to meals and they were always sitting together in the Media Lab for group work. They looked happy.

"I hate Abria holding his hand almost as much as when you were holding his hand," Declan said one afternoon while they were in Engineering learning about the Russian Empire. "You girls! I don't know what you see in him. And I don't get why everyone wants to spend time working on a hopeless case."

The only pleasant part about Abria and Kidd being together was all the extra time she had with Austin, Declan, and Fergie. Declan was back to his normal, cheerful self. Therefore, the four of them spent many hours thinking up new ways to prank Dino Roman and the other members of Archon.

"I don't either," said Elena. "I mean, I've learned my lesson."

"He's not good enough for you," Declan said. "So I don't know why you were surprised about him cheating."

Elena and Declan had never spoken before about how Kidd had treated her. She didn't really want to discuss it with him now and she wished that her face wasn't turning a bright shade of red.

"He's not good enough for Abria either," she said.

"I totally agree with that. But Abria doesn't really have a type. Sometimes she goes after the easy-going guys and now it seems she also goes after the silent, moody types," Declan said.

"It doesn't really matter," Elena said shortly. "Since I don't have group work with either of them, I don't have to see them much. In fact, I have a system all set up for avoiding them."

"Ransom, you're going to have to forgive them at some point. At the end of the day, they're our friends. Plus, Abria is my sister so it's not like she'll be out of my life. And, we still have artifacts to find together."

"If they were really my friends you'd think they could have waited a little longer before becoming clamped together at the mouth," Elena said moodily. "Also, she could have told me she liked him so I didn't have to find them in the hall that way. Too many paradigm shifts."

"What does that mean?" asked Declan.

The truth was that there had been secrets, secrets, and more secrets in Elena's life the past few years. Her parents hadn't told her that they'd been involved with a conspiracy to remove Imperator from power; Melly Linus had lied about living in Crowfield Plantation; Kidd had lied about the Tablets of Destiny.

Now, a new year had started and Pigg hadn't told her that he was addicted to pain supplements, Kidd had cheated on her, Abria hadn't admitted that she had feelings for Kidd, and Austin still hadn't fully explained why he and Fergie were always working alone together on something. She was starting to feel like she couldn't trust anyone or trust that anything was the way she saw it with her eyes. But, she didn't want to tell Declan all that.

"How about we talk about something else?" Declan suggested after noticing the look on her face. "For instance, I wanted to ask you to come to Harleston Village with me tomorrow. Imagine it! You, me, and one of those ice cream sundaes that you're supposed to share with three people, except I usually eat the whole thing myself."

When Declan said *Harleston Village*, Elena couldn't help but remember the last time she'd been there and how that one event had changed her so much.

"I don't know," Elena said uneasily. "I have a lot of class work to finish. That last lecture from Niva about killed the few brain cells that I have left."

But, after she noticed that Declan's face fell a bit, she added, "But maybe I'll meet you there at some point during the day. Where do you like to hang out?"

As Declan began to talk about all the different restaurants that he liked, Elena couldn't stop thinking about how distorted her view of life had become. Or perhaps it was distorted in the beginning and now things were becoming clear. She didn't feel confident.

Elena stood suddenly in the middle of Declan's sentence and said, "I'm really sorry to interrupt, but I have to be somewhere."

Elena raced out of the classroom and down the hall. She knew exactly where she needed to go. When she reached Austin's learning cocoon, she scanned her Trademark on the door and stepped inside. All the Optivision screens he was using suddenly froze.

"What are you doing in here?" Austin asked with a surprised look on his face.

"I don't know what to do!" Elena cried. She felt as though she would burst out of her skin at the very words that came tumbling out of her mouth. "I feel like I'm going crazy. I feel like everything I've ever believed about life and people was completely wrong. My brain is spinning out of control. I can't get a grip on anything. Everything has changed so much these last few years! How can anyone be expected to deal with all of this?"

Austin listened and then said thoughtfully, "Everything has changed, but I'm still here for you. And we'll deal with it like we deal with everything else. Together."

Elena wanted to reply calmly, but as the words were building in her mouth she was aware how foolish she sounded.

"I guess I had this idea that I'd be *enough* for one person. Like the way my parents were enough for each other. That if I had a boyfriend he'd only want to be with me and no one else." Tears swelled in Elena's eyes. "It was a stupid idea."

Austin laid a gentle hand over Elena's forearm. "But what if Abria is Wheeler's *enough*?"

Elena had been so busy feeling hurt that she'd never considered that someone else might be better for Kidd than her.

"They should have told you they wanted to be together," Austin said. "They were wrong to lie, but forgive them. They're our friends."

"When we first got together, I felt like we shared an understanding. Like Wheeler and I were hurting in the same way and we could be there for each other," Elena sobbed. "I guess I thought he could fix something in me, or maybe we could somehow fix what was broken in each other. I guess it doesn't work that way."

"No, it doesn't," Austin said. "It's time for Elena Ransom to learn that two broken people don't make one whole person."

"And now he's with her," Elena said, shaking her head sadly. "Which is just..."

"Lena, let's focus on how you can become whole again instead of what they're doing."

Elena stopped to take a deep breath. "How do we do that?"

"Well, to start, you're going to have to learn how to be honest about your pain and grieve through it instead of expecting that another person will take it away or heal it."

"I can't do that," Elena grumbled. "My dad and mom always fixed everything for me. They always helped me talk through what I was feeling. I never had to grieve anything on my own until they died and I didn't do that well. Remember?"

"You have to learn," Austin said. "And, you need to learn how to move forward calmly no matter your circumstances."

"Now you've gone too far," Elena hiccupped. "If you think I could ever be calm no matter my circumstances then you obviously don't know me as well as I think you do."

"Lena, you're strong and confident," Austin said boldly. "Your parents instilled so much security and conviction in you that it can't be challenged by boyfriends or friends or events that cause stress. I know you can find the place of peace because it's already in there."

"I don't really believe you, but thanks for the pep talk," Elena said, rolling her eyes.

Austin laughed.

As Elena crawled into her bunk that night, she let the Kairos slip through her fingers. She wanted nothing more than to be with her parents, to feel their presence and find the peace that Austin had been talking about.

In time, Elena was sitting in the warmth of her bedroom back in Atlanson. She looked around at all her familiar belongings and then gasped as she heard her mom's voice coming from the other side of the apartment.

Elena couldn't wait to see her so she took off running through the halls toward the front door. But then, Elena stopped short when she noticed that Emelie Pigg was standing in her living room. The little two-year-old boy that was standing beside Emelie was playing on a PocketUnit. Tiny the Humanoid was standing in the living room with Hannah Ransom.

"And what's your name?" Hannah asked the boy, but he was clearly too distracted by his game to answer.

Emelie Pigg's eyes fell on Elena and she instinctively looked down, noticing how childlike and small her hands appeared.

"His name is Gribbin," answered Emelie as she looked at Hannah.

"Ma'am, I must depart," Tiny reported in a formal tone. "I have orders."

"I am aware," Hannah replied and she dismissed the Humanoid as Emelie and a two-year-old Gribbin Pigg sat down on the couch.

Emelie looked again at Elena and Hannah followed her gaze until she noticed Elena standing in the hallway.

"Oh, Elena, please come over and meet Emelie and Gribbin."

Elena moved slowly across the room, feeling a mixture of curiosity and fear. She noticed that Emelie's eyes had moved from her to the mantel across the room, where Elena saw an object in the shape of a human heart that was encased in glass. Instead of pumping blood, the heart was glowing red. Elena's brow furrowed in confusion.

"This is my daughter, Elena," Hannah said as she pulled Elena into her lap. "She's also two-years-old. Though we're not fond of playmates yet."

Elena didn't mistake her mom's comment or look on Emelie's face. She knew by Hannah's voice that she did not want Elena to play with Gribbin.

But suddenly, they weren't in Elena's apartment any longer. Elena was standing with Pigg outside the front door to his apartment. He looked older than the last time she'd seen him and he was nursing a bloody nose.

When the door opened, Emelie Pigg stood there looking gruff. She ushered Elena and Pigg over the threshold. Elena felt panic build in her chest as she watched the front door close behind them.

"What have you been doing?" Emelie asked Pigg tersely.

"I was playing at the park when these boys came over," Pigg explained. "They were picking on me and then one of them punched me. But then, Elena showed up and fought them off."

Elena suddenly realized that Pigg was talking about the first time they'd met. It was in the park when they were five-years-old, right before their first year of school started.

Emelie wiggled her finger at the two of them and the children followed her through the apartment. Elena felt so confused by all the Egyptian décor as she walked behind Pigg into the kitchen.

"What do you have to say for yourself, girl?" Emelie asked as she plopped Pigg down on a chair and started to wipe the blood roughly from his face.

Elena suddenly hoped she could manipulate this Cognicross as she had in some of the others.

"Your Egyptian artifacts are rare," Elena said.

"Yes," Emelie replied vaguely.

"Did you live there once? In Egypt?"

"Yes."

"Was your son there with you?" Elena asked.

"Yes."

Elena's mind began to race. She was certain that part of the riddle of the artifacts she'd been working on with her friends was going to be answered.

"Where's Gribbin's dad?" Elena asked.

"He's not here yet," Emelie replied. "He'll join us soon. Would you like to stay as my captive until he arrives?"

Elena awoke suddenly, feeling strange. Her encounter with Emelie definitely felt like a memory instead of a dream. What was her mom trying to tell her now?

The bedroom was very quiet. She felt curious about the silence until she realized that this was their only day off of the week. She was sure that most of the other girls were already down at breakfast, including Fergie who was missing from her bed.

Elena dressed quickly and managed to avoid most of her fellow trainees as she hurried out through the forest to the Firebird Station.

Soon, Elena had the Ransom Dossier opened on the table in the Research & Development room. She flipped quickly through the pages looking for a very specific story. Eventually, Elena stopped when she came to one name. Agent X.

She read her dad's handwriting aloud, "Agent X was based in Egypt with partner and son. Agent X disclosed the location of the Cup of Jamshid to Imperator. Mission compromised. All evidence of the Guardian and his family has been destroyed. Agent X destroyed the location of the Feather of Truth. It is unclear whether or not Agent X possesses this artifact, but I will personally be watching to see if it makes an appearance. Agent X also killed her counterpart. No investigation could be launched because the city of Egypt was under duress."

"Destroyed the location of the Feather of Truth," Elena repeated.

Elena's mind swirled. Emelie Pigg had been in her dream with a young Pigg, but no dad. She'd seen the Egyptian artifacts. She'd asked Emelie questions, but now she needed to talk with someone about it. Only Austin knew about her Cognicross, but she began to feel that it was time to trust someone else with her questions.

And then, she remembered that Declan said he'd be in Harleston Village for the day. Elena tossed the Ransom Dossier into a rucksack and sprinted out the door.

The Harleston Village skyline was soon on the horizon. The streets were filled with students trying to get away from school. On one street, Elena managed to dart behind a vending cart so that Kidd and Abria could pass by without seeing her. Covertly, she made her way down the street to the restaurant Declan had described to her. And there she found him, sitting alone at a table with a Smartslate.

"You showed up!" Declan said ecstatically as he noticed her and pulled out a chair for her at the table. "I wasn't sure if you would."

"Well, you know how I hate to be considered predictable," Elena said with an uncomfortable smile.

They sat in silence for a few minutes until Declan finally asked, "Okay, what are you thinking about?"

"Pigg, actually. He's been weird the last few times I've seen him. Austin says he's on painkillers and he looks awful, but I can't get him to talk to me about anything except hacking into the school's mainframe for pranking purposes."

"Think about how he must be feeling," Declan said. "Especially since the school took him away from the thing he loves most in the world."

"Food?"

Declan laughed. "Yes, food."

Elena looked around uneasily.

Then, she whispered, "The thing is, I had this dream. But it was really more like a memory of Pigg's mom, Emelie. We were in my apartment when I was two-years-old. And there was a heart like object glowing red on the mantle. I think I recognized it as the Firebird Disc, though that really doesn't make any sense."

Declan nodded as if he was listening intently and trying to understand.

"My mom was there, too," she continued absentmindedly. "She always conducted herself with grace and dignity. I wish I could be more like her."

"Don't lose your spunkiness on the quest," Declan said with a twinkle in his eye. But that's when Elena realized that he didn't understand what she was trying to say.

"But then my dream changed. I was at Pigg's apartment when we were five-years-old. Emelie had all this weird Egyptian décor. So, I went to the Station this morning and I got the Ransom Dossier."

Elena took the book from her rucksack and flipped to the passage about Agent X. She read it in a whisper to Declan.

"Do you see what I'm trying to say?" Elena asked.

"Not really…"

"Emelie or Norman Pigg told Imperator about the Cup of Jamshid on Wheeler's farm. Imperator went there and murdered Wheeler's entire family to get the Cup."

"Wow! That's life changing info," Declan replied. "Let's go tell Austin."

"Do you know where he is?" Elena asked.

"He told me that he'd be at the Station with Fergie at some point today," Declan said.

"He and Fergie have been very secretive lately," Elena said bitterly. "I'm not sure I want to tell them anything."

"But you know we should tell them," Declan said. "There's no point to wait. So, let's go."

Even though Declan had warned her, Elena still felt irritated when she found Austin and Fergie alone at the Firebird Station. She could tell they'd been in deep conversation by the amount of artifacts and materials that was laid out on the tables in the Research & Development room.

"I'm tired of this!" Elena said bluntly as she and Declan entered the room. "Why are you two always alone? And what are you working on?"

"We have been working on a great many things," Fergie replied in a formal tone. "For instance, I have been teaching Austin the art of Cryptology."

"What? Why didn't you teach me?" Elena asked.

"I started teaching him after your parents were murdered," Fergie said.

"Honestly, we didn't think you'd need the extra distraction at the time," Austin said.

"We have also been researching where to find the Firebird Disc," Fergie added.

"Why didn't you tell me all this before?" Elena asked.

"Because, when we started the school year, it seemed like you didn't want to research the artifacts any longer. I mean, let's face it, you were happy to come to school and get through each day pranking people," Austin said honestly. "Then, after you told me about your intense dreams, I thought talking about the Firebird Disc might make your dreams worse."

Elena could feel her face growing warm in embarrassment. "I feel like a dimwit. I shouldn't have wasted so much time being distracted by Wheeler. I should'da been helping you. I should'da been fighting for my parents."

Austin looked at her sympathetically. "Lena, don't ever feel guilty about needing an escape from this. Taking a break was good for you."

"You and Fergie didn't take a break from working on it," Elena argued.

"Well, Fergie possesses certain qualities that help her remain neutral and never exhausted." He winked at her. "And, as for me, I kept going because I knew you couldn't."

"You don't have to worry about that anymore," Elena said resolvedly. "I'm back and I'm determined to be more helpful than ever."

"Me, too!" said Declan.

"I'm glad to hear it!" Austin said. "We've spent many hours decoding all the pages of the Alpha Manuscript to see how they correspond with all the other research and data we have collected."

"From the Ransom Dossier and the details we have learned about the Horn of Gabriel, we have ascertained the location of the Firebird Disc," Fergie said in a tone of formality.

Elena wasn't sure if what Fergie said was entirely true. She remembered overhearing them talk recently about how Elena had already discovered the location of the Firebird Disc from one of her dreams. Did Austin and Fergie locate the Disc based on a dream she'd told him?

"Whoa!" Declan interrupted. "This is too weird, because Elena was talking about a dream she had about the Firebird Disc."

"Really? What was it?" Austin asked.

In the smallest part of Elena's heart, she didn't want to tell Austin or Fergie anything more about her dreams. They'd kept secrets from her, so it only felt right to withhold a part of herself from them. Plus, it was clear that Austin had shared the dream about the wall with Fergie and she wasn't sure how she felt about that.

Still, as she looked at the eagerness on all three of her friend's faces she didn't feel right about keeping it secret. She reminded herself that she knew Austin wanted what was best for her, even when she didn't understand.

Elena took the Ransom Dossier from the rucksack and read her dad's handwriting aloud.

When she finished, Elena said, "We've read that passage many times before without knowing what it meant, but I know what it means now. I had a dream about it last night. I'm pretty sure Agent X is either Norman or Emelie Pigg."

Austin's brow furrowed in disbelief. "Are you sure?"

"Yes, my dream was a memory of Emelie and Pigg at my house and also at their house with all the Egyptian décor."

At once, Fergie accessed a map of Egypt.

"Look there," Fergie pointed. "One of the pyramids is completely caved in, but not the others. Does it remind you of something that happened in Istanbul?"

"Yes," Austin said slowly. "The cistern completely collapsed when we took the statue of the Horn of Gabriel."

"So, maybe Norman and Emelie were living in Egypt. The Feather of Truth was their artifact, but instead of keeping it hidden, they took it before they defected," Elena suggested. "But how can we know for sure?"

"What about Gribbin?" Fergie asked.

Elena looked at Austin with distress etched on her face.

"We can't tell Pigg that his parents were traitors," Elena said. "What they did led to the death of Wheeler's entire family. Pigg shouldn't have to live with that."

"Plus, I'm not sure we can even get to Pigg," Austin said truthfully. "He's under lock and key twenty-four hours a day in that programming room. I rarely see him anymore and when I do he never tells me what they're working on."

Elena wanted to tell Austin and Fergie that he'd been contacting her through the Optivision screen during her class work, but then she changed her mind.

"But what about Wheeler?" Declan asked. "Should we tell him what happened?"

Elena looked at Austin for an answer, but she was sure she already knew what he would say.

"Yes. We need to tell him as much as we know. Or else let him read it for himself," Austin replied.

"Austin, we should show them the location of the Firebird Disc," Fergie interrupted.

"You know where it is?" Elena asked, her brow furrowed in confusion.

"We think we do," Austin corrected.

Fergie grabbed an oblong piece of weathered leather that was closed with a red clasp. She set it on the floor, pushed on the clasp, and Elena watched as the

Catalan Atlas opened and spread itself across a large portion of the floor. She saw flags and shields bearing different crests, illustrations, text, continents, and seas. There were also symbols representing cosmography, astronomy, and astrology.

With an Optivision screen from her Touchdot, Fergie accessed the celestial ceiling patterns from Truman Ransom's office. As those hovered in midair over the Catalan Atlas, light spread out highlighting certain locations on the map.

"History tell us that there is only one place in the world that was a holy site for the three major religions of the past," Fergie said and she pointed to the map.

"The Western Wall in Jerusalem," Austin interjected. "That's where we need to go next. Though it will be difficult to get there considering we haven't had any time off from school since we started Level 4 training."

"So, you want us to go to this wall to find the Firebird Disc?" Declan asked. "And that will answer all our questions?"

"Maybe not all our questions," Austin admitted. "But we will be a step closer if we can find this artifact."

Austin and Fergie had certainly done a great deal of work, but Elena was having a hard time appreciating it. All she saw was more challenging work ahead of them.

"Given all the information we have gathered," Fergie said. "I believe we need to return to Tavington's farm and ask him again about the Tablets of Destiny."

"But, I think Imperator already has the Tablets of Destiny," Elena said. "Didn't Austin tell you about my dream?"

"He did, but we can still ask Tavington if he knows where we can locate it," Fergie said. "Even if we have to commandeer it from Imperator."

"But, if Imperator has the Tablets then he might already know our future," Elena said. "What if all this is just for him to get to me?"

"I told you before and I'll say it again," Austin said steadily. "I won't let Imperator take you. No matter what happens. I promise."

"Wait a sec!" Declan said abruptly. "Ransom's life is in danger and no one told me?"

Elena wanted to tell Austin again that Imperator was too powerful. That it would be impossible for him to protect her if Imperator really wanted to take her. But instead she said, "Let's hope we find the Firebird Disc before he does."

"So, I guess we need to call the others together and start making plans for our next treasure hunt," Declan said.

Elena sighed heavily. "I don't want to make plans with all the others."

But Austin was already shaking his head. "We have to tell Abria and Wheeler what we're doing, even if they don't want to come with us."

"It's not okay with me that they're together, but whatever, okay?" Elena said. "I can't control them. But I don't have to sit around making plans with them either."

"We've got to tell them, Ransom," Declan said matter-of-factly. "You know we do."

Elena only rolled her eyes.

¤ 21 ¤

Unexpected Leeway

The following day, Elena agreed to sit at the Firebird Station with Abria and Kidd so that Austin and Fergie could communicate the information that had been discussed about the Tablets of Destiny, Feather of Truth, and the Firebird Disc.

"It was Pigg's parents who betrayed your family," Austin told Kidd. "They told Imperator where your family was hiding."

Abria gasped, looking horrified, but Kidd's face was impossible to read.

"We've decided not to tell Pigg that his parents were traitors," Austin continued. "But it's your right to discuss it with him since your family was destroyed because of it."

Kidd paced the room up and down in silence.

"Anyway, if we ever get a break from school we need to get back to Atlanson to get the Independence so we can get to Jerusalem," Austin said. "That's where we think we'll find the Firebird Disc. At some point, we also need to go back to Tavington's to see if he can help us find the Tablets of Destiny."

Kidd stopped pacing suddenly and turned to him. "I'm not going with you this time."

Elena felt her face grow warm. She wondered if Kidd didn't want to come with them because of her.

"If it's because of what I said about Pigg's parents…" Austin started, but Kidd interrupted at once.

"I need to go back to my parent's farm."

"Okay…" Austin said leadingly.

"Ever since that Tribulation where you found that Kantele," Kidd started. "I realized that I need to get my mom's necklace."

Elena's mind was suddenly back in the Smuggler Station when Kidd picked up a small instrument that was threaded with strumming strings and was carved with strange symbols.

"One of the artifacts we're looking for is your mom's necklace?" Declan blurted.

Kidd nodded. "I think so. And I know it sank with the Smuggler Station, but I can't get it outta my head. That's really why I've been building the extra hovercraft. I needed a way to get there, but I didn't want to take the Independence by myself. I'll go while you're in Jerusalem and meet you back here."

Abria came close to Kidd and laced her fingers through his. Elena looked away as she said, "I'll go with you."

Elena crossed to the opposite side of the room slowly.

"I don't know," Austin said. "I'm not sure if it's good for us to split up. What if you have trouble and we can't get to you? Or what if the Independence crashes again? We'd need your help to fix it, Wheeler."

"Nah, you'll be fine," Kidd said. "You'll have Big Ears to help."

"He's not coming this time," Austin said. "I don't think we'll be able to get him away from school. They sort of have him *locked* in programming."

"Actually, I have my own path to follow, too," Elena added suddenly. "I want to go see Norman and Emelie Pigg. I'm going find out if they have the Feather of Truth. And then I'm gonna make them give it to me, even if it kills me."

"I'll go with Ransom to see them," Declan offered.

"Are you sure?" Elena asked.

"Yeah, parents love me," Declan replied with a toothy grin.

"These parents aren't like that," she said.

"Well, Fergie and I want to go back to Tavington's farm to ask again about the Tablets of Destiny. He may not tell us anything, but it's worth another try to me," Austin said. "So, we'll go to Atlanson with you, have our meetings, and then we can get the Independence and head off for Jerusalem together."

"How're you going to get through the force field around Tavington's farm?" Kidd wondered.

"Fergie designed a program for us to gain access," Austin said and Elena found herself wondering how long Austin and Fergie had truly been making their plans.

Abria looked around at them somberly. "It sounds like we're all going separate ways this, like, time."

Elena knew she should feel sad that they wouldn't be together on this next adventure, but instead she only felt relieved that she wouldn't have to see Kidd and Abria kissing in the halls of the Independence.

As their meeting ended, Austin and Fergie moved to one side of the room toward the pupil station while Kidd and Abria left together quickly through the front door. Elena took a chair in the kitchenette wishing that Pigg was with them so she'd have someone to be awkward with.

"What'cha thinkin about, Ransom?" Declan asked, pulling up the chair beside her.

"Oh, I'm not looking forward to seeing Emelie. I don't know if she's *really* Agent X because the Dossier said the agent's partner died in Egypt, but Pigg's dad is alive so that doesn't make sense. But she has all those weird Egyptian artifacts. And I don't *really* think she'll help us, but if there's the slightest chance that she has the Feather of Truth or can tell us where it is then I have to go.

"And then there's the whole thing with Pigg. I wish he could come with us, but it's probably better that Emelie doesn't see us together. And I don't want to tell him that his parents were traitors. And I'm so confused."

"Wow! That was a lot and I don't think you took a breath the entire time you were speaking," Declan said with a smile. "Listen, you can't control all of that. We're going to have to focus on making small steps forward, one at a time, and figure it out as we go along."

"I wish I could be calm like you," Elena said absentmindedly.

"Nah, I'm glad you're a rambling lunatic," Declan remarked. "It makes me seem smarter than I actually am."

■■■

The first day of the tenth month of school began without any hint of time off from Grimsby. The weeks of Tribulations had taken the Special Ops division to the boundaries of time and space in simulations that Sabrina Bauer and Brennan Colt had both called *excessive*. They had trained in every type of environment imaginable, under conditions of extreme duress and with many different styles of weapons that Dino Roman often used against them as punishment for not performing up to his standards.

The Level 6 Archon officers, Link Hawkins, Collum Duke, and Charleston Woods, were often in conflict with Roman over his methods and questioned his authority when he was out of line. However, since they were also trying to garner favor with the Headmaster and Hannibal for career placements they often didn't notice when Roman was abusing his position over the other trainees until after he'd gone too far.

Elena often found solace running in the woods or around campus with Austin during cool crisp evenings. For reasons she didn't know, he'd stopped spending so much alone time with Fergie. She didn't ask Austin what secrets he was still keeping from her, but now that they were spending more time together she was less curious. She was simply glad to have her friend back and enjoyed his company.

"Would you come to the Firebird Station with me today?" Austin asked one afternoon while they were jogging the campus. "Fergie and I have been working for many months on how all the artifacts fit together, but I wanted to say it out loud to you to make sure I have everything straight. I know you'll be honest if you see something missing in the plan."

"Yes, of course," Elena replied, feeling flattered that he wanted her help.

Soon, Elena and Austin were sitting alone in the Research & Development room. As Austin set out all the artifacts they'd gathered and opened up several Optivisions with data, Elena flipped through the pages of her dad's dossier. She remembered how far they'd come; from a small rumor that Hannibal once heard about an Amulet that would save them all from Imperator to an entire quest that had crossed continents and stretched the boundaries of their understanding of time and destiny.

"The parts of the Ransom Dossier, the Catalan Atlas, and the Alpha Manuscript that we've been able to decode give us the directions that we need and a framework for what we're looking for and where artifacts should be located," Austin began.

Elena looked over the Atlas, with its illustrations, different crests, text, continents, and seas, and compared it with Optivision of the artifacts they'd already found.

"We still don't know exactly what the Cryptext is for," Austin said as he grabbed a cylinder contraption with numbered keys that encircled the entire outside like a casing from the table. "But we do know that the ampoule from the Amulet we collected in New York City can reveal secret text from pages in the manuscripts."

Elena looked over the last few objects on the table. She saw the Horn of Gabriel, a purely white statue of an angel with a horn to its lips. And then her eyes landed on a wooden cup with a pedestal and stem that were carved into the shape of a twisted tree trunk.

"Did Fergie ever figure out what the Horn or the Cup of Jamshid were supposed to do?" she asked.

Austin shook his head and replied, "No, but each of these artifacts has a different code that we need for the key to defeat Imperator."

"So, the codes from the Amulet, Catalan Atlas, Horn of Gabriel, and Cup of Jamshid are all entered into the system," Elena said. "And we need to get the

Feather of Truth, the Firebird Disc, and the Tablets of Destiny and we'll be finished?"

"I'm hopeful that will give us everything we need to defeat Imperator," Austin said optimistically. "But then again, you still have to get Norman and Emelie to talk to you."

Elena laughed and said, "Well, you still have to get Tavington to tell you about the Tablets of Destiny, so it's hard to say which of us has the worst task."

Austin also laughed.

"Do you have an escape plan for Jerusalem?" Elena giggled. "Because once we've grabbed the Disc we need to expect an end-of-the-world type scenario."

Austin smiled and nodded.

"It all sounds really good," Elena said. "I think we're headed in the right direction, even though it's going to be strange to do all this without Pigg,"

"Yes," Austin agreed. "But perhaps when we get back we can make more of an effort with him, especially during the break before our Level 6 studies begin."

Elena hoped, rather than believed, that would happen.

"I'm going back now," Elena said as she began to stand. "Do you want to come with me?"

"Nah, I'm going to stay a while longer and go over this again," Austin said and she rolled her eyes at him.

As Elena neared the Station door, she realized it was opening and saw that Abria was entering. Unfortunately for her, there was nowhere to run unless she wanted to run directly over Abria.

"Oh good, you're here. I want to talk to you," Abria said.

"I have nothing to say to you," Elena replied, diverting her eyes to the floor.

"It's been weeks since we talked," Abria said.

"Are you still dating Wheeler?"

"Yes."

"And do you remember a conversation we had about how he was bad for me and I needed to not be around him for a while?" asked Elena.

"Yes," mumbled Abria.

"So, if we're friends and you're dating him then at some point I'm going to have to hang out with him in a social setting, right?"

"Yes."

"That doesn't work for me, Abria. Look, I'm trying to accept that you want to be his girlfriend. Now, you need to accept that I can't be friends with the two of you. Can you do that?"

Abria hung her head. "Yes."

Elena walked away feeling terrible. Losing Abria's friendship had been sad, but talking about it made things worse. And things continued to get worse for her as she entered the arena for their next physical training session.

"I've set up today's fighting schedule," Roman barked at all the Special Ops trainees. "Choose your weapon, then find your first partner and engage. The winner moves along the board until we have a final victor."

"This is going to take forever," Elena said as she and Austin went around the room to the wall of weapons. "I wonder if that means no classwork for the rest of the day."

Elena picked up a weapon. Then, she looked at the competitor's board and saw that she was paired up first with Kidd Wheeler. She felt her face burn red with anger and embarrassment. She marched across the arena straight to Roman.

"What's going on?" Elena spat at him.

"Excuse me, Goonie?" Roman replied.

"You put me up against Wheeler first? Why would you do that?"

"Does it matter, Ransom? That's the order so it should be good enough for you."

"Change it," Elena demanded.

Roman's brow furrowed, but he also had a hint of mocking in his eyes. "Get back over to your zone and start fighting."

Elena turned away feeling bitter, but steadied the weapon in her hands. If she was going to have to fight Kidd, she was determined to do whatever she could to beat him.

As she took her place in the fighting zone she realized that Kidd was already staring at her. It had been a long time since she'd looked him in the face. His eyes seemed sad, but she pushed her feelings to the pit of her stomach.

However, before they could even get started, Roman shouted, "Goonies!" Stand in formation."

Confused, Elena fell in line with all the other trainees, as far away from Kidd as she could get.

"As much as it pains me to say it," Roman shouted after all the trainees had assembled. "Headmaster Worthen Bentley has announced that you've earned some time off school."

Elena felt sudden relief. They'd been working non-stop since school started nine months ago. She was really looking forward to taking a break. Plus, this would give them the time they needed to search for the artifacts.

"The Headmaster has approved a one week furlough so you can visit your families," Roman said, though he didn't look pleased. "You have the night off from the normal schedule and you have the freedom to leave campus anytime, starting now. Dismissed!"

Elena's brow furrowed as Roman walked away from the trainees. She covertly watched him cross to the far end of the room where he joined the Headmaster and Hannibal. After a few moments, a tangled mess of curly rainbow colored hair entered the room and joined the meeting. She stared for a few moments hoping to catch Hopper's eye. When he finally looked in her direction, Hopper smiled and winked at her. Elena desperately wanted to know why Hopper had joined them and what they could be talking about, but her thoughts were interrupted by the sudden presence of her friends talking to her all at once.

"Our time off is unexpected," Abria said eagerly.

"And confusing," Elena added. "Why would they give us time off now? And look over there." She gestured with her head. "What do you think they're talking about?"

"We can't waste time worrying about that now," Austin said steadily. "Now that we've been given the time, we should leave as soon as possible."

As the others nodded, Elena hurried to the first cocoon she could find, hoping to speak with Pigg before they left. To pass the time, she opened a session of Booker's classwork and waited. Minutes passed.

Feeling bored, she accessed several other documents from her other Instructors. However, since she was only waiting for Pigg, the documents blurred against her eyes as she felt a swell of nervousness about the unforeseen events that were about to occur, especially since she wouldn't be with all her friends this time around.

She was about to give up waiting when Pigg's face suddenly appeared on the screen. Elena was shocked and horrified by his thinning hairline, his emaciated face, and his twitching eyebrow.

"This is a strange time for you to be doing classwork," Pigg said in a groggy voice.

"Yeah, I missed you," Elena replied. She tried to ignore the guilty look on his face as she added, "I wanted to let you know that we've been given some time off. We're headed to Atlanson tomorrow. I wish you could come."

"Me, too," Pigg said. "But they haven't mentioned anything about taking a break. It would be nice to be far away from this place."

"Pigg, do you need help?" Elena asked.

Her question seemed to rouse him a bit back to the reality of where they were.

"No, no. I'm fine. But I'll want a full report of your adventure when you get back. Don't leave out any of the life-threatening, hair-raising, blister-boiling, back-breaking, jumping out of a building, almost being smushed to death, details. Okay?"

Elena wanted to smile, but the look on his face was so strange. "Be safe, okay?"

"You, too," Pigg replied.

When his face faded away, Elena stood in the cocoon for a long time wondering if she should have told Pigg the whole truth. From his last statement, it seemed that he knew they would use their time away from school to find another artifact. But she wanted so much to tell Pigg that she was about to visit his mom.

Elena climbed in bed that night wondering if she'd have time to try and reach Pigg again before they left in the morning. But, all too soon, she was standing once again on top of a sand colored stone wall. She looked around the rotund temple with a gold-topped roof and acknowledged that she was inside the same dream she'd had several times since the school year started.

The same gunship landed at the base of the wall. When the door opened, she watched the imposing figure of Imperator step down to the ground. He was shrouded in a black cloak and wore a silver-studded mask that made him appear indestructible.

At this point, Elena tried to manipulate what she was seeing. She tried to freeze the door of the hovercraft, but several dozen robotic figures still emerged from the gunship and moved toward the base of the wall in perfect unison.

When Imperator appeared at her side, Elena tried to jump from the wall, but her feet wouldn't move.

"I have come for the Firebird Disc," Imperator declared in a superior tone.

"I'm not giving it to you no matter what you do to me," Elena said stubbornly. She wished that she could somehow manipulate more than her words in the dream, especially as Imperator came towards her because she knew what would happen next. She felt the squeezing of her neck and the tearing of her flesh.

Elena looked right and left to the walls adjacent to her, expecting to see her friends. But instead, there was nothing. When she looked back into Imperator's face, it had changed. Austin was standing there, but instead of his hands wrapped around her throat, one of his hands was covering her mouth.

The image alarmed her to such a degree that her eyes flew open. Instantly, she felt pressure on her mouth. She looked straight into Austin's eyes. With his free hand, he put a finger to his lips. Then, he released her mouth and wiggled a finger at her so she'd follow him.

Elena pulled on the first pair of jump boots she could find and followed Austin down the hall, over the balcony, and into the forest toward the Firebird Station. They walked along silently through the increasingly cool night air and Elena found herself wishing that she'd brought a coat.

When they finally reached the Station, Austin sat quietly on the couch. Elena sat beside him, their shoulders touching. She could feel his sadness and felt so confused.

"What's the matter?" Elena yawned, feeling suddenly tired.

"I feel afraid."

"Of what?"

When Austin didn't speak, Elena asked, "Are you thinking about your parents?"

"Why would you ask that?"

"I don't know," Elena said. "It just feels like it does when we sit in the park and mourn your parents."

"For some reason, I think that finding the Firebird Disc will lead me to my father." Austin sighed. "But, even if we get the Disc, we still don't have the Tablets of Destiny, or Wheeler's mom's necklace. And what if Emelie won't give you the Feather of Truth?"

"Don't worry, I'll make her give it to me."

"But, what if she doesn't have it? And what if we go through all this and we still don't know what everything means?"

"Listen, we have the Ransom Dossier and the Alpha Manuscript. We have the Catalan Atlas, the Horn of Gabriel, and the Amulet. We have the Cup of Jamshid, and the Cryptext. Wheeler will get his mom's necklace and hopefully that will help make some more sense of things," Elena said. "We'll figure it out at some point. It can't be a mystery forever."

"Look who's so optimistic all of the sudden," Austin said with a slight smile.

"I'm not optimistic, I'm delirious with exhaustion," Elena replied. "But I don't get why you're so worried all of the sudden?"

Austin was quiet for a moment.

Then, he said steadily, "Something momentous is about to happen. Something that will change the course of history."

"Does it involve me getting back to my bed?" Elena asked sleepily. "Because we have to leave tomorrow."

Austin smiled.

"Do you remember the conversation we had on the balcony back home? About helping people learn the truth?"

Elena nodded.

"Lena, I want you to remember what we're fighting for, no matter what happens going forward."

"Why would you say that?"

"Well, a few months ago you lost your way a little bit," Austin reminded her. "Don't forget it again. Always remember where you belong."

▭ 22 ▭

Furlough

"You're very quiet," said Declan.

Elena looked out over the city of Atlanson as she and Declan rode the elevator up the resident tower toward Pigg's apartment. They'd left Grimsby with Austin and Fergie an hour earlier, while Kidd and Abria were on their way to his family farm in the hovercraft he'd built.

"I know that Abria and Wheeler had to leave because we have such a short break from school, but it was so risky to let them go before they'd activated their Humanoids," Elena said.

"It was a *calculated* risk," Declan reminded her. "Fergie said that she'd be able to turn on their Decoys without them being here. And once all our Decoys are seen around Atlanson together, no one will even realize that they didn't come back with us on the train."

Elena sighed, feeling anxious.

"What else?" Declan asked. "Let's get it all out there."

"I can't believe we left Pigg at school. We should have tried harder to get him to come with us. And now, I'm thinking through our possible options. If Emelie is difficult, do you think it'd be totally wrong to tie her up so we can ransack the apartment?"

Declan chuckled as they stepped off the elevator into the hallway.

Elena drew a deep breath and whispered, "I can't believe I'm only asking this now, but do you have a weapon?"

Declan held up his fists and smirked.

"That makes me feel better," Elena said sarcastically. "When we get in there, try not to talk. I want you to constantly assess our surroundings in case we need to make a quick escape."

"Good idea."

Elena reached the outside of the Pigg's apartment door and rang the bell. She knew that Emelie was going to be able to see her on the monitor so she tried not to look as nervous as she felt. A moment later, the door slid open silently and Emelie appeared, looking so vicious that Elena's flesh crawled.

"What are you doing here?" Emelie Pigg said nastily. "And where is Gribbin?"

Based on Emelie's posture, Elena could tell that she had no intention of letting her and Declan into the apartment without Pigg so Elena stepped slightly to the left and pushed her way into the apartment as she said, "Pigg's at school."

"Oh, well come on in," Emelie responded in a rude tone.

Elena went straight into the sitting room where she found Norman Pigg sitting quietly, reading a book. She rounded back on Emelie and noticed that Declan was standing near the door in a position that indicated he could make a swift movement in any direction at a moments notice.

"Do you know why we're here?" Elena asked.

Emelie crossed her arms firmly over her chest and replied, "I haven't the slightest idea, but if you've gotten Gribbin into trouble again I assure you I will attempt to have you expelled from school."

Elena held up her arm and allowed the Touchdot to fly out from her Broadcaster. She accessed several Optivision screens with images of some of the artifacts and the Ransom Dossier and set them floating in midair near Emelie's face.

"Does any of this look familiar to you?" Elena said steadily. "The Catalan Atlas, the Ransom Dossier, the Cup of Jamshid, and images from the Bowen apartment."

Elena watched Emelie's face as each of the images appeared and continued to hover in midair. Pigg's mom watched the images with such an expression that it was impossible for Elena to know what she was thinking. Then, Emelie's eyes filled with outrage as they shifted from the images to Elena.

"You were a Renegade," Elena said plainly. "And you were a spy for Imperator. You knew about all the artifacts, didn't you? It was your job to know."

Emelie stood in silence, her eyes flicking quickly around the room as if she were trying to figure out an escape.

"There's a dot on the Catalan Atlas indicating that there's an artifact located in Egypt. We made plans to go there until Fergie Foreman pulled up the map of Egypt. Guess what we found?" Elena accessed an aerial map of the pyramids in Giza.

Emelie stared at Elena without speaking.

"We noticed that one pyramid is completely caved in," Elena continued. "It reminded me of something that happened in Istanbul when we retrieved the Horn of Gabriel. You know, don't you? You already have the artifact we need. You have it in your house. I've seen it before."

Emelie gazed at Elena in a threatening way.

Elena turned slightly and shouted at Norman Pigg, "Are you a traitor, too?"

Norman was stone faced and it was impossible to tell what he was thinking. Then, a shrill laugh of derision burst from Emelie's mouth.

"Freeze all motor fuctions!" she commanded.

Elena watched in dismay as Norman Pigg instantly appeared to be asleep. Declan shifted uncomfortably as the realization that Pigg's dad was a Humanoid began to register in Elena's mind.

"My dear husband died during the Exodus," Emelie said with derision. "But it was a good thing. Norman was uncertain about joining Imperator and what that would mean for Gribbin's life. He never had enough courage to do what needed to be done."

"Oh, but I bet you did, right Emelie? You've always been clear about what side you're on," Elena spat. "You're all about doing whatever you can to make sure you live."

"Not only me," Emelie said insistently. "Gribbin needed me to protect him."

"Oh really? So, he knows that you murdered his dad?"

Emelie pursed her lips together tightly.

"I read about what you did in my dad's dossier," Elena said boldly. "He didn't list you by name, but now that I know Norman died in Egypt it all makes sense. You betrayed Kidd Wheeler's family to Imperator, you stole your own artifact and you killed Pigg's dad. You're a murderer!"

Emelie moved across the room, passed Norman, and to the large picture window that took up the entire wall of the sitting room. She looked out towards the city in silence for a long while. Elena looked to Declan for answers as to what they should do next, but he only shrugged.

"Gribbin was nothing more than my insurance policy," Emelie said at long last. "I would have left him behind except I know your dad would not have allowed it."

Emelie continued to stare out the window, but Elena got the sense from her voice that she seemed relieved that she could share this information. And, far from being embarrassed by her lack of empathy, Emelie Pigg almost seemed bolstered by her despicable behavior.

The core of Elena's being began to bubble uncomfortably. She suddenly became worried about Pigg's safety. If his own mother would have left him behind when he was only two-years-old, what could she possibly have planned for him now that they all knew the truth?

"Give us the Feather of Truth," Declan said suddenly.

As Emelie turned away from the window her hand slipped into the inside of her gown. Elena and Declan instantly steadied into an attack position. Emelie cocked her head slightly. Then, she slowly drew a purple plume from her tunic. She extended it towards Elena carefully.

Elena reached for the Feather with her free hand. When she closed her fingers around it she felt a small tug and met Emelie's hardened eyes.

"Don't ever come back here again, girl," Emelie said so coldly that it sent a chill down Elena's spine. "Ever!"

Elena took the Feather into her hand. As she and Declan backed towards the front door, she took one last fleeting look at Norman Pigg who was still immobilized on the couch. She wondered how she was going to tell her friend that his dad was really dead.

"Did that seem strange to you?" Elena asked as they climbed back onto the elevator.

"Which part? The creepy Egyptian décor, the fact that Pigg's dad is a Humanoid, or the pleasant reception given by the hostess?" Declan asked sarcastically.

"I'm serious," Elena replied. "She *gave* us the Feather. For a woman who murdered her own husband and almost left her child behind, why would Emelie give this to us?"

"Maybe it's not even real," Declan suggested. "Fergie will be able to tell us."

"If she used Pigg as her insurance policy before, she's sure to do it again," Elena said uncomfortably. "I wonder what she has planned for him. It's not like she's ever been good to him before. But now that she knows that we know all this horrible stuff about her, Pigg's sure to pay for it somehow."

"We've got to tell Austin," Declan said as they stepped out onto Peachtree Street.

Elena and Declan moved swiftly through the underground of Atlanson, taking little notice of the pedestrians and holographic figures swirling around them. They soon went through the alley and entered the Sector 7 clubhouse. Elena was surprised to find that Austin and Fergie were already there.

"We thought you'd be gone a few more hours," Declan said.

"Tavington was brief," Austin replied. Then he looked at Elena and asked, "What's wrong? You look upset."

Elena held the Feather of Truth out toward Fergie.

"Emelie gave this to us without a fight," Elena said. "Austin, she murdered her husband in Egypt. Norman Pigg is a Humanoid."

Austin shook his head sadly. "Now it all makes sense."

"This is not the Feather of Truth," Fergie said formally.

"How can you tell?" Declan asked.

"These are not the correct series of symbols," Fergie said. "They do not correspond with any of the symbols obtained from the other artifacts."

"What a waste of time!" Elena stated.

"Don't worry. We'll get the real one," Austin encouraged.

"No, the tragedy is that we have to see that wretched woman again!" Elena said.

"What worries me the most is why Emelie gave you any information at all," Austin said. "Why would she do that?"

"That's exactly what I want to know. It was almost like she was proud of how horrible she is and how she outsmarted people," Elena said.

"Maybe she's still working for Imperator," Declan suggested.

"We should try to reach Pigg to see if he's okay," Elena said urgently.

Fergie opened an Optivision screen from her Broadcaster at once. "Gribbin, are you there?"

Elena waited impatiently. She chewed an entire nail off her left hand while Fergie tried a few times to contact Pigg from her Broadcaster.

"I'm worried about him," Elena said finally.

"Should we go back for him?" Delcan asked.

"There's not enough time to get him and get back from Jerusalem," said Austin.

"I'll try not to worry. I mean, he is at school," Elena said. "And Hannibal is there in case anything happens with Emelie."

"So, what happened with Tavington?" Declan asked Austin.

"Tavington still won't discuss the Tablets of Destiny, but then he just came right out and told us about the Kantele."

"The Kantele? What do you think it means that Tavington has the same info about that as we do?" Elena asked.

"It means we have a problem, but I don't understand how all the pieces fit together yet," Austin said. "We should go, though."

Elena, Austin, Declan, and Fergie made their way back through the city and into the drainage tunnel where they'd left the Independence before their Level 4 training had started. The masquerade was still activated so Elena couldn't see the hovercraft until Fergie activated it using her Touchdot. Then suddenly, a set of stairs materialize out of midair leading up to the main entrance to the hovercraft.

"You know, that's amazing every single time," Declan said with a smile.

A long time had passed since Elena had stepped foot on the Independence. After she'd almost drowned in the Smuggler Station, she was happy to leave it all behind. But now, being on the hovercraft again and knowing that they were searching for artifacts felt really natural to her. And as they walked through the halls with the lights flickering on automatically, she suddenly realized how much she'd missed being on the outside of the domes.

As they reached the command bridge, Elena watched Declan climb into the navigator's chair beside Fergie.

"*You're* going to operate the hovercraft with Fergie?"

"Yes," Declan replied, sticking his chin out proudly. "I may not have all the same reflexes as Wheeler, but I'm certainly better looking so that must count for something."

"You're full of surprises today," Elena laughed.

"Well, I'd hate to be considered predictable," Declan replied with a smirk as he turned toward the control panel.

Suddenly, the floor began to vibrate under Elena's feet. She watched Fergie access the maintenance data control system. Then, the door to the outside world slowly opened.

Every time Elena had ever left the domes before, the vibrancy of authentic color was always overwhelming to her senses and today was no different. The terrain was rich with a soft palette of greens and gold while pale sapphire water canals outlined the vast expanse of amber plains. The sky was maritime blue and the dazzling tawny sun reflected off the sides of the eminent Atlanson dome.

"Bowen, if you take the controls while we travel this easy terrain I will go to make sure that all of our supplies are ready for our eventual disembarkation," Fergie said.

"Sure, no problem," replied Declan.

"I'll come help you," Austin offered.

As Austin and Fergie left the command bridge, the world spread out before Elena through the front windows.

She couldn't think about anything except her parents. She'd been without them for three years now. It felt like a lifetime had passed and it also felt like their death happened yesterday. Time was funny that way.

Elena wanted so much to hold onto the memory of her parents, but part of remembering them also came with a price. Remembering them always forced her to acknowledge that she wasn't free. She wasn't free to live her own life. She wasn't free to choose her own future. Instead, she was always striving to bring justice to something she didn't understand.

"This place feels pretty empty without Pigg, Abria, and Wheeler here," Declan said.

Elena gave a non-committal grunt as looked out over the ocean that was now beneath them. The water that flowed in long blue waves of color was almost hypnotic. She thought about what it would be like to float aimlessly around without a care in the world.

"So, how are you doing?" Declan continued.

She could tell he was staring at her, but she didn't dare look at him.

"Today is the day, isn't it?" Declan continued. "The day you got news that your parents died?"

Elena looked up sharply. "How do you always remember the anniversary of my parents' death?"

"Your eyes change when you're grieving," Declan said plainly.

"I'm starting to forget them," Elena said in a barely audible tone, as if she were making a confession that she didn't want anyone to hear. Then, she caught the look on Declan's face and added, "I'm not forgetting the most important stuff they taught me, but I can't remember what my mom looked like when she was sleeping or the routine my dad had for getting ready for work in the morning." She let out a deep sigh. "And sometimes they'd dance in the kitchen while they were making breakfast together, but I don't remember exactly how he held her."

Declan selected the autopilot control from the Optivision screen at once. Then, he stood and pulled Elena up into a dance posture. She smiled as they began to sway around the bridge.

"I can't remember my mom's laugh," Declan admitted. "I wish I could."

Elena swallowed the rather large lump that was obstructing her airway and swiftly changed the subject so she could steady her voice.

"Where did you learn how to dance?"

"From the Humanoids," Declan said. "Kenneth and Anne said that it improved their functionality if they performed human like movements and activities. Who taught you to dance?"

"My dad." Elena smiled a little. "I never wanted to be left out when he danced with mom so he taught me."

Elena fell silent and so did Declan as they spun in slow circles around the room.

"So, what do you think Jerusalem will be like?" Elena asked in an effort to fill the awkwardness she was beginning to feel.

But, instead of answering, Declan hummed a tune they'd heard from the people playing instruments when they'd visited tunnels in New York City.

The sun was just starting to rise the next morning when the Independence made its decent from the clouds and into the broken city of Jerusalem. Fergie directed the hovercraft to a heap of rubble that overlooked an extensive stone courtyard. Elena could see a golden, rotund roof to her left and buildings to the right.

"So, what's the plan, Haddock?" Declan asked as their hovercraft came to rest.

"I've already packed up all the artifacts in my rucksack and then we're going to get out there and find the Firebird Disc," Austin said.

"Why are you bringing the artifacts?" Elena asked.

"I'm not sure," Austin admitted. "It feels like we might need them this time."

After Elena and the others stepped off the Independence, they crossed the courtyard toward the sandstone wall that rose out of the ground like a monument. The place had a reverent silence about it that Elena found almost comforting.

Elena walked toward the Western Wall until her nose was almost touching. Then, she looked straight up, feeling small. The wall was filled with slips of paper in every crack and crevice. Curious, she pulled one out. The paper was weathered and nearly falling apart, but still she could read part of a sentence in Aramaic.

"What are we looking for again?" Declan asked as he also grabbed papers from the wall.

Suddenly, Elena felt the Kairos begin to move beneath her shirt.

"Austin! My Kairos is working!" Elena said, but as she looked toward Austin she had a nagging feeling something was very wrong.

Austin was holding the rucksack of artifacts slack in his hand. He was staring off into the distance as if he were expecting something.

Then, a tremendous sound arose so mighty and powerful that Elena was knocked off her feet. She slammed her palms against her ears and looked around. She wasn't the only one on the ground. Austin, Fergie, and Declan were lying in heaps along the wall.

As Elena stood, she noticed that the noise was rolling towards them like a wave and it was coming at them from a tremendous haze of billowing black smoke. The clouds were rushing towards them, building and building.

"What is it?" Declan shouted over the noise. "A storm?"

"Based on the trajectory of the undulating and speed of the system I would say that what we are witnessing is an artificial phenomenon," Fergie said formally.

"Austin, what should we do?" Elena asked, but Austin only continued to stare as if he were expecting someone.

Then, he hurried toward her and said in earnest, "No matter what happens, remain silent."

Before Elena could even ask what he meant, a massive hovercraft broke through the cloud cover. She scrambled across the ground and pushed her back into the Western Wall as the gunship landed in the middle of the courtyard.

¤ 23 ¤

The End

Fear coursed through Elena's body. She could tell by the hovercraft's unique markings that it was a gunship. She'd seen images of it many times in the Ransom Dossier. She knew that only one person in the world used or needed a gunship. Imperator.

As Elena began to stand, she vaguely noticed that Austin started to move towards her in a protective way. And then, Declan and Fergie came toward her as well in the military style that they'd been taught at school.

After all this time, Imperator had finally found them. She knew that he wanted her. She knew it after she'd eavesdropped on her parents long ago, before she started Grimsby. She knew it by her recent dreams about him asking for the Firebird Disc. She knew it by the sense of dread that had made its way into her heart.

Elena's breath caught in her chest as the door to the gunship opened. But, quite unexpectedly, Headmaster Worthen Bentley stepped into the doorway. Elena thought for a moment that she should feel relieved by his presence, but his face was so rigid she knew they were in serious trouble. The Headmaster's collar was absolutely choking his neck and he had a look in his eye that made Elena slightly unnerved.

As the Headmaster reached the ground, Elena noticed that Hopper was also coming down from the hovercraft and behind him came Melly Linus! Of all people.

Feelings of confusion rushed over Elena. She looked to Austin, but his eyes were transfixed on the Headmaster.

"Headmaster Bentley," Austin said steadily, as a formal greeting. "I'm surprised to see you here. And with Hopper and Melly."

Elena felt him tense beside her.

"I think the time has come for you to end the charade, don't you?" Austin continued.

Elena's brow furrowed in bewilderment as the Headmaster pulled his high collar down. She noticed a thick, black band around his neck. He tugged on it once and the band detached with a pop.

Once the band was gone, Headmaster Worthen Bentley's face morphed immediately into a fierce, silver-studded mask. From behind him, Droidier soldiers began to descend the gunship plank.

A moment passed that seemed like an eternity where Elena felt her life sliding into some kind of new focus. She looked into Imperator's mask. She looked at the wall of stone behind her. Then, she looked back at the gunship. She'd been here before...in her dreams.

Or perhaps this scene had been written for the Cognicross in her head. But either way, Elena was clear on what Imperator had come for. He wanted the Firebird Disc. She honestly didn't know where it was, but she wasn't about to let her friends be tortured for the Disc.

"YOU!" Elena screamed at Imperator. "You murdered my parents!"

Elena made an attempt to rush towards Imperator, but Austin grabbed her around the waist and pulled her back.

"No matter what happens, remain silent," Austin repeated and he looked at her with such intensity that Elena closed her mouth.

However, as lie after lie began to unravel and explode in her brain, Elena wasn't sure that she could remain silent indefinitely.

"How did you find us?" Austin said somewhere far off in Elena's consciousness.

"You have been betrayed by a person who has been working for me for quite some time."

As Imperator turned his head slightly back towards the gunship, Elena saw Pigg step out with Emelie by his side. She couldn't believe her eyes. Pigg looked worse than he ever had before. Part of his face had been horribly disfigured, as though he had been burned and his skin melted. The fingers on his left hand were bandaged, but in his right he pointed a weapon at her friends.

"Gribbin was offered a seat at the high table in exchange for his cooperation," Imperator said in a low, clear tone.

Pigg didn't look as though he'd been given anything except an express visit through a torture chamber.

"If he was given a seat at the high table, why has he been tortured?" Austin asked calmly.

"I said he was *offered* a seat," Imperator said with distain in his voice. "Gribbin, it turns out, was inadequate."

Elena noticed Pigg's shoulders sag a little. But as the fire of betrayal began to burn out her eyes, she could have cared less how he felt.

"Yet, he has always been more than adequate for us," Austin said, his voice raised loud enough for everyone to hear.

Imperator sighed impatiently. "You already know I have no need for the others. I came for you alone. If you would like them to live, they are free to leave you behind."

Elena let out a sharp intake of breath that bordered on the psychotic. Then, a high-pitched laugh of sarcasm burst from her mouth as she stated, "No one is going with you!"

Even with all the armed Droidiers surrounding them and even though they were horribly outnumbered, Elena pulled the Kairos out from under her shirt, hoping that somehow it would magically change their circumstances.

Austin did not break eye contact with Imperator's mask as he said, "Bowen, right now."

Declan didn't say a word but, in one motion, he grabbed Elena. With Elena kicking and screaming on Declan's shoulder, Declan and Fergie began to back out of the courtyard.

Once they'd cleared the scene, Declan set off through the ruined city at a rapid pace. Elena was still writhing and begging Declan to put her down, but he and Fergie continued with long, sturdy strides. They cut down lanes, taking completely random twists and turns.

"How could you leave him there!" Elena screamed, clawing and scratching, trying to get away from Declan. "WE CAN'T LEAVE HIM!"

"Ransom! It's him or all of us!" Declan shouted over her.

"Then, let it be all of us!" Elena hollered.

Declan never responded, even with the profanity that Elena hurled at him.

At long last, Declan entered what looked like a stone cave. He walked down a flight of stairs and put Elena down on a flat surface though there was stone along the walls and ceiling. Elena tried to run for the exit, but Fergie grabbed her arm.

Elena wrenched free from Fergie's grasp and shouted, "I can't believe you left him there!"

"Elena Ransom!" Fergie said, her tone so sharp that the hairs on the back of Elena's neck stood on end. "We cannot follow where he goes. Austin Haddock has reached his supreme moment in time."

Kairos.

"No…" Elena whispered in disbelief. "That can't be."

But Fergie was no longer paying attention to Elena. She'd already opened her carrier bag and had pulled up several Optivision screens from a strange looking Smartslate.

"We were following orders, Ransom," Declan said seriously.

"Orders! What orders?" Elena shouted in his face.

"Austin gave us specific instructions," Fergie said confidently.

"I highly doubt that he gave orders to leave him there!"

"He gave the order to leave him and a separate order not to tell you," Declan informed her. "He seemed to think you'd overreact."

Elena gazed at him for a moment with an expression of pure loathing. Then, through gritted teeth she said, "I'm going back!"

In a stern tone, Fergie said, "Elena, you cannot go back there. We did not leave him. However, we also cannot save him later if we do not get away now."

"What are you even talking about?" Elena asked impatiently.

Then, all of the Optivision screens lit up with different points of view from the scene taking place between Imperator and Austin back at the Western Wall.

Elena's mouth fell open. "How are we seeing this?"

"I tossed the eight-legged androids out as you were thrashing around. Thank you for providing the perfect distraction," Fergie replied.

The scene was tense. Austin was on his knees with Imperator standing in front of him.

"I am trying to tell you that I don't know where it is," Austin said impatiently.

"It is pointless to try and deceive me," the Imperator responded. "For I have known for many months that *you* are the Firebird Disc. Rather, I suppose it's better to say that the key to the riddle is within you."

Austin remained silent.

"You must realize that I do not need you to be compliant in order to get what I want from you."

Austin still remained silent.

"Our father chose you," Imperator told Austin. "But he made a mistake."

"Father doesn't make mistakes," Austin declared. "It was your choice to abandon him. It is my choice to fulfill the prophecy."

"And how will you fulfill the prophecy if you are eliminated?" Imperator asked.

Before anything else could happen, the Optivision screens began to cloud with static.

"What's happening now?" Elena asked desperately.

"There is some type of interference," Fergie said, but then very quickly she added, "Listen closely. Austin asked me to insert a tracking mechanism into his body so we could locate him in case anything happened. We have been working on it together all year. That is why we always got quiet when you came around. And why we seemed so secretive to you," Fergie said as she tried to regain access to the Optivision screens. "Austin did not want anyone to know what we were doing. It was as if he *knew* this would happen to him."

"But won't Imperator be able to find the tracking thing?" Declan asked.

"Not this kind. It is a Fergie-first. They could never find it in a million years."

"Too much is happening right now!" Elena cried hysterically. "I...j-just...d-don't...I mean..."

Elena was silenced as the Optivision screens began to flash bits of the scene between Imperator and Austin again. Amongst the fragments of data, Elena could tell that some form of electric charge was emitting from Imperator's right hand. Austin screamed in pain as the charges entered his body.

Elena fell silent as her dear friend was being tortured. She didn't even bother wiping away the tears that spilled down her face because they were coming in a steady stream.

As Imperator extended his left hand, Austin's body rose in the air. He was shaking uncontrollably now. Then, Elena watched helplessly as parts of Austin flesh began to tear, like his body was being ripped apart.

"No! Stop!" Elena screamed.

Elena followed the trail of Austin's blood flowing through midair to the Alpha Manuscript that was hovering in front of Imperator. As Austin's blood touched the open blank pages, lines of text began to appear.

"Is he using Austin's blood to decode the diary?" Declan asked in horror, but Elena couldn't even think enough to put words together to answer him.

As Elena began to hope for some miracle of mercy, Imperator made one last hand gesture. Austin's body fell from the sky into a limp heap on the ground.

"Bring the body and the artifacts," Imperator said to Hopper and Melly as he reached for the Alpha Manuscript. Then, he turned away from Austin's lifeless body.

As Austin's lifeless body was lifted from the ground, Elena crumbled to her knees in grief.

"Does the Fergie-first work if Austin is dead?" asked Declan in a horrified voice.

"Yes," Fergie replied quietly.

Suddenly, the earth began to quake beneath Elena's knees. She looked up and could see from the Optivision that the Driodiers were struggling to remain balanced. Then, the sky turned as black as night. Inside the cave, the rock began to crack and dust began to swirl around their heads.

A new wave of panic clouded Elena's judgment. In the sudden darkness and desperation, her breaths began to come in shorter and shorter gulps of air. She couldn't quite take a full breath into her lungs.

Vaguely, she could tell that Declan was trying to talk to her, but he looked blurry around the edges of the hololight he held suspended above his head.

"I-I-Imperator k-killed h-h-him," she sobbed uncontrollably. "I can't believe he's gone."

Then, something pinched Elena sharply in the back of the shoulder and she cried in pain. She felt around and pulled a dart into her hand. As the dart fell to the ground, she noticed the end of a dart sticking out of Declan's chest. Then, she saw Hannibal emerge from one of the cavern walls.

"Hannibal, where did you come from?" Elena heard Declan ask from somewhere far away in her consciousness.

But Elena's eyes were already fuzzy. An unnatural light was spreading through her. As she slid to the ground, she saw Declan drop to his knees. Fergie was still standing, watching Elena in silence. Elena reached out for Fergie, but she didn't even have time to scream out in grief before she knew no more.

▢ 24 ▢

Undesired Facts

Elena's head ached. Her eyes were closed and all was dark and that suited her just fine. Opening her eyes seemed it would cause unnecessary dizziness. She lay still, not really able to form clear thoughts. It was nice not to think for once. Silence spread out. She had no concept of time or space. Then, quite suddenly, she began to feel warmth spread through her body.

The sensation reminded her of the spring picnics she once had with her parents at the park in Atlanson. Home. She could see the three of them in her mind so clearly, laughing, talking, and eating. And then, for some reason, she was suddenly sitting in the Galilee Province around a table with Abria, Kidd, Fergie, and Declan on another warm spring day. They were laughing, talking, and eating, too, but the scene seemed to be missing something.

Declan turned towards her suddenly and said, "We have to go."

He pointed to something behind Elena and she turned to see Imperator holding Austin by the arm. As she started to scream, Imperator scraped a knife across Austin's throat.

Elena eyes involuntarily flew open. Everything was blurry. As she rubbed her face tenderly, she noticed a strange, unnatural smell. She turned her head from side to side. She was lying in a bunk bed, covered with heavy blankets.

At first, Elena thought she was in the Firebird Station because it looked so similar, but then the light was somewhat other-worldly.

Elena rubbed her eyes and opened them again. She didn't seem to be dreaming. She swung her legs over the bed and touched the floor carefully with one toe, as though it may bite her. The floor was freezing even with her socks on.

She slowly stood. Then, her head swam and her legs trembled. She fell back into the bed. As she was beginning to wonder why she felt so awful, she noticed a strange, shiny light was dancing off the far wall.

"Okay, Ransom," Elena said aloud. "You need to make it to the wall so you can figure out where you are."

Elena turned her head. Slowly, the room slid more into focus and she found what could help her. She eased off the bed onto the stone cold floor again. Her arms and legs felt heavy. She slumped onto her belly and army crawled several paces, but even that was a challenge. She paused to catch her breath and then started to crawl again. She stopped frequently, but kept on until she finally reached a chair across the room.

After a great deal of effort, Elena managed to pull herself into the chair. She sat for a while trying to regain her strength.

"Hello?" she called out hoarsely.

Elena waited. When no answer came, she decided it was time to try standing again.

Using the chair as a crutch, Elena started toward the strange light that was dancing at the end of the hallway. The walk was not far, but she had to stop several times to rest.

After many pauses, she finally reached a vast round window. Elena blinked her eyes rapidly. Could it truly be what she was seeing? She hobbled towards the window and pressed her face against it.

On the other side of the glass was an expanse of clear blue water. A vast reef of coral and colorful fish stretched out before her eyes.

"Hey Freckles," said a resounding voice from behind her.

Elena's eyes filled with tears as she turned to see Kidd Wheeler gazing at her. Relief and delight brightened his face. He crossed the room and scooped Elena into his arms.

"I was so afraid!" Elena cried. "I was alone when I awoke and thought..." She pulled away suddenly, wiping her face. "Where are Abria and Fergie and Declan?"

"I don't know," Kidd admitted. "I don't know where we are or how we got here. I only woke up an hour ago. The last thing I remember is Abria and I swimming back to shore from the Smuggler Station. What's the last thing you remember?"

Elena felt suddenly weak again. Her knees buckled.

"What's wrong?" Kidd asked as he helped her to sit in the chair she'd used as a crutch.

Elena remembered Imperator. She remembered Austin suspended in the air. She remembered Hopper standing there with Melly, Emelie, and Pigg...Oh, Pigg! Her best friend had betrayed her. She remembered Declan carrying her away. She remembered Hannibal being there and a sharp pain in her shoulder.

Elena swallowed hard and asked, "What happened at your farm?"

Seeming to understand that Elena wasn't ready to talk about what'd happened to her, Kidd said, "I'm still not really sure. Abria and I dove for the Smuggler Station. Finally, we found my mom's necklace. When we got back to shore, we started to call Fergie. Then, there were lights in the distance. And Tiny arrived."

"Tiny? Tiny! My humanoid, Tiny?"

"Yes," Kidd confirmed. "I recognized her from the time I'd seen her in town with your family."

"What did she say?"

"Nothing. She didn't say anything," Kidd said. "She shot us with some kind of dart. I blacked out. And then I woke up here."

Silence spread out between them. Elena was trying to understand how her Humanoid, who had disappeared after her parent's death, had now suddenly reappeared. Her mind hurt as she watched fish swim in the reef beyond the window.

After a long time in quiet, Kidd asked, "What happened to you?"

Elena did not want to speak out loud what she'd been through, but she also didn't think it was fair to keep it to herself.

"We'd just gotten to the Western Wall when a strange hovercraft appeared. Headmaster Bentley arrived." Elena paused for a long moment. "The Headmaster has been disguised the entire time we were at Grimsby. He's really Imperator."

Shock registered on Kidd's face.

"And Hopper was working with him, and Melly, and Emelie and" — She let out a stifled cry — "Pigg betrayed us. He's been working with Imperator."

"Wait! Slow down. You're not making any sense. What are you saying?" Kidd asked in a desperate voice.

Elena took a labored breath.

"Imperator has been hiding at Grimsby for years. He knew about my dad's work with the Renegades, which he learned from Emelie Pigg. He killed my parents to motivate me to look for artifacts because my dad was hiding the Firebird Disc. Imperator was following us from the very beginning.

"He put the original Firebirds together. He had Hopper lead us to the Firebird Station. He watched us collect artifacts from New York City, Washington D.C., Istanbul, and your farm.

"Imperator removed Kate Bagley from our Unit and replaced her with Melly, the spy. He killed Fergie's parents to keep them from creating the Humanoid army that could defy him. And now he has Pigg working for him so he'd know where we were going next." She sighed. "He was looking for Austin the whole time. Only Austin."

"Why?" Kidd asked.

"Because Austin is the Firebird Disc."

"How can Austin be the Firebird Disc?"

Elena shrugged. "How is it possible that Austin and Imperator share the same father?"

"Huh?"

"I don't know. And I don't get it, but it doesn't matter," Elena said sadly.

"Why doesn't it matter?" Kidd asked slowly. "Where is Austin now?"

Elena's eyes filled with tears. She didn't want to say it aloud because that made everything real, but she knew it was the only way to help Kidd know the desperation of their situation.

"Austin's dead. Imperator killed him."

"That can't be true!" Kidd stated.

"It is true!" Elena cried. "I saw it happen."

Kidd seemed frantic as he began to pace the room. Elena didn't even care to watch him. The weight of all the lies consumed her. She had no energy to think beyond accepting that Austin had died. He'd died so they could get away from Imperator. He died so they could be free.

Elena vaguely registered that Kidd left the room. She simply sat in the chair and stared out the window into the water, wishing she could be one of the colorful fish swimming untroubled on the other side.

After a few minutes, or perhaps hours later, Elena heard Kidd's voice coming from somewhere in the distance.

"Pan Pan, Pan Pan, Pan Pan! Number 11241979 at 18.2871S by 147.6992E needs immediate evac. Over."

Elena wanted to care about what he was talking about, but even as he repeated the same information over and over again she couldn't bring herself to be curious about what he was doing. All she cared to do was watch the fish swimming outside the window. She was jealous about how simple their lives were.

After a time, Kidd finally returned to her chair by the window.

"We have to figure out a way to call someone. Someone needs to find us."

"What have you been using to try and contact someone?"

"There's a communications board in the other room, like the one at the Firebird Station."

Elena's eyes widened in horror as she realized what he'd been doing.

"You can't use that! Imperator will find us. He's connected to all of this. He knows everything!"

"We have to try something," Kidd argued. "We don't even know where we are. We have to get home."

"Home? Home is a myth," Elena replied "Besides, what are you so eager to get back to?" But then her face burned red with embarrassment as she realized that he probably wanted to get back to Abria.

"I would have thought you'd know better than anyone how important it is that we find Austin as soon as possible," Kidd said.

"Austin is dead! I saw him die," Elena said bitterly. And, although she desired to find his body with all her heart, she didn't want to share that with Kidd. So, she lied, "Finding his body won't help us."

"I know you want to give up and I understand why, but..." Kidd started, but Elena interrupted him.

"You have no idea how I feel so shut your mouth!"

After her outburst, Kidd left the room looking sad, but Elena didn't care.

At some point, she got up from her chair and wandered aimlessly around the Station using the chair as a crutch. She found the kitchen and pantry, a dozen empty bedrooms with bunks, and a room for development and research.

Finally, she came to a long hallway that was extremely dark except for a tiny light far in the distance. Elena followed the hallway slowly, wondering if there was someone standing at the end with a light.

At long last, she came to the rung of a metal ladder. The ladder was lit with a tiny light on each rung. Elena looked straight up, but couldn't see beyond where it vanished into the shadows above. She looked back down the hall to make sure that Kidd hadn't followed her. She listened hard with her ears until faintly she heard his voice.

"Pan Pan, Pan Pan, Pan Pan! Number 11241979 at 18.2871S by 147.6992E needs immediate evac. Over."

Elena looked at the ladder and swallowed the lump of fear growing in her throat. Slowly, she began to climb. But the farther she went the more desperate she became. Soon, she was almost tripping over her feet because she was ascending so quickly.

The little lights on the rungs were no longer shining, but she didn't care. She climbed on and on in the absolute dark. Finally, Elena smashed her head into something hard. She felt the metal above her head, moving her hands around and around until she realized she was touching a circle.

Scarcely daring to breath, Elena turned the metal wheel as hard as she could. She felt gritty resistance, but she kept on until finally she heard a click of unlatching. Elena pushed against the wheel as hard as she could.

First, a small beam of light spread through a crack. Then, more and more light came streaming through the space as Elena pushed the wheel harder. Now she could see that she was opening some kind of hatch door. Something gritty was falling through the opening, but she kept on until the door was finally ajar.

Elena pulled herself through the opening and onto a sandy floor that was dry and warm. Her brow furrowed in disbelief as she saw horribly weather beaten wooden walls and window openings with no glass. Behind her, Elena saw a door.

Elena tripped her way through it hoping to find something...someone. Instead, she came to a crushing halt. Her body spun wildly around as her eyes tried to make sense of where she could possibly be in time and space.

"Ransom! Ransom!"

Elena could hear Kidd calling her name from far away, but she couldn't even respond. Her mouth had gone dry and as she tried to shield the sun from her eyes she realized that she was uncommonly hungry.

Soon enough, she could hear footsteps on the metal rungs down the tunnel. But she was already sitting so comfortably that she didn't get up.

"What in the world!" Kidd said as he came through the shack door.

Elena watched him take in their environment from the shade of the coconut tree above her.

"We're on a very small island," Elena said. "Or we're in a Station and the island is the camouflage."

"This is insane!" Kidd said as he stepped through the sand toward the water.

"I'm actually feeling pretty good about it," Elena said. She closed her eyes peacefully and laid her head back against the tree. "I suppose it's going to be pretty awful to starve to death, but then again, I guess I could swim out far enough and let nature take its course. There are worse ways to die. Trust me."

"Get up, Freckles!" Kidd said in a harsh voice with a look of disgust on his face. "Come inside and help me get the communications panel working."

"No, thanks," Elena said coolly.

Kidd's look was unfathomable. "Haddock would be disappointed in you."

For some reason, Kidd's words pierced Elena's core. Maybe it's because she was so angry or maybe because his words were true, but whatever the reason Elena was on her feet and started towards him aggressively.

"What are you going to do? Fight me?" Kidd scoffed.

Elena made a fist as she went, but he'd already anticipated her approach. When she made her first swing he grabbed her around the middle and set her down as gently as he could, considering how much she was struggling. She made an attempt to get up, but realized that he really was a lot stronger than her.

"Just stop!" Kidd pleaded. "Don't do this."

"Let me up!" Elena screamed in his face.

Kidd released her at once. She didn't come after him again. The brief fire that had burned so brightly was extinguished and now all she felt was pain again.

"Would you please help me with the communications panel?" Kidd asked again. "We need to find out if there's anyone still out there."

Elena's heart was completely unwilling to help him, which is why she was sure it was the right thing to do. He'd been right. Austin would have been disappointed to know that, upon his death, she'd turned her back on everyone that he considered to be their family.

Therefore, she followed Kidd back into the Station and they stood around the communications panel.

"What's the code thing that I heard you say earlier?" Elena asked.

"It's a distress call that's used between hovercrafts," Kidd explained. "I read about it from a book in your dad's library."

Elena wanted to open her mouth to yell that he was never allowed to step foot in her dad's library again, but Kidd was already speaking into to the communications board.

"Pan Pan, Pan Pan, Pan Pan! Number 11241979 at 18.2871S by 147.6992E needs immediate evac. Over."

Elena waited, listening to what sounded like a dense fog of silence.

"Pan Pan, Pan Pan, Pan Pan! Number 11241979 at 18.2871S by 147.6992E needs immediate evac. Over."

"How long do you think we'll have to do this?" Elena asked.

"I honestly don't know," Kidd admitted. "I figured we'd take turns until someone replies."

"What if no one ever does?"

"We have to try."

For the next few days, Elena and Kidd used the distress call from the communications panel to try to reach someone. They took turns sleeping, fishing, cooking, and eating, but mostly all they did was repeat the distress call. That is, until late one afternoon.

Elena's frizzy red curls spread out on the table as she laid her head down wearily. She'd been repeating the distress call with her Trademark numbers for over an hour and had finally grown tired when suddenly she heard a faint noise of static.

Elena jumped up at once and called down the hall.

"Wheeler! I hear static!"

Kidd came racing into the room and began to push several of the options on the Optivision screen.

Then, out of nowhere, Fergie Foreman's face appeared.

"Fergie! Fergie! It's so good to see you!" Elena said, the edges of her words filled with relief. "Are you okay? Where are you? Where's everyone else?"

"I am attempting to trace the signal from your location," Fergie said formally. "It should only take a few more moments."

"Foreman, what's going on?" Kidd repeated Elena's question. "What happened?"

Fergie seemed hesitant to answer him. "I have deciphered your general location. Please stand by for instructions."

"Instructions? From who?" Elena asked.

But then she heard a loud commotion in the background of Fergie's transmission and someone called out, "Is it really her?"

Declan's face appeared suddenly by Fergie's side.

"You're ALIVE!" he shouted, grinning widely. "I'm so glad you're alive!"

And then Abria appeared beside him and squealed, "You're both safe! We were so worried!"

"Of course I'm alive and of course we're safe," Elena said disdainfully. "You were with us a few days ago. Tell Hannibal for me that it was a really kind of him to shoot me in the back like that."

Declan exchanged a worried look with Abria.

"What's going on?" Kidd asked.

"Where's Austin?" Elena interrupted. "I mean, where's his body."

"We don't know, Ransom," Declan admitted. "Everything has happened so *strangely.*"

Elena noticed her three friends exchange tense glances at once another. She was starting to feel angry at their silence.

"What's wrong?" she demanded. "What aren't you telling us?"

"Ransom," Declan said seriously. "You and Wheeler have been missing for three months."

Elena's mouth fell open.

"What are you talking about?" Kidd asked sharply.

"We have not heard from you nor been able to access your Trademarks anywhere in the world for the past three months," Fergie said in a monotone voice.

"After the thing happened with Austin and Hannibal, you disappeared," Declan said. "I mean, when I woke up you weren't there. And we were never able to find you."

"We've been so, like, worried about what happened to you!" Abria added.

"Now that we know your general location, we will come collect you," Fergie said.

"In what?" Kidd asked. "How can you come get us? The Independence was being tracked by Imperator."

"It's hard to explain unless you can see it with your own eyes," Declan said. "But we have access to more hovercrafts than you could possibly imagine."

"But what about communications?" Kidd asked. "Doesn't Imperator control all that as well? Won't he know that we're talking now?"

"Explaining where we are would be too complicated," Fergie reiterated. "But rest assured that we are safe and can communicate without Imperator's knowledge."

"Where is Imperator now?" asked Kidd.

"He's at Grimsby, same as always," Declan said.

"Still pretending to be Headmaster Worthen Bentley to all the, like, new students," Abria said.

Elena let Abria's words come together in her mind slowly. Not only had she been missing for three months, but Imperator had been at school the entire time abusing a new set of trainees.

"So, what's the plan exactly?" Elena asked abruptly as her face suddenly felt warm with anger.

"We can and will explain more when we see you," Fergie said. "But in the meantime, I really need you to tell me as much as you can about your location. Can we land there?"

As Kidd opened his mouth to speak, Elena turned her back and walked directly out of the room. She could hear Kidd and the others calling her name, but she didn't stop.

A minute later, Elena climbed back up the metal ladder and out into the island shack. She removed her shoes and socks. She stepped confidently through the front door onto the sand. The grainy graduals felt warm between her toes, but she didn't stop until her feet touched the water.

Elena stood still as the rippling waves pulled sand from beneath her feet. The constant sound of the water lapping against the shoreline was unfamiliar, but completely comforting at the same time. She looked out across the vast expanse of water.

"I've never seen anything more beautiful than this place."

Loneliness spread in her soul until it touched every piece of her.

If she really had been missing for several months, why couldn't Fergie and the others tell her what happened in her absence? Why did they keep insisting that it would be better for her to see what they were talking about instead of them trying to explain it to her?

She longed for the answers to so many questions. How could Imperator and Austin share the same Father? How could Pigg betray her? How could it be true that Austin was dead? How could she keep on living knowing that Austin was not alive?

In this place where time forgot, Elena felt desperate for the day that she would finally be freee.

THE ADVENTURE WILL CONTINUE!

What will happen next to Elena, Austin, and their friends?

Follow Elena Ransom's story at

www.elenaransom.com

Made in the USA
Columbia, SC
04 February 2021